Other Avon Books by
Earl W. Emerson

POVERTY BAY
THE RAINY CITY

NERVOUS LAUGHTER

EARL W. EMERSON

AVON
PUBLISHERS OF BARD, CAMELOT, DISCUS AND FLARE BOOKS

NERVOUS LAUGHTER is an original publication of Avon Books.
This work has never before appeared in book form. This work is a
novel. Any similarity to actual persons or events is purely coinci-
dental.

AVON BOOKS
A division of
The Hearst Corporation
1790 Broadway
New York, New York 10019

Copyright © 1986 by Earl W. Emerson
Published by arrangement with the author
Library of Congress Catalog Card Number: 85-90814
ISBN: 0-380-89906-X

First Avon Printing, January 1986

AVON TRADEMARK REG. U. S. PAT. OFF. AND IN
OTHER COUNTRIES, MARCA REGISTRADA, HECHO EN
U. S. A.

Printed in the U. S. A.

WFH 10 9 8 7 6 5 4 3 2 1

"The boys with their feet on the desks know that the easiest murder case in the world to break is the one somebody tried to get very cute with; the one that really bothers them is the murder somebody only thought of two minutes before he pulled it off."

—*Raymond Chandler*

Chapter One

THE HEADLINES READ: NORTHWEST TYCOON SHOOTS TEENAGE MISTRESS, SELF, IN BIZARRE SUICIDE PACT.

It was the sort of tacky emotionalism the papers gulped down whole, no matter how much they belittled the supermarket checkout tabloids for trashing people's lives with the same bludgeon of publicity.

The front page of the Seattle paper was loaded with pictures: a photo of the underage girlfriend swilling beer with her poorly dressed friends; a three-year-old photo of the ill-fated businessman grinning disarmingly as he accepted an award from the mayor.

The biggest picture was a ghoulish snapshot of the bodies being trundled out of the Trinity Building into the sunshine —one to the morgue, one to the emergency room at Harborview.

As in so many of my cases, I got involved on a whim.

Several days earlier the instructions had arrived in a cheap white envelope, handwritten in an effortless, flowing cursive I decided was that of a woman. After the building had emptied for the day, someone with a flair for the dramatic had poked the envelope through the mail slot of my cramped office in the Piscule Building.

It was early—a Friday morning in May.

Mr. Thomas Black—Investigator:
    Don't be alarmed at the quasi-outlandish nature of

this offer, but I am more than a little embarrassed about this whole affair and wish to manage it with the least amount of fuss.

Your name was mentioned by mutual friends as one who could be trusted implicitly.

I have no idea what your rates are or how far this money will take you. Until it runs out, please follow Mark Daniels and report on his movements.

He spends a great deal of his time in the office on Harbor Island, both before, during, and after the regular business day. He is a fanatical Mariners fan and he has a cabin on Lost Lake which he may visit from time to time.

There is the possibility that he is seeing women. Please report on this. Send your report to Post Office Box 3751. Thank you for your time and trouble.

P. S. We don't need pictures or legal proof, just reasonable certainty.

The note was unsigned. My guess was that a woman had written it. It might have been his wife. His mother. Mistress. Whoever she was, she smelled positively angelic. The envelope retained a whiff of thick and fragrant perfume intermingled with the unforgettable aroma of freshly minted legal tender. Paper-clipped to the note were five one-hundred-dollar bills, the notes stiff and unwrinkled.

Thumbing through the white pages in the phone book confirmed that a Mark and Deanna Daniels resided in town, at a plush location on Queen Anne Hill.

It had been a queer deal from the beginning.

It smelled like trouble. It smelled like a corny case from one of the old *Black Mask* stories. It smelled like a scorned woman or a jealous business partner or some other incredibly jumbled and messy domestic intrigue. I should have bundled the bills up, licked some stamps, pasted the twenty-cent darlings on and mailed the hodgepodge to Box Number 3751.

I didn't.

Early the next morning, Saturday, I hopped into my '68 Ford pickup and drove to the address on Queen Anne Hill, parking on a side street on the south slope. There were only two houses on this short cobbled dogleg of a street. Each of them sported a view some people would kill for.

The residences were uphill and thus higher than the street, but even from the roadway I could see the entire Olympic Mountain Range, Elliot Bay, the hump that was West Seattle, Harbor Island, and most of downtown Seattle, including the Space Needle and the bustling waterfront. To the east, the Cascade range was clouded over. It was enough to suck the blood right out of your heart.

Most of the neighbors were still knocking the sleep seeds off their faces when Mark Daniels emerged from his house and wedged himself into an ebony Volkswagen Rabbit parked in the circular driveway. I wondered why he didn't take the new Cadillac sitting beside it.

Slewing from side to side, the Rabbit skittered down the hillside on the twisty streets—streets damp from spotty morning showers.

Thoroughly familiar with his nimble little car as well as his labyrinthine neighborhood, he dropped me twice on the way down the slope. He finally jumped onto the Alaskan Way Viaduct and proceeded south. Only because traffic was skimpy and because I had a fair idea of where he was heading did I manage to stick.

I had done no preliminary research on this cat, so I didn't realize until I read it in the papers the next day that the mammoth building he drove to on Harbor Island—a building with attached warehouses and a dog food factory abutting it, a building that took up the better part of four full city blocks—was one that he owned half interest in.

A rustic wood-burned sign on the corner read Trinity Building.

Harbor Island is a vast flat tract of industrial area at the south end of Elliot Bay between Beacon Hill and West Seattle. It was an island only because the Duwamish River poured into the Sound on either side. It had once been miles and miles of tideflats and marshlands. The Indians had fished and clammed out there.

Reclaimed from the sea by overzealous landfill engineers, much of the city's deep port activity was handled from its banks. The ground rumbled ominously when heavy trucks rolled up the streets. Some scientific wag once claimed the lead content in the air down there—heaviest in the state—was enough to kill a congressman.

Daniels parked in a vacant lot that had been landscaped by professionals, festooned with young birches and dotted with rhododendrons in full flower. The stick-on clock on my dash said 7:45.

In his late thirties or early forties, Mark Daniels wore wool slacks and a pin-striped dress shirt without a tie, the sleeves rolled into wrinkled doughnuts just shy of his elbows.

Maintaining cover in that area was difficult because I was in a pickup truck—an old pickup truck. So I parked a hundred yards away and spied on Daniels through a monocular. He locked the Rabbit and disappeared into the complex through a side door. It was going to be a wait.

Of average height, he had a pudgy face, hefty forearms and a great solid paunch that rode over his belt. His wavy brown hair was short and styled, molting into a fashionable gray at the temples. Like a lot of men these days, he sported a neatly trimmed beard, the mustache shaved away. He had the walk and general picky avoid-the-mud-puddles air of a man who hadn't done any physical labor in twenty years. Or maybe ever.

Thirty minutes later as I thumbed through the paper and settled into the funnies, a late-model Mercedes sports coupe pulled into the lot. A tall, gray-haired man got out and shuffled into the building, disappearing through the same door as Mark Daniels. He left the motor of the Mercedes running. After awhile, in the undisturbed and deadly still morning air, I could smell tendrils of diesel exhaust from the Mercedes drifting up the street.

Looking drunk, the gray-haired man bumbled out of the

building, sidestepped into the lot, squinted down the road, then hastened back inside the brick building. Nobody could get drunk that quickly. He was a man out-of-sync with the universe—waiting impatiently for something that couldn't come fast enough.

Along with the exhaust, something else began drifting in the still morning air: the distant wail of a siren. I spotted the genesis in my rear-view mirror and watched the speck of flashing red light in the distance gradually evolve into a boxy aid car from the Seattle Fire Department.

Cutting its siren, it raced up the deserted street and screeched to a halt in the lot of the Trinity Building.

As if on cue, the old man blundered out a second time and distractedly propped the building door open while the two men from the fire department fetched their equipment in large black suitcases from the back of their vehicle. They hustled along behind him into the building.

Soon another white and red boxy fire department van pulled into the lot—the paramedics—and two more men hefted their suitcases of equipment into the Trinity Building.

It was only when I spied the blue ping-pong lights from a prowl car half a mile behind in the rear-view mirror that I clambered out of the truck and hustled into the building. The cop may only have been coming in for a blood run, but if it was for more than that, this would be my last chance to rubberneck.

Inside I found a long fruitwood receptionist's counter that had accommodations for two receptionists and a switchboard operator. Nothing was there but a coffee cup with lipstick on the rim that somebody had abandoned in Friday afternoon's melee. Beyond that, the room opened up into an enormous atrium that could have held four, maybe five hundred people in a pinch. Huge fig trees grew in concrete planters. Ferns dangled from perches built high into the walls. Colorful tulips grew in concrete planters along the walkway. There were three levels, open aisleways fronting the atrium in a rectangular arrangement, offices off each level.

Today's business was all being conducted second floor center.

Standing in the doorway, the old man was pale and sweaty and rigid, his back pressed up against the blond wood of the door. I skipped up the open stairs two at a time. It's funny what you can get away with if you act like you belong.

I strode through the doorway past the old gummer directly into the office.

The old man spoke to the firemen, "Is he going to live?"

"Don't know, Pops. You know who he is? You got a name and address? Next of kin?"

"Sure."

"He related to you?"

"You might say that." The old man swiped at his brow with a balled-up handkerchief. "He might as well be."

Intermingled with the smell of perfume, sweat, and urine, I could still detect a whiff of gun powder.

The office was neat and spacious, with Danish furniture and brushed steel fixtures, though the six bodies inside made it look smaller than it ordinarily would have. Four of the bodies were living, breathing firemen. One body was that of Mark Daniels, fresh blood streaming out of his scalp and down the side of his head, pooling on the carpet in a thick, goopy puddle. He had been shot in the temple. Three firemen were perspiring over him, inserting needles, taking hurried blood pressure readings, and chattering on their portable radios to a doctor at Harborview.

The sixth body was that of a girl who I guessed was about eighteen. No, make that sixteen. She was lying on the floor on her back.

One of the firemen stood apart from the others, gawking at her.

A dishwater blonde, she was short and chesty. She was naked except for thigh-length black silk stockings. Or maybe they were nylon. I couldn't tell without touching them and I wasn't going to touch them.

"I guess she's dead," said the fireman, without looking away from the spectacle.

"Appears that way," I replied. If you looked carefully you could see where the bullet had dug into the side of her skull at about the hairline and done a lot of damage behind her eyes, both of which were open. Cornflower blue. The left one was slightly blown.

A minute later two uniformed cops came in and the party began.

Chapter Two

KATHY BIRCHFIELD insisted on chauffeuring me. The car was new, a smart little apple-yellow two-seater, an import from over the water, and the payments had her on a stingy budget.

"I asked you out," she said, "so I'll pick up the tab."

"Like hell you will."

"I will. And don't be such a grouch. And thanks for coming, Thomas. I know how much you abhor parties and chitchat and 'too much silly talk about too much nothing,' as you call it. You don't know how much it means to have you for my escort when I need you. Really."

"Forget it."

I stared out the window at the houses we were passing in the twilight. Dressed to the nines, we were screwing up our eyes looking for an address on Queen Anne Hill only a matter of blocks from where I had picked up Mark Daniels over a week earlier. I was in a double-breasted suit Kathy had insisted on helping me select a year ago. The stiff collar of the shirt chafed my neck.

Kathy was poured into a slinky gold lamé dress that I had only caught a glimpse of through the folds of her full-length fur coat, a coat she had bought years ago at St. Vincent DePaul and redone—long before they had come back into fashion. Kathy had two bedrooms in her new apartment, one for herself and one for her clothes.

"This must be it," she said. "See all those cars?"

"I thought you said this was going to be a small gathering. There wouldn't really be anybody important here."

"Don't go getting scared."

"I'm not scared."

"You sound scared. More than five people in the room and you go bananas."

"I'm not bananas."

"Don't be a grouch. You'll love it."

"Oh tish." It was how her three-year-old niece, who had a longshoreman for a stepfather, said, "Oh shit." We used it between ourselves to show disgruntlement.

She reached past the gear shift knob and squeezed my thigh, making a superb mockery of Mae West. "Oooooooooooo."

"Tish."

It was a tall colonial, with white pillars bracing the front, antique lamps in the drive, a doorman—the whole bit. I knew the neighborhood vaguely from a case I'd worked when I was still with the city police. Across the street lived a retired United States senator whose maid raked in more money in a year than I ever had.

A conservative guess pegged the house as capable of holding two hundred people. We parked in the first available spot, which was four blocks away, and crossed our fingers that one of the spring showers that had been clobbering the city all day wouldn't drench us. They had valet parking, but Kathy wasn't going to trust her new car to some gawky college kid in coveralls.

Inside, we were introduced to the mayor, a couple of city councilmen and their wives, a city councilwoman and her husband. It was a political gathering having something to do with a sister city in Japan. There were some round-faced Japanese. I recognized several reporters from the local TV stations, all shorter than they appeared on the tube.

"Oh, Thomas Black," Kathy whispered in my ear when we got a breather from the initial flurry of introductions. I could tell from her tone that she was going to mock me.

"You look so big and handsome in that suit. I'll bet half the women here are dying to go home with you."

"Flattery will get you everywhere," I said, spotting a voluptuous blonde across the room.

Strawberry-blonde, really. She was in her mid-twenties. Several times I caught her looking at me. There was something about her—a certain twinkle in her sad eyes when she looked about, as if she were mildly amused by the world—and in love with it. My guess was she had a vivacious personality that for some reason was subdued tonight.

In her childhood her hair had probably been red. Time had transformed it to the fascinating shade of sun-ruined straw. We held each other's eye until one or the other of us broke—and my palms began to get real slippery. I had to meet this woman. Half the knowledge of the universe seemed to pass between us when our eyes met, like an electrical charge. There was a chemistry in the air and we both knew it.

She turned away and spoke deliberately to a sober-looking man at her elbow, a chubby chap who had been pried into a gray suit and strangled with an evangelical collar. After her escort answered her, she erupted into a low-pitched laugh. She had a laugh that flowed like water sloshing in a wooden tub. I could have listened to it all night.

"Kathy? You wouldn't mind terribly if we went home separately, would you?"

"Of course not. You know the deal. Suit yourself."

"You're a peach."

I moved across the room toward the blonde. Halfway there, Kathy apprehended me, grabbing my elbow and standing close, avoiding my face and talking at my arm like a spy.

"You're not making a move on *her,* are you?"

"The blonde, yeah. She's smitten with me. I don't really want to, but I feel it's some sort of duty, you know? Look at her. She's smitten."

"Thomas, she's with a clergyman."

"I'm with an angel. That doesn't mean anything. We can talk about relations—trade relations."

"You don't go to an affair like this and then samba over and try to pick up some society matron who is with a clergyman. Thomas?"

I looked over at the blonde. "It's not that I want to. Or even that I need to. It's an obligation, really. Do you understand what I'm saying? We're talking civic obligation here. My debt to the city."

Kathy smiled patronizingly. I had seen her use the same sorry smile over a gravestone once.

"Thomas! Why don't you wait a while? Maybe that's her husband. Besides, isn't he Sam Michael Wheeler, that preacher who's on the television all the time?"

"She's head-over-heels in love. Can't you see the way she's been mooning over me?"

"She's not, Thomas. You must look like somebody she knows or something, somebody she doesn't recognize in this context. Maybe you look like her dentist. Her sanitation engineer. The guy who snatched her purse last week."

"Funny."

Kathy shook her head. "Believe me, she's not in love with you."

"Do you know who she is?"

She shrugged. "I might have met her."

"Well, she's fallen hard for the kid. Married or not, I'm going over there sometime this evening so I can at least pat her hand and console her."

For the better part of ten minutes the pneumatic blonde and I flicked hot glances at each other. She meandered around the gathering beside the reverend and I meandered around beside Kathy, and then alone when my date began discussing politics with some of the local pompous and elected. Drinks were served. Canapés were munched. Jokes were told and acknowledged with polite tittering.

Everything was genteel except the blonde.

Her looks grew hotter and lingered longer than they had a right to. The more I thought about it the more I knew she couldn't be married, or even seriously interested in the reverend, not the way she was ogling me.

When the reverend left her side to fetch refreshments, I waded through the crowd toward her. When I turned around Kathy was giving me a funny warning look from between two short Japanese gentlemen, one of whom was himself having a hard time tearing his eyes away from Kathy's liquid gold gown.

"Good evening," I said.

Without really being a part of their group, the blonde had been listening to a conversation between several women standing in a nearby doorway. She was sitting on a shiny sofa under an oil painting. When I spoke she turned her head. The movement made a straight line of tendon run down her neck and into her blouse.

"I understand you work for some security outfit," she said.

"You've heard of me? I'm surprised."

"Somewhat."

"I work for myself." I sat beside her. Up close I could see that she was a large-framed woman, breasts like igloos. She wore a black skirt and a silk blouse in a shade of blue that looked like something on a swallow. Her legs were crossed and one calf was swollen from the pressure of her knee beneath it. Her greenish-brown eyes played over my face.

"Security work. That must be very exciting."

"Mostly it's just work."

"I can't help but think there must be an awful lot of adventure to it."

"About once every ten years." I was thinking about a pair of hoodlums who had tried to teach me to breathe underwater six weeks before.

"You don't know me?" she asked.

"I'm sorry."

"Haven't you been reading the papers?"

"After last Sunday I didn't have the stomach for it. I've been tossing them into the fireplace all week."

"That's right. You were involved in the investigation. You were mixed up in that shooting, but you didn't give the police anything. They were going to arrest you."

"I spent two nights in jail."

"Did you? I'm sorry about that."

I laughed. "It wasn't your fault. So what do you do?"

"A little sculpture. I dabble, really. I was an art major in college."

Across the room Kathy scowled at me and shook her head. It wasn't an admonishment, but an order. She was commanding me to leave this woman. I couldn't believe it. I winked at her.

When the reverend tried to ford across the room, Kathy intercepted him, detaining him for my benefit. She was, I thought, going slightly overboard.

"You here with your husband?"

"No. No. My husband has been . . . ill. He couldn't make it."

"Sorry to hear that." So, Kathy was wrong. She wasn't married to the man in the collar. She was out for a fling, had chosen me, and Kathy was making a fool of herself.

"I suppose that's your girlfriend in the gold?"

"A friend. She needed an escort tonight. She's going a little goofy right now."

"Just friends? That's hard to understand. She's ravishing."

"It's a long story. By the way, so are you—ravishing."

Her eyes smiled without the rest of her face helping any, and I noted how much green there was in the circles around her pupils. We were going to get along just fine. We both knew it, like some sort of cosmic inference.

Kathy and the man in the ecclesiastical duds reached us and stood over the couch. Kathy said, "Perhaps we should all adjourn to another room. The host has graciously made the library available."

Slowly swinging my eyes away from the strawberry-blonde, I said, "Kathy, I don't believe this."

"No," said the blonde, picking up my hand by the

thumb, standing and pulling me to my feet. "She's right. Come along."

Kathy gave me a look. I gave her a harder look. The blonde towed me away, the others trailing behind. It wasn't until we got to the door of the library that she dropped my hand, which had begun perspiring in her grip.

All four of us walked into the library. The lights were already on. The clergyman closed the door and stood against it and the four of us exchanged looks.

Chapter Three

THE BLONDE seated herself at a small, round table and switched on a Tiffany lamp, handling the valuable antique as carefully as if she knew what it was worth, as casually as if she owned it. There were five of the obstacles in the book-lined library and I moved so as not to blunder into one of them.

Diffused lamplight played on her face, and I noted for the first time that her cheeks were splashed with washed-out freckles.

They peppered the backs of her hands and arms, and crept down her neck into the swallow-blue of her blouse. As a child, she undoubtedly had been one of those milk-skinned redheads. Her twenty-five or so years on the planet had dimmed the freckles and leached most of the reddish pigment out of her hair. Piled on her head and secured with whalebone combs, it was an entrancing hue of gold. It seemed to change color with the light.

Hands balled into fists and rammed into my pockets, I bided my time and waited to see how Kathy was going to get her foot out of her mouth.

Kathy said, "Most of us know each other."

I glanced around. The clergyman nodded. The blonde gave me a vaguely nervous smile. It was the first time she had looked at all anxious that evening, no doubt disturbed that our smoldering yen for each other would soon be publicly exposed.

"Leech, Bemis and Ott is representing the case," Kathy

15

said. "I'm doing the preliminary background work. Thomas
Black, the gentleman by the door is the Reverend Sam Michael Wheeler. The woman he is escorting is Deanna Daniels."

It took a few seconds for it to hit me.

Kathy prodded my memory. "Mrs. *Mark* Daniels?"

"Oh, tish."

Smiling, Kathy reached over, picked my hand out of my
pocket, and fondled it maternally. Crumbs of comfort.

"Sorry to do it this way, but Mrs. Daniels wanted to look
you over before she hired us."

All that eye play in the other room, the staring I had mistaken for hot blood, for good old American lust, had been
nothing but a good old systematic professional evaluation.
Good teeth. Nice coat. Fetlocks healthy. Pack the animal
into the van, Roger. I looked around for a rug to crawl under.

"From what we've been told," said Sam Michael Wheeler, strolling across the room to Deanna Daniels and draping
his arm heavily across her shoulders, "from what we've
been told, in a situation like this the investigator is almost as
crucial as the lawyer. Of course, we're no experts. This is
the first time Deanna has been involved in something of this
sort. I've had experience in civil litigation. And, of course, I
was in the military for ten years."

I cut him off. "Comparing the military to a murder case is
like saying you know what an artichoke tastes like because
you once ate a piece of celery."

"Thomas . . ." Kathy lowered one of her looks on me.

The Reverend continued, "Deanna just wanted to . . .
check you out without any pressure. Don't you see?" He
gave me a glance that was partial smile, partial patronage,
and partial obsolescent aristocratic hauteur. It was a lethal
look that might work on a cowed congregation. In his forties, he had a full head of mustard-brown hair and a chubby
face that couldn't be called anything but boyish.

I turned to Kathy Birchfield. Since passing the bar a year
ago she had been working at Leech, Bemis and Ott, a well-

known firm of attorneys in Seattle. The invitation to work
for L, B and O had been a coup, and since she was the only
one in the prestigious house who wanted to sink her teeth
into criminal cases, by default she was getting those cases
when they presented themselves. While I wasn't considered
their official investigator by any means, the two times before that Kathy had needed someone, she had called upon
me.

"Well," I said, removing my hand from Kathy's grip and
folding my arms across my chest. "Did I pass muster?"

"I'm sorry," said Deanna Daniels. "We weren't trying
to belittle you . . . or anything. I just felt uncomfortable
hiring a firm without . . . I mean, I've heard wonderful
things about you. It's just that I had to see you. I go on my
gut instincts a lot. It's how I am. Now that I've met you I
feel silly. Of course you'll do."

Kathy said, "Thomas does work for Leech, Bemis and
Ott on a case-by-case basis, Deanna. We'll have to lay it out
for him and see."

Deanna bit her lower lip. "Sure. I remember you explained that at the office."

Pacing around the room, Kathy outlined the situation. I
couldn't help noticing that for a clergyman, Sam Michael
Wheeler's eyes lingered a little too long on the shimmering
gold dress. Maybe I was watching him too closely. But
then, he was only human. Even Deanna was looking at it.

"A week ago Emmett Anderson, Mark Daniels' longtime business associate, dropped by the Trinity Building to
pick up some papers. You were outside, Thomas.

"When he got upstairs he heard somebody groaning in
Mark's office. The door was locked from the inside, but he
had a key. You know what he found in there. You saw it.
Mark Daniels has been in a coma at Harborview ever since.
The doctors don't know when he might regain consciousness. Or even if he will. Meanwhile, the Seattle Police Department has built a case on him. If he lives . . . they
prosecute for murder."

Kathy glanced across the room to see how Deanna Daniels was absorbing this narrative. The Reverend rubbed the back of her shoulder in a comforting motion and she laid her hand on top of his, both their hands massaging lazily in unison. Despite her voluptuousness, I couldn't help noticing how thin her hand was.

"If he dies, Deanna stands to lose a good deal of insurance money. Life insurance doesn't pay off on suicides. And she may lose part of the business to boot."

"How does she lose part of the business?" I asked.

"Emmett Anderson and my husband have been together for years," said Deanna, clearing her throaty voice and avoiding my eyes. "They were very close when they first started out and they did most everything without putting any of it in writing. Some of the ventures Mark owned outright. Some Emmett owned. Most Emmett owned. We've only done a little investigating, but it would take an army of accountants to straighten things out if Emmett decided not to assist. I know that's hard to believe, but they started off small and most of the money in the beginning was Emmett's. When they got bigger they didn't see any reason to change . . ."

Kathy finished for her. "Legally, he could choke off the Daniels estate with next to nothing. At least we think he could. So far we're having a difficult time pinning him down on what he is planning to do. And Mark had run up some bills. He's behind on his child support. He bought a custom-made sailboat for a small fortune. He is up to his ears in debt. If Deanna doesn't get the insurance money, and doesn't get any of the business, she'll be out on the street."

"You could sue for your share of the business."

Kathy shook her head. Deanna said, "I'll have to declare bankruptcy. Going to court would take years. I could never pay it all off."

I looked at Kathy. "What do they have downtown?"

"The girl's body. The gun. It is registered to Mark. The fact that he knew the girl. She worked at the plant for three months last summer. And the note."

"What note?"

"He left a suicide note in the typewriter in his office."

I hadn't seen it, but there had been a lot of confusion that morning, a lot of other things to look at. Though I had searched, I hadn't seen the gun either. One of the paramedics had surreptitiously laid his coat over it until a uniformed officer showed up.

"Do you have a copy of the note?"

"We know what it says," said the Reverend Wheeler. "It was a family courtesy to provide it for Mrs. Daniels. Detective Crum was kind enough to do that."

"Ralph Crum?"

"I believe that was his name." The hand-on-shoulder business wasn't stopping and it was beginning to wear me down. "Do you know this Crum fellow?"

"What did the note say? Better yet, do you have a copy with you?"

"If you know this Detective Crum, it might make things more expedient. We weren't aware that you had contacts with the police."

"The note?"

Deanna stared at a Flemish tapestry hanging on the opposite wall. She quoted from memory in a voice flatter than a student saxophone.

" 'Deanna dear. Forgive me. So much of my life has been lived apart from you that now when you require so much of me I find it so very hard to give. This is something that's been coming on for a long time. Don't feel bad for me. Just forgive me. I'll love you forever. Mark.' "

"That's it?"

"That's it," said the Reverend Sam Wheeler, his voice a bit more chipper than I would have liked. I noticed he wasn't wearing a band on his left hand. Perhaps his plump ring finger had outgrown it.

"Mark didn't write that," Deanna said, springing up and moving toward me. The Reverend followed, grasping her by one elbow, acting as an anchor on her fervor.

"How do you know?"

"Because Mark didn't try to kill himself. He wouldn't. He just wouldn't."

"Was the note signed?"

"Typewritten. His name at the bottom."

"What about the girl? Do you think he shot her?" Tears began trickling down Deanna's cheeks. I was pouring salt into old wounds.

The Reverend took advantage of Deanna's momentary confusion to hug her to himself, a self-satisfied look on his mug. Any moment I expected him to start purring.

"Of course he didn't shoot her. Mark wouldn't shoot her."

I looked past the couple in front of me to Kathy who was watching the three of us, an indecipherable look marring her liquid violet eyes.

"No woman thinks her own husband would shoot anybody. Yet it happens every day. Tell me specifically why you think Mark wouldn't do such a thing."

"Aren't you being a little hard on her?" interjected the Reverend Wheeler. "This lady has had quite a week. She may lose everything this life has seen fit to give her. Her husband is lying half dead in a hospital bed in a coma that he may never wake out of. She only came to this party because I talked her into it. It's killing her to sit in the hospital alone and wait, Lord almighty, man, can't you see it's killing her?

"She's been almost a week without any real sleep. She needed to get out by herself, if only for a few hours. I practically forced her to come and meet you here. And now you're giving her the third degree like some sort of police-state baboon."

"It's okay," said Deanna softly.

"No, it isn't," continued Reverend Wheeler. "What do you think it was like for Deanna coming to this party where everybody knew what happened—to know that everybody was whispering behind her back? Answer me!"

"No," said Deanna. "No more, Sam. It's all right. In fact, I want to answer him. If I can't, then he's right: I don't have any right to hire him."

The bluster Wheeler had worked up seemed to sizzle away like air out of an old tire. He walked his hand from Deanna's shoulder to the back of her bare neck, where he cupped his meaty thumb and palm around the base of her skull and left it there like a man cradling a melon. She didn't seem to notice.

"Do you have reason to think Mark couldn't have done it?" Kathy Birchfield asked.

"That note. Mark had the typewriter in his office, but he only used it for business. Whenever he wrote anything personal he used a fountain pen. It was just his way. He loved fountain pens. He never would have typed a note like that. And those words—they just aren't his. I can't quite put my finger on it, but there was something clichéd about the way that note was written."

"Did you tell the police?"

She nodded. Kathy looked from Deanna to me and said, "We'll talk to them later, Thomas. Ralph Crum said he'd talk."

"Just one item before you get too wrapped up in this," said Wheeler, unctuously. "We understand from the news media that you were involved in some sort of mysterious activity out on Harbor Island . . ." He let it waft in the air, awaiting my—he thought—compulsive explanation.

I watched Deanna's eyes turn to mine and grow reflective. Chances were she had hired me to follow her husband. She uncrossed her legs and smoothed the thighs of her skirt. She was a large woman, extraordinarily well built and had the look of an athlete, a swimmer or an avid tennis player.

"That is to say, the day Mark was discovered by Emmett, you were there. You were apparently working on something. But you wouldn't tell the police. Is that correct?"

"You got it."

"What were you working on?"

I flicked a piece of lint off my left sleeve. I straightened my cuff. I looked at Wheeler, at his hand resting on Deanna's neck. I looked at Deanna. "I've got rules, Reverend Wheeler. One of them is not to compromise a client."

"Are you saying you were out there working on a case? For a client?"

"I'm not saying anything."

"We have a right to know. After all, Leech, Bemis and Ott are Mark's attorneys and they're hiring you to look into this. His life may hang in the balance. At the very least, his reputation. We have a right to find out just how much you're hiding."

Something in the green-brown of Deanna Daniels' eyes told me she wasn't exactly sympathetic with Wheeler's line of inquiry. Contesting it was a feat she didn't have the requisite energy for. Neither did I.

Wheeler continued, "We're paying your bills, fella. Now, cough it up. You can't hold out."

"Watch me."

When he got tired of glowering at me, which took longer than I thought, he turned to Kathy Birchfield for succor. She shrugged and said, "Thomas is very good at what he does. If there's something more to be found out about this case, he'll find it."

Deanna gave me a look that might have been gratitude— but was both melancholy and inquisitive in turn.

Wheeler walked to the door and turned around, the knob in his fist. We could hear people conversing in the hallway. "Coming, Deanna, honey?"

"In a minute."

"I'll meet you outside," said Kathy, following the glances that were passing between Deanna and me. I no longer wanted to think there were sparks, not with her husband five miles away in a coma, so I thought it was something else. Something primordial, something about a knight in shining armor, something about a man with a rope in his hand when you were sinking in the black night off the side of a ship. I had seen the look before—a dangerous situation which left a distinct and bitter aftertaste if things didn't pan out.

Chatter from the corridor grew louder through the half open door. Deanna stood, walked to me, raised her hand as if she were planning to touch me, dropped her hand and said, "There is one thing. How did the girl get there? And how did he have enough time to get into the mood? I mean, suicide is a big step. You don't just wake up in the morning and say, 'Okay, bang.' Do you? Also, the note said he had been thinking about it for a long time. He never mentioned anything about suicide. Never ever. You'd think he would have said something. Maybe once when he was drunk."

"Did he get drunk?"

"Not a lot." She avoided my eyes. "Once or twice a month maybe."

"You don't love your husband anymore, do you?"

Her words were clipped, almost angry. "Not anymore. Not for a long while."

She heeled around and walked out of the room. Outside in the hallway a young waiter in an ill-fitting white coat longingly watched her walk away, swept up in the perfume of her being. Me—I was going to need an inoculation against her witchery. Along with several booster shots.

Chapter Four

WORKING AN IMITATION antique crank phone in the hall-way, I dialed Ralph Crum. He said he was plowing through some paperwork, but would meet us in twenty minutes at a café on Third Avenue. It was a seedy greasy spoon and Kathy was going to draw a lot of looks in that liquid gold.

"I'll take a cab," I told her when she met me at the front door.

"I don't think so, big fella."

"Hey Pancho."

"Hey Cisco. I go weeth you."

"Okay. But keep your coat buttoned." On the assumption that I was kidding, she playfully closed a fist and rapped me on the shoulder.

Two angry rain showers doused us on our short journey, but the street was dry when we parked on Third Avenue. Seattle was like that. If you don't like the weather, stick around five minutes.

We commandeered a table by the window so Kathy could keep an eye on the grifters and panhandlers on the sidewalk—and on her new car.

"Sorry about the ruse," said Kathy. "I know how embarrassed you were."

"Nothing to it." I buffed a nail on my sleeve. "I wasn't embarrassed."

Kathy Birchfield looked at me as if I had just offered to work a variation of the pigeon drop on her favorite aunt. "You were, and you snapped at Wheeler because of it. He's a powerful and very influential man in this community. Besides, he's done an awful lot to improve life for certain segments of society in this town. I wish you didn't take such a sudden dislike to certain people."

"Naw, I wasn't embarrassed."

"Okay." She held up both open palms. "Thomas, I'm sorry. I just wanted you to know that Mrs. Daniels was very specific. You weren't to know anything about what was going on. Don't ask me why."

"I think I know why."

"You do? I've been wondering all evening."

"Forget it."

"I didn't want to embarrass you."

"The pinnacle of your emotional life is embarrassing me, Kathy, and you know it."

I looked away from a pair of middle-aged lovebirds necking in a back booth in time to see Kathy wiping a smirk off her face with an open hand. "Don't feel bad about it, Thomas. Deanna's always been the kind of woman men get brainsick over."

"Brainsick?"

The smirk returned in spades and above it her eyes were as amused as if I'd done a jig on the tabletop in a fig leaf. "You have to admit, you were a little green around the gills."

Kathy sipped at a Dr. Pepper and watched two men in ragged coats pushing a broken-down Dodge up Third Avenue, one of them steering through the open driver's window. Cars beeped. A lady Metro driver with a peroxide mop manhandled her bus around them, honked and flipped them off.

"Why is Crum talking to us?" We both knew it was almost verboten for a homicide detective to talk to defense attorneys about anything. They made their case and handed it over to the D.A. The D.A. might try to talk. Never the dicks from downtown.

"Ralph Crum figures the case won't get to trial and he wants to save us some grief."

"Why won't it go to trial?"

"Because of Mark Daniels' physical condition."

"You mean Daniels isn't going to wake up?"

"The doctor I spoke with gave him one chance in ten of regaining consciousness. At that, he may be a vegetable. In fact, they haven't even taken the bullet out yet. They feel it's much more likely that he'll just linger on for a few weeks, or months, and then die."

"Does Deanna know this?"

"We haven't discussed it. She may. She probably does."

"How much life insurance are we talking about?"

"Oodles. Three or four separate policies. I think it's over $600,000, all told. And his business holdings are worth more than that—if Anderson decides to do the decent thing and split it down the middle. The problem there is Anderson was real close to Mark's first family. He was disappointed when Mark divorced Helen and married Deanna."

"I bet a lot of people were disappointed the day Deanna got married."

"Funny. By the way, who were you working for? Were you following Mark, or the old man, Emmett Anderson? Or the girl?"

"Deanna asked me where the girl came from. Good question. She didn't drive there with Mark and there weren't any other vehicles around."

"You're avoiding the question," said Kathy. "Who were you working for?"

"Maybe later," I said, as Ralph Crum stormed through the front door of the café, spotted us and clumped over to our table. He shook off his trench coat, unsnarled an argyle scarf from around his neck and meticulously laid both items across a nearby chair. He scooted into the booth beside me, so that he could gaze across at Kathy. It was May and not as cold as he affected it was.

A small, blue-eyed, balding man, Ralph Crum was punctilious and invariably polite, even when he was arresting you for an axe murder.

"Sorry about last week," he said, piercing me with his wet blues. "I know a couple of nights in jail ain't no picnic.

It wasn't my idea. The boss gets a little heavy-handed. I think he's becoming political or something and this case has a lot of people watching it. I been interviewed more than two dozen times this week.''

"Free board and lodging for two nights? All the pinochle partners I could ask for? Are you kidding? I should have been paying you guys.''

Crum looked at me for a second, trying to discern how much was acid and how much was leg-pulling, then broke into a tiny wry smile. He took out a pipe and began working with the fixings. Crum was married, had four children and fell in love with Kathy every time he saw her. Maybe he forgot about her when she wasn't around, but when she was there, he was definitely in love. It was the only reason he was being so helpful.

"What do you want to know?" he asked, dipping a match into the bowl of his pipe and sucking.

"Everything you can tell us.''

"You're wasting your time. He's not going to live. If he does live, he'll be a rutabaga. We can't try a vegetable. He'll just lie in bed somewhere and round-the-clock nurses will feed him intravenously and wipe his behind and clip his nails. And he'll wither away. If by some miracle he does live, and he's not a rutabaga, we've got a case on him that is airtight.''

"What makes it airtight?''

Ralph expelled darkish blue smoke out the side of his mouth in spurts. "First, the girl worked for him last summer. He met her there, began sleeping with her, got upset about how things were going, and knocked her off. Then himself. He's got debts coming out his ears.''

"You have witnesses that he was sleeping with the girl?''

"We're getting to that. It was his gun. A .357 Magnum firing .38 specials. Two empty shells in the cylinder. She was shot from about two feet away. The barrel was only an inch or two from his head when he got it. The lab tests show the gun was in his hand when it was fired. In his right hand.

He's right-handed. He wrote the suicide note and left it in the typewriter.''

''That's all?''

Crum gave a snort. ''What else do you need? Hell, even I'd plead guilty if they had that on me. Okay. There *is* one more thing. He's a type B secretor. The girl had sex with a type B secretor sometime that morning. That's the icing on the cake right there.''

Kathy said, ''What's a type B secretor?''

''Approximately eighty-five percent of the population secretes their blood type in other bodily fluids. So even though we don't have a sample of blood from the man who had sex with her that morning, we know he was blood type B. And that he was a secretor. He could have been a type B nonsecretor. Or a secretor type A. Understand?''

''And Mark Daniels is a B?''

Crum nodded. ''And the man the girl had sex with is, too.''

''The fact remains,'' I said, ''that Deanna Daniels does not think her husband did it.''

''How many wives of suicide victims want to admit that it happened, Tom? Not many. Most of them think of it as some sort of indictment of themselves. As if they've failed somehow.''

''He was only in there a half hour,'' I said. ''You think she was waiting for him, he screwed her, then shot her, typed a note and drilled himself? All in thirty minutes?''

Crum shrugged. He didn't care if a man could do that in thirty minutes or if he could do it in thirty days. His case was airtight. We all sat there and mulled it over for a few moments. Crum ordered coffee and doughnuts from a young waiter growing a mustache that looked like dirt smudges. Outside the gritty booth window a pair of pigeons fluttered to the sidewalk and began strutting around in search of treasures.

''Who was the girl?''

''Nobody seems to know. According to papers we found in her purse, she was Debby Crowley, but last summer, when she worked in the Trinity Dog Chow plant, she went under the name of Beatrice Hindenburg. We've been trying all week, but we can't find anything on her.''

"Not even where she lived?"

Crum shook his head. "She's probably a runaway. Maybe from out of state. How do you trace a thing like that? She could have come from anywhere. Chances are her folks haven't even bothered to contact the authorities. We thought Daniels might be stashing her up at a place they keep on the lake, but we checked and found nothing. She was referred to the Trinity Dog Chow plant for temporary work by the Downtown Runaway Center. But their records are never what they should be. We couldn't get any name on her except Beatrice Hindenburg. No current address. No relatives. Nobody seemed to know where she came from. Maybe Alaska. We're getting a lot of runaways from ice country.''

"You think Mark Daniels was keeping her in an apartment somewhere?"

"Could be." Crum didn't seem real interested in the conjecture.

"But you haven't been able to find it?"

"Hell, we don't need it. We've got that rutabaga nailed to the wall. Screwed, blued and tattooed. He couldn't weasel out of this if he hired a thousand lawyers and ten thousand detectives.''

"It seems to me that if you found out who the girl was, you might learn a lot of interesting things.''

"Mmmm. Like what?"

"Like whether or not she had a jealous boyfriend. Like whether this was a long-term affair or a spur-of-the-moment thing. And where did the girl come from that morning? How did she get to the plant? You find a taxi or whatever that took her there?''

"Nope." Crum popped his eyebrows twice, acknowledging that I had a point, but that the point wasn't going to spur any untoward activity downtown.

Kathy turned from the pigeons on the sidewalk and

glanced from Crum to me and back to Crum. She wanted to say something. That was obvious. But she didn't.

Sliding out of the booth, Kathy said, "Thank you for your time. Hope you don't get into Dutch telling us all this."

"Don't even think about it." Crum stood and let me out, eyeing Kathy as if to memorize the details of her face. We didn't shake hands. He plunked back down, took a long gander at Kathy's dress through the folds of her coat, and said, "Open and shut. Don't waste your time."

"There's more to it than that," I said.

Crum popped his eyebrows again.

I said, "You ever get the feeling that all people are good for is filling up graves?"

Dunking a piece of doughnut into his coffee and shoveling it between his thick lips, Crum said, "Why, yes. I get that feeling quite often. How 'bout yourself?"

"Once in a while."

Kathy drove me back to the party, rolling the window down in her car so the night breeze would expunge Crum's pipe smoke from her fur coat. Though I looked, Deanna and the Reverend Wheeler had already left. We stayed late, very late. Kathy drove me to my house off Roosevelt Way, gave me a sorry look and an even sorrier peck on the cheek.

I skipped up the steps and went into my house, turned on the TV for company, thumbed open the phone book and scribbled Deanna Daniels' number. It was only natural Deanna would swear her husband was innocent. But some of the facts were skewed. She had a point about that. We would see.

I put the pad beside my bed. Then I undressed, brushed, took a leak, and trotted into the living room to flick off the set. Sometimes I used the electronic blabber like campers used the dampening sound of a nearby river or waterfall. White noise. I slept fitfully thinking about pneumatic blondes and giant rutabagas.

Chapter Five

THE NEIGHBORHOOD SPARROWS had just begun their morning serenade when a breeze rattled a tall forsythia against my window and dragged me up from a dream about a man trying to hang me.

I crawled out of bed, showered, shaved, and pulled a week's worth of newspapers out of the basket beside the fireplace, scanning them to see how much yummy scandal I had missed.

The Daniels case was the biggest scoop to hit this town in five months. I perused carefully, examining each page for peripheral articles. The only scraps I culled were some flimsy background items they had printed on Mark Daniels, how he had battled from the bottom of the pack to evolve into a corporate giant.

I snipped the articles out and left the clippings on the table.

It was eight-thirty when I slid into my pickup and drove to the Daniels house near the crest of Queen Anne Hill.

Anticipating the pall Deanna's presence—her unattainability—would cast over my psyche, I deliberately tuned the truck radio to one of those elevator-music stations that slowed down your blood.

The gray Cadillac was in the drive with a yellow personalized license plate that read DeeDee.

The ebony Rabbit I had tailed eight days earlier stood beside the Cadillac. A third car, a new Chrysler, was parked behind the Caddy. I walked over to it and stuck my hand out over the hood. Heat rose from the engine block. It crackled tinnily under the hood. I climbed the concrete steps, thumbed the buzzer and wheeled around to look at the world.

An Indonesian freighter steamed across the glassy sound toward the huge bright orange loading cranes on Harbor Island. Below on the hill, church bells pealed and ripped open the crisp morning air.

"Nice view, eh?" The voice was deep, much deeper than mine, and mellow enough to soothe the video hordes.

I turned around. Sam Michael Wheeler, replete with natty black suit and evangelical collar, smiled gamely at me. His collar wasn't strangling him like the one last night had. He wore them a size smaller for parties where he might turn up a sinner or two.

"Deanna in?"

"Morning. You have an appointment with Mrs. Daniels?"

"Nope."

Wheeler pursed his lips twice in succession, looked me over—I was wearing jeans, a polo shirt and Pumas—and, by way of answer, swung the door wide, beckoning with a sloppy yet flamboyant wave of his forearm for me to enter.

The odor of chlorine and the stifling humidity of moist warm air trampled my senses. Instead of a living room in the front of their house, they had an indoor pool, turquoise light radiating around the terra-cotta walls, marbling the ceiling. A determined swimmer could do laps. The surface was somewhat roiled, as if someone had been splashing recently. Small, puddled footprints on the walkway confirmed my thesis.

Piloting me past the pool into the house through a set of triple-insulated sliding glass doors, Wheeler, without turning around, gestured for me to sit. He then progressed through the room and out the far end.

The living room sported a wall-to-wall view of the pool area out the sliding glass doors, and—out another set of windows—a view of the bay and the snowcapped Olympics.

Across the Sound, a rain squall lashed Bremerton. The furnishings were all new, all neutrals, Danish and modern, lamps bobbling off the ends of curved brass poles. It was the kind of house somebody trying very hard to be chic had spent a lot of energy on.

Wheeler came back first, walking all the way across the room to the couch, and stood inches from my knees so that I couldn't have risen without bumping him. He had a duck walk, feet aimed northeast and northwest.

"Going up to the hospital this morning," he announced, a single note of glee buried in the carefully orchestrated bland harmony of his tones. "It's a trial. A real trial. But Deanna's holding up well. The woman has courage. You have to admire the woman. And poor Mark. It isn't often when you visit a man in the hospital that you've already written the funeral service. Half the state'll be there. I'll say one thing for Mark. He had friends in high places."

Sam Wheeler savored hospitals and tragedies and graveyards a little more than he should have. But then, why not? It was his business.

He smiled down at me. I curled the edges of my mouth up at him. He pivoted and swaggered across the room to a bank of family photos on a low table. Of medium height, he was a heavy man who seemed propelled towards blandness. His success in television ministry baffled me. But then, the camera often arbitrarily magnified one personality quirk and dwarfed the others.

"You, uh, have some business with Deanna this morning?" he asked, without turning away from the photos.

"Sure do."

"May I ask what it is?"

"Thought I'd get keys to the Trinity Building."

"I doubt if she has them. You planning to give the place a little inspection tour?"

"I might poke around."

"This morning?" Wheeler cocked his head around and riveted his dark eyes on me.

"Whenever."

The Reverend picked up a gilt-framed photo of Deanna in her high school days and fingered some dust specks off the face. He set it back, deliberately altering its position, although the setup had been very deliberate to begin with.

"You get the keys, I'll go with you," he announced.

"Not necessary."

"I know that building well. Years ago I worked out of there when my folks used to run a little mom and pop store. Bought ice from Mark. Nuts, they got a freezer big as a barn. I'd pick it up in my old truck and drive it out to Issaquah where my folks ran the junction store."

"You've known Mark a long time then?"

"Years and years. We went to school together. Been friends ever since."

"What is he like?"

"Heck of a man. Good head for business. Sharp, friendly, loyal. A good husband. Good father. The best. And generous too. I've got maybe ten, eleven suits and sports jackets he's given me. We're the same size and when he gets tired of something he gives it to someone. Some have never been worn."

"He play around?"

"You mean with other women?"

"Yeah."

"Mark was a complicated man. His minister is more than likely the last man he would have confessed indiscretions to."

"People have glimmers though. We know things without being told."

Deanna walked into the room before he could reply. Her hair was bundled in a towel.

As she sailed toward me, Wheeler docked with her and looped his right arm over her shoulders. She did not object.

Barefoot, her toenails painted the same rusty rose as her fingernails, she wore a pale lilac silk caftan. Faintly diaphanous, it was plain she wore nothing underneath. I thought Wheeler hadn't noticed because he was looking at an opposite wall, but when I followed his gaze, I saw he was watching her in a mirror.

"Thomas. How nice to see you. What can I do for you?"

"Honey," said Wheeler, squeezing her shoulders. "Mr. Black would like to borrow Mark's keys to the Trinity Building. I think he wants to do a little sleuthing." Wheeler chuckled, patronizing the child in the room—me. "Why don't you just give me the keys and I'll open it up for him? I know where just about everything is. All the revisions on the old buildings."

I stood up. "I'll go alone, if you don't mind. You must have a service this morning, or something."

"Obviously you don't know show business. My sermons are all taped. In fact, Sunday is my least busy day. I'd be more than happy to show you around. I can show you things you'd miss otherwise."

"Alone," I said.

"I insist."

"Sam," said Deanna. "I think Thomas wants to do this by himself."

"But I'll save Black some time. A great deal of time."

Deanna turned and padded off to fetch the keys. On the way out she caught a glimpse of her bouncing reflection in a full-length mirror. When she came back, she was wearing a terry robe over the caftan. Sam Wheeler reached out and palmed the keys before she could deliver them to me.

"We can drive in my car," he said, lurching toward the door.

I looked at Deanna. "You have another set?" I asked, coolly.

Wheeler turned around, a hurt look impinging his boyish face. He spoke peevishly, disbelieving. "You really don't want me to go, do you?"

"I work alone, Reverend Wheeler."

Pulling his heavy lips into a pout, Wheeler tossed the keys at me. Clinking in the space between us, they shot across the room and would have struck me in the face if I hadn't caught them. It was a good way to hurt someone and make it look like an accident. I looked down at the simple steel ring which held about thirty-five keys.

"Sorry," said Deanna, folding her arms across her chest. "I wish I knew which ones were for what, but I never could keep track."

"I'll make out."

"You should be okay on a Sunday morning. Nobody works on Sunday. The only person you might run across is Emmett Anderson. Just explain who you are and I'm sure he'll agree to let you look around."

"I'm working for Mark's attorney," I said. "He doesn't have the right to object."

"I guess not."

"Learned a little humility the other day," said the Reverend Wheeler, rolling on the balls of his feet, riding his paunch forward in front of himself like a pregnant woman. "I was watering the yard when I saw a cat under a rose. This was a particularly pesky cat who's been bothering us for years. I hissed at him but he only glared at me, glared at me like the very devil himself. I hissed again. Stamped my foot. He still didn't move. So I sprinkled him. He didn't move. Gave me the evil eye. Then I turned the hose on him full force."

Deanna cocked her head and listened attentively. I stuffed the bundle of keys into my Levi's pocket.

"When the cat was fully drenched, he started to crawl away. Only his front two paws worked. The hind legs were broken—he'd been run over by a car." Wheeler held a plump thumb and forefinger up to the light. "I felt about that big."

"That's awful," said Deanna.

"There is a point though, my dear. Things aren't always what they seem. Are they, Black? If we act humbly, we'll be on the right side every time. We get a little persnickety, why, things can go awry." His boyish smile was almost disarming. People didn't thwart his will every day. When they did, they listened to a sermon.

Deanna Daniels looked at me. I winked and walked past

Sam Wheeler into the pool room. Sam did not move for me to pass. It was hard to tell if he thought I already had enough room or if he was being persnickety.

"Nice pool," I said on the way out.

"You'll have to come over and use it sometime." Deanna followed me to the front door. "This is a sun roof. It opens up mechanically when the weather's nice. We'd love to have you up here."

I searched her smoky eyes for some evidence that my folly of last night was remembered, saw none, nodded, and descended the steps. She was still watching me from the doorway when I got into the truck, a longing in her eyes that I might have mistaken for personal interest if the circumstances had been different. When I got to the corner I looked back and she was still in the doorway, still watching.

I drove down the cobbled street. The Reverend Wheeler's story about the cat would have been a lot more impressive had I not heard a comedian tell it on TV the night before while I was looking up Deanna's phone number.

The Trinity Building parking lot was just as abandoned as it had been when Daniels parked in it last Saturday. I left my truck in the same stall he had used, earmarked Daniels-President.

After six or eight stabs with different selections from the weighty key ring, I got the side door open and went in, past the receptionist area and up the open carpeted stairs. If you looked closely, you could see the bloodstains in the carpet. They could have been marked his and hers.

The typewriter was gone, no doubt confiscated by the police. The carpet had been vacuumed, and the desk combed through. Except for a pair of unused tickets to a Mariners game last Thursday evening the place was sterile.

No address book. No list of appointments. Not even a package of chewing gum in Mark's desk. All personal items had been confiscated. All except a glossy eight-by-ten portrait of a smiling Deanna on a rustic-looking lakeshore dock. She wore shorts and a halter-top and looked a few years younger. I turned away from it. I was already overdosed.

I spent half an hour wandering through the maze of offices, nosing around, fumbling through people's desks. I found a paperback novel about half-naked slave women from another planet in the bottom drawer of one of the secretary's desks. That was it.

The huge office complex was joined to a cold cement-floored warehouse stacked high with cases of canned dog food. It held maybe four truckloads, with pallets and space for eight more.

I shambled through the dark warehouse and out into the dog-food factory through an enormous sliding fire door. The whole place smelled like machinery and some sort of soapy antiseptic.

High windows along all the walls filtered in enough daylight so that I could see without groping for the light switch. A man was standing in front of me.

He was small and dark and Asian.

A needle-sharp meat hook glittered in his fist.

Behind him four other short Asian men stood in a broad semicircle, as if they had been waiting for me. Presumably they were about to pluck and butcher a big chicken. This bird was about six-one and weighed around one-eighty.

"Morning," I said, giving a small beauty-queen wave.

Nobody blinked. They were like statue targets in a pinball game, frowns painted on their brown faces. Behind the leader with the meat hook, three of his cohorts held short lengths of lumber. The fourth had doubled up his fists into tight little roots. A tic festered in one dark eye.

"Morning," I repeated, smiling and nodding. I was doing a lot of nodding. "Nice day. I'm an emissary for Mark Daniels' lawyer. I'm working for Mark Daniels. You boys must work here. Nice place to work?"

The man in front, the one with the hook, stepped forward in snakeskin cowboy boots that had five-inch heels. They were tiny enough to be women's boots. He was a foot shorter than me. All of them were. When he got just out of arms' reach, he began slashing at my face with the meat hook, advancing a step with each swipe.

I kicked out at his knees and missed. He lashed to and fro with the meat hook until it sang in the air like a birch switch.

The men behind him fanned out and scurried toward me, soldiers following their platoon leader.

I thought they were merely trying to unnerve me until the leader snagged a piece of my polo shirt and ripped it with the hook. He took a small, very painful snip of my chest with it. He was quick. Quicker than shit.

Chapter Six

I COULD FEEL BLOOD sluicing down my belly and into the rim of my jeans. My guess was each of them knew six different brands of karate.

They advanced. I was gunless and getting scared.

Like a nerd in his first self-defense class, I leaped up, yelling and gesticulating with all the absurd menace I could muster.

"Yah!"

Startled, all five of them hopped backward a pace.

The fire door behind me had slid shut on its weight, all avenues of escape gone.

Ripping a forty-pound dry chemical fire extinguisher off the wall, I jerked out the pin. I held the handle and body in one hand, the hose and nozzle in the other, ready to press the trigger with the heel of my palm.

They looked at me as if they had never seen a fire extinguisher.

"What is this? A Tupperware party?" Each of them took a step forward. "I'm working for Mark Daniels' lawyer. Do you understand?" Each took another step forward.

The hardest-looking of the lot was the leader. He bore the bleak, scarred face and dead eyes of a skilled mercenary—no—of a torturer. The four chaps abetting him looked like farmers from the Mekong Delta, recently emigrated with enough English to get them a basket of Bok Choy at Safeway and a tank of unleaded at the local service station.

Dangling the nozzle, I reached into my snug jeans pocket, used two fingers and tweezed out the lump of keys.

"These," I said, "were given to me by the wife of your boss. I didn't break in. I have keys. You do work here, don't you?"

Without taking his black, otherworldly eyes off me, or even blinking, the leader spoke in a birdlike Asian dialect. Two of his pals grunted in reply, nodding. All of them were nodding.

"Beautiful," I said. "I'm off the hook . . . so to speak? Everything is hunky-dory? You understand? Comprende? Friend?"

Stepping forward, the leader flailed the meat hook at my face. He swung at me six or seven times in quick succession. I yo-yoed my head backward each time he swung and felt the tiny spurt of air from the hook on every swipe.

In unison, they moved toward me in tiny mincing steps. They were closing in. I backpedaled to the fire door and tried to elbow it open so I could squirm through. It was too heavy.

Then I thought of a great trick.

I flicked the keys at the leader. They struck him across the bridge of the nose and clanked on the concrete floor. Flecks of blood appeared on his nose. The trick worked just great. He didn't bat an eye, just whipped the meat hook again. Whoosh. Whoosh.

Ducking backward and upward, I knocked the back of my head on the steel fire door and crushed the firing mechanism of the extinguisher at the same time.

It wheezed for a split second before it coughed a cloud of ultra-fine powder into his face. The swirling dry chemical mixture caught him wrong because he began hacking right away—must have aspirated some of it. I cocked one leg up and kicked him square in the sternum.

He went reeling, knocking one of his soldiers down with him.

Two unlaced K-Mart jogging shoes with the heels crushed down stood where the second man had been.

The man on my far left ran at me, whirling the piece of board in his hand high over his head. He didn't realize how tall I was, how long my legs were. Back braced against the steel fire door, I kicked at him sideways, striking him across the ribs and sending him sprawling. I heard the meaty sound of ribs cracking. These men were tiny.

The two men in the middle were getting very nervous. Jabbering in dialect, they came at me together, one swinging his timber high, and one low, hoping teamwork would succeed where individual initiative had withered. I blocked the low one with the extinguisher as I sprayed the upper one with a burst of whitish dry chemical. It blinded him. I bashed the low man on the skull with the bottom of the extinguisher. He went down fast.

The man I had kicked made his way to his feet, grimacing, limping and clutching his fractured ribs. The leader got up, clopping his cowboy boots on the concrete floor, white powder drifting off his body in tiny clouds.

"Give up," I said. "No more fight? Fight no good. Somebody get hurt. Nobody wants to get hurt. You get hurt. I get hurt." The leader flicked open a gleaming seven-inch switchblade and passed the meat hook to his other fist. *"I* get hurt."

Three of them came at me while a fourth—in whiteface, his ears plugged with the gunk—tried to knuckle the powder out of his eyes.

"Hey, listen guys. Tell me what the problem is. I'm not trespassing. Do you think I'm trespassing? I'm not. Talk to me." But they didn't talk, only moved in. "You want to buy a *Watchtower?"*

I emptied the dry chemical extinguisher, but they knew it was coming and winked against the spurts of suffocating powder, choking and blinking, but refusing to be intimidated.

I grabbed the extinguisher in both hands and used it as a shield, kicking at them below it. I caught one in the knee and he backed up. I booted another square in the solar plexus. He did a reverse rumba and tumbled out of the fray.

They poked, slashed, swung at me. I fended them off.

My old mutt had been in a position like this once, warding off a pack of neighborhood dogs, battling them to a standstill and then snarling at them for forty minutes until I found him and pelted the bastards with rocks all the way back into their yards.

We must have remained there, the five of us—one was unconscious at my feet—for a good two minutes before the steel fire door behind me slowly slid open, making ominous grinding noises.

A tall, stooped old man—the man I had seen last Saturday, the man who had discovered Mark Daniels and the dead girl—stepped through the opening and took a good long look at all of us.

"What the hell is going on?"

The Orientals looked confused, then shamefaced. The leader glanced at the old man and back to me, his face ranging through a variety of nervous mannerisms.

"I asked you a question, Hung. What the hell is going on here?"

It took the leader a while before he could tear his inky eyes off me and reply. "Man here fire dis building."

"What?"

"Torch. He is hired torch. Fire up dis building. Enemies have hired so Hung is out of work."

"Whose enemies, goddamnit?"

"Hung's enemies . . . from home."

Taller than me, the old man cocked his head back an inch and squinted through the lower portion of his wire-rimmed spectacles. Black spokes in his eyes radiated out of the cerulean blue. "You a hired arsonist?"

"My name is Thomas Black. I'm a private investigator working for Mark's lawyers, Leech, Bemis and Ott."

"Oh, hell. I saw you last week. You was here at the killing."

"I was working on something else then."

"Put that goddamned knife away, Hung," said the old man, strutting through the group as if he were a bowling ball rolling through pins, sauntering past them for twenty yards. Hung folded the blade and pushed it into his pocket, then reluctantly walked over to the old man. They had words for several minutes while the three remaining men picked up their friend and slapped his face.

Stained concrete floors. Corrugated aluminum walls. Three-story ceilings. The building didn't have anything in it but space heaters and various unidentifiable machinery, rollers for assembly packaging, and rows and rows of empty shiny tin cans in feeder funnels that ran the length of one section.

The two men conferred, one tall and ashen, the other small, brown, diminutive. When they were finished, Hung heeled around and walked angrily away, avoiding my eyes, his back stiff, his face rigid. The four men in front of me hustled after him, one of them carrying the shoes I had kicked a man out of. A moment later I heard a door clang shut.

"Sorry about that." The old man took the extinguisher and set it in the middle of the walkway so he wouldn't forget to have it recharged. He then slapped away some of the chalky dust that had roiled up onto his slacks.

He stared at the blood on my shirt. "The Nip nipped ya, huh?"

I looked down at the red dappling my polo shirt and shrugged. "Let me get you to the first-aid station. Over here in the foreman's office. Slap a dressing on that. By the way, my name is Emmett Anderson. Folks call me Andy. You might have heard of me. I'm Mark Daniels' business partner."

"Thomas Black," I said, gripping his hand, which was weak, his palm sweaty.

He was tall and thin and old and gangly. He walked in a characteristic bowlegged cowboy slouch. He had been everywhere and done everything and he knew it.

Knifing a key into a windowed door of a cubicle built off the main room of the factory, he switched on the lights and dug a first-aid kit out. I hoisted my shirt while he taped a bandage onto my chest.

"Kind of a nasty gash," he said, stashing the kit away. "Your man there is kind of a nasty guy."

"Hung? Don't mind him. He made a mistake. Don't know what's going on, really. He told me somebody phoned him at home and warned him some of his old enemies had hired a torch to set this place up so he wouldn't have any job. Nor his brothers. Two of them fellows were his brothers. The other two work here. It's plausible. Why? You wanta prefer charges on him?"

"Not today."

"Couple months ago his uncle got blowed up in Texas in some factory gig. Something to do with Anglo-Asian tensions. So he had cause. He's one of our lead men. A good worker. And he's intelligent."

"You have a lot of Vietnamese working here?"

"Vietnamese, Laotian, Cambodian, Filipino. Most of 'em are direct off the boat. That's why Hung is such a good man. Speaks seven languages. We couldn't get along without him. One of Mark's friends got us into it, hiring boat people. Did it as a favor at first. But hellfire, these people are better workers than most of the whites. And they're loyal. You saw how loyal. So we been hiring almost nothing but. Damn fine workers."

"How'd you happen to show up in the nick of time?"

"You accusing me of something?"

"Just wondering."

"Hung's wife got scared and called me. They know me. I been over to dinner. We have a big company picnic out at Mark's place on the lake every summer. Hung's quite a guy. He was a colonel in the South Vietnamese army. You oughta hear some of the war stories he tells. Used to hunt tigers in Nam. Was an engineer. But he can't qualify here."

"So he works in a dog food plant?"

"We got a fella here was a doctor in Cambodia. Another was a professor. By the time they learn the language and get their families settled it's five or ten years. Then you're talking another five or ten years of education to qualify for our system. If you're already thirty or forty when you come here, that makes you forty or fifty when you're going back to school. It ain't worth it. Most of 'em stay in menial jobs.''

"Who phoned Hung?"

"He didn't recognize the voice. Said it was a white guy, though. Said a guy was going to burn the plant to the ground. He highballed it down here and brought his friends. I don't know what the hell they were going to do to you, but I wouldn't put anything past Hung. Good thing I came along.''

"You been having plant troubles? Anybody ever threaten to burn the place down before?''

"Nope.''

"Mr. Hung is a pretty dependable guy usually?''

"Mr. Doan. Hung Doan is his name.'' The old man peeped at me over the rim of his bifocals and smirked. His teeth were long and yellow. He looked at least eighty years old. But he might have been in his sixties and sick. He moved with vigor, but each time he did so he took stock and breathed heavily. "Keep looking for a Hung Low, but all we got so far is a Hung Doan. These people are strange on names. One named a daughter was born last year Snow White. Snow White Bui.''

"He's dependable, though? Hung Doan?''

Emmett combed his hair with one knuckly hand and said, "That's a matter of opinion. I wanted to fire Hung, but Mark wouldn't stand for it. We had a young guy come in here applying for a job once. Can't recall his name. Vietnamese. He saw Hung out there on the floor and he about went nuts. After we calmed him down enough so he's speaking English again, why, he told us Hung had killed his mother and father and half his village with a bayonet. Said Hung was some sort of sadistic terror specialist for the South Vietnamese Army, got a kick out of watching people die in the most gruesome manner possible.''

"He have any proof?''

"This little guy that accused him, he got out of the country with his wife, five kids and a bag of clothing. Three of the kids died on the trip to the ocean to get a boat. Naw. He didn't have proof. We called Hung in afterwards and asked him about it. He got a little shifty-eyed, denied it, but we couldn't really do anything but fire him. And Mark wouldn't have it. He didn't think it was fair to take a man's job on the accusation of a complete stranger."

"What about you?"

"Never have trusted Hung. Mark dies, I'll fire his ass." His eyes got filmy thinking about Mark's death. "There's just something about Hung. I believed every word that little fellow applying for the job said about him. He wouldn't work here. Was scared to. We got him a job over in a fish packing plant on Airport Way. But I believed him. Mark did, too, I think. He just didn't believe it was fair to fire Hung. Not without proof. Told me he was going to investigate Hung himself. Last week they had a couple of meetings. I don't know what about, but Hung didn't look too pleased coming out of Mark's office."

"From what I read, you and Mark have built yourselves up into quite a proposition. You personally hire people to work out here in the plant?"

"This plant is only a fraction of what we've got. Mark and I own a cannery in Tacoma, a wood mill in Everett and a few other things. Whenever anyone is hired or fired, we take a personal interest in it. That's part of the secret of our success. People. We know everybody that works for us."

"You been with Mark long?"

" 'Bout twenty years. Started right here in this plant. I was the manager of a small trucking company. Mark was a junior exec. We always got along famously and when I got some money saved up, enough to take out a loan and start something on my own, why, I asked Mark if he didn't want to team up."

"Sounds like you're real close."

"Up until he got his divorce three years ago. I never did agree with that. Mark . . . Mark was like a son to me. Still is, I guess. When I went in there last Saturday and saw him lying in a pool of blood, I just about cried. I really did.'' He had cried, but maybe he didn't remember. Or maybe the old buckaroo just didn't want to admit it.

"He have any enemies?''

The old man picked up a rubber mallet someone had left on top of a cardboard box, walked away from me and dropped it into a nearby toolbox. "What are you working on, anyway? You said you was hired by Mark's lawyers?''

"I'm trying to help devise a defense for Mark.''

"Defense?''

"If he recovers they'll try him for murder.''

His exclamation was drawn out and musical, and the only reason I recognized the word—which took five seconds to say—was because I had heard others mouth it the same way. "Sheeiiit.''

"He have enemies?''

"Mark? A jealous husband or two. Mark was a cocksman. Don't know why. He wasn't like that in the early years. He just . . . I never did figure it out. He started caring more for that gutwrench in his pants than his wife and two kids. Happens to a man.''

"He having an affair with the girl we found dead?''

"Couldn't tell ya. He knew I didn't approve so he rarely talked to me about other women. Knew he was stepping out when he was married to Helen. I don't know about *this* marriage. Tell you the truth, I don't think the cops know either. We hired the girl last summer. Had to look her name up in the files. Beatrice Hindenburg. But the cops called her Deborah something or other. Couldn't find where she lived. I know they couldn't 'cause they came back askin' more questions about her late as Friday.''

"Did Mark know her last summer?''

"Was right over in that room there with me when I hired her.''

"You did all the hiring?''

"Took turns.''

During our talk we had been strolling toward the rear of

the plant. We went through an opening in the concrete wall and into an area that looked like a loading dock. Across the dock area was a large door to a freezer, a freezer big enough to drive a car into. Several cars and a few trucks to boot.

"This is it," said Emmett Anderson. "This is where the whole thing began. I sneaked up to Mark's office one day when we were still at National Truck out in the north end and said, 'I'm quitting, sonny. Gonna start up my own firm. You in?' All he said was, 'When?' Got a streak of wildness in him. A gambler. I put up the money in the beginning, then we turned it into a joint venture."

"Andy, why don't you sit down for a minute?" I gestured at a stack of cartons.

Anderson shuffled over and carefully squatted on a carton. "You noticed, huh?"

"You look a little winded."

Wheezing, he inhaled and exhaled in his own perfected rhythm. After a long while he looked up at me, his eyelids closing down on that cerulean blue, and said, "You know Mark never knew. Years ago he would have known. We were close then. But now, I got maybe six months to live and he hasn't an inkling."

"He might beat you."

"I ain't racing, but he might. Hell of a note. Hell of a note."

I leaned against the stack of cartons. Everything in the plant was neat; everything in its place. The rubber mallet Andy had found was an anomaly. Preciseness in an operation as large as this one didn't just happen. It filtered down from the top.

"Cancer," said Andy. "And don't go feeling sorry for me. I don't mind. We all gotta go sometime. I would rather know when and how than have it spring up on me some night while I'm riding the old woman. I always have hated surprises. Love to gamble, but hate surprises."

"Mark's wife is worried you won't divvy things up fifty-fifty if Mark dies."

Andy took off his eyeglasses and wiped them on his shirt.

He inspected them against the light from one of the high windows. They trembled in his fingers. "I'll bet she is. I'll bet she's mighty worried."

"You holding a grudge against her?"

He shook his head, hooked the glasses back around each ear and stood up laboriously. He moved to a large sliding steel door with more agility than I expected. Opening a padlock on the door, he slid the door open. I helped when I saw how heavy it was.

"Let me show you this place. It's my baby. Always will be. It's what made me and Mark. We bought it from a family thought it was the stupidest investment they ever made. Thought they were skinning us. Sold it for twenty-four thousand bucks. Thought they just stole the pants off a couple of hicks from hicksville. Hellfire, the land alone was worth more than double that."

He gave me the royal tour, treating me as if I were an out-of-town dog food manufacturer. I didn't need a tour of a dog food plant, but I was beginning to like Andy and he was here alone on a Sunday morning and he wanted to show me his baby. So I tagged along after him and gawked, billing and cooing at the appropriate moments, genuinely impressed with his business acumen, with the histories of various machines and processes. He knew it all, every aspect of the business. I was impressed with his baby and the love he had for it.

Chapter Seven

ANDY PARADED ME through every step of the process. The complex was even larger than I imagined.

Attached to the huge square modern office building and its atrium was the warehouse stacked high with cartons of cans. Adjoining that, the dog food factory. Trinity Dog Food: Best in the West. The factory itself had been expanded and augmented like a jigsaw puzzle gone wild until it was more than quadruple its original size. It looked like the inside of a domed stadium. Outside, a hundred feet behind the factory was another huge pink cement-walled complex which the Trinity Corporation rented out to various industrial companies. Sandwiched between the two buildings in the grass lay a set of railroad tracks that ran unobstructed for five hundred feet.

I looked out at the windowless building behind the plant and beyond the shielded strip of tracks. "Seems like someone could drive a truck back here on the weekend and unload a warehouse without being seen."

Andy peered at me over the tops of his spectacles. "You're dead right. Coupla those places across the way been cleaned out. Had to install a complete burglar alarm in the building to keep our leases. Cost a bundle."

"You don't have a system here?"

"Who's going to hijack dog food?"

"How many entrances are there into the office building where the shooting was?"

"Counting outside where you parked? Six, seven maybe.

There are three doors from the parking lot. On the third floor one of the halls has a door that leads here. We never use it, but it's unlocked most of the time. On the main level there must be . . . Let's see . . . the fire door we used. Two others.''

"Kept locked?"

"Not always."

Rail cars hauled the meat and grain to the loading dock at the back of the factory. On one side was a storeroom for the grain sacks, on the other a freezer as big as a house. Andy took me into it. The ceiling was thirty feet over our heads. Ice hung from it like crystal stalactites.

"Colder than a witch's titty, eh? Between thirty and forty below in here. Keep it that way for the fish. Take a deep breath. It'll freeze the boogers right where they be.''

"This where Sam Wheeler used to buy ice from you?"

"You know Sam? We got some trays back there we make ice in. Don't use 'em much anymore. Buy? Hell. That sniveling little pissant never paid for a thing in his life. Cheapest bastard you ever met. Mark used to give it to him.''

One section of the freezer was hung with beef quarters in racks. The main section was stacked with whole chickens and fish in packages, piled almost to the ceiling in spots.

The old man showed me where they hurled the fish or chicken or beef into bladed machines that gobbled it and spit it out in chunks dinky enough for the smaller machines to digest. They had one machine—a gigantic meat grinder built like a car engine with a huge squarish smooth-sided funnel on top—that could chew up an entire beef quarter, bones and all. He showed me where the grain was cooked, how the meat and grain were mixed, mashed and stirred together to formulate the different recipes. They even had a head chef. He guided me through every step in the process, visiting each machine in turn. I didn't have the time, but hell, he was dying.

"Started off twenty years ago,'' he said. "Nobody ever heard of Trinity Dog Food. Now we're the leading seller on the West Coast and sliding into the markets in the East.''

After he had walked me through the canning process, we sat down in the glass-walled office off the factory floor.

Emmett Anderson offered me a swig from a bottle in a desk drawer. When I declined, he fished out the makings and built a cigarette in his knobby fingers, sealing it with his tongue. It had been a long while since I'd seen someone do that.

"Gonna die," he wheezed. "May as well die with my vices intact."

When he had pretty much caught his breath, I said, "This Beatrice Hindenburg who worked here last summer. How did you come to hire her?"

Andy shrugged, placed his hands on his knees, pistoned himself to his feet and walked over to a battered army-green file cabinet. He riffled through it for a minute, then pulled out a loose-leaf file. "Beatrice Hindenburg. Somebody called on the phone and asked us to look at her. Don't recall who, now. I think that was it. You want the address she gave us?"

"You give it to the cops?"

"Last week."

"If they couldn't find where she's living, I won't either. I'll copy it, just in case. Anybody around here close to her? A co-worker?"

"That I couldn't tell you. Can't even remember where she worked. I'll call Hung. Just lives up the hill. He'll remember." A few minutes later Andy cradled the telephone receiver and said, "Ingrid Darling. Hung says they used to eat lunch together. Maybe even drove to work together."

"She still work here?"

"Nope. Just a summer worker like the other. A young girl. They was both young." Remembering the massacre last Saturday, he shook his head and inhaled on the cigarette which hadn't left his lip.

"Can you get Ingrid Darling's address?"

"I'll show you what we had." It was on Capitol Hill. He also gave me her mother's name and street number in Ballard, a section of the city down by the docks.

Before I left I had Andy draw up a list of people Mark knew. The tally was extensive. I had him put a star beside the name of those Mark knew well and two stars beside those he had known for over five years.

I drove to a hardware dealership, waited for it to open, and had a disgruntled clerk reproduce every key on the steel ring Deanna had given me. Eyes like slats, the clerk kept gawking at me; thought I was some sort of housebreaker. At the Daniels homestead the Cadillac was gone. No one answered the bell. I poked Deanna's keys through the mail slot.

It took me all the rest of that day to exhaust the list of Mark Daniels' friends. I contacted most by phone, a few in person, and couldn't locate four. Most were business acquaintances, were shocked about Mark's predicament and were far too obliging to a stranger on the telephone claiming to be working for Mark's attorneys. Loose lips sink ships. But the shock of Mark's predicament had shaken loose a lot of things.

The most productive calls were to two of Mark's drinking companions, two men he had known while working for National Trucking. Both still worked for National and once or twice a week during the season they picked up Mariners' games together. Once a month they would get bombed. Both men assured me that Mark stepped out on his wife when the occasion presented itself. One told me he knew for a fact Mark slapped Deanna around from time to time.

"You mean he hit her?"

"Sure. Used to whop Helen all the time, too. That's why she divorced him."

At five in the afternoon I changed clothes, grabbed a basketball and dribbled it three blocks away to the school. Seven high school kids were lounging around shooting baskets and lying to each other, waiting for another body to show up so they would have even teams. We played for an hour and a half. When the clouds rolled in and primped the city in a misty gray, when it started drizzling, two of the boys went home. The rest of us rearranged the teams and played on in the feathery mist. I played until my feet were sore and my legs were rubbery.

Late in the evening I reached Deanna at home. "Deanna. Thomas Black here. How's your husband?"

Her voice was fuller than I remembered. "Thomas. He's fine. I mean, he's the same. At least he's not deteriorating."

"How are you?"

"I'm okay, I guess."

"I need a list of friends Mark knew. I want to talk to everyone."

She didn't provide nearly as many names as Andy. She could only cook up three names to place a star next to. The others she called acquaintances. Only one of the names was on Andy's list: one of the drinking partners from National. After cross-checking the lists I was struck by the fact that the Reverend Sam Michael Wheeler was on neither.

I called, spoke to people, left messages, and spoke to more people. It was Monday just before noon when I felt I had plumbed as far into Mark's life as any of his friends were going to let me. I had interviewed fourteen people on the telephone and visited five in person.

I reached Kathy Birchfield at work, and offered to take her to lunch. We met in a small Mexican restaurant on the waterfront. Juan's. ("Have a juanderful day.") Next to our window a hulk of a ferry was moored. It bobbed on the tide as we ate, making us both slightly queasy.

When Kathy sat down she eyed me for a long time before she spoke, "Hey, Cisco."

"Hey, Pancho."

"You still love me?"

"Always."

"No, I mean after what happened the other night. You know? When you turned yourself into the court jester to Deanna Daniels' Queen Guinevere."

"Would you get off that?"

Kathy lowered her voice an octave and imitated my speech only too well. "I think she be smitten, girl. I really think she be smitten with me."

I gritted my teeth, picked up a spoon and plunged it into my gazpacho. I glared at Kathy as long as I could hold it and then laughed.

Kathy waited a beat and laughed, too. "She's not your type, Thomas. Those big brassy women never go for you. It's the tiny delicate women who find you attractive."

"Like you?"

"Like our waitress. Or haven't you noticed?"

"She's just trying to get a tip. They do that."

"You still think Deanna has a thing for you, don't you?"

"What?"

"Don't give me that jive, Thomas. Once you get your mind fixed, you're jinxed for life. I know you secretly think she has the hots for you. That's what you think, isn't it? Sure, it is. You're even blushing."

"Private detectives don't blush."

"Must be a heat rash, then."

"Want to know what I found out about Mark Daniels?"

"I wanted you to take me with you, Thomas. I thought you were working for me."

"Solo. I work solo."

"Can't I go on part of it? I like to watch you work and there's absolutely nothing going on at the office these days. Business law is dreary."

"Old man Anderson told me he thought of Mark as a son, but that's not what other people say. Maybe they were like a father and son once, but two weeks ago they got into a knock-down drag-out fight that was so loud one of the secretaries phoned the police."

"A fist fight?"

"Just shy of that."

"Maybe . . . ." Kathy picked up a fork and toyed with an enormous tostada. "Maybe Mark was moody enough to kill himself. Maybe he really was moody enough to kill himself."

"Most of the people I talked to were aware that Mark dallied with the ladies. But nobody knew of any current amours. I couldn't find anyone who had ever seen him with

Beatrice Hindenburg. Or Crowley. I did talk to a sales clerk at Nordstroms one of his buddies said he had 'planked' a couple of times. She wouldn't fess up.''

''But?''

''But you could tell she knew him from the way she evaded my questions. She had an engagement ring on. I believe that might have explained her reluctance to talk about an affair with a married man.''

''So he played around. A lot of men play around.''

''Mark Daniels beat his first wife. My guess is he beat his kids, too. That's why his first wife left him. He had an explosive temper that flared up and then was gone in just a minute. He beat Deanna, too.''

''Thomas, are you sure?''

''According to my sources, the last time was only a few weeks ago.''

Chapter Eight

I SAID, "I don't think Mark was ever depressed in his life. Moody. Angry. Rowdy. Violent, when he thought the time was right. But nobody ever told me he was depressed."

"People don't have to be depressed to commit suicide, Thomas. They could be angry maybe."

"Maybe."

"He beat Deanna? I don't believe that."

"Sent her to the emergency room six months ago. Whopped her so hard he broke one of her teeth. Sprained a wrist. She left him for a week."

"Why did she go back?"

"I really couldn't say."

"She must love him a whole heck of a lot."

I shrugged, remembering what Deanna had confessed to me Saturday night when we were alone. I wondered now why she had confided in me, someone she had only known a few minutes.

"Wait a minute, Thomas. If it wasn't a suicide-murder, what was it? Are you saying Mark had people who hated him enough to sneak in there and shoot them both, to kill an innocent person to get at him?"

"Or the girl did."

"I never thought of that."

"Or it could have been a burglary, something like that."

"But it sounds like Mark probably has a lot of enemies."

"He quarreled, he blew up at people, but he apologized, always tried to make it good. And most of the time he was

generous. He never fleeced anybody in his business dealings. I don't think anybody holds any grudges."

"With him in the hospital, who would admit to a
grudge?"

"Only a fool."

"But the police said the gun was in Mark's hand when it
was fired. How do you get around that?"

"It could be accomplished. Mark and the girl step into the
room. Somebody stands behind the door with the gun they
found in Mark's office, lets the girl walk in unharmed, then
presses the pistol to Mark's head. Pop. They take the gun,
fit it into Mark's hand and shoot the girl. It can be done.
With luck it'll make a nice neat frame."

"Like this one?"

"If this is a frame, it's as neat as they come."

"Wait a minute. The suicide note in the typewriter. A
burglar couldn't have done that. He wouldn't have known
Deanna's name for one thing. Didn't it have her name on
it?"

"I believe it did. That's a good point."

"And the girl was naked. And Mark wasn't. How do you
account for that? Ralph Crum said she'd had sex recently."

"I can't account for any of it right now. Could be whoever shot Mark raped her before he killed her. But that
makes the timing even tighter."

Kathy finished her meal without another word. She
watched the traffic, both auto and foot, on Alaskan Way.
Before we left she slipped a tip under my plate for the waitress.

"That's too much," I said. "Way too much."

Kathy gave me a bawdy wink and wandered out to the
cashier. "We don't want her to think all that eye business
was wasted."

"Life is a bitch," I said to the waitress on the way out.

The co-worker Emmett Anderson had told me about, the
friend of Beatrice Hindenburg, still lived on Capitol Hill.
She had neither moved nor found another job.

Her apartment was in a shabby two-story building several blocks from the community college. In the street I could smell diesel exhaust from city buses and, from a nearby bakery, the overpowering aroma of yeast and sugary doodads in ovens. I parked illegally in an alley, jogged up the stairs and rapped on her door, which was half-open. I had the feeling it was always half-open.

Ingrid Darling was tall and thin, almost spindly, with good bones. Her rear was tailored for sitting astride a horse. Her blade-shaped face was so pale it looked bloodless. Dull brown and stringy, her hair hung straight down her skull like wet yarn. She wore jeans and a short-sleeve sweater, the fabric speckled with tiny fuzz balls. Looking at the bones she called arms, I wondered how well she had been eating lately.

Without opening the door further, she stood hipshot in the doorway, swaying to an Oak Ridge Boys album that strained the outer limits of a tinny stereo across the room. "Yeah?"

"Ingrid Darling?"

"Call me Kandy, okay? Kandy Darling. Kandy with a K."

"Sure, Kandy." I handed her one of my cards. She read it, shimmed it into her tight jeans pocket and nodded. "Another one, huh?"

"Can I come in?"

"Suit yourself." She walked away from the door and across the room where she rolled the volume down on the stereo, then hitched across to a single bed, picked up a blouse, surveyed it, folded it sloppily and patted it down into a ragtag suitcase that had seen better days. "Moving out. Been here almost a year, and when you have three roommates in a place this size, I'm tellin' you, it gets on your nerves. So Hazel asked me to move out and I told her that's what I was planning all along. If she thinks I want to stay here with these loonies, she's nuts. I mean, I don't even talk to any of these girls anymore."

"You work for Trinity Dog Food last summer, Kandy?"

"Trinity? What a job. We had to take the bus out there

every damn morning at quarter to six. You ever take the bus to Harbor Island?''

''Who's we?''

''Bea and me.''

''Beatrice Hindenburg?''

''Um hmmm. Course, working there wasn't too bad, except for the noise. More money than I made anywhere else.'' She glanced furtively at me. ''Almost anywhere.''

''She ever call herself Deborah Crowley?''

''She called herself Mickey, and Gerry, and Kiki, and all kinds of things. I think Deborah Crowley was her favorite. She thought it sounded like a movie star or something. But her real name is Beatrice Hindenburg, and don't let nobody tell you no different. I seen her write that on a letter to her mom in California.''

''You know her mom's address?''

''Nah. I just seen the one letter. Didn't pay no attention.''

''Know what city?''

''Naw.''

''What was she writing her mom about?''

''Bea was on the streets, same as me. She just ran farther, was all, from somewhere in Southern Cal. She wrote 'cause her little brother was having a birthday and she wanted to give him something. She loved her little brother. Had a few bucks, but she didn't know how to wrap up a present and mail it, you know, so she put ten dollars in an envelope, wrote a note for her ma, and mailed it. Her ma wrote back that she was takin' the money for rent Bea owed her. Bea like died over that. I mean, shit man, how much rent could she owe? She ran away from home when she was fourteen.''

''You know why she ran away?''

''Her old man was hittin' on her. You know.''

''Her *dad?*''

''You sound like you never heard of such a thing. I know five or six girls on the street left home for the 'xact same reason. And he wasn't no step-dad neither. He was the real shillelagh.''

''The cops been talking to you?''

"Why would they? You trying to get me in trouble or something?"

"About Beatrice. Nobody's spoken to you about her?"

"Coupla months ago."

"Don't you read the papers?"

"I don't read so well. My teachers were all a bunch of jerkoffs."

"What about the news?"

"We don't got a TV. We listen to the Boys mostly." She cocked a thumb at the stereo.

"Beatrice is dead."

She stared at me as if I had slapped her across the face. Her gray eyes were like small orbs of a black and white TV on the wrong channel. "What'd you say?"

"She got shot a week ago Saturday. I'm investigating it."

Kandy dropped onto the bed, bouncing, and said, "Oh man. That's gross. That's really gross. I can't believe it. Bea was a nice kid. That's bad. I mean, I finally got my life together, you know, and then I hear all about this. Man, this is rotten. I got this boyfriend . . . I mean I can't tell my mother or my friends about him 'cause they wouldn't approve, know what I mean? He's an older guy. We're movin' in together. Just him and me. It's what I've always wanted. And now I hear this about Bea. Who did it, man? Who would shoot Bea? A pimp?"

"They think it was a suicide pact between Bea and her lover, a man named Mark Daniels. One of the owners of Trinity Dog Food."

"Mr. Daniels?"

"Was he involved with Bea last summer?"

"You mean was he gettin' any off her?"

"Was he?"

"I doubt it. He drove us both home from work once. Bea was staying here then. Took us to a tavern and bought us both beers. Bea got a kick out of that 'cause we're both underage. Didn't faze me. My boyfriend buys me beer all the time."

"Bea lived here?"

"For a few weeks. Then when she quit Trinity she moved downtown somewhere. I never seen her much after that."

"Was she hooking?"

"Come on. A runaway? We gotta eat. Besides, Bea liked the life. I mean, she really liked the streets. Them weeks she worked at Trinity, she was miserable. She missed the street. She wanted to do right, but she really missed the action."

"What about a pimp?"

"Not that I knew of. She was kind of a hit or miss kid. Sometimes she'd work. Sometimes she'd go hungry. Scared of what might happen, if you know what I mean."

"Who talked to you about her?"

"A detective, man. Just like you. Older. Big guy. About your size only he was fat. I got his card here somewhere. He told me to hold onto it and if I thought of something else to call him and he'd pay me. You gonna pay me for this?"

"What'd you have in mind?"

She raised her eyebrows, as well as her voice. "Five bucks?"

I took a bill out of my wallet and handed it to her. She pulled it tight between her two hands and examined it like a child.

Though there had been an indefinable tension in the room since the moment I had stepped in, a personal and sexual tension, she was one of the least sensuous, least sexual people I had ever met. There was an almost sleepy, androgynous quality to her mannerisms and looks.

"You got any more money?" She ran her tongue around her lips in a complete circle and gave me a look she had culled from a movie house down on First Avenue. Her tongue had huge pores on its pink slimy surface.

"Where are you moving? In case I have more questions."

"Can't tell. I got your card. I'll call you in a week or so."

"Can you find the other detective's card?"

She turned, bent over and began pawing through the heap of articles on the bed, finally retrieving it from the pages of a paperback that looked as if it had never been cracked open. The book was titled *How To Name Your Baby*.

The card read: Seymore "Butch" Teets—Investigations-Private.

"What'd this fella look like?"

"Like my father. Ancient and all broke down. Wore one of those goofy hats, you know, like they wear in the old movies. Started pawing me once he found out what he wanted to know. I threw a pot of cold coffee on him."

"What did he want to know?"

"Same stuff you been asking. About Bea."

"Two months ago?"

"About that."

"And the cops never showed up here?"

"Could have. I'm not around much. After today, I won't be around at all."

On the way out the door I turned around and said, "How did you and Bea meet?"

"Don't really remember. On the street, I guess." I suddenly glimpsed some remnants of shame in her eyes.

"How'd you get jobs at Trinity?"

"Oh, that. The Downtown Service Center. In Pioneer Square. The Wheel works there. He got the jobs for us."

"The Wheel?"

"Reverend Wheeler."

"Reverend Sam Michael Wheeler?"

She grinned up from her clothes folding, almost a smirk. "That's the one. Why? You know him?"

"Do you?"

"Naw. He just got us jobs."

Chapter Nine

PRIVATE DETECTIVE Seymore Teets catered to clients out of a seedy office off Nickerson. Humming with flies, the place was two blocks from the ship canal.

Tilting a slat-back chair on its hind legs, he sat with eyes glued to a dog-eared Classics Comic—*A Tale of Two Cities*. He was as fat and ugly as a fisherman's cat. A snap-brim fedora was perched on his large head, just like Kandy had said. He was smoking a stogie, pursing his meaty lips and blowing plumes of smelly smoke past the rim of the comic. His hands were big and broken-looking, like an ex-boxer's. On the wrong side of fifty, he looked like he had lived every year twice.

He made me wait while he finished the page.

"Good writer, eh?" he barked, banging his hand down hard on the empty desk. "Eh? That Charlie Dickens could really spin a yarn."

"So they tell me. You Seymore Teets?"

"Call me Butch. What'cha need? I do it all. Strong-arm? Find a lost kid? Tail your wife? Tail your boyfriend? I even catch lily-waggers. Twenty bucks an hour plus expenses. I know, it seems like a lot, but you gotta consider the overhead and the years of experience backing up my every move."

"I'm Thomas Black. I'm . . ."

"Who? Black, huh? I seen your name in the papers." He snapped the brim of his hat loudly with one finger and wobbled the cigar around in his teeth without dropping it. "You don't look so tough. Saw you in court once testifying. Musta been about a year ago. You don't look so tough.''

"I've been eating a lot of A-1 sauce."

He teetered backward on his chair, gnawed on his stogie and tucked either side of his jacket back so that he was sure I knew he was wearing a revolver in a shoulder holster. It looked like a .38 snub-nose. They punched holes in you as easy as any.

Broad and fat, his face was corrugated. The creases were deep enough to wedge pennies into. A shock of wavy brown-gray hair peeked out from under the fedora. His piercing brown eyes didn't want to let me look away.

"You were asking around about a girl named Beatrice Hindenburg a while back. Anything ever come of that?"

Butch Teets got up and walked around the desk, moving like a poorly executed caricature of John Wayne. "Who wants to know?"

"Who do you think? I do."

"Who are you working for?"

"Who were you working for?"

"No, I asked first, smart guy. Who you working for?"

I smiled, but I could see it was a no-deposit smile. He would never return it. "Let's write down the names and seal them in envelopes."

He watched a fly buzz slowly through the air between us, then shot out one meaty hand like a snake's tongue and caught the fly. He crushed it, eyeballing me all the while, then dropped the crisp corpse onto his desk.

"That's quite a trick," I said. "I can juggle a little. Want to see?"

"Maybe you think I'm so old I can't outrun my own farts," he said. "And maybe things aren't what they used to be, but don't underestimate me. I got five submachine guns dumped in different parts of Half Moon Bay. I'm one of the last survivors of the Siskiyou dope wars. A lotta old geezers around today got rheumatism now 'cause they underestimated me. Got it?"

"Tish," I said.

We were belly to belly, mine slim and hard, his round and hard. He had stashed the cigar in a sawed-down beer can he used for an ashtray. His breath reeked of cheap tobacco and cheap beer, too fresh to have been from last night. Sometimes heavy drinkers sweated the beverage. The telltale spiders of a chronic drinker dappled the bridge of his nose and his upper cheeks.

"Listen, punkola," he said, grabbing the lapels of my sports coat so hard that I could hear small pieces of the material tearing. "I ask you a question, I want a goddamn answer. Who hired you?"

I cocked my right arm back and slugged him in the gut. He folded so violently our faces almost collided, then he took a few steps doubled-up, as if he were walking on stilts. I waited to see whether he was going to pull out the gun.

He stood partially upright and said, "Whoo. Boy, I guess I'm outta practice. I really opened myself up for that. You're tougher than I thought."

"Must be the hula lessons."

He hobbled across the floor to a washroom, closing a door with a frosted glass panel behind him. "I'll be back in a sec," he said. "Gotta spruce up."

Out the window behind his desk I could see the mast on a schooner traversing the locks on its way to the Puget Sound. Somebody was going on vacation. Up to the San Juans for a few weeks of campfires, scuba diving, crab pots, and sand in the socks.

I found a rubber band in his top drawer, along with a blackjack, about forty stray bullets and some nudie magazines. The guy really played the part. Cutting the rubber band in half with a pair of blunt-nosed child's scissors, I turned to the windowsill. By stretching the band tight, sighting down the taut line, edging it close to unsuspecting bluebottles and then letting go one end, I killed four of the buggers in less than a minute. I dropped the rubber band into his wastebasket and spilled the flies onto his Classics Comic.

When he came out his face was dripping water and soap.

He mopped it with a nubby towel that had Munson Motel printed on it.

"Beatrice Hindenburg," he said. "Worked for her father. He's in California. He's still paying child support on her and he's pissed. I hadda find her and prove she wasn't living with her ma in Southern Cal."

"How'd he come to hire you?"

"Used to work out of L.A. Moved up here for my health. Been sorry ever since. This whole state is full of ex-Californians, like a blight. Drive to the end of the loneliest logging road in the Cascades and you'll find a parked car with California plates on it. Hell, I'd rather take the smog than the fungus that grows up here in all this rain."

"I'm working for Mark Daniels. The one in the papers. I'm trying to find out what I can about Hindenburg and Daniels."

"Yeah, I seen where she got blasted by that guy. Shame. She was just a kid."

Butch Teets meandered around his desk and gaped at the line of dead flies on his comic.

"Can you tell me about it?" I asked.

The dead flies had him confounded. "What all do you need to know?"

"Where did you track her to? And what did you see?"

Teets brushed the flies off the table with the thick edge of his hand, then filed the comic in a drawer in his cabinet, a drawer that contained nothing but comics, dozens and dozens of them.

"A motel out in the North End. Out off Aurora. They used to show dirty movies on TVs over the beds, but they've cleaned up their image."

"You tracked her two months ago?"

"Yeah. About. How did you know?"

"You spoke to somebody named Kandy. She told me about it. Recall the name of the motel?"

"Sure, we'll go out together."

"I'd rather just have the name."

Bracing himself against the desk top on his huge tanned

knuckles, Butch Teets glowered at me. "Sure you would. But I know better. You're on a case, clown. And where there's a case, there's money. And where there's money there's Butch Teets. I want in."

"In what?"

"Whatever you got going. I got caught a little short this month and I need a piece of the pie. Whatever you got playin', it's fifty-fifty."

"I'm working for an attorney. There's nothing more to it."

"Hell, boy. You think I was born yesterday? You're working a flimflam and I want in."

"What'd you see at the motel?"

Butch walked over to a table in the back of the room and rustled through a disheveled stack of newspapers. Finally he came back with a front page of the *Times,* the one with the pictures of Beatrice Hindenburg-Crowley and Mark Daniels. He pointed to the picture of Daniels with a blunt fingertip. "Him."

"What about him?"

"He was with her. Had some sort of love nest set up. What was he . . . forty-five years old? And she was sixteen, seventeen? Wait, her father told me she was fifteen. Can you beat it? If I wasn't the consummate professional, I would have gone in there and beat the tar out of him."

"How long did you follow her?"

"Coupla days. Her father wanted me to tail her a week, but two days was all I needed."

"How'd you find her?"

"Her dad had a letter from the kid he'd stolen from his ex-wife. The return address was a house in the U-district. Hindenburg was using it for a mail drop. I waited around until she showed up for her mail, then tailed her. The afternoon I picked her up, she met Daniels in a little coffee house in the U-district and he drove her out to this motel. They stayed there five or six hours. He went out once for a six-pack and came back. He left her alone there at maybe ten, ten-thirty that night."

"You follow him home?"

"Didn't have to. I was after the girl. Fact is, I didn't even know who he was till I seen it in the paper this week."

"How many times did you see them out there?"

"Twice. First, I thought she lived there, but she didn't. I never did figure exactly where she was living. Think she just bummed around. One friend's apartment one night. Another the next night."

"You know where any of these apartments are?"

He shook his head.

"What do you know?"

"Let me in on the scam and I'll tell you."

"You talk to the cops about this?"

"Yeah, but they weren't interested in what I had to say."

"Why not?"

"Me and cops . . . we don't get along. Got a history of not getting along."

"Where is this motel?"

"Follow me."

"I'd rather you just drew a map. You got crayons, don't you?"

"Tag along after me or you don't find it."

The fly corpses really had him on the ropes. Before he left he peered down into the wastebasket at them, then opened the top drawer of his desk and flung a handful of dully clinking bullets into his jacket pocket.

He drove a junky old Ford Falcon that spewed so much oily smoke from under its belly I was afraid a cop would stop him before we got there. I followed him across the Aurora Bridge and out of the city. He drove at breakneck speed, a regular California daredevil. I had to run innumerable amber lights to stay with him.

The Galaxie Motor Court Inn had seen better days. It was a block off Highway 99 in a grimy area of drive-in burger joints and small businesses getting squeezed out by conglomerate stores and bland shopping centers designed by bland technicians. A block away a weary residential section began.

Teets parked his Falcon in a no parking spot, fiddled with his shoulder holster so every kid within two blocks knew he had it and beat me through the front door of the manager's office.

When I got there, he had a wallet flopped open and a fake badge showing, opposite a pair of cheap handcuffs.

"You're not going to use that?" I said.

"Let a consummate pro handle this, would you?"

We heard the throaty, wall-rattling sounds of a large dog barking. A door ten feet behind the counter in the tiny office popped open and a full-grown German shepherd charged out, barking and lunging at Teets. He ignored me. The dog dashed straight for Teets, as if he'd been waiting all day for him to show. His teeth had been borrowed from a crocodile. They were bared, saliva drooling out between them. This sucker was hungry.

I catapulted myself up onto the counter, pulling both feet up behind me. Teets tried the same thing, but there was only room for one.

Chapter Ten

THE LADY WHO lunged out of the back room baby-talking and grappling with the German shepherd had ex-prostitute written all over her. Let's be generous: ex-showgirl.

In her fifties, she had an hourglass figure—only the hourglass was plastic and someone had left it in the sun to warp. She wore snug jeans and a tight magenta sweater. An unnatural blondish-white, her teased and sprayed hair looked bulletproof.

Teets peeled himself off the wall and gave her a boldly appreciative once-over while she ran the dog into the back room. When she closed the door and faced us, her mustard-colored eyes inspected the buzzer and bracelets Teets was flashing.

"Are you the manager?" I asked, but Teets overrode me in a booming voice.

"Police Department. You run this crackerbox?"

"I own the Galaxie Motor Court Inn, yes. What can I do for you gentlemen?" A hint of loneliness lurked behind the eyes.

Teets nudged me and said, "You got pictures?"

I showed her a photo of Mark Daniels I'd clipped from the newspaper, and one of the girl. The girl's wasn't so hot. She had been dead a few hours when she posed for it.

"You know these two?" Teets asked.

Studying the photos for several long beats, she said, "What's this in connection with?"

Teets took out a small notebook and began writing. "You got a name?"

"Olive Peyton."

"And you own this place?"

"My husband left it to me when he died."

"I'll just bet he did. You want to keep it?"

"What does that mean?"

"It means we have questions for you. It means we ask and you answer."

"Excuse him," I said, in softer tones. "His mother dropped him on his head one too many times." Teets glanced at me warily. "We think this man and this girl may have been staying here. You recognize them?"

The bottle blonde looked at me as if she were really seeing something ten feet behind my head. I had the feeling nothing I could do or say would affect her.

"Don't pay much attention to my people. But yeah, I think maybe I do. He pays while she waits out in the car."

"You sure it was these two people?"

"Him, I'm sure of. Round face. The beard. The eyes. It's him. Her? I couldn't be so certain."

"I am," said Teets. "It was her."

I kept my eyes on Olive Peyton. "When was the last time you saw them?"

"Two weeks?"

"How many times have they been here?"

"Don't know. Two dozen maybe. A dozen with her."

"What do you mean by that?"

"He's been coming for years."

"With other women?"

She nodded and patted her coiffure. It moved in one piece, like a helmet. "Always with a woman."

"Know his name?"

"I know what he writes in the register."

"What's that?"

"M. Daniels."

Teets and I looked at each other. "How about his car? You write the license number down?"

"I never bother. Not with the regulars."

"He have a favorite room?"

"Right across the way. Twelve?" She pointed a finger with a nail that had been chewed to the quick. "Give you the key if you like. There's nothing in there. We keep our rooms tidy and we keep them antiseptic."

"Let me look at your register first." I made a list of all the dates when the signature M. Daniels cropped up. In six months of bookings I found it sixteen times, always to Room Twelve, always in the evening or late afternoon, and always one night at a time.

"Tallyho," said Teets as we left, tipping his hat.

Outside in the courtyard I looked at Teets. "You get his license plate?"

He shook his head, eyes on the manager through the curtained window. "Had it once. But my notes are always messy. It's back at the office somewhere. If I had six months, I could find it for you. What's the point?"

I forged across the weedy macadam. Teets lagged, peeping through the curtains. "What's the matter?" I said.

"Think maybe I'll go back in there. That little lady's got an itch I think I can scratch."

"What are you talking about?"

He was incredulous. "You didn't see the way she was looking at me? I thought you were a trained observer. I feel sorry for you if that's how you see things. She needs me to slip her this old bone. You didn't see that? Brother, I feel sorry for you."

"Are you crazy?"

"Hell, man. You got eyes, ain't you? She saw my Smith and Wesson. It gets 'em hot. A man with a gun is something to behold. The fragrant and manly aroma of gun oil is an aphrodizzzzzziac for women."

"You're crazy, Butch."

He gave me a rakish look. "She ain't no great shakes, but she's better than a poke in the eye with a sharp stick. Women worship us comic book heroes."

When I glanced over my shoulder, he was standing beside

the manager's hut, peeping through a half-drawn blind. I
would be back for him. Even from where I was, I could hear
the locked-up shepherd woofing.

The Galaxie Motor Court Inn was laid out on an enormous lot, the single-story buildings constructed in rows and
set up in a pattern almost like a Nazi swastika, narrow alleys
just large enough for a car to squeeze through alongside each
building. My guess was Olive Peyton's husband had died
ten years ago; and when she buried him she buried the maintenance schedule in his blazer pocket. The paint was peeling
and several shabby doors needed replacing because irate
tenants had booted shallow holes in them.

Twelve had a double bed, a shower, a hot plate and a refrigerator that must have been a year or two older than I was.
I snapped on a Philco radio that had wood parts in it and
waited to see what sort of music the last visitor had preferred. Crystal Gayle crooned a soggy ballad at me.

Twelve was an end unit. I went next door and knocked on
ten. This one had miniature cactus plants growing in plastic
pots on the windowsill, the curtains drawn and pinned shut.
Moisture and a bluish-green mold were heavily beaded up
on the inside of the window. A bumper sticker pasted across
the top of the door read, "Jesus Saves." Black moss clung
to the shaded porch and yellowed copies of the local free
Wednesday afternoon shopping news had piled up.

Though I heard movement inside, nobody came to the
door. I knocked again. Nothing. I waited a full minute and
knocked again. Louder.

"Morning," I said, when the door finally squeaked open
on a chain. Her skin was so pale it looked like wax. She was
no larger than a child and had matted, close-cropped black
hair and a well-established mustache. A geek. In the window behind the cacti a geek man, who looked as if he were
her grown son, appeared. "I'm wondering if you live
here."

"Who's askin'?"

I handed her one of my cards. She read it slowly and
handed it back, handling it with the tips of her long-nailed,

dirt-crusted fingers. A fetid aroma began sliding out the door and into the court. Her boy gave me a rigorous and goofy look.

"We live here. Son and me."

"Have you ever seen either of these two people?" I unfurled the newspaper clippings and held them up for her.

"I seen 'em." Her words came out like pellets of hatred. "Come here and raise a ruckus. Play that damn music. Sittin' up all night drinkin' and carousing. Sometimes he'd bring two girls. Satan's work. He'll be burning. Mark me on that. Them guitars is instruments of the devil. My momma told me that and I ain't never forgot."

"He play a guitar?"

"Just the radio. Radio play the guitars."

"Country-western music?"

"That's it. Satan's work. We seen 'em. And we heerd 'em through the wall."

"What'd you hear?"

The door began inching closed. "You ain't from Satan yerself? Is you?"

"Me? No ma'am."

"You an angel of God?"

"You couldn't really call me that, no."

"Git."

"If you remember anything about what went on in there, would you call one of the numbers on this card?"

"Git." The door slammed in my face. I pushed the card under the door. In the window her son was scratching the nits in his crew cut with dangling fingers like a chimp, flashing me the goofiest grin I had received all week. He disappeared from the window, as if he'd been yanked. Mother and son. Geeks.

All was quiet at the manager's hut. I opened the door and glimpsed Seymore Teets standing in the back room, the door ajar. So—he had gotten all the way into the back room. It looked like a rather strange courtship ritual. Long teeth bared in a tall and unnatural grin, Teets appeared to be debating whether to go for his gun. I couldn't see anybody else in the room with him.

When I got closer and hung the key on the wall rack, I spotted the dog, inches from his crotch, fangs exposed, mouth slavering, body poised to leap and rip, giving Teets a simple but effective lesson in comportment. Some canny trainer had apparently taught this pooch to go straight for the nutsack.

I found Olive Peyton in another room off the manager's cubicle, blithely stuffing laundry into a paint-chipped Maytag. "Your animal is causing some real concern to Mr. Teets," I said.

Olive Peyton gave me an icy look, then went back to punching laundry into the machine. She switched the machine on and sashayed out a back door to the complex.

I found my way back to the detective.

"Teets? What was the address of the mail drop Beatrice Hindenburg was using in the U-district?"

Whispering, he gave it to me.

Detective and dog were still doing their tango when I left. Neither looked to be enjoying the siege, but then, I doubted if either of them knew how to break it off. I certainly wasn't in a mood to lose fingers trying. The last I saw of them, they were still drying their teeth at each other.

"Have a nice afternoon, comic book hero."

I drove to Queen Anne Hill and rang the chimes on the Daniels place. Nobody was home.

Parking at Harborview was scarce. I found a spot around the south side next to the boarded-up windows of the county medical examiner's office and went up to the second floor. Deanna was in the waiting room off the intensive care unit, thumbing through a magazine. She wore a plain skirt and, under an open sweater, a purple leotard top that clung like a membrane.

"Thomas." Whipping the magazine aside, she stood, rushed me, snaked her arms around my waist and hugged her face against my heart.

"How's Mark doing?"

"The same." She released my chest but kept hold of my wrists, looking up into my eyes. She was a touching kind of person. She touched both men and women when she spoke to them. I wasn't used to it. "I'm so glad you came here. I feel so alone. And . . ."

She was warm and soft and fragrant and more vulnerable than any woman I'd been around in a long while. I was a perennial sucker for vulnerable women.

"Are you all right?"

"I'm bearing up."

"Mark and you weren't getting along so famously, were you?"

She examined my eyes for a while. "No."

"You left him?"

She nodded, reluctant and a trifle embarrassed.

"He beat you?"

"You know about that?"

"I know about a lot of things. Mark isn't such a nice guy. I found a motel this afternoon where he took women, lots of women. Beatrice Hindenburg in particular."

"That means he was seeing her." I nodded. "Then maybe he killed her?"

"Who knows?"

Deanna sagged against me and murmured heavily.

"Deanna, do you still think Mark couldn't have done it?"

She hesitated. "He was wrong sometimes. But this whole deal is screwy. I know he didn't do it. Suicide just wasn't in Mark. I could believe almost anything else. I believe he had the girl. That he had other women. I might even believe . . . if the circumstances were right . . . that he shot that girl. I found out after I married him two years ago that he got divorced because he couldn't keep his fists off Helen. He even hit the kids. I could believe a whole lot of things, but not suicide. And not that note."

"I obtained a list of dates that he was at the motel. Never on a weekend. My guess is he used the office on weekends. Was he gone a lot?"

"Sometimes we might not cross paths for days. But I had

a busy schedule, too. I was taking some courses. I was sculpting. We were both busy.'' I had her look at the dates. They didn't mean anything to her. ''In our hectic routines, I doubt if I could trace down one of these. Neither one of us kept an appointment book.''

''Someone said you have a boat.''

''Mark ordered a sailboat—for $112,000. We haven't seen it yet. Teak decks. It was extravagant.''

''Where'd he get the cash?''

''I'm beginning to find out Mark was an expert when it came to juggling funds from one project to another. He borrowed on our house and then hocked some of my jewelry for the down payment. He wanted the boat for me. At least that's what he claimed. Said we needed someplace we could go together to get away from the worm races. That's what he called it. Worms racing for dollars. Now that I think about it, maybe he just wanted it as a place to take his girlfriends.''

''Where else might he have gone with a woman?''

Backing off my chest where she had been mumbling into my jacket, Deanna leaned back and peered into my eyes. My inquiries, this entire discussion, was stinging her, whittling down her strength.

I apologized. ''We'll talk about this some other time.''

''I don't think I'll have the fortitude some other time. He might have gone to the lake. In fact, I can't believe he would bother with a motel. Our place on Lost Lake is less than an hour from here. Why didn't he go up there?''

''Maybe he did.''

Deanna looked at me, her greenish-browns as chagrined as greenish-brown could get. Then her look turned steamy. Or I thought it did. Maybe I was only wishing. Looking at her invariably caused my mind to wander. I was reminded of a wacky divorce I'd done some investigating for, in which each partner slept with the other's best friends, all of the other's best friends, just to get even. It had been the sexiest case of the year. Until now.

Brushing my cheek with her fingertips, Deanna laughed a

giggly, nervous laugh that made me want to drop all my reservations and give her a buss on the tip of her nose.

"How do I get to this lake?"

"I'll take you. You'll never find the place on your own. We've given directions, sketched maps. Only one in ten finds it."

"Maybe I'm one in ten."

"I'll take you. If you want, we can have dinner up there. The freezer's always stocked. There's a microwave we can use."

She lowered her eyes. I couldn't believe the sheen from the windows on her blonde hair done up in a sweeping pile. Sometimes it looked golden, sometimes strawberry, and in some lights it was almost ash-colored.

Before we left, Deanna and I walked arm in arm into the ICU ward, one of her pneumatic breasts pressed into my elbow. Some women you could caress or hold when they were in trouble. Other women you couldn't touch without the touching becoming something else. For me, Deanna was one of the latter. I began to sweat a little.

We sauntered down one hall, up another. All the rooms were open, and most had patients in them—patients with tubes inserted into various parts of their bodies. I was surprised that most of the occupants were elderly. I had expected a lot of young trauma patients.

We stopped in front of a room that had three or four machines hooked up to a bearded man in a white hospital gown. The patient was Mark Daniels, his head twice its normal size swathed in layers of white gauze. His skin looked ashen, almost yellowish. A bag of clear silvery-looking liquid was suspended over his body, dripping something through a line in his arm at the inside of his elbow.

Deanna held back at the doorway, gnashing her lip. I went in and gazed down at him. He had tubes in both arms and one down his throat. A Bible lay next to his bed.

"Sam Wheeler leave this?"

"I never saw much of Sam until this. But he's been a

good friend. I'll never forget him for the last week. He's been with me almost every day except today."

Mark's doctor wasn't in the hospital so I spoke to the floor nurse, a jolly woman wearing a short, mannish haircut and horn-rimmed glasses. "He say anything since you got him? Anything at all?"

"No. The Reverend was in here talking to him for a long time yesterday, but as far as I know he didn't answer back. You know the Reverend?"

I nodded.

"He has a theory about talking to head cases so they can hear you. I don't know. Maybe there's some point to it. He was in here babbling for over an hour. As far as I know, nothing came of it."

"What about when the patient first came in?"

She shrugged. "You might want to ask downstairs in the emergency room."

Deanna waited while I went downstairs, where I bumped into a helpful nurse in the emergency room. "This is the shift that was working when he came in. You might want to talk to Danny—the one across the aisle with the mustache. He's a doctor's assistant down here from Alaska getting some experience. I remember he worked on him."

Danny was short and pleasant and looked for all the world like a young doctor. It was an appearance they cultivated: the mustache, the beguiling mixture of innocence, dedication, bookishness and eyes that tried to say I've-seen-it-all, and somehow failed to say anything. He rubbed the black hair on one of his arms as we spoke.

"The guy upstairs with the bullet in his head?" I said. Danny nodded. "I understand you were here Saturday when he was brought in?"

"Yeah, I worked on him. The medics intubated him, but they didn't do a very good job. We had to do it over. Wasn't really much for us to do on that one. I'm still waiting for a good accident where we can crack the chest and do some open heart. Have they cut him yet?"

"Not yet. I was wondering if he regained consciousness while he was in here."

"He mumbled a bit."

"You remember what about?"

"I remember it well. It kind of got to me. Not right then. We were all busy at the time. But it hit me later when I had a chance to think about it."

"What was it?"

"He said, 'The Lord is my shepherd.' He said it three or four times. Said it almost like he was trying to convince somebody of it, you know? 'The Lord is my shepherd.' "

Lost Lake was situated just across the border of King County, in lower Snohomish. We drove in my truck. Deanna seemed out of place in a 1968 Ford pickup, but only for a minute. Her perfume reminded me of something, another time, or place, or maybe another woman, but I couldn't quite put my finger on it.

If we had dinner together up there, it would be dark before we returned to the city. She was distraught and vulnerable and I wasn't sure if I was ready for what might happen at the lake.

Chapter Eleven

BOUNCING ALONG in the beginnings of the rush hour maelstrom, we braved irate truckers and errant bus drivers. We talked only about inconsequentials, but there was something about Deanna's vivacious prattling and laughter that made me stop and think. I liked it—I liked her—but I couldn't figure her out.

The lake lay past Maltby on a bumpy macadam road. Lost Lake Road. Quaint.

A dinky thing, only a few dozen acres, Lost Lake was shaped like an egg, was sunk into the earth, trees towering along its banks. In some states they would call a puddle like that a sinkhole.

A narrow roller coaster of a road circumscribed the basin. The Daniels' summer house was on the southeast corner of the lake, couched in a stand of alders. She had been right. I never would have found it on my own.

We parked in the sloping graveled drive and she climbed out my door behind me.

It had been sunny and pleasant when we left Seattle, but we had driven into a blanket of fog. A cool fuzzy drizzle, almost too faint to see, wafted through the air.

"It's really not that much," she said, looking up at the weather. "It belonged to Mark's grandmother. Two bedrooms. He's left it pretty much the way it was when she passed away. What makes it neat is the lake. It's all private except for that little strip of public fishing across the way.

There aren't any strangers down here. Except us. We don't come often enough to know anyone real well.''

It was early afternoon and the local flora looked lusher and more verdant under the oppressive fleecy haze than it would have in sunlight. Even the sky itself seemed to be cast in a greenish tint. The clouds were a uniform gray, low and melded into one big suffocating umbrella. A musician from Florida had once told me he had never experienced drizzle before coming to Washington. It was so fine it feathered your eyebrows like overspray on a careless painter and you could stand in it an hour before you actually got wet.

She gave me the royal tour. The house was plunked smack in the middle of an acre and a half of trees, only a hundred feet from the water. The unpretentious front lawn sloped down into the lake, clumps of tall weeds dotting the shoreline. A small homemade raft was anchored fifty feet out, buoyed by fifty-five-gallon drums. Inside an old shack tacked onto the side of the house, I spotted a red canoe and paddles.

I saw half a dozen houses surrounding the lake, each spaced a football field or more from its neighbors. The surface of the water was unmarred by wind or tide. Near the base of the Daniels' lawn a fish broke the mirror effect with a lazy flip of its tail.

"Trout," Deanna said, reading my mind. "The locals plant perch, too. It's really idyllic. Wish we came up more often." She keyed open the front door and we went in.

Slinging her purse onto a hutch near the front door, Deanna scurried around checking the utilities, inspecting the refrigerator, cracking the kitchen window an inch or two to air the place out. The living room smelled of cheap perfume and beer, as if we had just barged in on a pair of illicit ghost lovers.

"You and Mark are going to get a divorce," I said, "aren't you?"

"I wouldn't say this to anyone but you . . . If he lives, yes, I'll divorce him. I hope he's not . . . I hope he doesn't recover and need constant care. People will think I'm running out. Yes. We're through. He's . . . he's not what I thought he was. He lied to me about why he got divorced from his first wife and he's been lying ever since. He used to hit me. I was so shocked I didn't know what to do."

"I'm sorry."

"Then there were the other things. This sleazy man came up to me in the hospital and told me he had worked for Mark. Said Mark owed him over $25,000. Mark always told me he didn't owe a dime to anybody. He was always bragging about that. I believed him. I thought the house was almost paid for."

"It's not?"

"After he went to the hospital I called the mortgage company. We owe four months of back payments. Twenty-seven hundred a month. Can you believe that? He wanted me to think he didn't have a care in the world, that nothing had ever gone sour for him. I think I might have loved him more if a few things had gone sour."

"They're sour now."

Her mouth twitched so that I thought she might cry. "Yes."

Deanna took a deep breath, gathered her resources, looked at me, then waved her hands. "Live and learn, I guess. Only trouble is, I never seem to learn." She sat down on a sofa that had frayed arms. "When I was in college I worked in a shoe store in Ann Arbor. The dictum was, one shoe at a time. Don't let anybody try on two shoes at once.

"You know me. Dumb Deanna they call me. One day this couple walks in, both well dressed, obviously moneyed people. They asked for matching alligator shoes. His and hers. Dumb Deanna, I bring out the shoes, fit them each with both shoes. Then the lady turns to me sweetly and asks if I can't get one size smaller so she can see if it fits better. She could hardly squeeze into the ones she had, but I figured the customer is always right. I walked all the way into the storeroom before it hit me.

"Pow. Right out the door, lickety split. You never saw a couple run so fast. When I got out onto the sidewalk, they

must have been two whole blocks away. They took my job
with them. One shoe at a time. A little common sense. A
little perspective. But that's never been me. It was the same
with Mark. I gave him both shoes. Dumb Deanna. The story
of my life.''

She scrunched her hands into shoe shapes and wriggled
them.

Was she giving me both shoes, too?

I stood over a cherrywood cabinet stereo, opened the top
and picked up an album cover from a Loretta Lynn record.
Two other Lynn records were on the turntable. ''Mark liked
country-western, eh?''

''Mark? He didn't care for any kind of music. Never listened to the radio, even.'' She cupped her hand to her ear
when she said listened, miming, then laughed when she
caught me observing the signal.

''This must be your album, then?'' I flagged it at her.

Deanna shook her head, looking grave but unflappable.
Then she realized the implications and jumped up. ''Never
seen it before!''

''It's not Mark's?''

''Mark never bought an album in his life. Country-
western is the last thing he'd buy. In fact, none of the punch
buttons on his car radio were tuned to anything. He didn't
like excess noise, he said.''

''When was the last time you or Mark were up here?''

''About a month. Unless Mark came up . . . you know,
with another woman.''

''Mind if I look around?''

She assisted, pawing through the belongings in the house,
squeamishly but thoroughly inspecting the bedding in both
bedrooms, peeking into the closets, while outside the wintry
cloud loomed over the house and lake. It took ten minutes.
Nothing seemed amiss.

''Somebody's been in this house.'' Her nervous laughter
bubbled out of a quaking chest. I went to the doors and
checked the locks. There was no sign that anything had been

forced. I went around and inspected the windows one by one. Nothing.

"I smelled beer and perfume when we came in."

"Did you?" Deanna said distractedly, pulling pots out of a cupboard. "What do you want for supper? You have to excuse me. When I get stressed out like this I have to be busy. Chicken or steak?"

"Chicken is fine. They were careful, though."

"Who?"

"Whoever was here. They didn't want anyone to know. The beds have been carefully remade with fresh linen. They only left the albums. It was almost like somebody cleaned up in a hurry and forgot them."

"It's creepy," Deanna said, setting about fixing supper, using the motion to ward off thoughts about her husband with other women.

All I could think was that Mark had been up here with Deborah Crowley-Hindenburg or someone else, apparently a country-western fan. Nothing else made sense.

While Deanna fried up a batch of chicken and talked to me over her shoulder, I stared out the kitchen window at the lake and the lushness surrounding it. This was what they meant by lincoln green. Sherwood must have been this color before the air pollution and the wars and the condo developments.

On the far side an old man sat in a webbed garden chair, concentrating, a fishing pole dangling out over the water. A boy younger than school age drove small wheeled things in the sand at the old man's feet, as intent on his traffic as the old man was on the motionless cherry bobber.

I lifted a set of 8-power binoculars off the windowsill, removed them from their case and scanned the opposite shore, slowly working from one end of the lake to the other. A trio of mallards paddled around in the shallows at the bottom of the Daniels' lawn.

Before I got to the end of the lake something warm and soft and aromatic leaned down against me, nudging my cheek. When I turned my head, Deanna ran her hands slowly down my shoulders and languorously across my chest. It was a big move for a woman to make on a detective when her husband was in a hospital bed and she wasn't quite sure how the detective felt about her. But then, maybe I had inadvertently given away some of it with my eyes. Or a lot.

"You're not married, are you?" she whispered.

"Nope."

"Been?"

"Not in this lifetime."

"Why not?"

"Came close a time or two. Things didn't work out."

"What about Kathy Birchfield?"

"What about her?"

"I thought she . . . I mean, you get on so well. You seem like you've known each other for ages. I thought you were living together. Or something."

"Kathy and I have a platonic relationship. Always have had."

"Are you seeing anybody, then?"

"Not a soul."

"Would you mind seeing me, maybe, a little bit?"

"I've been thinking about that since the first time I saw you."

"You sure?"

"I like you, Deanna. When this is over, yes, I'd like to see you."

"Why do we have to wait until it's over?"

She bent over me and kissed me a sideways kiss, long and steamy, tasting of the salt and radishes she had been munching. I felt like somebody had dropped a bowling ball on my head. If I slept with her, I'd probably stroke out and wake up with half my body frozen and nerveless.

"What was that for?"

"Just 'cause."

I twittered my eyebrows in my patented Groucho imitation. She gave me a quicker, tidier, less serious kiss and backed away to tend the dinner. "You must think me an awful vamp to do that when Mark is . . . hooked up to all those machines.''

"I don't know if I do or not.''

"Tell me when you make up your mind. I want to know the instant you make up your mind.'' We looked at each other so hard the windows started fogging over. Humming to a popular tune on the radio, she looked away.

Things looked brighter and bluer in the field glasses, the optics of the glasses screening out much of the green in the air. I could see the mist drifting like particles of smoke in a projection room. I skimmed the lakeshore one more time and then focused on the surface of the water.

I spotted it out by the homemade raft. It wasn't very noticeable and if I hadn't been the suspicious type, I wouldn't have thought anything about it.

Whoever had been in the house had left two items, not one: the album, and what was out in the water.

"Does that canoe in the shed keep your feet dry?''

Deanna half-turned and shot me a quizzical look. "Sure. Take the paddle with the blue tape around the handle. The other one's cracked.''

I barged out the back door, clumped through the damp grass and pulled open the rickety door to the shed.

The canoe was beautifully constructed, wooden, forty years old, and much lighter than it looked. I hoisted it up and carried it on my shoulders Indian fashion. When I jogged back up for the paddle, I could see Deanna's strawberry-blonde head bobbing in the window preparing dinner.

I poled off, took two short powerful strokes and glided out to the raft. If I hadn't grabbed hold of the rough, unfinished boards on the raft I would have glissaded all the way across the satiny surface of the lake. I maneuvered around, peering intently into the glassy depths. Without a light, without sunshine at my back, I could see only about four feet into the bluish-green.

It was right where I had seen it in the binoculars, only now it was deeper. I rolled my shirt-sleeve up and plunged my arm into the shoulder socket, dangerously tipping the canoe. My face was so close I could smell the surface of the water. Ducks. The cold water caused me to shiver.

My fingertips grazed something. It felt airy, like undulating corn silk. Or floating hair. Yes, that was it, hair throbbing back and forth gently in the almost motionless water.

Even holding my breath and dipping my head and shoulder into the lake, I couldn't quite get hold of it. Nor could I pierce the murk enough to see what it was, but my heart was racing.

Chapter Twelve

PADDLING BACK TO SHORE, I nosed the canoe into the base of the lawn where it thumped hard, screeching against the gravel and jolting me. I raced up the lawn to the shed.

Hunched inside the musty, cramped shed in the monochromatic murk of the afternoon, I scavenged some rusted fence wire, worried a three-foot piece off and angled one end into a needle-sharp makeshift grappling hook. I slogged back to the canoe and stroked out to the corn silk. Piloting around in circles, it took me a while to detect it this time. The mass seemed to be sinking deeper. In another few minutes we would need scuba divers.

I dipped the hook into the water and finagled, jigging it around in the depths. After about two minutes I snagged something. Jerking, I set the hook. The wire wasn't very stout and the hook on the end was feeble at best, so I hauled it up slowly, reeling it in like a careful fisherman working up a hundred-year-old sea turtle.

The mass bobbed to the surface the way a swimmer gasping for breath might. Only she wasn't gasping, didn't breathe, just rolled over and stared at me out of her wrong-channel, black-and-white TV eyes.

As I stared at her, she slowly began drifting back down into the water.

My grappling hook had snared her through a piece of her chin.

Bits of lake goo in her hair, Kandy looked even more cer-

vine and lanky than she had this afternoon when I had given
her the five dollars.

Naked from the waist up, she had been pummeled se-
verely around the face and eyes. Her cheeks were reddened
and puffy, her skull lacerated in several places. Ribs showing plainly, breasts like nibs, she looked hungrier and
knobbier than ever. She was so pale she didn't look real.

"Ingrid Darling," I said. "What have you let them do to
you?"

She had made good time. In just a few hours she had finished packing, met her sugar daddy, and come up here
where somebody beat her to a pulp and then tied her neck to
a rock and gave her one last swimming lesson.

The rope had unknotted from around her gangly neck, but
you could still see the pinkish-red tracks embedded in her
pasty skin.

Threading the hook through a belt loop in her jeans, I
wired the other end to a piece of bracing on one of the seats
and paddled awkwardly back to shore. The old man and the
boy across the expanse of silky water had taken no notice of
me and my passenger.

Deanna was more observant. Or perhaps she had been
keeping track of the expedition from the start. She leaned
against the jamb in the kitchen doorway, staring in disbelief,
tears running down her freckled face, flour soiling her hands
and forearms.

When she plodded barefoot down the damp grass, I saw
why she had been outside, why she had spotted me and
Kandy. In one hand she had a fistful of tiny flowers, butter-
cups mixed together with delicate flesh-colored pansies. In
fact, the pansies were closer to the normal color of human
skin than the dead girl was. She had come out to pick a bou-
quet for the supper table. Everything was going to be perfect
for our tête-à-tête.

"Oh God," she said, when she got closer. "Why, she's
only a girl. What happened to her?"

Disembarking from the canoe, I stepped into the water up
to my ankles. I leaned over and gently slid Kandy's belt loop

out of the hook and then steered her lanky cadaver up onto the grass on her back. She was barefoot, clad in the same skin-tight jeans she had worn earlier. The zipper was at half mast. I had the feeling someone had tried to dress her hurriedly. Or that she had tried to dress herself and got caught at it. Her thin soaking wet hair was pasted to her scalp in strands.

"Thomas?"

"Are you all right, Deanna?"

"Thomas? I feel so lightheaded. Thomas, I don't understand this at all. Where on earth did she come from? Who is she?"

"I interviewed her a few hours ago about Beatrice Hindenburg, the girl your husband was supposed to have killed. She used to work with Beatrice at Trinity. Name is Ingrid Darling."

"A few hours ago?"

"Yeah."

"That means someone was just here!"

"We must have just missed them."

Deanna tiptoed around on the wet stones until the slack, pummeled face was upright in her frame of reference. "I've never seen a dead body before. Except at funerals. And that's different. She's so . . ."

"Unremarkable?"

"Yes. How in the world did you find her?"

"I'm real lucky that way sometimes."

"Have you ever . . . have you ever seen a dead body before?"

Reluctantly, I nodded, bent over and pulled the canoe away from Kandy's legs. "Just about my share."

"Do they always look like this?"

I stepped closer to Deanna Daniels. Her chest was heaving faster and faster. I was afraid she would vomit on the cadaver.

She was slipping into shock. Suddenly her greenish-brown eyes swung up onto mine as if she were drowning and

I were her only hope. She rushed into my arms. I kissed her cheek gently. It tasted salty, yeasty.

Pushing her off slowly, I said, "Go in the house and call the county sheriff. Say we pulled a body out of the lake and we think it was murder. Tell them how to get here. Tell them they're going to need divers and lights. Then make a pot of coffee. We're going to have a lot of visitors in a very short while."

"What are you going to do? We can't just leave her here, can we?"

"It doesn't make any difference to her, Deanna. Not anymore. I'm going to paddle across the water and ask that old man if he saw anything. I'll be right back."

"Thomas?"

"Take it easy, Deanna. People die every day."

"Not at my house."

"Everything will turn out."

"Mark didn't do this?"

I shook my head. "I spoke to this girl today. A few hours ago. In fact, we probably just missed her murderer, maybe even passed him on the highway."

"You think this is connected to Mark and that girl?"

"I don't know, Deanna. I really don't."

A barn swallow swooped out of the sky at us, chirping and snapping up insects in its beak. Birds seemed to love this sort of weather. I shoved off and twisted around once to watch Deanna flouncing up to the house in the wet grass.

There was something about our discussion that had bothered me. She had made a big production about never having seen a dead body before, yet there had been something in her demeanor, a momentary flash in her eyes, that told me she had been lying. She had seen a body before. Or bodies. Why would she lie about a thing like that?

I stroked across the lake and drifted to within a few feet of the old man and the boy. The moppet looked up at me and grinned, twirled a toy fire engine in his chubby little fingers. "Pretty nice," I said.

The old man smiled a weary smile and turned his sooty eyes onto me.

"You see anything across the way today?" I asked.

The old man shook his head.

"How long have you been out here?"

"Hour. Hour and a half." He held up a string of five perch, their orange fins bright in the dim afternoon, as if he measured time by how many fish he caught. Then he dropped the line gently back into the shallows.

"Do you remember if anyone was over there?"

"They don't usually come up here but once or twice in the summer. Stayed a week once. Since the old woman died, we rarely see a body over there. My stepson, Jason, mows the lawn for them."

"We found a dead girl in the water," I said. "She was put there today. Thought you might have seen something. Or heard some screaming." The boy looked up at me, eyes wide, and I was sorry I had said it.

"Maud did say something as we was comin' down here. Said she thought she seen somebody swimming. Thought she seen somebody splashin' around. But her eyes is bad. A mite nippy for shenanigans like that."

"Thanks. The county sheriff will probably talk to you later."

"I'll be here. Name's McDonell. Willy and Maud. Live right there." He pointed to a shingled house in the trees. A visit from the county sheriff would probably qualify as the excitement of the century.

Gliding back to the Daniels place I observed the trails in the wet grass. From out on the lake I could see plainly where Deanna had walked down from the kitchen door and then gone back up, using almost the same footprints. I could see my three trails, one with the canoe, one for the paddle, and a third for the wire that I formed into a grappling hook, all overlapping one another. The rest of the dewy, fog-misted lawn seemed untouched. But then, whoever had dumped Ingrid Darling into Lost Lake might have done it before the clouds had settled down and feathered the landscape.

When I scooted the canoe up onto the lawn, a flock of Evening Grosbeaks were perched in a tree over the water, cheeping loudly. Big, yellow-bodied birds, they sounded like chicks chirruping through megaphones.

Ingrid Darling, bedraggled and defiled, hadn't moved. I grabbed her cold shoulders and heaved her up another few feet, so that her toes weren't dangling in the water. She couldn't have weighed more than a hundred pounds . . . sopping. She felt like a big lump of damp clay.

The sheriff's deputy who took charge of the investigation was a bombastic man, slovenly dressed in his uniform and sloping Sam Browne belt, who focused his shrewd eyes on Deanna and the purple membrane of her leotard top as often as he could and slurred most of his words. Even with a murder on his hands, she was something he wanted to remember. I didn't blame him. His thinning black hair was wet and combed straight back, the same as the dead girl's. We told him what we knew, what time we had arrived, who the dead girl was, and what we were doing there. Though he didn't voice it, he didn't believe we had come up to search the house. He was certain we were there for a lovers' tryst.

After disgustedly forking the chicken out of the pan into the garbage, Deanna had topped off a brushed-steel carafe with hot coffee.

Deputies burned their tongues on the java, searched the house, confiscated the albums, took fingerprints and discovered a pair of tiny black lace panties tucked down in the sheets of one of the beds. Deanna said she had never seen them before. One deputy upended the garbage can outside and, using his flashlight, sifted through the rubbish.

Two hefty off-shift deputies showed up with scuba tanks and portable lights. After going through the twenty-minute ritual of peeling their suits onto their limbs and testing their regulators, they waded out and plunged into the water. Ten minutes later they brought up a hunk of angle iron with a strip of clothesline tied to it. It was hardly enough to have held down the corpse after it bloated. Whoever had killed

Ingrid Darling had been rather inept. Didn't know a lot about death.

They took our statements in the house and abandoned the crime scene. The last person off the property was the county medical examiner. She was a few years younger than me. Flaming red hair, lips painted a shiny dark crimson, cheeks heavily rouged. She wore earrings that looked like tiny silver tambourines.

She didn't even pretend to be glum over the prospect of an autopsy.

I asked her if I could have the results.

Ripping a card out of her wallet, she handed it to me and said, "Call tomorrow sometime after ten. I do 'em first thing in the morning. I should know by then. Ask for Carol Neff."

"Dr. Neff?"

"Yeah, but that doctor stuff is a lot of bull hooey. Just a bunch of overtrained nitwits indulging in God complexes. Call me Carol."

She was the only one of the Snohomish officials who didn't seem disgruntled to be working with a private detective from the big city. In fact, she seemed overjoyed. But then, she seemed overjoyed about everything, especially tomorrow morning's session of slice and dice. Before she drove off she said, "I like the young ones. Most are so old. The young ones . . . it's almost like working on real people. It's good to get them prime like this, too." She grinned and gunned her station wagon out of the driveway.

I didn't know whether or not to say "you're welcome." What was the protocol? After all, she had more or less thanked me for handing over a nice, fresh, relatively unscathed corpse. I would send her a card.

Chapter Thirteen

THE DRIVE BACK to Queen Anne Hill was dark and gloomy.

We got sidetracked in Woodinville and picked over a dinner at a steak house I had heard good rumors about. The rumors were wrong. The service was hit-or-miss and the food was bland and tasteless.

The dead girl had put a pall over us, but now it had been almost three hours and we both needed relief. As if by tacit agreement, we spoke of other things, sliding the afternoon into the distant past.

Midway through the meal I spilled my water glass onto my shirt, then soaked both my napkin and hers mopping the puddle. I asked her if she had anything else. She dug a handkerchief out of her purse and handed it to me. I sponged up the spots on my shirt and shimmed the heavily perfumed hanky into my pocket.

Deanna, silent in the truck, became loquacious with food and drink in her system. She hadn't eaten all day and she wolfed down her meal, then entertained me with half a dozen hilarious stories from her childhood. Chutzpah. Pizzazz. She had them both in quantities I admired.

It dawned on me during the conversation that she was unconsciously working some sort of voodoo, had set the cross hairs on me and was squeezing the trigger mechanism. I felt like a snowbound deer, helpless, about to be gutshot. I felt as if I were going to like it.

"You know why I like you, Thomas Black?"

I shook my head.

"You're a loner, aren't you? If you see a queue, you go the other way. If there's a crowded bus and an empty bus, you take the empty one. When a salesman tells you his model is the most popular model to ever come down the pike and John Doe and all of his neighbors have already bought one, you turn around on your heel and walk out of the store."

"You're very astute."

"I was a saleswoman for years. I worked in retail sales. I even sold computers at the beginning of the boom. That's where Mark met me, in fact. He was buying a Northstar system for the company. I learned to size up men a long time ago. I had four brothers, two older and two younger, all rascals, and they kept me on my toes. You're good for me, Thomas, because I'm a joiner. Too much of a joiner. I see a line in front of a movie house and I want to go stand in it. You want to run for your life and I want to join it. You detested that party the other night, didn't you?"

"As parties go, it wasn't bad."

"You hated it. I could tell you were uncomfortable. Being around you refreshes my perspective, makes me think twice about what I'm doing. I don't know if I could live with you, but I like being around you. I'll bet you're a detective because it's a job for loners?"

"Or maybe I'm a loner because I'm a detective."

She laughed, a vivacious, rafter-shaking laugh. "It just seems like being a loner would be an advantage in your profession. Is it? Tell me all about it?"

"Not tonight, Deanna."

"But how did you get into it? Were you in the CIA or something horribly sinister like that?"

"I was a Seattle policeman for ten years. That's all."

"Why did you quit?"

"It's a long story. I shot somebody. It kind of broke me up for a while there."

"I bet you don't carry a gun, then."

I shrugged, wondering why she would care, although a lot of people asked me that. She smiled it off.

"Just wondering. I couldn't feel a gun on you."

Maybe Teets was right. Maybe guns turned the dames on.

"Most of the time there's no need."

"Someday will you tell me all about it though? I want to know everything."

I smiled weakly. "Someday."

The conversation tapered off during the drive.

At Harborview we both went upstairs to the intensive care unit and checked on Mark. A Filipino nurse squinted at us out of pretty, unsmiling eyes and said he was the same.

I escorted Deanna downstairs to the public lot where she had parked her Cadillac. Under a street light she opened her front door, then turned and looked up at me. Her pinned hair seemed almost red under the street light. Her eyes cajoled me, blotting out the rest of the world. "Thomas?"

"Ummm."

"Promise me something?"

"Um hmmm."

"When it's all over? I want to see you."

"Um hmmm."

"Promise?"

"Hmmmm. It's the Bushido of the private eye. We practically never go back on our promises. Never. Practically."

She laughed, kissed the point of my chin, and slithered into the front seat. When she wheeled out of the lot a young intern in a flapping lab coat gave her the once-over, gaping until she was gone. She was more than a beautiful woman in a flashy Cadillac. She was the sort of dreamy vision guys saw on the street and remembered for weeks every time they made love to their wives. I waited until she was safely out of sight before I went to my truck.

I drove home at breakneck speed. I had scrounged a dry shirt and dry socks from Mark Daniels' supply at the lake house and they had been nagging at me to take them off. The socks were too tight and the shoes were still damp. The shirt was enormous, bagged out like a blowzy maternity dress in front of my gut. Mark had an atypical figure, short arms and a huge and long torso. The shirt had been altered accordingly.

Flipping on lights in my dark house, I changed into a sports shirt and a slightly sullied suede jacket I had inherited on a case two years ago. I peeled off the socks and put on a thick cotton pair, along with another pair of shoes and trousers. I rang up my answering machine at the Piscule Building downtown. The recording was blank except for some dirty jokes a giggly, nasal-voiced teenage boy had phoned in. He had been plaguing my machine for months. When I got time, I was going to track him down and wash his mouth out with an entire bar of Lava.

I took a quick leak, then picked up the anonymous letter I had received two weeks ago—the letter that had set me onto Mark Daniels in the first place.

I sniffed the letter. I pulled the handkerchief I had kyped from Deanna out of my pocket and smelled that. I had to repeat the test three times before I was certain.

The fragrance was the same. I didn't know what it was called, but it was the same. Odds were Deanna had been my anonymous employer two weeks ago, and that she had hired me to tail her husband and report on his philanderings. That had been my first guess, of course, but I needed evidence.

For someone with no guilt on her conscience, she was being coy. It made perfect sense for a guilty party. Guilty of what? But I didn't want to believe that. It despoiled a future I was slowly conjuring up, a future with a vivacious strawberry-blonde bubbling around in it.

It was a shade past nine-thirty. With luck, a few night owls would still be prowling about.

I drove to the address that Butch Teets had given me that afternoon, the address Beatrice Hindenburg had used as a mail drop.

Sandwiched between two brick apartment buildings with open balconies, it was a woman's boarding house, shabby, three stories, two blocks from the University of Washington on Ravenna. Even though it was growing late in the rest of the city, the U-district was humming.

Two young women squatted on the unpainted front stoop under a dim light, reading to each other out of a yellow text-book. They wore coats and slippers and I had the feeling they couldn't find anyplace inside, or else they were waiting for someone.

"Either one of you know a Beatrice Hindenburg?"

A brunette in what looked to be a grown-out mohawk, orange and greenish streaks down the back and one side, turned her face up to me and answered. She spoke English.

"She got killed, mister. It was all over the KOMO news. Somebody shot her in the brain. Her boyfriend. Then he tried to commit suicide."

The other woman, all in black, including jet black lipstick and charcoal eye shadow, spoke bluntly. "I think it was sick. The whole thing makes me want to puke. The state of this world."

"Well, it could have been romantic, you know. It might have been. We don't know all the details. We don't know what they were thinking. It might have been romantic." The woman in the mohawk looked like someone whose own life lacked romance. Her eyes had a difficult time staying on my face, shifting to my chest and twittering about the street.

I displayed my license. "I understand Beatrice used this as a mail drop."

"She got her letters here, if that's what you mean. Only she didn't get very many. The mail's all stacked on a table in there every morning, and she hardly got anything. Once in a while a letter from California."

"Why did she use this address?"

"Couldn't tell ya. Used to live here. For about three weeks, I think. Mrs. Workman hadda kick her out when she found out how young she was. She's all heart, that woman."

"Mrs. Workman in?"

"Sure."

I rang the bell and spoke to a gaunt woman in horn-rimmed glasses, her graying hair pulled back and knotted into a severe bun. She didn't bother to look at my license when I flipped it out. "Beatrice Hindenburg," I said. "She used to live here?"

"Till I found out about her sneaking ways. She lied about her age and she stole a ring from me and some money from one of the girls. I tried to keep it quiet. Just threw her out was all. Same night I caught her."

"But she gets her mail here?"

"Yeah. I didn't see what harm that would do. Besides, the mail came, she picked it up more often than not from one of the girls while I was out. What could I do? I hate to send letters back to the post office. You know how they are if you get on their wrong side."

"Yeah, I know. They'll dogear the corners on your magazines for a month of Sundays."

She nodded in dizzying agreement.

"Did you know she was dead?"

"Who's dead?"

"Bea Hindenburg."

"Bea? Why . . . no. What happened?"

I told her, then advised her to phone the homicide section downtown. She didn't look as though she would take my advice. "Wait a minute," she said, and scuttled away from the doorway into the interior of the house. She scuffed back breathlessly and handed me a letter, a squarish envelope with a child's scribbling on it. It was addressed to "B. Hindenburg." No return address. Postmarked Cupertino, California.

"Give this to the police," I said.

"Forget it." She drawled her syllables out into a long, assertive whine. "You take it and give it to them. I have enough trouble around here getting mail for people who've moved out without getting mail for dead girls, too. The door clicked shut in my face.

Tramping down the hill to my truck, I hefted the letter. The postmark was four days old. One sheet inside. A child's writing. What could it hurt? I fished a pocket knife out of the glove box and sliced open the envelope. It didn't take me long to wish I hadn't.

Dear Bee,

Thanx for the gum. I never got gum in a letter befor.
It was cappish. The train book you sent got here al rite
and i am having a grate time with it. I love you. I wish
you cood cum bak home. I wish Bill wasnt so meen to
you when you been here. Rite me in a letter when you
will be coming home. I can wait.

XXXXXXXXXXXXX
OOOOOOOOOOOOO
Yur best brother—Ronny

It rocked me. If I hadn't run across his letter, who knew how
long Ronny might have waited for an answer? Last Saturday
morning she had been a naked blonde with cornflower blue
eyes and a hole in her skull. Now, for the first time, she was
a real person. A real person who still received mail from a
little brother who obviously didn't know she had already
lain, drained and pale, on an eight-foot stainless-steel tray
for a week.

If her mother had possessed a letter for her divorced father
to pilfer, it was a letter her mother had, in turn, highjacked
from Ronny. And Ronny, I guessed, was using the home of
an aunt or a friendly neighbor to receive his letters and
presents.

Bill must have been the mother's new boyfriend. It
wouldn't be too difficult for the cops to track down all the
Hindenburgs in the Cupertino area.

I would turn the letter over to Kathy Birchfield in the
morning. Giving it and the mail drop to the police might
produce some interesting trading material.

On a hunch I drove to the Downtown Service Center. Ingrid Darling had mentioned them briefly because they had
been the ones who secured jobs at Trinity for her and Beatrice Hindenburg. I had heard a lot of good things about the
Downtown Service Center, a privately funded foundation
dedicated to helping young people in trouble. Once a year
one of the local TV stations presented a mini-telethon to aid
it.

Mostly they helped street kids, kids who had run away from home, kids who were selling their bodies on First Avenue for enough change to buy lollipops and maybe an umbrella to keep Seattle off their backs.

I parked a block away in Pioneer Square, the refurbished section of downtown Seattle, with buildings seventy and eighty years old, redone in their original state. I hiked to the Service Center. Though it was after ten at night, the place was lit up like a Christmas tree.

Chapter Fourteen

THE DOWNTOWN SERVICE CENTER was housed in a two-story brick building, catty-cornered from a computer store, not far from the Kingdome.

I recalled a blurb about a year earlier in one of the local slicks about how the neighboring businesses were trying to coax the Esterly people, the people who had founded it, to move out, asserting that an endless stream of vagrants was tarnishing the image of the region.

I plunged into the well-lit main entrance, past a couple of teenage boys bivouacked on the spic-and-span floor of the lobby, reading aloud snatches from a science-fiction paperback titled *Vacuum My Skull*. I noted that, although they were both high-school age, they read using mouths and fingers.

A woman in wire-rimmed glasses and a hooplike, ankle-length dress, sandals protruding from the bottom hem like broken fence slats, peeped at me.

"May I be of assistance?"

Self-sacrifice was printed all over her.

Flopping out my license, I waited until she was properly and thoroughly impressed and said, "I'm working on a murder. About a year ago you people referred two girls to Trinity Dog Food. Remember that?"

"Try another one. Every detective who comes in here tries the murder bit. Even some of the fathers looking for their runaways claim they're working on murders." She showed me a piece of her tongue at the edge of her mouth.

"How about white slavery? We don't hear that but once every month or so. Try that one."

I smiled at her but her eyes had been purged of humor.

"Beatrice Hindenburg and Ingrid Darling."

"Never heard of them."

"Somebody here has heard of them."

"Let me take you to John Esterly."

In a businesslike lope, she led me down a pine-walled corridor to a cubicle at the end. Rapping smartly on the door, she pushed it open, the flab on her bare arm jouncing to the movement. She smelled of wildflowers and I could have sworn she had honey on her breath.

"John? There's somebody here to see you." She vanished in a puff of sweet incense.

I put my hand out and introduced myself, explaining briefly why I was there and who I was working for.

A young-looking man, John Esterly was about the same age as me, early thirties. His handshake was clammy and soft. Built like a lodgepole, his face was long and lean, but cheery. His gray eyes twinkled. Several inches shorter and forty pounds lighter than myself, I judged that he was one of those rare individuals who could take a deep breath, relax, and still sink to the bottom of a swimming pool. Not enough fat to float. But he wasn't fit. The turkey-wattle under his chin and his matchstick limbs attested to that. Long hours of soaking up other people's worries had taken its toll.

His desk was a mountain layered like geographical strata. If he wanted something from last week he would look an inch down. From last year, dig another foot.

"Darling and Hindenburg. Let me see. Darling and Hindenburg."

Propelling an old-fashioned tilting office chair around on its chittering casters, John Esterly began scooping slabs of paperwork off his desk and teetering them on a nearby bookcase that was already about to tumble. A wall behind me was door-to-corner and floor-to-ceiling sociology and popular self-help books. If an earthquake hit, the boys with the body bags would never excavate us.

"Those names I know."

"Hindenburg was killed last week. The second one, Ingrid Darling, was just discovered this afternoon at the bottom of a lake. It hasn't hit the papers yet."

"Is that right? Well, you're johnny-on-the-spot, aren't you?"

"Trinity Dog Food," I said, trying to keep him from getting sidetracked. If he insisted on burrowing through the morass on his desk, we might be there all night. "Listen, I'm kind of tired. It's been a long day. Is there . . ."

"I know." John Esterly wheeled his chair backward, swung around and pulled open a drawer in a file cabinet. He riffled some cards. "Sure. Trinity Dog Food. It's owned by Emmett Anderson and Mark Daniels. Right?" I nodded. Esterly looked past my head at something in the doorway. "Speak of the devil. There's the man you want to talk to. Right there."

I pivoted in my seat and met the Reverend Sam Wheeler's gaze. He gave me a fierce, fleeting look, as if to say he had banked on never seeing me again.

When he finally used it, his smile was lopsided, foxy and almost genuine. "Sure thing, Tommy. Be right with you. I have a counseling session going on right now. But I'll be in my office." It took me a few moments to realize Tommy was me.

I got up and closed the door behind him. "He set up the deal with Trinity?"

"Yes, he did, in fact. He's been close personal friends with Mark Daniels since about a year before God was born. The Reverend's got a lot of contacts. It's good to have him working here." Esterly beamed.

"He a partner, or what?"

"The board consists of my father, who founded the Esterly Center, my mother, and myself." John Esterly smiled at me. There was not an ounce of selfishness or ego in him. I was almost ashamed to be in the same room with him. On the way home I would flagellate myself with a scourge, beat my head against the dashboard. "People like the Reverend Wheeler donate their time and services. But I have to admit, they don't come out of it empty-handed. The Reverend gets a lot of mileage out of this in his radio and TV sermons. It's a fair balance."

"Does he spend much time here?"

"Depends on what you mean. He meets troubled kids. Sometimes he works with them here. Sometimes he gets them into a foster home, or back with their parents, or whatever. Maybe a job like he got for Bea and Ingrid. He's streetwise. He knows what these kids will respond to."

"What about Ingrid Darling and Beatrice Hindenburg?"

"They used to hook downtown. You're right. It was about a year ago. Sailors and out-of-towners mostly. Came in here because one of them got beat up. I can't remember which. The Reverend can tell you more. He got them the jobs. I lost track of them myself. We were just getting the overnight center started up out north. It was a hectic summer."

"The Reverend, huh?"

"Mr. Black? I can see by the look on your face you have reservations about the Reverend."

"You're good at reading faces, Esterly. Better than most."

"A talent I picked up on the streets. I'll vouch for him. Sure, he's made some money at it. And he comes on a little cold sometimes. But I've seen him on Pike Street at three in the morning caring when nobody else would. I've seen him take a fifteen-year-old junkie to his own home and keep him there until he could straighten out his life. He may have his quirks, but he's got what we need down here: He cares." I tipped an imaginary hat at John Esterly and moved to leave. "Wheeler's office is up a flight, directly over this one."

"Thanks."

After I climbed the pine stairs, I spotted Wheeler at the

other end of the corridor, near the steps that led down to the front lobby. Rocking on his heels, pushing his maternity gut in and out, he was consoling a youth in tight jeans and a pea jacket a size too large. Some might say he was consoling. Some might say he was lecturing. The skinny youth was distraught, bawling.

I couldn't catch all of what he said. Something about things being a big circle. Slipping the kid a bill from his wallet he sent him off with, "Remember, success means getting up one more time than you fall down. That's all. You can do it. I know you can."

I didn't see for sure the denomination of the bill, but it looked like a single. A dollar bill was going to do him a whole hell of a lot of good.

Wheeler chugged down the hall toward me. His smile was as broad as it was phony. "Tommy. Tommy," he said. "Come into my lair." He laughed artificially.

I trailed him into an office that was a replica of Esterly's pigpen downstairs, except that the Reverend kept his pristine almost to the point of obsession. He sat down behind his desk and took an accounting book out of a drawer, meticulously penned an entry and put it back. Reparations for the bill he had given the boy would be forthcoming.

Wheeler gave me a brittle look and tilted his chair backward. He knew just how far to tip it without sending it over.

"You should have come to me," he said soothingly. "Should have come to me if you had any questions. Want to know about Bea? I can tell you."

He stropped his pudgy hand across his cheek, a sapphire ring on his pinky. It might have been imitation sapphire, but I doubted it. He wore a simple short-sleeved sports shirt. It was the first time I had seen him without his collar.

"So tell me."

"Bea got smashed up by some john last year and decided to cash in her chips for a while. You know, play a safer game. She hitchhiked up from Oregon. One of her rides pulled off the highway and raped her. Real sad story. Had been streetwalking in Portland. Was running away from a small-time Oregon pimp, if I recall. We managed to get her an apartment and a job at Trinity. But she didn't take. Sometimes the rot gets so deep in their souls you can never get it out. It just didn't take. She was on the streets the night she quit Trinity. In fact, I saw her with one of our more influential local citizens, driving off in his car.''

"Not Mark Daniels?"

"No. No." He laughed politely at my naiveté. "He must have come later. I've been doing a lot of thinking about it and I think what happened was, Mark must have given her some clue when she worked there. You know, made an offer, or patted her on the fanny, something like that. Then she went back to the streets and when things got rough again, she went to Mark. He must have been seeing her on a semi-regular basis, don't you think?"

I decided the Reverend Wheeler didn't have to know anything about the Galaxie Motor Court Inn.

"What about Ingrid Darling?"

Wheeler's chair snapped forward. "Darling? How does she play in this?"

"I thought you got them jobs together at Trinity. Esterly said they came in here together."

The chair rocked back again, seesawing. "Yeah, I guess maybe they did. We get so many different kids runnin' through here, it's hard to remember all the details sometimes.''

"What about Ingrid?"

"Far as I know, she's still working at Trinity."

"Not since last summer."

"Really? I didn't realize that." Wheeler formed his thumb and forefinger into pliers and began worrying a whitehead on his neck just over the collar. "That's really news to me. I'll have to check up on her and see how things are. We generally run follow-up checks, but you know how it is. I talked a kid out of suicide last night. After losing my good friend, Mark, I don't know if I could stand by and see another suicide.''

''You haven't lost him yet.''

''No, and I've got my fingers crossed. I pray for him almost hourly.''

For which outcome, I wondered, recovery, or rutabaga city. ''You think it was a murder-suicide, then?''

The whitehead exploded between thumb and forefinger and the Reverend winced at the sudden pain. ''Maybe. I'll be honest with you, Tommy. I've wanted to see this investigating you're doing quashed.''

''Why?''

''You know Deanna and Mark were having troubles? He slapped her around. Boxed her ears. That sort of thing. Did you know she once picked up a pair of scissors and tried to park them in his chest? Did you know that?''

''You're the first to mention it.''

''She did. She claimed she was only defending herself, but I don't know. Mark was beginning to think her ladder didn't reach all the way to the attic. Another time she tossed a pot of boiling water at him. Temper, temper. I guess she chased him all over the house with those scissors. When she couldn't catch him, she started hacking up his clothes. Actually, this shirt here was one of them. I don't know why he wanted to throw it out. It only had a little nick. She's a sweet kid, Deanna. She's got an Irish temper, but she doesn't mean it. Whatever happened to Mark, the way he treated his ex-wife and kids and all, I don't like to say this, but maybe it was divine justice. Maybe it was. I'd hate to see Deanna in court, though. That's all.''

''Are you saying you think Deanna sneaked out two weeks ago, caught her husband and the girl and shot them?''

Wheeler shrugged. ''Not saying anything. I just think sometimes poking around does more harm than good.''

''What about the suicide note?''

''Things like that have been faked before.''

''Why would Deanna call attention to it? Why would she

say she thought it was a fake if she was the one who shot them?''

"Whoa there, boy. I didn't say she shot anybody. You said that. Don't go putting words into my mouth. If you want to know what I really think . . . I think Mark killed the girl and then shot himself. That's what the cops say. What makes you smarter than the cops? If you're concocting some weird plot, if your mind works like that, why, I've got some real estate in Nevada I want to sell you. Course, it glows in the dark, but I'll give you a real deal." His laughter was mellow and fabricated, steeped in rancor.

"Know anybody else who knew Beatrice Hindenburg? Besides the Darling girl?"

"Not really. Bea tended to be a loner. So did Kandy, if you want the truth."

I drove home, jogged three miles on the dark streets, showered and hit the sack. The jogging wasn't enough, but it was all I had time for. A good night's sleep was what I needed. But I didn't sleep well. I had nightmares about fishing and bringing up corpses, all pretty, young bloodless girls. My last dream before waking was a saga about the big nuclear barbecue. In the morning the pall was still over me. I was standing in front of the bathroom mirror trying to paste my hair down with a wet comb when the phone jangled me out of my stupor.

I answered it in the living room, momentarily blinded by the strong sunlight beaming through the gauze curtains.

"Thomas?"

"Kathy?"

"You don't sound so good."

"I feel like I've been thrown by a horse. What's new?"

Kathy hesitated. "Mark Daniels died about half an hour ago. The hospital just called."

"What about Deanna?"

"They said they called her first. I haven't spoken to her yet. I'm not sure what this means. I guess we'll still need you. There obviously won't be a murder trial now, but there's still the question of it being suicide. Deanna stands to collect almost $600,000 if it isn't suicide. How are you doing?''

"Going to be in the office?''

"All day.''

"I'll be over sometime this morning to fill you in.''

"See you then, Cisco.''

I climbed into my truck and drove in the bright sunshine to Queen Anne Hill. A handful of flesh-colored pansies Deanna had picked yesterday lay wilted on the dashboard. A five-car non-injury smashup on 45th with accompanying gaper's block slowed things. People in this state weren't used to this sunshine. It blinded them. When it came out they piled into other cars, utility poles, and even slow-moving houses.

Chapter Fifteen

THE BLUE SKY was stunning.

The well-swept narrow streets on Queen Anne Hill were lined with professionally manicured trees and expensive new cars, everything crisp and dazzling and undented in the unexpected sunshine. Record-setting rains had been dousing the city throughout May and everything had stayed green and gray.

Across the street from the Daniels place a Japanese gardener in a pleated uniform the color of chlorophyll medicated a row of birches, dosing them from a sprayer. Deep in my throat I could taste the tang of chemical toxins.

I shambled up the front steps and ran into Emmett Anderson erupting out the front door.

If I had been on the ball, I would have recognized the Mercedes abutting the sidewalk when I drove up. I had seen it weeks ago at the first murders. But I wasn't on the ball; I was stumbling around in a purple haze.

The old guy didn't see me until he was a step or two away, his gray eyes milky with tears.

"Morning."

Anderson stepped aside and swiped at his face, boosting his glasses up out of the way. When he moved his hand they clunked back down onto his nose. A bandage was pasted to his knuckles. He was the rough-hewn sort who would always need a ready supply of dressings. He stammered, "You heard, I 'spose."

"Yes."

"He was like a goddamned son to me. I couldn't have loved him anymore if he was my goddamned son."

I decided not to bring up the squabble they had had two weeks ago, the knock-down-drag-out brawl.

"Too bad," I commiserated.

"I'm closing the plant. Everything. At least for a month. Paid leave for one and all. Can't stand to see it. Fact, it hasn't been running all week. A goddamned shame. Now look at me. If somebody had to get shot, why couldn't it be me? I ain't got that long to go anyway. This may sound like bull hooey to you, but I goddamned wish I could trade places with the bastard. Hell, I ain't doing anything here but hogging space, breathing good air meant for someone better. Mark had a whole lot of good years left in him."

"The girl probably had a few, too,"

Tugging on an ear that looked like gum rubber, Anderson said, "Never thought I'd live this long." He gazed out across the rooftops at the sound. "You should have seen the hell I raised when I was a young 'un. Rumrunners. We used to run it in from Canada. We had two big speedboats specially made. Coppers used to chase us for miles, but their boats never was as fast as ours. We used to tease 'em, slow down and keep just out of range. Took a bullet in my thigh once. I still got the scar. We were hellions."

"Sounds like maybe you were."

"And then Mark works honest his whole life. Never cheats a soul. Only problem is he gets het up over a little pussy now and then. Bang! When he's least expecting it, right in the brain pan. What turns a body to do something like that to hisself? And to his family? It don't seem fair." He hobbled down the stairs, pirouetted and looked up at me. "She ain't what I would have expected. I only met her once before—at the wedding. Helen was always my favorite. Now I'm going over there to see if I can do somethin' for the kids. But she . . ." He nodded up at the Daniels house. "She ain't what I expected."

"How's she taking it?"

"See for yourself," he said gruffly. He swiveled and headed toward the ex-wife and the kiddies.

"Emmett?"

"Son?"

"You going to play fair by her?" Emmett didn't even turn around this time. "You going to split things the way Mark would have wanted?"

It took him a lot of groping before he found words, slurring his reply. "People always told us we was crazy to keep everything so informal, that we was askin' for big trouble."

"So?"

"They was right." He plodded down the steps, tramping heavily to his Mercedes.

I yelled at him, "You don't do fair by her, that automatically gives you a motive. You know that, don't you?"

"He did it to hisself!"

"We'll see."

I had to push the bell four times.

Waiting on the stoop, I listened to a starling shriek on a nearby phone pole. Emmett Anderson drove away slowly, rigid in his bullet-gray luxury car, not deigning to look up at the house. Next door a young man emerged in tennis whites, swinging a racket in a wooden holder, whistling. He smiled my way. He hadn't heard.

When Deanna cracked open the door she was wearing a floor-length silk robe, her hair tucked into a rubber swimming cap that had pink plastic flowers attached like Satan's horns. Her eyes were not teary. Not even fuzzy.

"Come in."

I stepped into the pool room and watched her lock the storm door and then the front door, turning and bouncing her backside against the knob.

"I'm sorry," I said.

Her eyes shot me an intrepid look, tried to hold it and disintegrated. She broke down and sobbed, her face destroying itself and turning ugly—slimy with grief. I reached for her but she put out a hand to fend me off. "No, don't hug me

now. Just . . . Thomas. I need you so badly. I'm afraid of
what might happen. And it wouldn't be right.''

She slipped the robe off her shoulders onto the floor, glissaded two giant steps and dove into the pool, hardly rippling
the glassine surface. The robe lay on the floor like the husk
of a ghost. Too robust for a bikini, she wore a one-piece
bathing suit cut very high on the hips. I watched her swim
two laps, her motion easy and fluid. Gliding the last few
yards, she winged her arms onto the ledge below me, suddenly full of lassitude. She blinked the chlorinated water out
of her eyes.

''Will you stay with me?''

''Deanna, you should be with friends, someone you've
known longer than me.''

''I haven't known anyone longer than you, Thomas.''

''But . . .''

''I've known you a thousand years. And my friends? All
these society freaks around here? They all dash away when I
say boo. I need somebody to be with me for a few hours. I
don't want to talk about Mark or this case or anything. I just
want to swim until I'm exhausted, and I need somebody to
swim with me.''

She gave me a doughty look and I thought of Wheeler's
story about her hounding Mark around the house with a pair
of scissors, snipping his clothes into bite-size pieces when
she couldn't snip him into bite-size pieces—capsizing a pot
of boiling water onto him. I wondered if Wheeler had been
setting me up with a bunch of blarney.

''I was there,'' I said. ''Where Mark was shot. Just a few
minutes later.''

''Yes. I know.''

''Somebody hired me. It was an anonymous note with
five hundred dollars cash in it. The note was hand-printed.
Somebody wanted me to follow Mark and report on his
philanderings.''

Deanna tucked an errant strand of blonde hair back up under the bathing cap, unconcerned. ''Did you ever find out
who it was?''

"I had my suspicions. I didn't know for certain until last night." Plucking the hanky I had taken in Woodinville out of my pocket, I waved it at her. She watched it, pursing her lips. "The perfume on this is a perfect match to the perfume on the letter. You hired me two weeks ago to follow your husband, didn't you?"

Deanna shoved off, taking a couple of casual swipes at the water, swimming on her back, studying me. "Thank you for sending the five hundred back. I had to sell jewelry to raise it."

"Why didn't you tell me you were the one?"

"You never asked."

"Would you have admitted it?"

"I was ashamed. For a long time I thought our marriage was made in heaven, that absolutely nothing could go wrong with it. Then he beat me up, broke my teeth, cracked my ribs. He was an animal. It pained me to hire you. In fact, it hurt more to do that than it did this morning when they called and said Mark was gone. Funny how things like that work."

I watched her porpoise around in the water for a few minutes.

"Swim with me, Thomas. Please?"

"I'm not real keen on skinny-dipping."

"There's a selection of suits in the changing room." Her smile was a cross between a tease and a smirk and I had the feeling she had been dropping it on chagrined males for years and years. Forming a scoop with her hands, Deanna shot a spurt of water at my legs. It came in a heavy stream and drenched my left cuff.

"I didn't come to lollygag around in the pool. I came to see if I could help."

Her voice grew serious and a trifle frosty. "You want to help. Jump in. That'll help. People grieve in their own way. This is my way. Don't send me flowers. Don't say any prayers. Jump in."

The sun's rays angled through the glass roof and crawled

down the far wall. The blue, choppy surface of the pool marbled the walls and my body with indirect sunlight.

I walked around the pool and went into the adjoining room. Deanna, treading water, gyrated around and followed my progress, her sorry smile firmly in place, wet eyes like green stars. I went into the changing room, unlaced my shoes and heeled them off. Then I took off my jacket, tie, shirt and undershirt, folding them neatly over a chair. Peeling the bandage off my chest, I stole a look at myself in one of the ubiquitous floor-to-ceiling mirrors. I was like a pop-eyed cod brought up not on a lure but by sheer hocus-pocus.

Sometimes I had the uneasy feeling Deanna used men like a cripple used crutches; always one within easy reach. I still wasn't certain if I was a temporary haven for her, or something else.

I slipped into the suit, trotted out and into the pool room. I took several running steps and leaped into the choppy water. It was warm, very warm.

And, except for myself, empty.

Rising to the surface amid a billion bubbles, I shook my hair out and said, "Oh tish." I spun around, treading water, inspecting every corner of the room. Before I finished, something big and heavy cannonballed into the water next to my face, rocking the pool. I caught a fleeting glimpse of white thigh, elbow and breast. She surfaced beside me and began swimming laps, pounding at the water.

I swam with her. It took almost an hour in the short pool for her to exhaust herself.

We ended up on the mats beside the pool at the shallow end, the sunshine radiating on our bodies, drying us quickly.

"You take many cases?"

"I take a few cases. I tend to get consumed by them."

"Where do you get your money?"

"I'm on a pension. I don't need much."

Running her fingernails across my shoulder, she spoke in a husky voice, "I thought you would have a lot of scars."

"You like scars?"

"Yeah. Don't they usually have a lot of scars? Detectives?"

"Some do. I met one yesterday who's probably got hundreds."

She laughed. "But you have hardly any."

"They're all inside, sister. On the walls of my heart."

She laughed and bussed my brow. "Here's one." Peering down, she examined the wound on my chest. "But this is new. No fair. I wanted some real old scars. You know, jagged things that look like you got them with whistling swords—fighting a duel in Heidelberg. No fair."

Stretched out side by side, I leaned on one elbow and locked eyes with her. She grew quiet, pulled her bathing cap off and let acres of hair cascade down across her shoulders and back. It was the first time I had ever seen it loose. I reached out and touched it, handling it like a national treasure, totally bewitched.

I leaned over and kissed her lips, tasting the chlorine. She kissed me back. We molded our bodies against each other.

"We shouldn't be doing this," she gasped.

"Really shouldn't."

I was hopelessly hooked. Deanna was a riddle within a riddle. And she was plucky enough that this cockamamie passion didn't seem all that farfetched. If another woman had done this the morning her husband died, it would never come off as anything but illegitimate sex—too pernicious to describe. With Deanna, somehow, it seemed ordained from the moment we met, something that had transpired in that first hot exchange of glances at the party.

We were nearing the delirious point of no return when someone slammed a car door outside and shuffled up the steps to the porch. Half the roof sections over the pool had been mechanically opened to take advantage of the weather, so sounds outside were much louder and closer than they should have been. We froze, both of us heady in the guilt of potential community thought. Deanna sniggered. I couldn't tell if it was hysterics or what.

"Dummy up," she said, though I hadn't spoken. She sniggered harder, jiggling against me.

I had to hold my hand over her mouth to keep her from bursting into gales of laughter.

The chimes rang in the house, then we heard the spang of someone rapping hard on the outer door.

A man's mellow voice said, "Deanna, honey. I know you're in there. Deanna, I've come to be with you." We lay still, children caught counting stolen cookies under the stairs.

When I looked up, I could see the muzzy silhouette of the Reverend Samuel Wheeler standing at the door, nose pressed like a dog against the frosted glass. Surely, he had spotted my truck. After a few minutes he went away, his muted footsteps raspy in our aerie.

Outside a car motor turned over and slowly hummed away down the street. An English sparrow chirruped.

I stood up and Deanna followed suit, shaking out her hair. It was the flute and I was the swaying cobra.

"Thomas? What would you say if I asked you to drop the case. Let's go somewhere, okay? Let's go to Reno and play the tables for a week. Doesn't that sound like fun?" She traced a line from my shoulder down my chest and around the ridges of my stomach. "Thomas? For me? Can you do that for me?"

I picked her up and carried her through the house until I found a bedroom, kicking the door open. She was heavy. I laid her on the bed and collapsed on top of her, both of us feeding a hunger that had been with us too long, both finally satiated.

It almost cleared the cobwebs.

We lay in bed and talked about inconsequentials for ten minutes. Then she said, "Thomas?"

"Yeah?"

"I want you to quit the case, okay?"

"That's not the way I'm constituted."

"Just quit. Couldn't you do that for me without asking why?"

"You'll lose 600,000 bucks in insurance."

"Emmett Anderson dropped by just before you got here."

"I spoke to him."

"He's obsessed with this. He thinks there's some sinister plot against Mark. He had a gun with him. He's going to find Mark's killer."

"He intimated to me that he still thought it was a suicide."

She thought that over. "He was all mixed up. But I'm afraid he'll do something crazy."

"Andy won't hurt me."

"For me?"

"What about the money?"

"Money doesn't mean anything to me anymore. I was poor when I met Mark, and all this didn't make me happy. I can be poor again. Besides, if Anderson doesn't give me Mark's share of the business, the insurance money will just go to paying bills anyway. I won't have anything left. I'd get the same result declaring bankruptcy."

"And if Anderson does share?"

"Then the insurance money would only be a drop in the bucket. I'll never have a financial worry again."

She turned and propped her head up on one elbow. I watched her rounded, sweaty contours. "Please give it up for me?"

"Why do you want me to quit it?" I could only think of one reason and it wasn't good.

"I don't know if you'll understand this, but I've had enough. The last weeks have been the sorriest of my life. And it seems to get worse all the time. I can't take the pressure. I'd rather just walk away from it and forget the whole thing. Quit. Please, quit."

I gave her a kiss, which turned into a grappling hug, which turned into something else. Afterward, I showered, borrowed a towel and traced a route back to the changing room to reclaim my clothing. When I had finished dressing,

Deanna came out and slipped into her silk robe, carefully backhanding her tresses out of the collar.

"What's the Reverend to you?" I said.

"Nothing. Why? He just came when I needed him. He's been a family friend for a long time. Mark's family."

"Has he said anything about all this?"

"Very little. Mostly he's tried to comfort me. For a man of the cloth, he's really not very good at it, but he's always been a media type. I think he had his last congregation over ten years ago."

"Do you trust him?"

"He's one of the sweetest men in my life."

I wanted to ask if she had slept with him, but I bit my tongue. This was not the time or the place.

Reluctantly, Deanna showed me Mark's things. She must have been thinking I might get it out of my system right there. It took almost an hour to sort through them. When I opened a trunk and took out some mementos of their wedding, she sat heavily in a brocaded chair and shed a few tears.

I leafed through his high school annual and saw that he had been on the baseball team. So had Sam Wheeler. They had gone to high school together. That meant they went a long way back, farther than I did with any of my friends.

Deanna said, "Friends in high school. Can you believe that? God, all my friends from high school are still back in North Dakota. We only had seventeen kids in our graduating class. Most of them are still working the farm."

When I was finished, Deanna took me down the hallway to a room where the wall-to-wall carpeting had been taken up. It was a workshop, cluttered with half-finished heads and torsos, sculptures. She was a sculptress, working mostly in clay, which she then cast in bronze or brass.

She looked up from a damp glob of greenish clay she had been kneading earlier that morning. She punched it viciously. A glimmer of her famous Irish temper shone through her motions. Her words were bitter.

"You caught me. This is my conceit. Deanna the artisan. Voilà."

"These are very nice." I reached out and touched a bronze child's head. Actually it looked clumsy and amateurish, but what could you say? "I don't know a lot about art, but I like these." Deanna shrugged. "Would you do me sometime?"

She spoke impassively, spent. "You really want me to?"

"After we get things cleared up. Yes. I'd like that."

"All right."

I hefted a piece of dried clay.

"You're still going to work on this business, aren't you?" Something in her tone warned me.

"Yep."

"I don't want you to."

"I know."

"I could fire you. Leech, Bemis and Ott are my attorneys. I could fire you."

"Sure."

"Why do you say it like that?"

"I've been fired before. Look, Deanna, I'm going to see this through. Somehow I feel responsible for that girl up at the lake. If I hadn't questioned her, I don't think she would be dead now. And besides that, I was attacked Sunday morning. I'm going to find out what that was all about. An explanation has been given, but it doesn't satisfy me. I've got something at stake here myself now."

"But you were doing it for me! It was my case!" She was growing shriller.

"Now, I'm doing it for me."

"You won't be paid!"

"That won't stop me."

"You're a bastard! A goddamned bastard! I asked you as nice as I could. How could you do this to me?"

I pivoted and walked to the door. A heavy gob of clay sailed through the air and whacked the wall next to my head. Either she was used to getting her way or she was taking

Mark's death harder than she thought she was—or both. I looked at her over my shoulder. Loose hair awry, eyes blazing, robe half open, she was more beautiful and appealing than ever.

Chapter Sixteen

When I arrived at the offices of Leech, Bemis and Ott near University Village I slipped quietly into the men's room and cracked open my shirt. The wound on my chest had been oozing pus since my dunk in the pool and I was afraid it would mat the shirt to me. Carefully, I applied a dressing I had appropriated from the glove box of my truck.

Kathy Birchfield was seated at her desk, a sheaf of papers in her hands. Behind the papers she was holding a library copy of *A Distant Mirror: The Calamitous 14th Century* by Barbara Tuchman.

"Good book," I said.

"Have you read it?"

"I told you about it. Remember?"

She stared up at my damp hair. "Just get up?"

"Not really."

"Your hair is wet." Her tone was both suspicious and sardonic.

"I, uh, worked out before I came down here."

"Must have been quite a workout. You look like you've been through the ringer. You jog to the top of Mount Rainier carrying barbells, or what?" The corners of her mouth curled limply in mild amusement. I had the feeling she somehow knew about Deanna and was toying with me the way an expert angler who had already bagged his limit toyed with a trout.

"It wasn't much."

"Maybe you're just upset about this case. You get strung out sometimes."

"Me? I never get strung out."

"Deanna just called."

"Did she?"

"Wants you off the case. She wants us to stop investigating altogether. What happened?"

"Nothing."

I was breaking a custom between us. We generally told each other about our love affairs. It had been a tradition since the time we had met and I was still in the SPD and going hooly-gooly over the boy I had shot.

A sixteen-year-old delinquent had been driving a stolen Volvo at me, trying to mow me down. I shot him through the windshield—in the eye. After I agonized several hours in the hospital corridor with his distraught and condemning family, he died. It broke me, plain and simple.

It broke me.

But nothing in our rules said I couldn't hold off telling her about Deanna. At least until my body temperature dropped back down to a 105 or so.

"Maybe we should go over and speak to Mrs. Daniels together, thrash this out? I'm not quite certain where we all stand now that Mark has passed away."

I sat on the edge of her enormous desk. "We might wait a day or two."

"We might?"

"Deanna and I had a minor falling out."

"A tiff? Is that why she sounded so upset on the phone?"

"Could be."

"What happened?"

"Nothing."

"You still think she has the hots for you?"

I shrugged.

"Oh, Thomas. I just got a horrible idea. You didn't make a pass at her, did you?"

I said nothing, just gritted my teeth and cursed her gift of ESP.

"You're so bullheaded· about things like that. You still think she . . . Thomas Black! Did you go over there the morning her husband died and make a pass at her? You did, didn't you?" I winced. "You're unbelievable. You really did, didn't you?"

I closed the office door so the rest of Seattle wouldn't eavesdrop on her unsavory accusations. "It was not what you think."

"I'll just bet."

"Life is a bitch, okay? Mark died this morning. Yesterday I found a friend of the dead girl. Her name was Ingrid Darling. She wanted me to call her Kandy with a K. I went up to her place on Capitol Hill and interviewed her. Then Deanna took me out to their summer place on Lost Lake to check it out—you know, in case Mark had been using it for trysts."

"Sure, Thomas."

"I thought there might be something lying around to help. There was. Ingrid Darling. She was floating in the lake."

"Sure, Thomas." She fixed her eyes on me. They were the sort of violet you could wallow in. "What do you mean in the lake? Dead?"

"Somebody beat her up and tied a clothesline to her neck; snagged the other end to a piece of angle iron."

"Oh, God. Do you know who?"

"Somebody who isn't a sailor. The knot came undone and she floated to the surface."

"You always seem to find bodies. It's like you have your own divining rod to . . ."

"Don't say it."

"To death."

I chucked the letter from Beatrice Hindenburg's little brother, Ronny, onto her desk. She plucked it up, opened it and read it. A unique combination of angst, wet eye shadow and sparkling tears began polluting her face. "Oh, Thomas. You're going to have to call these people. You're going to have to explain it all."

"I can't explain any of it."

"But you have to call."

"I've already made my share of phone calls. Why don't we give it to homicide? They're getting paid to phone relatives and listen to all that weeping. And maybe you can milk some more information out of Ralph Crum. Trade him. Stuff like this is always good for trafficking with the cops. You can swap the address of Beatrice Hindenburg's mail drop, too. In fact, I have the name of a detective who followed her around for a couple of days. Give it to him in small doses and see what he coughs up in return." I jotted down names and addresses on a blank pad on her desk.

"But we're not on the case anymore."

"Just give it a whirl. See what pops up."

When she left the room to freshen up and contact Crum, I asked if I could make a long distance call.

"You're not phoning another woman?"

"I'm ringing up a Hollywood agent to see if I can break into the movies." She made a face.

The jaunty voice of Dr. Carol Neff, the medical examiner for Snohomish County, answered on the first ring.

"Yes?" She turned it into a three-syllable musical extravaganza.

"Thomas Black here. The one who found the girl in the lake yesterday?"

"I'm glad you called. You might be able to fill in some missing pieces. She was prime, all right. I figured in her late teens. Her parents told the sheriff out here she was sixteen. She had sex maybe an hour before she died. Her appendix had been removed over a year ago by some quack with jittery hands. And she'd borne at least one child. Poor thing."

"What did she die of?"

"Hypoxia. We thought it might be drowning at first. You see, most drowning victims actually suffocate. Lack of oxygen. But she didn't drown. There was no water in her lungs, but then that's not startling. You pulled her out not too long after her heart stopped. A lot of the time there's no water in the lungs. They have what we call a laryngeal spasm and they actually choke. No water—they choke. But she didn't die like that. She had subcutaneous emphysema in the soft tissues of the neck. Her trachea was pretty well crushed. The reason water didn't enter her lungs was because she was already dead when she went into the lake.''

"Somebody strangled her?"

"Maybe. But I think it was more like somebody slugged her in the windpipe, crushed it that way. Not a pleasant way to go. Probably lingered several minutes or longer before she died. Possibly with the perpetrator standing by watching."

"Hell of a way to go."

"There was something else, too. I couldn't figure it out for the longest time. Her body temperature just didn't correlate. If you saw her alive just hours before, she should have been much warmer. She should have been several degrees warmer, according to all my charts. Then I found something interesting on the back of one hand, on her thigh and on one cheek and ear. All on one side of her body. I couldn't figure it out for the longest time, follow me? A lot of what you find in this game depends upon what you're looking for. And I wasn't looking for anything like this. Had she been up in the mountains?"

"Why?"

"She was frostbitten. Not bad, but she was frostbitten. I thought perhaps she had been lying in the snow, or on ice. It's just about the only thing that would fit. My guess was that's why her body temperature was off. She shouldn't have cooled off so quickly, not even in the lake."

When Kathy came back into the room she was almost as gloomy as I was perplexed. "Ralph Crum didn't have anything to barter with. He really didn't. In fact, they're going to close the case. It's going to be officially classed a murder-suicide. That means Deanna won't get that insurance money. And he said he would call the girl's parents in California."

I stood up and began meandering toward the doorway.

"Thomas? Where are you going?"

"Ingrid Darling was frostbitten. Isn't that strange? Frostbitten. It gives me an idea."

"What?"

"At Trinity Dog Food there's a freezer."

"You don't think somebody at Trinity . . . ?"

"It's a big one, as big as a house. Maybe bigger. When I
was in there the other day with Emmett Anderson it was 40
below. He told me that's what they always keep it at."

"But Thomas? With all the people around? I mean, nobody's going to hide a girl in a freezer in a dog food plant.
Are they?"

"The plant's been closed all week. Anderson told me that
this morning."

Before I could stop her, she grabbed her purse out of a
drawer. "Can I come with you? I know you like to do things
alone, but can I come? Just this once?"

"Don't you have clients to talk to?"

"This is for a client."

"Your client fired us."

"She fired you. I'm still her attorney."

We took my truck, Kathy refusing to wear her jacket. The
sun was warming up to its task now and it was promising to
be the hottest day in May.

"If we take your truck," said Kathy, "how am I going to
get back?" She was resentful that I didn't want to ride in her
new sports car.

"I'll drive you. Or you can use your broomstick." She
laughed. Kathy did a shtick as a clown in her off hours, and
several weeks ago at the Seattle Center a tot had asked her if
she weren't a witch. He was too young to know the difference between a clown and a witch. It had become an oft-
repeated gag between us, especially since her remedial ESP
was so often witchlike.

When we got to Harbor Island the traffic was mostly
loaded gasoline tankers from the tank farms on the island
and other heavy trucks. True to his word, Emmett Anderson
had given his plant workers the week off. There were only

two vehicles in the lot and one of them was parked off in a corner.

The other was a small, foreign pickup topped with a canopy. Maybe one of the janitors. A bumper sticker read, "Don't be a knockin' if this crate's a rockin'."

"Thomas, if it's all locked up, how are you going to get in?"

I grinned evilly.

"You're not going to pick the lock? Thomas?" Kathy had irrational fears of being arrested with me. The legal system meant everything to her and she would never have been able to live down a record. Certainly not as long as my memory remained intact.

I flexed my mouth and made my grin as wiry as possible. She almost didn't come to the office door with me. At the last moment she relented, springing out of the truck and trotting after me.

"This better be legit," she said. But I had already opened it and dropped the keys back into my coat pocket.

"Was that legit, Thomas? How did you do that?"

"Keep up. You're missing things."

A sign on the door said: "Due to the misfortune that has befallen one of the senior partners, Mr. M. Daniels, this plant will be shut down until further notice. Those applying for work, summer replacements or otherwise, may phone Emmett Anderson at his home. 737-4567."

"Can you believe that?" I strode into the musty office and headed toward the door to the warehouse. "All this trouble and Andy takes a stance like that. Those applying for work may phone him at home. That eggsucker never has forgotten the little guy. What a deal."

"Thomas? How did you get that door open?"

"Keep up with me and you'll know how these things are happening."

"Thomas? Are we in here illegally? If we're in here illegally, I'm going to have to leave."

A man who looked like he belonged to the foreign pickup outside met us in the hallway next to the warehouse. He didn't bother to ask who we were. It was evident from his cart of brooms, detergents and fox tails he was a janitor.

We zipped through the plant without turning on any lights, through the warehouse, across the vast expanse of the Trinity Dog Food plant to the indoor loading docks. On the other side of the docks, past a yellow forklift, stood the ten-foot-high door to the freezer.

"You weren't kidding," said Kathy.

"Inside it's even larger than it looks."

I popped the door open and a blast of arctic air rushed out and almost smothered us.

"Do you have your gun?"

"It's only a freezer, Kathy. What can happen in a freezer?"

"What if we get locked in?"

"There's no lock on this door. Even if there was, you couldn't shoot if off. If the handle doesn't push, you can beef the door open with your shoulder. It's not any tighter than your Amana at home." I stepped into the freezer, found the lights, shut myself in, then opened it from the inside. Satisfied, she tiptoed in with me, hugging her arms across her breasts, across the light poplin material of her blouse.

The first section of the freezer was stacked with twenty-pound bags of chicken parts, the stacks four, six and eight feet high. They had enough reserves to feed a small city. The rest of that first room was hung with steer quarters, two racks high. I couldn't see how they retrieved them from the higher rack, but I was sure they had some slick system. Anderson had everything in the plant figured out. Kathy gaped at the twenty-foot-high ceiling and its stalactites of ice.

"They won't fall on us, will they?"

"You see anybody around here with a big hunk of ice stuck in him?"

"Not yet."

"Trust me."

"How long are we going to be?"

"Keep up. You won't miss a thing."

"I didn't think a person could get cold this fast. This is just like stepping into a Minnesota winter. If someone had told me I would have thought they were being foolish. But I'm about ready to die. My ears hurt. Brrr."

"Just a few minutes. You can wait outside, if you like."

"No, I have to keep up."

"You're a peach."

"Yeah, a frozen cobbler."

The second half of the freezer was stacked high with brown sacks. Frozen beef parts. Frozen sacks of fish. In the far corner the piles went almost to the ceiling. Against one wall I spotted three cases of candy bars, one half broken. Whoever supplied the machines in the plant kept their stores in here. Why not? I picked up a Butterfinger and tapped the tin-lined wall with it. It felt like a steel pipe.

I was looking for someplace where a body might have been stashed, someplace relatively safe from prying eyes. In the second section of the enormous room there seemed to be a gap between the stacks and the far wall, an aisle. I jammed my benumbed hands into my trousers pockets and walked around to the far wall and the gap.

The area between the stacks and the wall was cluttered with old machinery, machinery I assumed had been used in the freezer at one time for various processes. Making ice. Or whatnot.

I sidled among the obsolete parts and found several long trays once used for producing bulk ice. Someone would run a hose in, fill the trays, and leave them overnight. In the morning the huge cakes could be wheeled out on skids or on forklifts, then chipped, chopped, or delivered as is.

At the end of the row, at the very corner of the freezer, and also the very corner of the building, a tarp was stretched across several more boxy appliances. They appeared to be more bulk ice-makers.

There was something funny about the tarp. It didn't carry the patina of frost on it everything else in the cavern did.

"Thomas? I'm freezing."

"In a minute." I edged through the junk and picked up a

corner of the tarp. I flipped it off in one clean movement, a magician clearing the tablecloth without disturbing the dishes.

"Oh God," said Kathy, peering over my shoulder. "What is it?"

It was a block of ice in a tin-lined wooden frame about seven feet long, three feet wide and two feet deep.

Lying in the center of the block of ice was a man. On his back.

He stared up at us as if in repose. The man was stiff as a frozen halibut and just as dead.

"You keeping up?"

"Oh God. I wish I'd stayed at the office."

"That's what you call a stiff."

"Don't make jokes. Who is it, Thomas? Do you know him?"

"His name is Seymore Teets."

Chapter Seventeen

"GET SERIOUS, Thomas. Is it real? A dummy? Do you know him?"

"You mean, is it real, or is it Memorex?"

"Don't be funny. I'm getting frightened."

"He's the detective I told you about. He followed Beatrice Hindenburg around for a couple of days. Died like a comic book hero, eh?"

"When did you speak to him?"

"Yesterday. He was all right then."

"Things are happening so fast. This is scary."

I knelt on the crumpled tarp and fingered the glazed surface of the ice. It was solid and glossy to my touch, smooth as polished marble. My fingertips began to adhere and I jerked them away. Virgin ice.

"Thomas, I'm frightened. I feel something. There's something wrong in here."

"We just found a dead man."

"No, worse than that. Something else."

"Seymore Teets, the great flycatcher. He won't catch any flies in there."

"Don't be flip. I mean this is serious. I'm having one of my premonitions. We're in big trouble. We've got to get out of here."

"You serious, Kathy?" I looked up at her. I didn't believe in ESP or any of that hokum. Just the sixth sense Kathy had. That I believed in. I had seen her miraculous prognostications come true too often. She had prophesied accidents ahead of us on the freeway, even to the color of clothing the victims would be wearing; had accurately predicted I would find bones in a cave in the mountains on one of my cases. When her powers were oiled and working, they were uncanny.

"There's . . . I think we're going to die. You and me. Together."

"When?"

"Soon."

"You are serious."

"Let's get out of here."

Teets still wore his gun. Peering through the magnifying ice, I could see the serrated hammer in the holster where his coat had fallen back, probably when they had hosed water onto him. His hat was crushed under his head. Whoever had done him violence had concealed it well. There weren't any marks visible. Only a bluish tinge to his face. Halfway between his nose and the surface of the ice a tiny off-white card was frozen, one of his calling cards, as if he hadn't been able to present it fast enough.

I lifted the heavy tarp which rustled like thunder in another city and draped it back over the ice casket.

Stiff-limbed, hugging herself, Kathy was already stumping to the big door. She lambasted me with a look when I got there. Kathy was good at leveling people with one hard look.

"Very funny. How did you do it?"

"What?"

She cocked her head at the door. I tried it and found it unyielding. I tried it again, throwing my shoulder into it this time. Still immovable. I kicked it, then jammed both palms against the tin and shoved until my shoes skidded on the floor, a growing panic infusing my motions. Somebody was playing a very macabre practical joke. It didn't budge. I might as well have been pushing against the Great Wall of China.

"It's locked, Thomas."

I looked at Kathy, grinned and said, "If you wanted to cozy up to me, all you had to do was ask."

"Okay, now show me where the other door is."

"This is it. *Uno.* The only one."

Staggering toward me, she burst into tears, her frame shuddering at the shock of our plight. I squeezed her shoulders and pulled her to me, cuddling her slender chattering physique against the wool of my jacket. She was freezing. I could feel the numbing cold in her flesh under the blouse. I doffed my sports coat and drew it over her shoulders, cinching it tight at her neck.

She snorted an unladylike snort, wiped her nose on both sides of my tie and said, "Thanks, Thomas. We locked ourselves in, didn't we?"

"There's no way to lock it, Kathy. My guess is somebody drove that forklift over and wedged it against the freezer door."

"We're being killed, aren't we?"

"That's one way of looking at it."

"I've never been killed before."

"I have."

She peered up at me, sniveling. "How was it?"

"Tons of fun. If you survive you get a merit badge."

Wiping an eye, she said, "What's the best part?"

"The best part is when your next birthday rolls around and you're still counting gray hairs."

Her voice got very tiny. "I don't have any gray hairs."

"You will."

I reared back and pushed on the door again. Kathy hollered, but we both knew her tones wouldn't penetrate that thick, insulated freezer door. I gestured for her to help me push, and she did, with no visible effect. I scanned the perimeter of the door to see if there was a warning bell or some way to dismantle the door. There wasn't.

"What are we going to do?" Effortlessly she dropped into a heavy Mexican drawl. "Thees is my dream, Cisco. Don't you know? I dream we stiff like frozen herrings. Hey, Cisco?"

I rubbed my hands together briskly. It didn't warm them, only pumped cold air up my shirt-sleeves. "At least we won't attract any flies."

She started bawling again. I cupped her face and brought it close to mine and tried to think of something very wise to say. When I wanted to be, I was a regular cheerleader. "Kathy, we're not going to die in a dog food freezer. All right?" She nodded feebly. "Some pussball out there is trying to get us and he's not going to."

"Pussball," Kathy repeated, teeth sounding out a rat-a-tat-tat. My icy hands on her face had chilled and unnerved her even more.

A fiberglass-handled fire ax was slung on the wall ten feet from the door, a permanent fixture in the place. By the look of it, it had never been used. I hefted it, knocking a ridge of ice off the haft. If I was careful and didn't smack the handle too often, it might hold up to a pounding. If it didn't, we were both going to end up in a bag of party cubes.

"What are we going to do?" said Kathy.

"We could wait him out? Write notes in case we don't make it. That way the cops would find out, eventually." She shook her head soberly.

"We could sabotage the freezer. Find the coils and break them. But even then, it would probably take a week or more for this place to thaw out. I'm not sure how long we would last. Maybe ten, eleven hours." Kathy shook her head.

"We could go back and thaw out Seymore. He had a gun on him. It might even be loaded." Kathy shook her head.

"I might chop through this door, but there's probably someone out there waiting with a six-pack of Coors and a loaded Mauser." Kathy shook her head.

"I could go in the back and chop a hole in the wall and sneak around and break the bastard's neck. What do you think?"

Kathy nodded vigorously.

"Break the bastard's neck?"

"Chop our way out the back," she stuttered.

While Kathy scrounged around for some gloves, I began

hacking at the wall behind the hanging beef quarters. Pacing myself, I swung in a rhythm, trying to preserve the ax. It was a genuine fire ax, a blade on one side, a pick on the other. It was easy enough to bash a hole through the tin and through six or eight inches of insulating material, fragments of which orbited around my work space like billions of microscopic planets. I breathed through my nose as much as possible and finally ripped the seam on my tie and knotted it around my face, using it for a face mask. One end had snot frozen to it. My hands were so cold I could barely fasten the granny knot.

When Kathy couldn't find a pair of gloves I had her begin tunneling into one of the piles of bagged beef from the top, carving out a niche for us to hide in when and if our assailant decided to burst through the door and finish us off.

"Do you think whoever killed Teets is outside?" Kathy asked.

"Who else?"

"Maybe it was that janitor. Maybe he got uppity because we didn't introduce ourselves?"

"He's number two on my list of suspects."

"Oh boy. Suspects. I like this." I could see that the shock of our predicament was beginning to wear thin.

"When I was here at the first of the week a gang of Orientals attacked me. The leader was a guy named Hung Doan. He's the foreman here at Trinity. Seems to take an abnormal interest in what's going on around the plant."

"You think he's outside?"

"Number one on my list."

"Did somebody follow us?"

"Maybe. Maybe they were just waiting for somebody to run across Seymore."

"You think it was this Hung Doan guy?"

"Or one of his henchmen." As I chopped, I detailed the scuffle with Doan and my first meeting with Emmett Anderson.

It didn't take her very long to scoop out a hidey-hole on the second tier of beef sacks. Kathy, whose cheeks were turning purple, kept her eye on the large freezer door. I shivered and swung the ax. I took a few breaks, striding back over to the freezer door and testing it. It remained unyielding. I was getting colder and colder. At this rate, even working as hard as I was, my blood would freeze through in another three hours.

Kathy rummaged around for something to keep us warm. She found that the tarp covering on Teets' ice casket was pinned down on one side by the cake of ice. Neither of us had anything sharp enough on our person to sever the heavy material. Finally she ferreted out a scrap of burlap and handed it to me.

"What's this?"

"Tie it over your head. Most of your body heat escapes through the top of your head." I did as she advised. "The Easter bonnets are nice this year," she cooed.

"I thought you wanted to play this serious? We're going to die, remember?"

"I now have implicit faith in your ability to get us out of this. You're *my* comic book hero."

"I'm going to write that in my diary tonight before I say my prayers."

I struck the wall with the ax. I wasn't so sure anymore. If we were still in here tomorrow at this time we would both be dead. Kathy first. She had fewer clothes on and her body mass wasn't as great as mine.

The inner wall, the wall that ran between the inside loading dock and the freezer, we didn't dare breach, as whoever had sealed us in was probably out there waiting. Besides, as I recalled, it was over three feet thick. Maybe a solid three feet. Maybe not. And now this wall was proving much thicker than I had imagined.

Kathy took turns chopping and acquitted herself well, her breath wafting out in curlicues, tendrils of perspiration rising off her back. It gave her a chance to build up some body heat and it gave me a breather. Blisters were burgeoning on both hands. A woodsman, I was not.

Peeling strips of burlap off my makeshift babushka,

which actually seemed to be helping me keep warm, I wrapped them around the fiberglass handle of the ax. It gave me an improved, if somewhat slippery, grip and cushioned the chafing somewhat. The blisters continued to puff up, swelling and throbbing in cadence to my pulse.

We peeled the wall away, leaving shards of tin and ragged hunks of insulation materials at our feet, then hit a layer of timber. I couldn't believe it. Actual timber. It turned out to be about four inches thick and a little on the rotten side. It took twenty-five minutes to get through it, to clear a hole three feet by three feet. On my right hand a blister had popped and was bleeding.

Excavating the final shreds of broken timber out of the hole, we discovered a layer of old brick.

"Oh, tish," said Kathy when she saw the mortar and brick. She was really getting numb; I could tell by the way her mouth wrapped itself clumsily around her words.

"No, this is good," I said. "This must be the outer wall. I just hope there's nobody standing out there with a gun."

"Do you think they can hear the chopping?"

I hadn't thought of that.

I chopped away at the bricks, using the pick end of the ax, which was pretty well dulled now. The crumbling bricks made a new sound, a plinking sound, one we weren't used to. After I dismantled two rows, I was able to hook the head of the ax over individual bricks and loosen them. Behind the bricks was a space about three inches wide and then more bricks—another complete wall of them.

Kathy slumped down and began sobbing. I sat down beside her and took a breather, quick serpents of vapor huffing out of my mouth. The fiberglass floor was unbelievably cold on my buttocks. "Somehow," I said, "I'm getting the feeling I'm somebody's cat's-paw?"

"What's a cat's-paw?"

"A dupe. A sucker. The nerd in college who shows up nude at the formal party at the sorority and gets arrested because somebody told him they were having a nude dance."

"Cisco?"

"Pancho."

"How long does it take to freeze to death?"

I stood up, reached down, grabbed one of her hands and pulled her to her feet. "Not real long if our butts are stuck to the floor."

"No, how long? Really?"

"We're getting out."

She nodded weakly. We had been in there for over an hour, and at this rate, surviving until supper would be a miracle. I let Kathy wield the ax again, until she heated up and some of the purple leached out of her complexion. She was much clumsier now. When she was finished she handed it back and said, "You know, Thomas, I love you."

"Sure, sister."

I began hacking. She hadn't done any damage to the second row of bricks, had only enlarged the first opening. I chipped out most of the first brick in the second thickness, then held up the ax and felt the head. It was wobbling. "Thomas, I mean it. I love you."

"I love you too, sister."

"Will we always be friends?"

"We always have been."

She rushed me, clasping me hard around the waist, pressing her head against the wound on my chest until, even in the cold, it ached. "Kathy, Kathy, it ain't that bad. Once my mother told me not to touch my tongue to the walls of our home freezer." She looked up at me, an odd mixture of amusement and grief on her face. "I was about ten. 'Don't put your tongue on that freezer wall,' she said. I was home alone. I couldn't resist it. I licked the freezer wall and there I was, alone in the house, my head in the freezer box, my tongue glued to the wall of the freezer."

She laughed, a nervous laugh that reminded me suddenly of the way Deanna Daniels always laughed. "How did you get out of it?"

"I didn't. I stood there with my head in the freezer until my mother got home and poured water over my tongue."

"How long was she gone?"

"I dunno. About two days."

Kathy snickered again and then broke out into downright guffaws. "Okay," she said. "You win. We're getting out of this."

"Good girl."

I swung the ax and the head flew off, spinning down into the slot between the two brick walls.

Kathy and I looked at each other.

One brick in the second wall had cracked with the blow and was almost destroyed. I rammed it with the fiberglass handle. It seemed to move. I rammed it again. Again. The fiberglass handle sent jolts through the bones in my arms.

The brick stirred, moved again and then popped out. From where I was standing I could see a strata of sunlight blazing onto the street outside. I glanced over at Kathy. "Oh, tish."

Dejected, she said, "Another wall?"

"Look, as my one last civilized act, I'm going to make your life complete."

"What?"

"You can have my body. Take me, I'm yours."

"Thomas, you ass." She bumped me aside and bounced up and down, peeping out the hole in the wall at the sunlight. "We did it. We did it."

I poked another brick out of the second wall, and another. Soon we had a two-foot-square hole through tin, insulation, one-inch boards, plaster and lathe, timber, and two walls of brick. It had cost us an hour and forty-five minutes, some tears, several blisters and one fire ax. The hole had started off four feet by four feet and had narrowed down at each successive level until now it looked like a giant ragged funnel.

Checking the freezer door one more time, I jogtrotted back, whirled the burlap off my head and laid it across the scalloped ridges of tin and splintered timber. I vaulted into the hole and scrambled headfirst through the opening.

The tunnel turned out to be five feet above the ground. I was halfway out into the sunshine when a parcel delivery truck slammed its brakes on in the street and the driver stopped to gape at me. I wormed out, and dropped to the ground in a flower bed of wilting tulips. I was too numb with cold to feel any pain, though the fall tweaked my back.

I clambered unsteadily to my feet, saluted the driver in the street, grinned maniacally and turned to receive Kathy from the bowels of the Trinity Dog Food plant freezer.

It was only when I realized how dotty my grin was that I knew I had escaped that icy dungeon. I took a deep breath and suddenly felt the warm air permeating my lungs. From forty below to seventy above. We could easily have laid there all night: frozen chicken parts, frozen beef parts, frozen detective parts and frozen lady lawyer parts. Two hours in the meat locker had seemed like two days.

Kathy Birchfield squirmed out feet first, looking very unladylike from my angle. The delivery driver got a big kick out of that, catcalls and hoots of glee echoing in his closed cab. She fell into my arms, spotted the cheering truck driver and gave him a salute virtually identical to the one I had presented him. He laughed and drove on.

Cheeks still purple, body trembling, mouth quivering, Kathy said, ''I thought we were dead.''

''I don't think I'll ever be too hot again.''

''If I'd been in there alone I would still be in there. I owe you, Thomas.''

''Don't be silly. You never would have gone in there alone.''

''No. You saved my life.''

''You know I hate mawkish women.''

We walked across the street like sailors just off a schooner, trying to get our land legs. I scouted a weatherbeaten building of corrugated aluminum and steel, and we went in. It was a junk salvage company. An old man in muttonchop whiskers whose face was all grime and soot said we could use his telephone. I rang the police and told them we had found a body and gave the address.

Staunch and pleased with ourselves, Kathy and I went out and stood in the sun for a few moments, surveying the damage we had done across the street. From here it looked as if someone had fired a cannonball into the brick wall. The hole looked clean and precise, except for the bricks and mortar littering the tulip bed.

"Stay here until you see cops," I said.

"Where are you going?" She reached out with a quivering hand and picked flecks of burlap out of my hair.

"To find out who's waiting outside that freezer."

"But the police will be here."

"Yeah, and they just might frighten our pigeon away."

The fiberglass ax handle was still in my hands. On the way across the street I flipped it end to end in one hand, trying to bring the dexterity and quickness back into my limbs. I walked briskly, then broke into a jog, warming my blood up. I might have gone round the back to the loading dock—I had a suspicion that's how our boy had gained entry—but I couldn't be certain the loading dock door wouldn't be locked, and it was a long walk back around to the front. I headed directly for the front.

The foreign pickup was gone. In its place stood another vehicle, one I regrettably recognized on first sight.

Unlocking the office door, I blocked it open for the cops, sneaked in, listened, then went through the warehouse. I crept across the shadowed floor of the empty factory and found the pigeon in the loading dock.

I had figured it right. The forklift had been driven up against the freezer door, pinning it tight by running the forks up and punching them into the center of the freezer door, making big dimples in the tin.

His back was to me, a pistol in his right fist, a squarish amber liquor bottle in his left.

Slipping off my shoes, I stalked toward him, tiptoeing, then shuffling and finally running silently. I was only five feet away when he swung around and pointed the pistol at my heart.

I swatted at the pistol with a tennis swing and batted it out of his fist. Thunking the floor, it spun away and skidded out of sight. It sang on the smooth concrete floor.

"Nice job, Andy. It almost worked."

Emmett Anderson looked at me as if I were a slobbering cretin and had just climbed over the fence at Western State Hospital. "What the hell you talking about?"

"Don't fool with me, Andy. I'm ticked."

"I can see that." He took a swig from the bottle. "You damn near broke my hand with that ax handle."

Chapter Eighteen

"SOME BIRDBRAIN locked me in with your doggie biscuits."

"If you were locked in, how come you're out here and the door's still jammed?"

"I broke out the far wall. With this." I shook the ax handle in his face.

"You busted our fire ax."

"Life is a bitch, eh?"

"Don't look at me. I didn't lock you in no freezer. Why the hell would I do that? You think I'd punch a couple of big holes in my own door?" Emmett Anderson sauntered in his bowlegged slouch to the forklift, where he squatted on a fender and guzzled his alcohol. He hoisted the amber bottle in offering to me.

"We assumed whoever did it would be out here waiting with a gun. You know, in case we figured some way to nibble through the door."

"Fetched that gun out when I seen the forklift. Went back to my car and got it. The whole thing looked fishy. I seen your truck out in the lot and I smelled trouble. But then I got in here and seen the forklift. That door was open too." He nodded at the huge loading door behind me. "Hell, I just now got here."

I twisted around and saw that the loading dock door was still partially open, a sliver of snowy sunlight dazzling the billiard-smooth concrete inside.

"Shit, boy, I was just now having a little refreshment and

149

lookin' things over. You stayed back in there I woulda had that forklift moved in another sixty seconds.''

"Maybe."

"Fuck you and the horse you rode in on. I don't give a shit. How long were you in there, anyway?"

"Coupla hours."

"Where'd you get out?"

"The outside wall." He gave me a querulous look. "It's going to need a little patching."

"Damn fool. That's the thickest wall in the whole city, maybe the whole state. I'll get Doan down here to brick it up." He sipped from the bottle. "I knew you had all your shit in one sock the day I met you."

"Thanks, I think."

I walked over and picked his gun up. He didn't budge from the forklift. When I came back, the pistol in one hand, the ax handle in the other, he said, "I suppose you'll want to know just exactly who had access to this place."

"You're awful sure you'll be cleared, old man."

"Mosey outside and lay your hand on the engine block of my rig. If I been in here two hours waiting for your head to pop up like the ground hog, that engine block will be colder than a witch's tit."

"You're saying it's not?"

"Don't burn yourself."

"Okay, I'll bite. Who has access to this joint?"

"I do." He grinned and peered at me through the lower portion of his bifocals, tipping his head backward. "Deanna Daniels does. Mark's ex, Helen, does. She used to work in accounting when we got swamped. I should think Helen's new husband has a key, though I never seen him around. My foreman, Doan, does. Two managers under Doan have keys. The janitorial staff. There's two of them with keys. And most of the office staff has keys to the office. It's just a walk into here from the office. Hell, we haven't changed the lock configuration in fifteen years. No telling who else kept their key."

"Maybe we should get the phone book out and make a list of who *can't* waltz in here?"

" 'Spose we should change the locks."

"Does Deanna Daniels ever come?"

"Been in from time to time. I seen her in here a couple of weeks ago."

I stumped over to the loading dock, wedged myself into the crack with my back against the wall and bench-pressed the huge sliding door open. Thirty yards away another peach-colored structure lay parallel to the Trinity Building, the two forming a long corridor in the grass. Rusted railroad tracks nestled between them. It looked as if someone had parked a vehicle in the weeds not long ago, but then I was no forensic specialist. My hunch was that the police wouldn't pursue the crushed grass, there being entirely too many avenues of approach to the freezer. To them, the likelihood that Teets' killer had come in this way would appear remote.

The cops trooped in with Kathy in tow. Emmett Anderson gaped at the uniforms and said, "What the hell's going on here?"

"There's a frozen gumshoe in your freezer. These fine gentlemen want to take a look."

After shaking his head in consternation, the old man hopped up into the driver's seat, fired up the forklift, reversed it, lowered the blades and backed it off into a corner. None of the police officers dawdled in the freezer. We told them where to find Teets, and they wandered in and hustled out shivering a few minutes later, rubbing their hands together. A balding detective asked Anderson if there wasn't some way to turn the freezer off while they poked and probed the crime scene.

"Sure, boy," he said, alienating the cop with his conceit. "You want to lay out 140,000 bucks for thawed meat, be my guest."

I sneaked out to the parking lot and rubbed my hand across the hood of Emmett Anderson's Mercedes. The wax job was thick and slick. He was right. The engine block was hotter than a two-dollar pistol after a Saturday night hoot.

But it didn't mean anything. He could have locked us in, gone, and come back.

Ralph Crum showed up, looking haggard and very ruddy in the warm weather, his baby blues watery, showering longing looks on Kathy when he thought nobody else was looking. I followed him into the mammoth freezer and watched him stand over the frozen detective.

"Looks weirder than hell," I said.

"Yeah, kind of like something from a Superman movie, huh?"

"Maybe from a comic book."

"Looks almost like a gangland thing, doesn't it?"

It wasn't until he uttered the words that I recalled Emmett Anderson's rumrunning days. I didn't mention it. I wanted Crum to send his evidence specialists out into the space between the two buildings to try to get a fix on whatever vehicle had been there. I calculated that if his thoughts got too cluttered, he wouldn't do it.

I had underestimated him. He deployed someone to secure the name of the janitor who had been servicing the building earlier, and began compiling a list of possibles who might have been in the building yesterday or last night. One man was assigned to comb the grassy lot between the buildings. I told him to look into Anderson's criminal past.

"I don't want you dabbling in this, Black," he said, leveling his jetstream blue on me.

"You're going to have to reopen the Daniels-Hindenburg case."

"Maybe."

"How can you say maybe? Teets had followed Hindenburg. Somebody murdered him. I was working on the Daniels-Hindenburg thing. Somebody tried to make a six-foot icicle out of me. How can you say maybe?"

"Easy. Maybe." His words were soft and understated as he watched a host of cops loping in and out of the freezer. He took my statement, took Kathy's statement, and grilled the old man.

Before I left, Crum marched over to me and held up a fist-ful of candy bars. "What's this?"

"Dunno."

"We found a little hideaway up in the stacks of frozen beef bags. Found these in it. It was a camp like kids might make."

I laughed. "Don't worry about it. We did it."

Crum said, "There are a lot of unanswerables in cases like this, Black. Don't get yourself killed looking for an unanswerable. 'Kay?"

When we left, Emmett Anderson was slouched against one wall, iron-willed and isolated from the hustle and bus-tle, thumbs hooked in his belt loops. He looked like a cow-boy long past his prime, a cowboy who had forgotten to die.

I drove Kathy back to her office in the University District. "So who locked us in?" she asked.

"You're the one with ESP."

"Thomas, you know it only works once in a while. Never when I want."

Swinging around in a large circle in the parking lot out-side the offices of Leech, Bemis and Ott, I waited for Kathy to get out of the Ford. She turned to me and said, "Be care-ful."

"Me?"

"Yeah, you, bozo breath." She smiled a timorous smile. "Okay. Promise me you'll be careful."

"Sure."

"And . . . Hey, uh, I would have succumbed in there if it hadn't been for you. I really would have. I would have gone to pieces and just plain shivered to death. Thanks."

"Don't even think about it."

She reached across and tweaked my cheek, hard. "And thanks for the date, too. You really know how to show a girl a good time."

The door clicked shut on me before I could think of a reply.

"Smartass." I wheeled out of the lot.

Kandy Darling had died from a blow to the windpipe, possibly a karate blow. Mark and Beatrice Hindenburg had been shot in the Trinity offices. Teets had been quick-frozen in the Trinity freezer. My guess was someone had only been storing him, the way they had probably stored Kandy before taking her up to the lake.

Kathy and I had been attacked in the Trinity plant.

Trinity was one line. Karate was another. At the point where they intersected a man was waiting for me. I couldn't help thinking his name was Hung Doan. Who would know karate better than a colonel in the South Vietnamese army? And he had access to the plant. He knew all the dead people except maybe Teets, and for all I knew, he had known Teets, too.

While the cops had been cantering through the plant looking for clues, I had gone to the glass-walled office in the dog food plant and secured the address and phone number of the head honcho, Hung Doan.

Crum didn't know anything about him, yet.

Doan resided in a huge complex of apartments in the Rainier Valley, affectionately branded the Ho Chi Minh Condos by some of the cops in the area. They also called it the boat village and gook city, depending upon their mood or temperament or who spit on their windshield last.

Ten years ago the complexes had been built, financed and sold as condominiums to mostly white clientele. When the osmosis of the central area began spreading south, the whites fled and sold out to blacks. After the collapse of South Vietnam, Washington State became one of the three primary receiving stations for refugees. Asians began settling the area and pushed the blacks out.

There had been a scandal in the papers a couple of years before. Several Asian gentlemen had cultivated opium poppies on the dirt terraces they had carved out on the hillside behind the condominiums. In some of the hill tribes opium had been raised, not with the intent to trade drugs, but as a part of the family medicine plot. When they were uprooted by war and famine and plopped down in Seattle, it was only natural to plant a garden. Bok choy. Onions. Garlic. Poppies. A genuine clash of cultures.

I kept thinking about the man who had come to Trinity looking for work and who had gotten so nervous and over-wrought when he spotted Doan. If the man had been correct, Doan had been a genuine despot in the old country, a journeyman torturer who delighted in his craftsmanship.

By the time I got there wispy clouds were strung across the sky, ruining our sole peek at spring this month.

The building was in better shape than I expected. Three stories, it was constructed in a long half-moon shape. Outside hallway balconies ran alongside the doors to each apartment, balconies that were roofed and enclosed in wire fencing, painted a faded plum color. It let the air circulate but kept the kids from falling overboard.

Doan lived on the top floor center.

I abandoned my truck next to a tricked-out AMC Gremlin with slicks and lots of tacky artwork on the sides, and worked my way up the interior of the complex to Doan's apartment. A smiling Asian boy let me through the locked gate at the base of the stairs without question.

Foreign dialects assailed my ears, quick and chittering, as I passed several open-doored apartments. It was three in the afternoon and most of the men were off sweating somewhere for the sahib.

The woman who answered my rapping was not what I expected.

Tiny, oriental, hard-eyed, she looked almost Spanish, her black hair teased into a stiff bouffant. She spoke meticulous English, with only a few mispronunciations. If her speech patterns hadn't been so cultured and precise, I would have thought she might be a reformed madam. Or maybe a not-so-reformed madam. The most noticeable thing about her was her tight skirt and unbelievably pointed bosoms, housed in what could only have been an extremely old-fashioned, stiff brassiere. It had probably been shipped from Vietnam with her.

She eyed me. "Yes?"

"Does Hung Doan live here?" Two small children

played with daichis on the rug in the apartment behind her, flinging them to the floor with glee.

"He's out right now. He'll be back in a little while. He went down to his work to repair a hole somebody make."

We must have crossed paths about the time I was escorting Kathy back to work. I glanced at my watch. It wasn't likely they would complete the job on the wall, just jury-rig something to tide it over for the night.

"I'll wait out in my truck."

"No, no." She had been sizing me up carefully. "You come in and wait. My husband be home soon. You come in. Are you friends with my husband?"

"Not exactly."

"I know he wouldn't want you to stay out in the truck."

"You never know."

"No, you come in. Come in." She motioned to me, waving her arm like an oar, a flashy turquoise ring swallowing most of her dinky hand. I ventured in. The moppets on the floor stared up at me with delicate eyes and the woman said, "This is a friend of your uncle's. He's going to wait here."

In silent unison they stood and lined up beside their aunt, brown eyes glued to me. I suddenly started to feel a little queasy, like I had eaten too much fatty meat and was waking up in the middle of the night, sweaty and sick and looking for someplace to empty my guts. It was a nice little family and I was here to put a great big hole in it. I stayed nauseated until I went around the table to the sole couch in the room where she was motioning for me to sit. As I did so, I happened to look through a partially open bedroom door and saw an AK47 assault rifle leaning in a corner next to a mattress on the floor. The rifle sent a spurt of adrenaline through my system and the queasiness evaporated.

"Hung is expecting you?"

I shook my head. Not only was he not expecting me, now, with his wife and the children here, I didn't know what the hell I was going to say when he toddled in. How many people did you kill this week? Who showed you how to make detective-popsicles? How would you like a trip to a nice big American prison?

"Has your husband been home all day?"

She smiled. Her teeth were crooked in a jumbled way I wasn't used to seeing, but the smile was as cheery and inviting as any that had ever greeted me. "I think so. He got a vacation. I teach at the school so I only got home, oh, about an hour ago."

"You're a teacher?"

"I teach English. I taught high school in Vietnam."

One child, a boy of about five, sidled over, politely folded both hands on my knee and set his chin on top of his hands, gazing up at me. The woman reprimanded him in another tongue, a sharp, grunting, guttural language.

"It's okay," I said. "I like it." I ruffled his hair and wondered if his uncle was going to try to kill me when he got home. The freezer in this place would hardly hold a pussycat, much less a big old detective. Maybe he would trick me into sticking my tongue on it.

The four of us sat there for a minute or two, studying each other. I said, "How long have you lived in this country?"

It was like pulling a rip cord on a parachute. She had a canned spiel and I had pulled the trip wire. At first I resented it, was bored and slightly vexed, but she was unimpeachably sincere. She had witnessed horrors I could only imagine, was from a culture I couldn't even guess at—a culture that had flourished when the Puget Sound country was a haven only for Indians. As she spoke, I began to have more respect for her, for her courage, her strength and her ability to cope. I began to hope I was wrong about her mate.

"In Vietnam my husband keep asking during the last week if he can send his family away. We have five children and his father. The communists will surely . . . you know. So we need permission to get on one of the planes. We lived in the compound in Saigon and the communists were closing in. Everybody is very scared. People commit suicide. Many people we know kill themselves.

"My husband's best friend filled a bathtub with gasoline

and sat in it and lit himself. It was a very terrible time. But no permission and no permission. We can hear the fighting outside the city. Then my husband, he gets permission. In ten minutes, we can go. I have time to pack only clothes for the kids. And some pictures. Just a few pictures. We lose everything. And two of the children are in diapers so it is mostly clothing for them that I take. And his father is very old, almost ninety. So he cannot walk without me to lean on. My hands were full.

"But the most trouble, the most trouble for me is getting permission from my parents to leave. They did not want me to leave the country. They will never see me again. Never see their grandchildren again. It is very sad for them and they do not understand. It took me a long time to convince them to let me leave. I had to beg them many times."

"You had to ask your parents?"

"Oh, yes. I cannot go without their permission." I stared at her. She didn't know how incomprehensible such a thing was in this country, a country where Lizzie Borden and others had been taking parental liberties for years.

"So then your husband came with you?"

"Hung was a colonel in the army. He couldn't come. He stayed. I went to Air Force base in Philippines. I was there four months before I know if Hung is alive or dead. And his father is sick. He is sick all this time. And I am in the hotel with these little children and his sick father. And every night I cannot sleep because I worry. It was a bad time."

She kept talking, telling me how lucky they were.

Life is a bitch. If her husband really had been guilty of atrocities in Nam, chances are she knew nothing about them, nothing at all. She came from a people who obeyed implicitly. Obeyed their parents. Obeyed their husbands. She probably knew even less of his affairs here.

She was explaining about the system of sponsor families in the U.S. and how much trouble they had had with their sponsor family when we heard somebody at the front door.

Two men chitchatting in Vietnamese walked down the corridor and emerged into the living room.

It was Hung Doan and another Asian man, a man I had never seen before. He looked like an executioner, small, compact, with mean, sunken eyes and a glinting gold tooth in the front of his mouth. He was taller and larger than Hung Doan, and I noticed immediately that he made a habit of keeping one hand buried deep in the pocket of his leather jacket. I had known gunmen who did the same thing.

Without a second thought Hung Doan turned around, raced down the hallway and out of the apartment, hollering over his shoulder in Vietnamese. His wife bestowed a horrified look on me and fell back against one wall, cradling one of the children in her arms. The boy on my knee looked appalled at first. Then grinned.

"I just want to talk," I said, rising slowly. But the apartment door slammed shut on my plea.

Locking eyes with me, the executioner backed up into the shadowed entranceway, blocking my exit, crouched, hands outstretched. His long-nailed fingers were curled into serpentine shapes, as if he might be required to gouge out an eyeball and some brains in the near future.

I looked at Hung's wife. "What did he say?"

"Maybe you wait a while and then you go?"

"What did he say?" I yelled.

"He said you are here to arrest him for drugs."

"What'd he tell this guy?" I nodded at the man in the corridor.

"He said to stop you. He had to get away and hide things. He said to stop you."

I started down the hallway toward the hunched executioner. "Is your husband dealing drugs?"

"Maybe. Sometimes. I don't know."

I marched down the hall, feinted once and put my fist into the face of the man barring my path. The blow knocked him back against the door, where he bounced onto the carpet like a child's sand-filled balloon punching bag.

The little scamp behind me said, "Hot diggety, dog diggety. Wowee. Did you see that, Auntie Sue?" Over my shoulder I saw him perform the same stunt, a perfect mimicry.

What a deal.

On my way out I noticed the back of the man's head had punched a melon-shaped crater into the door.

Chapter Nineteen

OUTSIDE DOAN'S APARTMENT I stopped and listened for the sound of running footsteps. There was nothing but traffic hissing a few blocks away on Rainier and a stinky city breeze humming through the plum-colored mesh.

Below I recognized the squeaking as the gate to the half-moon complex opened and Hung Doan clumped across the concrete bridge, prowling the parking lot.

Automatically centering his eyesight on his own apartment door, he twisted around and spotted me first thing.

He drew something small and dark out of his jacket pocket and extended his hand toward me, pointing the innocuous black object.

A popping sound. A ta-whirr on the plum-colored wire mesh. Pop. Pop. Small white puffs of smoke wafted from the object in his fist. Ta-whirr. Chunk. Something sounding like a very heavy bug slammed into the wall behind me.

He was shooting. The black item impaled on his fist was a Saturday night special. And that wasn't a discount at the local cathouse. What a deal. I was getting slower every day. Five years ago I would have hit the deck before he got off the first shot.

Dropping into one very quick reverse push-up on the cement floor, I dilly-dallied an appropriate interval and then peeked through the gap at the bottom hem of the plum mesh.

Doan was disappearing into an ink-black Dodge van with

161

one of those open vents cut into the roof. It was hard to be sure at this distance but I scratched what I thought was the license number into my notebook and started to climb to my feet.

I got almost into a half-crouch when Doan's compatriot came blasting out of Doan's apartment and bowled me over.

Startled, he backed away and clawed in his pocket. The blow from his knee into my ribs had knocked me into the mesh. When I had righted myself, I could see that he had a very ugly-looking knife in his right hand. A switchblade. The business section was long enough to pierce my chest clean through to my back and still have something left over to trim dental floss.

"Your friend is gone," I said, cocking a thumb at the van which was racing out of the parking lot, its tires shrieking like tortured cats. "No need for this."

I edged away, praying that I could backpedal out of this predicament. He trailed me, looking all the more like an executioner. No chopping block or heavy-bladed hatchet for this man. No sirree. This knight of the inner city could cheerfully lop off your head with a toad stabber.

We moved a step at a time, a rhumba student and his teacher picking across the painted footprints.

Behind the executioner an Asian woman who had been industriously stirring up small dust clouds on the concrete walk in front of her apartment caught a glimpse of his knife, of my sour-pickle face, and rushed into her apartment. The door boomed shut behind her. I could still hear her burbling a hundred words a minute in a language from the other side of the earth.

"Take it easy, fella," I said. "I'll remember your birthday next year. Okay? No wonder nobody comes to your parties."

A squiggle of blood had coursed out his nostrils and met another, wider swathe of crimson at the edge of his mouth. When he opened wide and flashed his pearlies, it looked as if he were sucking a mouthful of ketchup. The executioner's smile. His language was clipped, economical and right to the point.

"You be wearing your guts for a bow tie, mister," He said.

"Nice sentiments. But my spring wardrobe is just about complete. How about next season?"

As I finished my sentence he lunged forward, jabbing with the knife, nicking my belly. He was fast. As fast as anyone I had seen recently. Faster and trickier than Teets and his fly-catching burlesque.

I nodded at him.

"I already had this jacket tailored. Thanks anyway."

He sprang forward when I spoke, again hoping the distraction of my words would give him the edge. He swiped once, twice, three times, thrusting each time, keeping his body positioned well back of the knife.

Beside me was a small room. Inside was the mechanical ker-chunk ker-chunk noise of a washing machine. The laundry room. I heard voices advancing up the walk, the chittering of women and children. I feinted at the executioner, a right hook that I pulled before he could cut me, and used his cautionary counterfeint to snap my head to the side and check out the laundry room. It was a mere cubicle, eight feet wide and twelve feet deep holding two washers and one coin-operated dryer.

The voices behind were converging on us. The man in front of me would have no qualms about maiming third parties and I had visions of wide-eyed hostages, squealing mothers and other scenes from a foreign war.

I backed into the laundry room, quickly glancing from side to side for any domestic article I might turn into a weapon. You know the type—a chain saw somebody had already warmed up, maybe a bulldozer, a Thompson submachine gun with a full clip.

As soon as his small body blotted the light in the doorway, I hurled a glass ashtray at his face. He ducked his head to the side in a lightning quick move. This sucker was fast.

I gripped the metal handle of a garbage can lid, jerked the singing lid off the can and shielded my left side with it.

A gaggle of women and children appeared in the doorway behind my tormentor, peeping over and around to see what he was butchering. When they saw the big Christmas ham they murmured to themselves in a foreign dialect.

I grinned. I was like that. Detectives had to be cool under pressure.

None of them gave any signs of understanding English when I said, "Would you ladies mind calling the police?"

He cocked his head at the doorway and I made a move at him. I was going to pulp his brains with the garbage can lid. Instead, I skated on some damp soap flakes and went down hard, thumping my knee on the floor and pulling a muscle in my groin.

He strutted closer, a look of utter contempt contorting his bloody face. I had never seen a man who could sneer with as much heartfelt ecstasy as this man.

He was thinking to himself, how the hell did he let a gumball like me punch him out back in Doan's apartment. I was beginning to wonder the same thing.

Twice he slashed, both times making tinny cymbal sounds against the lid. I fell into the corner on my rump and scooted myself up the wall the way a rock climber might in a natural chimney, until I was on my feet again. At least for now. I gave him a ga-ga look. His expression had not changed once.

He slashed. I fended.

The people behind him in the doorway had evaporated. I guessed from their tepid expressions they had no inclination whatsoever to advise the police about the skirmish in their laundry room.

He slit the air in front of my nose. Another inch and my

nose would have been flapping like the tongue of a baby's shoe.

Bracing the lid in my left hand, I threw a hook, lid and all. I managed to smash it against his knife and fist, making a muted bonging noise. He backed up, favoring that wrist. Then he switched hands with the knife. Great. A switch-hitter.

I didn't even see him move. I was watching his eyes.

Weren't the eyes supposed to telegraph the blow? They didn't. His face didn't alter one iota. Nor did the rest of his body even twitch. It didn't even shiver.

The knife just flicked out and bit me in the right shoulder.

A jolt of pain shot through to the bone.

"Mommy," I wailed. "Geez, that hurts. Why did you do that? Oh, man, I need an ambulance. I'm going to bleed to death. You hurt me." I began crying, letting my right arm hang limp and useless. What an artiste. Surely, I would be nominated for the Maltese Falcon at this year's detectives' banquet.

The only clue I had that he was buying it was that he stood a little straighter, his eyes got a little sleepier, and the knife hand drooped a fraction of an inch. Just a fraction.

He stepped in close enough to knot up that bow tie he had promised me.

Using the wall for an anchor, I swung a right hook, aiming for the center of his face. I put all my heart into it.

If this wasn't good, my heart would end up on the floor in a puddle anyway. He caught my move, feinted, and began jabbing upward with the switchblade.

Too late.

Smack.

I hit him in the middle of his nose and mouth and just kept on driving right through him, as if I might send his head sprawling all the way to Tacoma. It was like striking a water balloon filled with blood. The little executioner flew backward, leaving his feet and landing hard—flat on his back.

Dazed, bloody, eyes watering, nose spurting, he still had a grip on the knife. I stepped in and booted his arm.

The knife flew out of his hands and he curled up like a worm some sadistic kid had plopped onto a hot plate. I peered down my nose at the tear in my jacket on my right shoulder. It stung like hell and I had almost screamed at the pain of it when I scrunched up my muscles to punch him. But there was no blood. At least not on the jacket.

He was crawling in the direction he thought the knife had flown. He wasn't moving gracefully, or even very quickly, but he was going after the weapon. I hit him in the spine with the edge of the garbage can lid. Then the shoulder. The neck.

I frisked him. I found nothing except a packet of Marlboros and a wallet with $700 in it. I put it all back, picked him up by the scruff of his neck and his belt and packed him into a side-loading Maytag dryer. He went in as limp and compliant as a jellyfish washed up on the beach. I slammed the door behind him. Inside, he twitched once.

I placed the lid back on the can as well as it would go, found his switchblade, folded it and plopped it into my pocket. Then I located a clean cotton cloth diaper in a plastic laundry basket. I sopped up some of the bleeding on my shoulder with it, wedging it under my jacket.

Maybe I could have quizzed him, but I figured he was at least fifty per cent tougher than I was, and I knew I wouldn't have said a word, so I let it go.

On the way out I flicked off the lights.

I felt woozy. I wondered whether I was going to be depressed over this one. I wasn't a killer. I knew it. Whether it was compassion or a moral sense or what—I really couldn't say—I had not been bothered enough to dissect it. I had slain only one person in my life and I was determined to keep it that way. Maybe I had been around when a few others died, but I only counted the one. But every once in a while I got crazy and mauled or got mauled by some goon. Usually we deserved what we dished out to each other, or worse. But that didn't alleviate the personal misery I felt afterward.

On the winning end of the stick or not, I felt filthy. Afterward for a time, my life seemed to flatten out. Life was supposed to be an upward journey, always finer, more beautiful: wiser, more loving, calmer, more peaceful. Onward and upward. The flattening effect was worse than depressing. And I knew it was coming again.

When I looked back down the corridor, Doan's little moppet nephew was peekabooing out the doorway of the apartment, doting on me, a broad smile insinuating itself on his face. I waved two fingers at him and was gone.

It wasn't until I was ensconced in my truck that I pulled my shirt out and found the gash across my belly. It wasn't deep. A quarter-inch line running horizontally across my gut. I took a few minutes, pulled a dressing out of the glove box, and taped it on. I had a torn chest, a knife wound to the shoulder and a lacerated stomach. But I was winning all my fights. At this rate I only had to win a few more before I'd be underground.

I drove home. I limped out of the truck under my neighbor Horace's steady gaze and cloaked my bloody shirt with the flaps of my jacket. After a case a year ago when I had gotten beaten up pretty bad, Horace—retired, bored and snoopy—had snidely accused me of being a masochist, of belonging to some sick club of perverts where I hung myself on a nail and let people poke and prod and flail with sharp instruments. He didn't take my detective business seriously, was always looking for another excuse for my activities: dope dealing, burglary, selling white women to the Arabs. Horace's retirement was kept lively by my comings and goings.

"You been out huntin' wild boars?" he asked, glee ringing in his tones. "They'll gore ya like that, you let 'em get in close."

He had seen the blood tracking up my shirt and hands.

"I've been down at the pet store twisting heads off canaries. Manny's was overstocked. How about your place? You got too many?"

Horace cleared his throat and spat across the fence into my rose bed. His home was a madhouse of squawking aviators from far-off jungles. I had been in there once, years ago, and counted eight cages. I think he had more now. One of the birds had been wearing a tiny sweater.

Stripping out of my bloodied shirt, rumpled slacks and sweaty undershirt, I eased a dressing onto the slit in my shoulder and awkwardly taped it in place. It was beginning to stiffen. I had punched the executioner pretty good after he'd jabbed me, but it was getting more and more tender. I knew that in a few hours a mere tap would make me retch. A blow to the shoulder would put me down for the count. I would get it attended to. But not now. Now, before the cops got the same notion, I had to go see what the flycatcher had left for me.

Outside, Horace was galloping around his yard behind a new power lawn mower that needed a governor on the engine.

Although it wasn't yet four o'clock, the gentle heat of the day was beginning to dissipate. A nonporous layer of grayish clouds was scudding in from Iceland just as a special treat for me. It looked like volcanic steam, heading in from the north.

On the drive I tried to take stock, but little came of it. Hung Doan would slither into the woodwork, at least for a while. He wouldn't have to report to work again for a month, so it was going to be hard to nab him. I still didn't know what I wanted to ask him, even if he had certain ideas of what he didn't want to say. Except that it was beginning to look more and more like he was implicated in this.

Could it be that Mark Daniels had caught Hung Doan peddling drugs? That he had threatened to turn him over to the police? That Doan had assassinated Mark and the girl?

But how did Kandy Darling figure in the imbroglio? And Teets? That poor old sagging detective with booze on his breath and bullets in his pocket. What had Teets seen that had gotten him dunked into that icy coffin?

His agency opposite the ship canal was only a minute away now. I might find out there, if the cops hadn't already ransacked it.

Chapter Twenty

SQUATTING SMACK in the gut of a sleepy residential neighborhood, the Teets Detective Agency was on the second floor of a run-down triangular structure. The tan, gritty siding material on the outside of the building was split and peeling. It resembled a big hunk of chocolate cream pie that had been forgotten at a picnic and had hardened in the sun. A cracked upper window was stitched with clear tape, snakeskins on the window. He had probably ruptured the glass swatting flies. To the locals, it had to be an eyesore.

I parked in the prickly shade of a blue spruce two blocks away.

Finagling a warrant to search this place would eat up a couple of hours and my guess was the cops wouldn't feel it was worth dithering over this late in the day. They would have to find a judge and then buck the get-home-and-grab-a-beer traffic. I would have the hero's office all to my lonesome.

In the musty interior stairwell I stretched up and walked my fingers along the dust-coated sill above the door. I flipped the mat over and sneezed at the storm it sent up. No key. Under a ledge farther back in the hallway I launched myself upward and did one long and laborious chin-up. Dust devils chased at my hard-breathing face. I finally unearthed his hideout key eight stairs down, cleverly secreted behind a knot in the wood.

I unlocked the door and cached the key away again, jigsawing the knot back in.

The lazy buzzing of a gaggle of fat bluebottle flies harmonized with the noises of my intrusion.

Butch Teets had left a window partially open, but the joint still reeked heavily of the man: the tang of tobacco, of booze, the stale, sun-dried paper smell of comic books and newspapers, and the musk of very idle and very lecherous thoughts.

The yellowed pine desk was chipped and scarred. Its drawers were littered with food wrappers, paper clips, bullets, packages of condoms with the cellophane seals still intact, several Washington county maps, a tattered map of L.A., and two half-full bottles of gin.

The file cabinet had four rickety drawers. The top two were crammed with comic books, most of them dogeared from endless readings. The third drawer contained his sparse case material in file folders.

I quickly jerked open the bottom drawer before pawing through the case material. It was empty except for a worn shoulder holster with a broken buckle, two blackjacks with fish scales on them, a stiletto and some rusted wiring that looking like it was meant to be part of a bomb. His junk drawer.

None of the file folders in the third drawer down were marked, so I began at the back and worked my way forward. Gauging by the dates on the receipts, Teets had been working in Seattle for only two years. Either he hadn't kept complex footnotes on his cases, or he hadn't had very many cases. He must have been near starvation. No wonder the first thing on his mind when I showed up was skullduggery.

A little graft, some scam, a pinch of extortion was probably all that kept him in bullets and booze and the Classic Comics version of Charles Dickens.

Midway through the folders I stumbled upon one teeming with pornography.

None of it was commercial. Just seamy stuff he—or other detectives—had amassed on cases. From the time span indicated by the styles in the photos and the dates on the letters, he must have swapped some of this trash with other investi-

gators who had subsisted on messy divorce cases back in the
Forties and Fifties when adultery was a common stipulated
ground for divorce—back in the good old days when door-
busting and flashbulb popping were popular rites.

Nowadays, the more common use of detectives in divorce
was to track down hubbies—poor-pays. Or to locate stolen
children in custody squabbles.

These photographs were more comical than lurid.

Comical or not, it took me two run-throughs to lose interest in the bundle.

Included were glossy snapshots of several minor Hollywood actors and one actress who had made it to the big
leagues a few years back and then had retrogressed to TV.
She had held down a bit part in a series until a year or two
ago. The guy putting it to her looked twenty years her junior. Gigolo-city. My guess was that more than one of these
snapshots had been the cornerstone for blackmail in L.A.
County.

The folder on the Hindenburg case was almost empty,
consisting of scraps of notebook paper with assorted scribbled snippets of information on them. Everything was
tossed in helter-skelter as if an angry child had done his filing.

I took the folder over to the desk and plopped down with
it, laying out each piece separately until I had a rectangular
mosaic.

Teets had been a disorganized slob. No wonder he didn't
work more than a couple of days a week. Skip tracing and
runaways should have kept him solvent, even if he never
took on anything else. If this was all he had on Hindenburg,
I was astounded that he had even been able to scrawl a report. Maybe he hadn't. I could find no carbons.

I saw the address of the mail drop Beatrice Hindenburg
had been using in the U-district. The name of the motel.
Mark Daniels' name. Hindenburg's father's address in California, along with a phone number. And another name I had
never seen before scratched on a corner ripped out of a
glossy magazine.

Roy Earlywine.

His address and phone number were printed beneath. He lived in West Seattle, only a few minutes from the Trinity Building on Harbor Island. It was a strange piece of geography called Pigeon Point.

Riffling through the remaining file folders in Teets' battered cabinet, I didn't find anything else of interest.

I copied the address of Hindenburg's father in California and Roy Earlywine's address on Pigeon Point. Then I left.

I drove through the congealing mush of rush-hour traffic, trying to hold my temper. I got all the way across the Spokane Street Bridge without junking my truck or tooting my horn.

It took me a few minutes to unriddle the maze of detours on the other side of the bridge.

Traffic had been a snake pit in this area ever since a freighter rammed the old drawbridge in 1978. It was said that this traffic corridor saw more cars a day than any other stretch in the state except I-5. Now they had almost completed the new high span, a huge concrete arch erected to the god of commerce, the Detroit rush hour.

I steamed up a bitch of a hill and coursed around a sleepy little neighborhood at the top.

It was a relatively flat bluff; only the residences on the rim had a view.

Pigeon Point overlooked the bridge, and the industrial tideflats. In fact, using a telescope and given a clear day, Trinity and the Daniels' house across the bay could both be seen from here.

Just up the hill from the steel mill, these had all been mill houses originally. A few of the homes were cared for, well-tended gardens being cultivated in the cruddy May afternoon, but most of them were Middle-American Junky. The Earlywine residence was an exception.

It was plopped on a tiny spur street that stretched right out to the northern edge of the bluff. In fact, it was difficult to imagine—in this slide-prone area—that in a few years the structure wouldn't suddenly vanish. Some windy December

in the midst of a rainstorm it would go whoopee all the way
to the bottom of the hill and skate into the river.

Earlywine greeted me at the door with a batty grin that I
was certain never removed itself from his face. He was a peculiar man, elfin, balding, toothy, his mouth a mere doodle
until he opened it and blinded you with all that gold bridge-
work. Though he was undoubtedly retired, he wore a
generic green work shirt, matching work pants and muddy-
brown brogans. From the first, he looked upon me as an
ally.

"Hey there," he said, overflowing with ebullience. "Afternoon, afternoon. What can I do you for?" He chuckled.

"You ever talk to a detective named Seymore Teets?"

"Who? Is this a joke? Got Prince Albert in a can? Yeah,
I've heard that one before. Seymore Teets. That's good."

"He called himself Butch."

"Butch?" His eyes traveled up and down my frame.
"Butch? Of course. You a friend of his'n? Come on in.
Sure, I remember Butch. It was kind of a strange transaction
'cause I seen him through my scope there and then 'bout half
an hour later he comes knockin' at my door. Ain't never
seen anybody do that before. Said he caught a glint off my
scope. The man has good eyes. You imagine that, from all
the way down beyond West Marginal, clean up to here?"

He ushered me into his house and to a sitting room off a
balcony. The wooden balcony had nothing below it but
rustling treetops and below that, traffic: cars and boats, and
a policeman racing across the waterway, blue and red lights
winking at us.

What magnetized me, though, was the mammoth telescope mounted on a tripod. It was set next to the balcony
door so that in foul weather one could gaze through the
glass.

It was a marine telescope of some sort, only went up to a
120 power. It had a huge eyepiece. Earlywine giggled when
he saw me gaping at it. He was the kind of guy who spent a
half-hour telling a grocery clerk he had never seen before all
about the tumor on his colon. Gas station attendants he saw

regularly were considered best friends. His barber was in his will.

"You must be a detective, too. That's the same damn thing Teets headed for. Just like a homing pigeon. Zoom. Right for that scope."

I introduced myself. "Roy Earlywine," he said, extending a dry hand.

"I'm interested in what you discussed with Teets."

"Wasn't much. 'Bout two months ago. Must have been the first of March or the tail end of February. See, I seen him down there. I keep a mighty keen watch below the bridge." He rubbed his hands together.

"It's a spoonin' spot. Don't you know? I seen more . . ." He gave me a conspiratorial wink and peered around the house for the old woman. "I seen more fuckin' and suckin' down there in the last thirty years than you could shake a stick at. You look through this scope here, you'll see what I mean. Hell, I don't need no television when I got this. Fact is, I hardly never go out. The old lady can't figure it. She thinks I watch boat traffic on the Duwamish."

He gestured for me to peek through the scope. I walked over, bent, and placed my face up to it, half expecting my eye to get blackened.

Earlywine was just the type to pull that tired gag. It was blurry until I screwed down the adjustment knob. He had it fine tuned to one of the crews working on the new bridge.

"Let me get it right for you," he said, shouldering me away. He smelled of weeds and trees and throat medication.

When he freed the scope it was centered on a female worker on the bridge, wearing tight jeans and a flapping tool belt.

"Ain't them steel workers something?" He gulped.

"What about Teets? Where did you see him?" Using an expert facility borne of years of patient self-tutelage, Earlywine swung the scope down, zeroed in on his target and surrendered the instrument to me.

At this range and low power the distortions from heat waves were almost nonexistent. The scope had sucked a piece of land underneath the old Spokane Street Bridge up to my eyes, making it look close enough to be just across the room. The packed earth had that parched-flesh color to it.

"Nobody there right now," said Earlywine. "But that's where they park. Come down to spoon where they think nobody can see 'em." He tittered. "You won't believe some of the hijinks I seen down there. I mean, it'd keep you entertained for a month of Sundays. Right in broad daylight, too, if you can believe that. There's one couple, must be skipping out at lunch hour. They show up every Monday and Thursday, just like clockwork. Sit in his camper and spoon. Pretty soon they slide up through the rear window of the cab into the back. Usually they park so I can see it all through the windshield. Now, last week the light struck it wrong and I couldn't see so well. It gets a little bad in May and then again for a week or so in September."

"What was Teets doing down there?"

"Seen a pair of kids down there once. A pair in the front seat, a pair in the back. They went at it and about every five minutes the kid in the front would hop over the seat and trade rides with the kid in the back. If that don't beat all." Earlywine's smile was frozen, his gold-laced teeth slightly bucktoothed. His deep-throated chortles sounded like something from after midnight at the zoo.

"You said you saw the detective down there. What was he doing? Did he have a woman with him?"

"Woman? Hell, no. He was just poking around. Turned out he was followin' this lady in a Caddy. They was a couple of my regulars until just recently. For some damned reason they used to show up early in the morning. I guess people have to be naughty when they got the time. Threw my schedule all out of whack. I like to work out in the yard in the mornings. Havin' to sit here and wait for them threw a real crimp in my day."

"A Cadillac?"

"Brand new. Leastways, I think it was a Cadillac. Them new cars is so danged hard to tell apart anymore. That detective fella was the one—I guess—told me it was a Caddy. He

was down there poking around. Had a fellow once used to
go down there almost every morning and pick up used co-
nundrums. Know what I mean? Picked 'em up with a stick
and dropped 'em into a little paper bag. Never could figure
out what his game was.''

"So Teets saw you up here?''

"Mother McCree, he did. First time that ever happened,
too. He had a pair of bitsy field glasses hanging around his
neck and he went down to where they parked and just started
a-swinging around the territory. Pretty soon he fixed on me.
Dangdest thing you ever saw. About a half-hour later he
shows up at the door. He wanted to see the whole setup. Just
like you.''

"What'd he ask you about?''

"Just that Caddy. Wanted to know how many times a
week it showed up. That sort of thing.''

"Think you might recognize the driver?''

He shrugged, smirked and spoke softly. "Maybe not with
all his clothes on. Course, he liked to strip the girl naked and
leave most of his things on. Kept that cowboy hat on most of
the times I seen him.''

"Cowboy hat?''

"Big. You know. Ten-gallon jobbie. With one of those
brims that bites down in front, like that there supersonic airplane the French made.''

"The Concorde?''

"Yeah. The brim bites down just like that.''

"Same girl every time?''

"Not him. Had all sorts. Young though. Always young.
Why are you after him? He some sort of criminal?''

I unfolded my newspaper clippings of Hindenburg and
Mark Daniels. "Recognize either of these?''

"Her?'' He shook his head. "Him? I suppose that might
be him. Sure, that's him. The beard.''

"Did Butch show you any pictures?''

"Nope. He sat there and gawked through that scope for a
good three hours though. Didn't see nothin'. You almost
have to live with it to make it pay off. You know, take a

peek every half-hour or so when you're passing through the room. I ain't been living on this point for thirty years for nothin'."

"You ever see this same fellow driving another car?"

"Don't think so."

"How about a Volkswagen Rabbit? You ever see him in one of those?"

He shook his head. "Them Rabbits has got a lot of glass. Somebody gets a-humpin' and a-sweatin' in one of them and you see it all. Lots of glass. Love 'em. I would have remembered if I'd seen him in one of those."

Odd. According to his friends, Mark Daniels drove the Rabbit exclusively. The Cadillac was Deanna's car. The way I understood it, he only drove it when they were going somewhere together. It seemed more than unlikely that he would drive his wife below the bridge to make out in the car. Only a nut would do a thing like that. Maybe he was borrowing his wife's car to impress his dates.

So if Teets had tailed Hindenburg to the bridge, Teets had either made a mistake—had tailed someone else with Hindenburg—or Daniels was routinely borrowing somebody else's car. Several of his friends had Cadillacs. But that didn't make any sense. Why under the bridge? He had the office he could go to at night. He had the love nest up at the lake. He even had the Galaxie Motor Court Inn.

What was wrong with him that he would be penny-pinching underneath a bridge with the trolls on the hill scoping out every move he made and following along in their paperback copy of the *Kama Sutra?* Penny-pinching? Nothing that I had found out about Mark had indicated he was cheap. Just the reverse. Daniels had always been generous to a fault, except for the Galaxie Motor Court Inn, and I attributed that to his desire for secrecy.

I was staring at the sawtooth tutti-frutti cityscape when the old man interrupted my reveries. "You care to sit here a spell?"

"No, thanks. This fella always wore the beard?"

Earlywine scratched his scalp and then rammed an index

finger into his ear and screwed it around until he had enough wax to roll up into a ball between his fingers. He rolled and thought and then dug into the mine again for more raw material.

"Now that you mention it, I don't think he did. Come to think of it. When he first started coming down there he never had the beard. Then he had it for a while and then . . . I don't know, but I would swear he come once or twice without it. Them whiskers a-his must grow awful danged fast."

"Probably some sort of tonic," I said, moving through the living room to the front door. "By the way. What color was that Cadillac?"

"Gray? Steel gray."

"Think it might have been something else? A Chrysler, maybe?"

"Sure, coulda been. I didn't watch the car that much."

I got into my truck and jumped back into the stream of rush-hour commuters, bucking the tide this time, heading back into town.

Gray. Steel gray. Deanna's Cadillac was steel gray. For that matter, with her hair done up differently each time, Deanna could easily have passed for a succession of different girls. Trouble was, Wheeler's Chrysler was steel gray, too.

Chapter Twenty-one

THE REVEREND SAM WHEELER lived in Renton, a burgeoning bedroom community off the southern tip of Lake Washington. I had never visited the Reverend in his digs. Maybe this evening would be a good time, if he wasn't entertaining too many insurance salesmen, or converting too many tearful runaways.

All I had propelling me was a description of a car that may or may not have been his—I figured a Chrysler was easy enough to confuse with a Caddy (and his car was gray)— along with my complete and unreasoned dislike for the man.

With my tender right shoulder, it was growing difficult to steer, and I was doing most of my driving now with my left hand. The pain had blossomed into something I wouldn't forget soon. I winced when I worked the gearshift on the column, even moaned to myself when I thought nobody in another car would see me. Some people got caught singing to themselves in the car, some picking their noses. I didn't want to get caught moaning.

It would be a long night.

It was a new house in a look-alike development. Some harebrained genius with an itch in his wallet had chopped down all the trees and, skimping by using only one set of plans, had nailed up sixty look-alike ranchero-style houses in drab pastel hues. In front of Wheeler's dream box were two skinny ornamental cherry trees in circular flower beds along with a slab of putting turf trucked in from Portland. You could tell how old these projects were by the age of the trees in the yards. This one was about six years. Behind the house was a narrow strip of woods awaiting the next sharp-eyed developer and his bulldozers.

Wheeler's Chrysler was in the drive, looking more like a Caddy than ever. Beside it sat a sporty new Mazda.

Cruising past, I caught sight of a heavyset woman in the kitchen window, her hair clipped so short they wouldn't bother to crop the stubble when she enlisted. Her age made her a stronger prospect for Sam's wife than his mother, though she looked more like the latter, her expression luster-less and weary, features sagging in the twilight.

I didn't see Sam. Deanna had told me they had no children.

Two miles beyond their house I hit a shopping center and tanked up on hamburgers and soft ice cream cones. I slipped into a convenience store and selected a cheap pair of sun-glasses, a dippy plaid golfing cap, and to assist in speeding the night along, a couple of magazines and the evening paper.

Then I went to a phone booth, thumbed a quarter in and dialed my business number. The whiny kid had left another session of smut on my recorder. "Hey, mister detective. Did you hear the one about the four high school boys who hitchhiked to Tijuana to catch the donkey act? One took a dog, a cat, a rat and a mouse." The finish of the joke didn't impress me. Each joke he put on my tape was more gross than the preceding one. I would nab him. When I got time I would track down and apprehend the little bastard. I phoned Leech, Bemis and Ott and asked for Kathy. The nasal-sounding switchboard operator told me she had gone home for the day.

I drove back past the Wheeler house. Nothing had changed. Making certain the snout of the truck was hidden, I reversed into a gravel road six blocks south, slumped down until my wounded shoulder was in a comfortable posture, and munched from a can of unsalted party nuts.

From here I could only cover half of their possible exits, but it seemed the more likely direction of travel. The major highways and the shopping center were both this way. When I finally logged the time into my notebook, it was a shade past six o'clock.

I slouched in my plaid hat and cheesy sunglasses and watched the tail end of the world race home to gobble dinner and de-flea the dog. The sunlight might last another hour, maybe less.

When the sporadic traffic abated, I paged through the paper. Butch Teets had made the last column of the first section, directly over a sexy ad for women's lingerie. He would have liked that. The article didn't mention that he had been found frozen in a block of ice, just that his corpse had been discovered at the Trinity Dog Food plant. There was no mention of the two other bodies that had been discovered there a week earlier.

Shortly after 8:30, Wheeler sped past in his Chrysler. I recognized his profile in the diaphanous dusk. He was alone in the car, driving like a volunteer fireman on his way to a conflagration, except that he was wearing a ten-gallon cowboy hat, the brim turned down in front, like a Concorde superliner.

I turned over my engine, but before I could head for his house to reconnoiter, another vehicle passed in front of me, traveling the same direction Wheeler had. It was a dark gray Mercedes 380SL—Emmett Anderson's car. And Anderson was behind the wheel, sitting forward, nose up almost against the windshield, a hound after the fox. Interesting. I let them flitter away.

I drove past Wheeler's house. The Mazda was still slotted in the drive. The curtains were pulled, the living room lights low.

A couple of hours of electronic diversion and she'd hit the sack. If I didn't poke fate in the keister, I might be there until dawn waiting for my chance to slip a lock and paw through Wheeler's Bible clippings. The area was too open for a daylight burglary. And if I kept the place staked out from my truck for that length of time, somebody was bound to spot me and grow suspicious. Then, too, my arm was growing steadily more painful, throbbing with a heavy dull ache that had struck up a cadence to the tune of my heart-beat. Later I might not have the mobility. Besides, things were breaking fast. If my assumptions were correct, a lot of interesting artifacts might be obliterated before the sun popped up.

A foray into another person's house was something an ethical detective had to think twice about. And I did. I always thought about it—*twice*. My problem was, I had performed the abomination so frequently it no longer seemed abnormal. Sometimes I even felt a pang of guilt, but it rarely slowed me. And it never dampened my enthusiasm. Poking through somebody else's life was one of the prime thrills of the job. If the police were allowed to toss the home of everyone they suspected, their success rate would rocket twenty-fold. More often than not they had a gut feeling about who they were after, but just couldn't hatch any evidence.

I trekked all the way back to the shopping center. Looking up Wheeler's number in the Renton white pages, I dialed and cooked up a spiel while I listened to the buzzing.

"Mrs. Wheeler?"

"Yes." Her voice was husky and smoky, as if she did a lot of screaming or sucking on cigarettes. Or both.

"This is Officer Raphael from the State Patrol. I don't want to alarm you, but a man has been in a minor traffic accident. We've got him here at Valley General and he's taken a little bump on the noggin. He doesn't quite remember who he is at the moment."

"Sammy? Sammy's been in an accident? Is the car all right?"

"Mrs. Wheeler, we found your phone number in his things. But he doesn't seem to have any ID on him. At least we couldn't find it. Do you think you might know this man?"

"That's my husband. He always drives like a maniac. He's not . . ."

"Just a bump on the head, Mrs. Wheeler. He will need

someone to fill out the forms and take him home. He's in no condition to drive.''

"He always speeds. I told him. Is the car all right?''

"I couldn't say. Trooper Hanford is handling that end of it. When can you be down here?''

"Twenty minutes. I'll be there in twenty minutes. Damn. He let the insurance lapse. I knew he shouldn't have done that.''

On the drive out I passed Mrs. Wheeler who was looking grim-faced and distraught and bending the steering wheel of her sporty little Mazda. She had decamped in such a mad scramble she had forgotten to flip her headlights on. I blinked her and peeked in the mirror to see if it took. No dice.

Twenty minutes out to the hospital. Five minutes to discover it had been a fraud. Maybe longer if she were inept and began phoning other hospitals instead of calling the State Patrol direct. She didn't look inept. So, twenty minutes out. Five minutes of screwing around and twenty minutes back. Forty-five minutes. I set the stop watch on my digital. I would vacate the premises in twenty-five.

The biggest problem would be if she got really cute and dialed the Renton cops from the hospital to warn them a burglary was in progress at her place. Or if Sam returned.

It took eight minutes to locate the road behind the development. I parked under cover of some twelve-foot-tall Scotch broom.

Taking a small flashlight from the glove box, along with my all-purpose sawed-off crowbar on a loop, I navigated through the thinning woods until I could see the line of lights on the other side. Not bad. I was only three houses too far south.

A dog on a chain next door yapped. I hurled a piece of cold hamburger from my dinner at him. He gobbled it, woofed once, and stood wagging his tail, silent, waiting for me to pitch another morsel. Like a lot of us, he could be bought.

She had left the lights burning. Blistering my fingertips, I unscrewed the back porch bug bulb until it winked out. I tried the door. Bolted.

It took only a second to locate a sliding window she had neglected to secure. I popped the screen off. It was a small window, chest height, the room behind it pitch-black. Probably a utility room. No need for my flashlight yet. I would crawl in and land on the washing machine. A cinch. When you'd been at something as long as I had, you learned things.

I wormed through the window feet-first, one-armed and awkward because of the soreness and growing stiffness in my shoulder. Immediately I sank up to my hips in what felt like a hot mineral spring.

It smelled as if I had been dipped in a huge bucket of luke-warm piss.

I took a step to the east and sank deeper.

Stifling an almost overpowering urge to yelp, I pulled my flashlight out and evaluated the situation.

"Oh, tish."

I was up to my belt buckle in a hot tub. They had dumped some chemicals into it, thus the peculiar unnerving odor. Life was a bitch.

Wading to the wooden edge and gripping the rim, I hoisted myself out and dropped onto the floor, my shoes sounding like a cow chewing her cud each time I took a step. I grappled with a towel in the dark and dried myself off as well as I could.

Ever try toweling your pants off when you're still wearing them?

Eleven minutes had elapsed. It had only taken me three to bamboozle a dog, break into a house and plunge into their hot tub. In another ten maybe I could take advantage of the cat and plop into the septic tank.

I sloshed to the back door, cracked it open and set it so it would lock after I went out, readying my getaway. Then I replaced the window screen and straightened up the mess I had made in the hot tub room.

My footsteps were loud and watery as I tiptoed around the

house, watchful for a guard dog. I knew they didn't have any children, but I wasn't sure about bloodthirsty canines. A year ago a pit bull had snapped at my buttocks from behind a couch when I was prowling somewhere I wasn't supposed to be prowling. I whapped him with my sawed-off crow bar and accidentally broke his neck, killing him. I had been forced to carry him out in a gunnysack and bury him. I don't know what his owner made of it. Lock your dog in the house; go to the store and come home to find he has vanished.

Usually I could smell a dog on the premises, or a smoker, even a doper; but tonight all I could smell was the humid and salty chemical bath I had just immersed myself in. My sloshing, sodden clothes reeked.

Everything on the main level of the house was her territory. It all had her stamp. The elegant and spindly gold-colored furniture. The kitchen, so jammed with convenience items she had no counter space. But most of all, the living room with its organ—a simplified musical arrangement of "Raindrops Keep Falling on my Head" splayed open on the music holder—and rows of softball trophies lined up on the granite mantel. There were photos of Mrs. Wheeler with three different women's softball teams. Photos of her as a child, alongside her mother, and one of her graduating from college. Her entire life was chronicled in the room, with nary a hint that Sam Wheeler existed. Strange.

Moving quickly, I frisked the bedrooms. Skulking from room to room, I looked for his lair. His hangout. It turned out to be a nook over the garage up a set of stairs off the living room. Sam Wheeler was using it for a den. One entire wall was lined up with packaged gifts of the type promoters gave away at weekend-condominium sales meetings. Coffee makers. Ice-cream makers. Inexpensive power tools. Some of them even had the promotional trappings still taped on. Ponderosa Pines Lodge and Condos. Fir Trails Living.

Miserly to the last, Sam had wrapped some in Christmas wrapping paper and stowed them in the closet. Only seven months early. The Reverend Wheeler braved all the promotional hype, accepted the free two-day vacation with a sincere look on his mug and collected his booty. If they were giving, he was taking. I sorted through the name tags, but couldn't find mine. Tish.

The roll-top desk was not locked. I went through it quickly. On top sat an eight-by-ten of Deanna Daniels. It was signed "With love, DeeDee." It could have meant nothing. Or everything. Her face gazed out at me while I burglarized Wheeler's den. I glanced back at it from time to time, wondering about this morning's frolic.

The desk didn't have anything in it that I thought I needed.

On the stereo in the back of the room a record album had been abandoned. The Oak Ridge Boys. He listened to country and western. That meant something. Three pairs of hand-tooled cowboy boots were lined up along the wall. On the top shelf of the closet, along with prewrapped Christmas presents, were several cowboy hats and, hanging on a hook, three or four gaudy bolo ties.

I looked at my watch. Sixteen minutes had elapsed. Nine left.

It irked me that I wasn't making progress. I didn't like anything about Sam Wheeler and now I didn't like anything about his house. It was too neat and it was segregated into male and female sections in such a rigid manner I knew something had to be drastically wrong with their marriage. But so far I hadn't found the incriminating items I had hoped for.

His papers were either published copies of sermons other ministers had given, highlighted in yellow grease pen—the portions he was going to purloin—or various financial documents. He had over $18,000 in a money market fund. In one mutual fund he owned over 30,000 shares. I didn't know what the market value of the shares was, but it had to be substantial. Over $100,000 worth, easily. There were several other share certificates from mutual funds. And a Keogh account worth over $150,000. The man had raked in his spoils.

Everything was tidy and in its place. Even the book of carefully clipped and filed coupons. Fifteen cents off on asparagus soup. Twenty-five cents off on single-ply toilet tissue. If there was a penny to be saved, Wheeler saved it.

I glanced at my watch. If I was going to get out of the house within the safety margin, I only had three minutes.

A small, flat metal box next to the telephone contained a note pad. I held it up to the light and saw the impressions from the last message he had scribbled. Ripping the page off, I tucked it into my shirt pocket.

Behind the desk on the wall was a cork board. Most of the notes were telephone numbers and business cards, but one scrap of paper said: Deanna Ascue—Purdy Correctional Center, spring of 1978 to January of 1979. Deanna Ascue? That couldn't be the maiden name of a woman I was growing attached to?

The steamer trunk in the bottom of his closet had a bulletproof padlock on it. I had seen them shooting steel-jacketed bullets at one on TV so it had to be bulletproof. I tugged the trunk out into the light and levered the hasp off with the crow bar, prying until I had torn an ugly hole in the lid where the rivets had been. Any hope of keeping my break-in covert was gone now.

I had broken the lock and it was probably filled with Bibles.

Inside I found three pairs of handcuffs, some old sweaters and a mashed spot in the clothing where it looked like a large book had lain until recently. The imprint in the sweaters was very clear.

Below the cuffs was a photo album, aged, the binding cracked. The Wheeler family album. The front page was devoted to yellowed newspaper articles about a husband-wife murder-suicide that had occurred forty years ago in Ravensdale, Washington. Wheeler had been raised by stepparents. When he was a child, his real mother had been murdered by her jealous husband—Sam's father—who, in turn, sent a bullet through his own gums and into his brain pan. A toddler at the time, after the murder-suicide Sam had been found asleep in another room by curious neighbors.

Fleeced by fate, Sam had lived his life under a cloud. The scenario two weeks ago at the Trinity Building had been a rerun of the Reverend Sam Michael Wheeler's own private nightmare.

I shifted my weight and I looked at my watch. Twenty-seven minutes. The cops might be here any second. I was cutting it close. Far too close.

Chinking open the blinds at the window, I glanced up and down the street.

It was just bald-ass luck that I looked out when I did.

Blue lights flashing a quarter of a mile away. The Renton police were on to me. Without sirens, they were racing up the street to apprehend the intruder. Perhaps gun him down. I had maybe fifteen seconds to escape.

Mrs. Wheeler was an alert hombre. She must have phoned the police as soon as she got to the hospital. Or maybe one of the neighbors had seen something suspicious. I had switched on a light or two. Damn, I was getting sloppy and careless in my old age. Kathy, who thought everyone over thirty was senile, had been warning me for five years about Alzheimer's. Breaking and entering. Tish, I could get a year in jail for this, maybe two.

Two at a time, I descended the stairs to the living room. I missed the last step, stumbled, twisted an ankle, and smashed into the wall. I hobbled to the back door, clicked it shut behind myself and sprinted in an ungainly gait to the woods.

I didn't slow down when I heard the deep-chested barking behind me.

A German shepherd. A police tracking dog.

Chapter Twenty-two

I SLAMMED THE DOOR of the pickup shut a split second before an indignant German shepherd galloped out of the brush and performed a little fox trot on his hind legs. His plump front paws chiselled curlicues of red paint off the side panel of my Ford.

"That's a new wax job, buddy."

Tongue lolling out the side of his ragged, yellowing molars, drool yo-yoing off his toothy jaw, he woofed in my face while I hastily cranked up the window.

After I had a sheet of safety glass between the Alsatian and myself, I woofed back, turned the engine over and eased the clutch in, trying not to churn up too much dust with my exit. The dog vacillated next to the Scotch broom and blackberry thickets, barking.

No shamus steaks tonight.

The officers had to be a good ways behind and if I was lucky they wouldn't figure out I was scramming in a vehicle until it was too late to pursue. They were probably still back at the house inspecting locks and cupping their hands against the windows. Years ago when I was wearing a uniform, that's what I would have done.

Not that they could trace me; I had worn rubber gloves during the burglary.

It wasn't until I was driving under the dirty, shadowy air of Seattle again that I began to relax. My right shoulder was killing me from slamming into the wall. Until now the pain had been blotted out by massive doses of uncalled-for adrenaline.

On Beacon Hill I parked in front of a Chinese restaurant. I went in to see how greasy the earpiece on the public phone was. My pants were still damp and sticking uncomfortably to my legs, but the people in the dark restaurant didn't seem to notice.

I pushed some coins into the black box and dialed.

"Kathy?"

"Thomas? Where are you? I've been calling madly all over town trying to find you. I've had a real bad feeling all afternoon. You all right?"

"Who rode a horse named Tarzan?"

She thought a minute. "Ken Maynard."

"You just won a free plane trip around Wayne Cody."

I told her where I was and asked her to meet me there.

"Are you in trouble?"

"I'm a little bruised, but no trouble. I ran into a minor snafu, but I'm out of it now."

"I never should have let you roam off on your own after we found that dead detective today. Your stupid machismo—code of the West and all that. You're out to avenge him, aren't you?"

"Listen, Mark Daniels didn't commit suicide. Somebody murdered him—and murdered the girl, too. I think I know who."

"Who? Can you prove it?"

"There's so much involved I don't even know where to start. I need you to kick this around with me. I always get ideas when I'm talking to you."

"Thomas, you're not still trying to pin some of this on Reverend Wheeler?"

"Whoever."

The line was silent for a few moments. "Thomas, you didn't like him from the moment you laid eyes on him. Some sort of male territorial dispute is my guess. Over Deanna Daniels. Don't quibble when you know I'm right. I took psychology in college. We're not that far removed from the apes. You know what the odor under your arms is for, don't you?"

"A signal to change my shirt?"

"The sweat glands are what apes use to stake out their territory, just like cats when they go around spraying. Apes rub their underarms on leaves and things.

"You males are all alike. You think I didn't see what was going on? Reverend Wheeler had her. You wanted her. He had staked out his territory. You wanted it. Well, it wasn't going to work out. You should have seen that from the first."

"You read me like a book, Kathy. Just come on over and see me."

"What . . . are you wearing a raincoat?"

"You *wish.* I'll order you a fortune cookie. If you leave now, you can make it in fifteen minutes. My head's spinning and what I need is for somebody I trust to talk this through with me. I'm right on the verge of busting this whole thing wide open."

"The detective and the girl at the lake? I spoke to Ralph Crum. The detective died the same way the girl did. A blow to the windpipe. They're connected to Mark and the Hindenburg girl?"

"Hop to it."

I slumped down in a booth under an ornate fire-breathing dragon stippled into the wall.

When the lady in the red silk sheath minced to my table I ordered tea. The dinner hour was long gone and most of the hired hands were in the back chewing the fat.

After the tea came I absent-mindedly inquired of the waitress if I could borrow the pencil stub tucked over her ear. She gave me a queer look and lined up the stub beside my teapot. After I scalded my tongue on the tea, I took out the slip of paper I had taken from the pad in Wheeler's study.

Selecting a steak knife from the silver setting the waitress had left, I chipped away at the pencil lead until I had enough pulverized graphite. Then I dabbed my index finger in it and rubbed it across the paper.

The etchings were pale, barely readable. I darkened them with the edge of the pencil. It said Trinity. There was a number: 9:30. And a name. I X-rayed it at the light, scanning the faint scrawls.

Then I bolted from the restaurant.

The wide-eyed waitress rushed after me and caught me at the door. I pushed a five-dollar bill into her hands and said, "A pretty brunette is going to show up in about five minutes. Tell her I had an emergency. Tell her not to worry."

As if English were a second language for both of us, the waitress nodded dumbly.

The Trinity plant was a place with a hex on it and I almost couldn't believe what I had read on the note paper. The name was barely distinguishable so there was a good chance I was in error. It had to be a mix-up. Sure, it was all a misunderstanding.

Spokane Street whisked me to Harbor Island quicker than I thought possible. It was 9:25 when I bolted out of the restaurant and 9:33 when I parked in the Trinity lot. Leaving my truck door ajar so as not to make any unnecessary racket, I switched off my headlights and trundled across the lot.

I could see that the lights were on in the warehouse, and farther back the lamps in the dog food plant were blazing, too. Inside the office building, only the lamps over the reception area were lit. The offices off the open balcony were all dark and shadowy except for one. It had belonged to Mark Daniels.

Quietly I ascended the carpeted steps and tiptoed down the hallway. The door was half open and the only sound coming out of the office was a radio tuned to some broken-voiced, sad sack crooner moaning about his cheatin' woman—a country-western station.

Crouched behind the desk, she was going through Mark's drawers, stuffing items in a series of cardboard boxes, her hair floating down past her waist, brushing the floor. She was dressed in khaki pants and a bright, short-sleeved blouse.

As soon as I saw her, the morning's clinches blurred through my mind at twice the speed of light. I remembered legs and kisses and hugs and stupid whisperings that had seemed momentous at the time, but rang with insincerity in my already-fuzzy memory. Rings around her eyes, she looked weary and saddened. I wanted to walk over and take her in my arms. I didn't budge.

When Deanna looked up at me she gave a start, traced her tongue around the outline of her fuchsia lips. "Thomas? How did you know I was here?"

As she spoke, she glanced behind the door. I followed her eyes.

The man said, "Howdy."

Grinning, Sam Wheeler stood behind me in cowboy boots, faded jeans, a rustic-looking shirt with a bolo tie knotted at his neck, topped off with a fancy, chalk-colored cowboy hat. Spiffy. He was duded up for a square dance. He imbued the manner of a TV newscaster who was shooting for the top of the heap—Network: He was genial, charming, and a bit opaque. He folded his arms across his chest and continued grinning, a twisted mixture of frenzy, gloating, and bald discomfort.

"Fancy meeting you here," he said, enunciating out the side of one cheek. Suddenly he was all apple pie and, wet and bruised as I was, I felt like the grease monkey who had stumbled into the wedding.

Gracefully, Deanna stood and, using the flats of both palms, smoothed the wrinkles across the front of her slacks. She took a wide swing with her head and flipped her hair behind her shoulder.

"What brings you here?" she asked, a hitch in her voice.

"I could ask you both the same thing."

"We're just . . ." Her mouth and throat went dry. "We're just cleaning up a few . . . a few things."

"I bet you've got a lot of things in your life you want to clean up."

Deanna shot me a hurt look and then glanced at Sam Wheeler.

Wheeler spoke, his words confident and brash. "Don't get uppity, Black. You don't have any business in this place or with this woman. You've overstepped your bounds one too many times.''

He moved toward me.

"I'm going to find out the truth about Deanna's husband.''

"Everybody knows what happened. It's an open book.''

"It will be very shortly.''

"What does that mean?'' Wheeler stepped closer. He was one of those rare scalawags who didn't seem to know when they were violating somebody else's personal space. Without fail, every time we met he blundered into mine. He stepped into it now and it was all I could do to keep from putting my fist into his face.

"Thomas, I asked you not to pursue this. I begged you.'' A tear squeezed out of Deanna's eye and starred her blouse. She looked like a woman standing over a fresh grave.

"Hear that,'' said Wheeler, tersely. "You've just been decommissioned. Buzz off.''

"Sam.'' She shook her head and repeated herself, speaking much more softly. "Sam.''

He looked at her and sneered. I wanted more than ever to plant a handful of knuckles into that smarmy face.

"Please leave, Sam. Remember what we said? Please leave.''

"You don't want me to go away, DeeDee. Things are going to be tough for a while. You don't want me to go away.''

"Get out, Sam!''

He pivoted and ran his pale blue eyes over my face, sizing up the opposition. "I could say some things.''

"You wouldn't, Sam . . .''

"Sure, I would. I'll bet Tommy here doesn't have an inkling, does he?''

"Sam, don't do it.''

"Why not? Some big secret? I could tell him a whole heck of a lot of things that might open his eyes.''

"You mean you might tell Thomas we had an affair? I was just about to do that myself.'' Deanna swerved her eyes frantically between Sam Wheeler and me, trying to gauge the voltage and meter of the electrical current in the air. She needed to know where she stood with *one* of us. I couldn't tell which one concerned her more, but her eyes seemed to be spending most of their time on me.

Sam didn't move. He didn't have to. I had been on the verge of lambasting him since I had walked into the room. What set me off was the mere cant of that goofy, thick-lipped smirk.

"Sure thing," he said glibly. "DeeDee's been my little sweetheart for quite some time now."

Swinging from my belt, I caught him under the chin with a steely left. It was just as much of a stunner to me as it was to him. I didn't even realize I was doing it until it was over.

He staggered back two or three steps, wiped his mouth, a look of fear on his mug. Blood wormed down his chin from a split in his lower lip. I almost laughed. What was an out-of-shape fat man going to do to me?

He turned his back on me, and too late, I realized it was a karate move, a very advanced karate move. You've seen it—the one where the man turns his back on his opponent only to pick up speed and swipe his head off with a high sweep of his leg.

Two walls and the ceiling lunged at me simultaneously.

As it happened I thought it must have been a freak earthquake mixed with some sort of extraterrestrial experience.

Then the floor reached up and snatched me hard, banging me with about a ton of force. When I tried to get up I found that I was lying partially under Mark Daniels' desk.

Woozy, eyes unfocused, I cocked my head up and thumped my forehead on the sharp corner of the desk. Sam Wheeler was standing over me, blood dripping from his chin, crouched in a battle posture, both arms winged out for combat.

"Get out, Sam," Deanna seethed between clenched teeth. "You are no longer welcome here. Now, get the hell out."

By the time I cleared the cobwebs and sat myself on the stainless steel and leather couch, the door was closed and I was alone in the room with Deanna Daniels. All I could smell was perfume and blood and maybe a little fear. My own. It seemed like I was losing all my recent skirmishes.

Life can be a kick in the chops sometimes.

Chapter Twenty-three

SHE SAT ON THE COUCH beside me—so close her weight sank me against her until I could feel the pleasant warmth of her thighs through my still-damp pants.

Ministering gently, she walked her fingertips across a part of my head that—from the inside—felt like a truck tire some ignoramus had chewed up on a curb.

"That awful boot of his made a nasty mark," she said, making me feel like a baby. It was a feeling I could grow used to. "Are you all right, Thomas? You had a faraway look in your eyes."

By degrees I screwed up my face and brought her into focus, forcing my roiling thoughts down to a mere simmer. In a minute I would get up and start a minor war with a small country. In a minute.

"I thought you were twins," I quipped. She laughed a quick, chittering laugh.

"Sam's a surprise a minute, isn't he? Somebody who knew how to fight taught him everything."

"So I see." I was lucky he hadn't gone bonkers and gouged out my eyeballs. Years ago I had seen a man in a back-alley brawl tap dancing on a pair of eyeballs. It wasn't pretty. Right now I felt like those gritty eyeballs.

Deanna had fetched a washrag and dampened it at the sink during the interlude when my brain was barnstorming the hinterlands. As she sponged off my feverish brow, I realized my neck was shot through with excruciating pinprick pains.

My right eye, swelling like the rupture in an inner tube, was taking in less every moment.

"Don't feel bad," she said. "You got in a good one."

"A good what?"

"A good lick. You gave him a real smart rap on the chin. It almost knocked him out. For a minute there I thought he was going down for the count."

"He seemed to have plenty of spunk left when *I* last saw him."

"You did fine."

"Did somebody kick me or was that a lettuce truck?"

Though I had initiated the joust, she was on my side all the way. Unhorsed and thoroughly thrashed as I was, here the fair maiden sat patiently at my side, comforting and consoling, patting me, soothing. Somehow it didn't vitiate the pain and humiliation.

"My arm was hurt earlier, see. And I haven't really been feeling all that hot. I've been running around all day . . . off my feed. A guy stabbed me this afternoon . . ."

"You don't have to make up excuses. I don't think any less of you because of what just happened."

The fat little pig, I thought. Where on earth had he learned something like that? Punctured ego. She was right. She was looking at me as if I were a prideful little boy who had taken a spill off his first two-wheeler, and what made it even more agonizing was that she was right.

"The little porker creamed me."

"Sam told me all about it. He was a fat kid and it seemed no one ever liked him. He used to get beat up about once a week. When he was a teenager he took every self-defense course there was. He still practices an hour a day, kicking and punching. That's where he met his wife—in a self-defense course."

I decided to make things better.

"How could you sleep with a jerk like that?"

Her vivid face went blank and, for a moment, I thought I had lost her for all time. Strangely, the thought panicked me. I stammered.

"What I meant was . . ." Smooth as silk; that was Thomas Black. Maybe I should write a book: *How To Win Any Woman With Nine Simple Words.* You silver-tongued devil of a detective, you. "By the way. Where did that little fat boy go?"

"Don't worry," Deanna said, flopping the washrag onto the desk. "I sent him packing." She gave me a look, a forgiving look; the old Deanna. She giggled. "And I doubt if his wife will show up."

"He'd never be able to do that move again. He just caught me off-guard was all. And I have this injury, see . . ."

"Sure, sure, sure," she said, stroking my brow with each word.

I stared at her. I was thinking a lot of thoughts, most of them not very generous, and they must have shown through the bruises on my face.

She looked away. She fluffed her blouse. She fiddled with her hair. She did everything but greet my eyes. I was angry with her because I was the big strong he-man and she had just saved my butt. If she hadn't been there, Sam might have done a lot of ugly trajectory experiments on my bones. It angered and frightened me to have been at the mercy of a pineapple like Wheeler. And the fact that a woman had rescued me was not encouraging. It made me angriest of all that she had slept with him. I had had my suspicions earlier and now my brain was rife with unwanted visions. She was athletic in her sex and it painted horrid pictures in my mind.

Staring at her hands while she fidgeted with the hunk of diamond on her ring finger, she said, "I believe I know what you're thinking. It didn't have anything to do with us. In fact, it was over before I met you."

"You spent a hell of a lot of time with him."

"It was just that Sam didn't know it was over. And after Mark's *incident* . . . I didn't know what was going on for a while there. You see, I went to him weeks ago when I thought Mark was stepping out on me. Mark beat me up and I thought he was seeing other women and I went to Sam for counseling."

"Sure, and he took advantage of this soft little cookie?"

"Yes, he did. He did! I was all mixed up. I didn't know where to turn. I was scared. You bet he took advantage of me."

"That's very hard for me to believe, Deanna."

"Why?"

"Because you're a big girl now. You know who you are and what you want. A guy like Sam doesn't come out of nowhere and cow somebody like you, not unless you're a willing participant."

"You *should* believe me. It's true. I've been reading about it. It happens to all sorts of women. It's a regular cliché in the counseling literature. The counselor who talks his patient into bed. 'We can work better together if we're closer as human beings.' "

"Is that what he said?"

"Something like that."

"And you fell for it?"

"That's right! I fell for it. Don't be so damned self-righteous."

"What made you think Mark was playing around in the first place?"

"I don't even know if Mark was playing around. That dead girl is the only real evidence I have."

"You just suddenly got suspicious?"

"Something like that."

"And you hired me anonymously?"

"I heard your name mentioned years ago when I went out on a blind date with a cop. Then I heard you mentioned again at Mark's attorney's."

"Somebody told me you had a temper yourself. Said something about you chasing Mark around the house with a pair of scissors."

She shrugged. "When somebody outweighs you by eighty pounds and they start knocking you around, you tend to want to fight back."

"Your maiden name wouldn't be Deanna Ascue, would it?"

"Where did you hear that?"

"A birdy."

"It was all a mistake, okay? I suppose you know it all?"

"Just about you doing time in Purdy."

"I was young and stupid, okay. Having an affair with my boss. He was twenty years older than I was. His wife went nutso and came after us with a gun one night in my apartment. She shot him. Killed him. Then she and I struggled and she got shot, too. I got the credit for the whole thing. I served time for manslaughter."

"But you were innocent?"

Deanna swung her greenish-browns around to give me a steely look. "If you loved me, you wouldn't ask a question like that."

"Don't expect miracles. I've only known you a few days, Deanna."

"Now, I suppose you think I sneaked out here, came in the back door and gunned down Mark and the girl?"

"The thought has crossed my mind."

She pouted, her cheeks drooping as if wires were attached to them, little gremlins tugging the wires at their whim.

"You don't know what was involved. I was so alone. I was so mixed up. And Mark was always off somewhere either at work or out to a ball game with his buddies. I was like a fifth wheel. He made me quit my job. He made me sell my Volkswagen. It was almost like I was a prisoner or something. In fact, I guess I was ready for something to happen when I got involved with Sam."

"Wait a minute. He knocked on the door this morning, didn't he? And the way he called out to you, it was almost as if he were expected. You had it all set up this morning to do your laps with him, didn't you? And then I came in and you decided I was more the thing for brunch. Cancel the ham and eggs. Think I'll have blackberry jam on rye toast this morning." Like a landlubber aboard ship, I carefully navigated toward the door.

Things were even more convoluted than I had imagined. Now I knew why she had been so adamant about getting me off the case. She hadn't wanted me, among other things, to find out about her and Sam. Had she been so involved with the Reverend that she killed Mark so they could carry on? Or had *he* killed Mark so they could continue? Had she been involved in the shooting?

At the door I took the knob in my hand and warmed it for a long while.

She was at Mark's desk and began mechanically sorting through the items she had laid out, pretending that I wasn't in her universe. I watched her for a long while.

"Deanna?"

She tidied up the articles she was stacking in the cardboard box, sniffled, and pointedly ignored me.

"Deanna? I'm sorry."

Turning her back on me, she opened the drawer in a small cabinet. She pulled out a photograph album and casually split it open. "Oh my God!"

"I've had a bad day, Deanna. I know that's no excuse but I'm a little dragged out. I broke into Sam's house about an hour ago."

Pivoting, she turned to me, her eyes puffy with crying. "Oh my God!"

I went to her and looked at the album, taking it out of her grief-stricken hands. She plunked down in the executive swivel chair and stared at the seventeenth planet in somebody else's solar system.

It was an album of Polaroid nudes. All teenage girls. Seven in all. The only ones I recognized were Beatrice Hindenburg and Kandy Darling. I quickly flipped the album over and scanned it for identification. Printed in block letters across the front of the cover with a blue ink pen was the name: M. Daniels.

I held it up for Deanna to inspect. "Is this you husband's album?"

"I dunno."

"How about this printing? Do you recognize it?"

It took her a long while to break off her conference with the gods. When she did she squinted at the name on the cover and said, "I dunno. It might be Mark's. He printed like that sometimes, I guess."

There were seven different sections to the book, a concoction almost like some oversexed adolescent pervert might glue together. The girls had been made to pose in the back seat of an automobile I didn't recognize, in a funky motel room which might have been the The Galaxie Motor Court Inn, or anywhere, and in this very office. All of them were young, too young for this sort of boondoggle.

"Have you been in here before, Deanna?"

"Not since it happened."

"I have. I didn't see this."

"What does that mean?"

"It means somebody put it here. And recently."

"The police might have taken it during the original investigation and brought it back."

"Yeah, they might have. But they didn't."

"Who did?"

"Somebody who wanted you to find it. Somebody who wanted you convinced that Mark was playing around, that he actually did kill himself. Maybe it was the somebody who pulled the trigger on your husband."

Deanna looked at me, searching my eyes. Then she stood up, packed the belongings she had gathered together, dumped the album into the carton and walked to the door with it.

"Deanna?" She opened the door. "I'm sorry about what I said to you. I shouldn't have snapped. I was way out of line."

"Sure, Thomas."

I watched her toss her luxuriant tresses across the shoulder of her blouse.

"Why was Sam here with you?"

"He's been ..."

"What? What has he been doing?"

"He's been pestering me. He wants to go to bed with me again. He says he can counsel me better if we're on an intimate basis."

"He's got his techinque down pat, doesn't he?"

"Please don't make fun of me."

"So what was he doing here?"

"This was neutral ground. I called him up and told him we weren't going to be seeing each other again. He began arguing. I told him to meet me over here so I could say my final goodbye to him. I didn't want him at the house again."

"You told him? Then what?"

"He stood there like a zombie. He didn't move and he didn't speak. Then you came. You goaded him. Then you hit him. He was already in a sour mood."

"Taught him a lesson, eh? Don't tangle with Thomas Black unless you want face wax all over your boots."

Deanna didn't smile. She twisted the knob, opened the door and went out, leaving only a dazzling whiff of her perfume to linger, dazing me with the keen memories it resurrected.

It took me a long time to get up the gumption to move.

I had made a mess of things.

Deanna was down on me.

Sam Wheeler was off in the dark beyond somewhere waiting for another chance to avenge his lost love and kick my head across the parking lot.

Things were getting muddled and I was too tired to sort them out.

Switching off the lights, I trudged downstairs and walked to the door. Deanna's Cadillac was gone. But Sam's look-alike Chrysler was still there. I turned and peered around the darkened office and atrium area. Nothing.

But there was something else, farther out in the parking lot, behind some alders: a Mercedes. I hadn't noticed it when I came in. Emmett Anderson's Mercedes. I could have sworn it hadn't been there when I arrived. It was empty.

He spoke from behind me, from inside the office complex.

"Okay, mister tough guy. Let's see what you're made of."

He pranced through the doorway from the warehouse, a fat and sassy cat stalking a mole. I was the bedraggled mole.

Chapter Twenty-four

I WAS WET AND WEAK and weary and my body was beginning to fester. I didn't need this. I didn't need a nighttime confrontation with *The Omnipotent Master of Kung Fu.*

Certain prissy and self-serving men could swagger with their bellies. A few pregnant women and some cops who swilled a lot of suds were good at it.

Sam Wheeler was better than most.

He dogtrotted toward me, his swollen watermelon gut held out pompously in front of himself like athletes held out their chests. Flushed and ruddy-looking under the haze of artificial light from the receptionist's desk, his face took on the aura of a glazed plastic mask. The weird mask of a boy's face that an old man might wear for a grizzly joke.

The lights in the warehouse behind him were blazing. No doubt he had been prowling through the factory . . . maybe prepping the freezer . . . getting it ready for another frozen dick.

"Got a little shiner there, huh pal?" he said, smugness seeping out of every pore.

"It was a nice little dance step. Well-executed with a good landing. The Yugoslavian judge gave you a 9.6."

"Quite the wise guy, aren't you, Black?"

I could have made a dash for my waiting truck, but he would have caught me when I slowed to open the building door. He was poised for flight on my part. It was funny how angry a smack in the kisser could make some people.

Though I had been cradling my sore right arm for the past

few minutes, I let it dangle, then shook it gently to get some blood in it. The pain was sharper than I imagined it would be.

Anderson was in the plant somewhere. I wondered if Sam knew it.

"Is this what they teach in the seminary? How to brutalize people?"

He snorted. "What are you worried about? Big strong piece of macho meat like you."

"Bible study has done wonders for your personality, TV star."

"I can quote a verse from every chapter in the Bible. Go ahead. Quiz me."

"I'll leave that to the little old ladies you gull and who send in money out of their social security along with a batch of brownies. I thought Deanna told you to leave."

"I never got any brownies."

"What were you doing in the factory?"

"Heard a noise. Just checking it out."

"The same way you were checking it out that Saturday morning with Beatrice Hindenburg?"

"What are you talking about?"

"You know damn well what I'm talking about. You were in this plant the day Mark and the girl were shot."

"Profanity doesn't impress me, Mr. Black. In fact, you won't impress me no matter what you do. And what is this fiddle-faddle about me being in the plant? An allegation like that is as stupid as it is ridiculous. It was a suicide."

"And so was Kandy Darling's death? And Butch Teets'? All suicides? A rash of suicides? Must be something Big Brother sprinkled into the food dyes, huh? Very convenient."

"You don't hit me in the mouth and get away with it, Black."

"This is all about a slap in the kisser. Sure. It doesn't have anything to do with the way your parents died."

That jibe stopped him in his tracks. I had been slowly backing up and he had been slowly pursuing, but my wisecrack halted him in his tracks. "What do you know about my parents?"

"Your dad got a little funny in the head and shot your mother, didn't he? Then shot himself. A thing like that lurks in your subconscious. Maybe someday when the opportunity presents itself, you might reproduce it, eh? A scenario like that sticks with a guy and someday he might see something close . . . and reproduce it. Like maybe with Mark and the girl."

"Nobody knows how my parents died."

"*I* know, Samuel. I know."

"My wife has never even been told. Where did you . . . ? You didn't . . . There's only one place you could have found that out." His baby-blue eyes widened as he stared at my insolent grin. I had to make it good. The way he handled himself in a bout it might be my last chance to be sassy. "Why, you bastard! You broke into my place."

I winked and tugged at the hem of my trousers. "You pee into that hot tub to get it to stink like that or what? You and your wife play golden showers?"

He was sputtering with anger. "You s-s-sneaking, lying bastard. You're so anxious to tie this business up . . . to confirm your silly little paranoid theories, that you broke into my place. Black . . . you're worse than a sorry excuse for a human being. You're despicable cow dung."

"Ow," I said, wincing at an imaginary prick of pain. "I'm going to need a psychiatrist to get this out of my system, Sam."

"Bastard."

"You counsel those little runaways and then when they're ripe for the plucking you sleep with them, don't you? Nice job. Good hours. Free sex?"

"If you want to play mind games, why don't you go play them with the little girly you had at the party. The goddamn lawyer with the twitchy butt."

"Profanity does not impress me, Mr. Wheeler."

Seeing that he was about to launch an attack, I made a hasty move for the doorway but the chubby man scurried forward and cut me off, his hands cocked like the dangerous weapons I knew they were. I backed into the atrium, into the gigantic waiting area with the long low couches and glass magazine tables. Now that he had cut off my retreat, Sam slowed down, relishing our sport of cat and mouse. It's always fun to be the cat.

"The album. That was your album, wasn't it? I saw a mark in your trunk where a book about that size had been hidden. Deanna told you to meet her here and you rushed over and slipped it into Mark's things. A neat trick. Very convincing too. If I hadn't already searched Mark's office once, I might have fallen for it."

A tic made both his long-lashed eyes squint and release, but not quite in synchronization. "Album?"

"You know what I'm talking about, fat boy."

"This is just between you and me, buddy," he said, stalking me, moving in a waddle.

How could a man that clumsy-looking fight so proficiently? All he had to figure out was where he wanted to stick me and how hard he wanted to do it. I wasn't a fighter. I won most of my scraps, but that was because I was careful in my selections, because I fought dirtier than I looked like I would, and because I had a rouser of a sucker punch and used it without waiting for my conscience to give the high sign.

Backing up, I reached into my jacket pocket and discovered the switchblade I had confiscated from Hung Doan's partner. I clutched the closed knife in my left fist, a talisman, an ally, a lump of surprise that I would try out as a sap and use for more vicious enterprises if that didn't work.

"You seduced Deanna when you were counseling her. You seduced the runaways, too, didn't you? The good Christian preacher. This isn't going to look good on the evening news."

"It ain't gonna be on the evening news, buddy boy."

"And then to cap things off, when Deanna told you to meet her, you rushed over and hid that album upstairs as if it belonged to Mark."

"What album?"

"The nudes. You don't have to play dumb, Sam. All you have to do now is kill me and you'll be scot free. Pretty good deal, huh?" I grinned. I was like that. Sometimes I made up little rhymes I wanted to say in front of the firing squad.

"Don't be absurd. I'm not going to kill anybody. I'm going to teach you a lesson, is all. A gentleman's lesson in manners. And as far as that album is concerned, you're right, I did put it up there. I wanted DeeDee to find it, but I didn't want to be the one to give it to her. Mark handed it to me weeks ago. Mark came to me for help. His whole life was jammed up. He had troubles with girls . . . young girls. He couldn't keep his hands off them. It was Mark, not me, you boob. He came to me for help, don't you see?"

"You were hitting on the teenaged girls you were supposed to be counseling. Beatrice Hindenburg. Kandy Darling. The four or five others that you had strip down so you could immortalize them in smeared Polaroid. You must have been using Mark's office. Years ago you hauled ice out of here. You had a key. You knew the routine. On a Saturday you thought you were safe. Nobody would be coming to work. Just sneak up for an hour or two of the old in-and-out on Mark's couch. Then Mark walked in and ruined it. He was shocked. Maybe he even threatened to expose you to the world. Mark was going to ruin you. So you ruined Mark."

"You . . . actually think I assassinated Mark?"

Plunging recklessly ahead, I said, "You counsel young women. Some of them are ripe for the plucking. You are tempted. So you succumbed to your temptations, you play bouncy-bounce one evening. You have a girl. And another. Pretty soon you're on a steady diet. But you're a cheapskate. You park under the Spokane Bridge and do gyrations in the back seat, but then they start building a new bridge and the place loses its sheen. Too many people. Too much dust. So, cheap as you are, you borrow your friend's office. Simple. One morning he catches you at it. You know that if the world at large ever heard about your secret life, your career would be ruined. So you take the easy way out and shoot Mark. Then you shoot the girl.''

Wheeler snorted a snort of contempt, of indescribable and unutterable disdain for me, for my theory, and for the fact that I was still squandering valuable oxygen meant for him. He contemplated my face carefully before replying, a half-smile of inexplicable contentment warping his thick, buttery lips.

''You detectives,'' he said. ''You really take the cake. This is good. This is really good. I'm going to have to use this in next week's sermon. You think I . . .'' He broke off and began giggling hysterically. He laughed long and hard, bobbling his rigid gut in one movement.

I let him finish the performance, if it was a performance. I didn't know anymore.

''Mark was having all sorts of troubles. He was bickering with his partner, Anderson. He had found out somebody in the plant was smuggling drugs. He didn't know what to do about any of these things. So he came to me. I tried my best, but I guess I failed him. *Mark* entrusted me with the album. He gave it to me out of shame.''

I shook my head. ''This just isn't hanging right, Sam. You were the one sleeping with the young girls. I know you were. You were Kandy Darling's sugar daddy. You took her up to the lake and you killed her, didn't you? Did she guess about you and her friend Beatrice? Did she get too close to the truth?''

''You're deluding yourself, Black. How do you account for the dead detective?''

''Easy. He was trailing Beatrice. He got your license number when he was tailing her, but he thought the car belonged to Mark Daniels. He just never bothered to check. Then after he met me and began to think there might be some hard cash in it, he backtracked and ran your plate. Knowing him, he probably tried to blackmail you.''

''Don't you think if I had really done all those things that I would admit it right now? I mean, after all, I could take your head off at the shoulders anytime I wanted.''

"You don't look like a confessor to me, Sam. You'll go right into your casket swearing you never played with yourself."

"I never did." He wriggled his nose nervously like a rabbit. He would never admit anything. Not playing with himself, and certainly not murder. But he was beginning to lose some of his composure.

"Ever since the day I graduated from high school I have desired nothing out of life other than to guide my fellow man to the Lord Jesus Christ. And you stand there and have the gall to accuse me . . . Do you want to know where that album came from? Mark Daniels gave it to me a week before he died. He told me he thought the old man, Anderson, was mixed up in this drug deal. He said some of the Orientals in his plant were selling heroin and he thought Anderson had something to do with it. He knew Anderson was sick and Anderson was taking the stuff for the pain."

Wheeler was beginning to make some sense. The way he was explaining it could easily have been the way it happened. Maybe he didn't seduce young girls. Maybe he had only seduced Deanna. And maybe Mark had come to him and had given him the album. I was beginning to see there was more than one way to put this jigsaw together.

And, of course, the morning of the first murders, who had been the first person on the scene? Anderson! I had watched him drive up behind Mark Daniels myself, had watched him go into the building and then summon the police. He had admitted himself that in his earlier years he had been a cutthroat. Daniels and Anderson had quarreled the week before the deaths. Maybe they had quarreled about the drug dealing.

The slow realization crept over me that what I had been uttering might just be totally preposterous, that I might be sucking on my own shoe leather in a moment.

There was a persistent ring of sincerity to Sam Wheeler tonight.

I hadn't noticed this particular strain in the man before,

but then Kathy had been right, I had been nursing a grudge ever since I laid eyes on him.

Beatrice had been sleeping with Mark Daniels. She just happened to get in the way. Kandy Darling must have been sleeping with the old man. He had killed her when she started cogitating too hard about her friend Beatrice's death. Or maybe he just panicked and slugged her in the throat. And Seymore Teets had cottoned to the drug dealing somehow and had wanted somebody to divvy up his share of the booty.

Teets had gone to Anderson and Anderson had iced him, so to speak. That accounted for why Anderson had been outside the freezer when Kathy and I broke out. The lying old booger had locked us in. Then he had gone somewhere in his car and come back to check. That's why the engine had been warm.

Sam Wheeler had moved very close now, watching my eyes complacently. I had the unopened switchblade in my left fist, had been planning to use it like a roll of quarters, to toughen my fist and harden my blows.

There was just one last nagging loose end. Where had the old man learned to kill with a blow to the windpipe? That seemed like something a martial arts expert would know, not an old man, even if he had been a hooligan in his youth. And the country-western album? These pointed to Sam, not Andy.

As I mulled it over, Wheeler's eyes enlarged and the gray pupils shriveled to pinpricks.

Was it my imagination, or did he have the cold and simultaneously frenzied stare of a snake about to strike? The well-modulated voice burst forth. "The Lord is my shepherd."

If I hadn't been so sore and tired and unguarded I might have escaped the blow entirely. I saw it in the nick of time. Not in time to escape, but in time to keep from being killed.

Wheeler hardly moved his body at all. Nor did his eyes flinch.

When he flicked his right hand at my throat, his fingers

were bent at the second joints into a deadly slicing axe of a weapon.

His intention was to shatter my trachea.

Kandy Darling's trachea had been smashed. Teets had died the same way.

Twisting, wrenching around, I belly-flopped onto the floor, grasped my neck with my bad hand, and bellowed like a strangling calf.

Collapse that rigid tube and you strangled to death. While a crowd gathered and some well-meaning soul who had seen too much phony emergency work on the tube said, ''Give him air,'' you just plopped down on the spot and slowly asphyxiated. Two minutes. Three minutes. Four. Flopping and gasping, clawing and scratching to open a pipe that was squashed flat. It was a hell of a way to go. Bluer than blue.

The gargling desperation in my snores sounded bad even to me. Though he hadn't crushed my trachea, any blow to the neck is painful, is bound to rupture vital targets. I was seeing stars. Tish, was I hurting, unworried about what was next on the agenda. Maybe he didn't realize he had missed. Maybe I could pretend to turn blue.

He booted me in the kidneys. The toes of his cowboy boots felt like needles. He kicked me in the spine and shoulders and hip and anywhere he could get a good shot in. The bastard was going to put the boots to me until I was dead. Turning blue wasn't fooling anyone.

''The Lord is my shepherd,'' he said, and then proceeded to repeat himself over and over, a litany of pain and destruction and obfuscation.

I could clearly hear Sam's stepfather decades earlier invoking the scriptures when he dragged the young whimpering Sam out to the woodshed and whaled the tar out of him.

That was the last thing Mark Daniels had said in the hospital. It hadn't been an invocation. It had been a clue. It had been the last phrase Mark Daniels had heard on this planet.

''The Lord is my shepherd.''

Chapter Twenty-five

HE HAD ALMOST conned me out of it, but not quite.

When he punched me it was because he knew I would have jigsawed the pieces back together—later—after I had time to reflect. So he simply moved first.

The famous Thomas Black Sucker Punch had been delivered to the originator. That was like Alfred Nobel getting blown up by TNT. Ben Franklin getting electrocuted. Henry Ford getting run down in four o'clock traffic.

I rolled across the carpet like a fallen tree that hadn't been debranched yet, my movements bumpy and uneven. He followed clumsily, kicking and missing and swiping at the air. Finally, I screwed myself behind a steel and leather sofa placed out in the open, bumped my head as I squeezed around it and pushed up to my feet, free. I could barely breathe, but I grasped my neck using both hands and pretended that it was even worse than it was. I was a pretty doggone good thespian when I needed to be. This stunt would give me a breather. I might even buy enough time to think up a plan.

He soared over the back of the sofa, feet poised to strike, screeching at the top of his lungs. He wasn't giving me time for diddly-squat. I dodged, wheeling to the side. A slashing foot brushed the hairs on my temple.

Before he could get his bearings and rise, I kicked at his kidneys. But in my haste and furor I missed, striking him squarely in the spine. He flopped forward and did a fancy

215

tumbling move and finished up on his feet, weight balanced, facing me.

"The trouble with these oriental fighting arts," Wheeler said, "is a guy never really gets a chance to use them. You won't believe how many times I've waited for somebody to jump me. But nobody's ever been stupid enough to do it."

"Until Kandy Darling and Teets," I said, grinning so hard my gums hurt.

"Until *you,* buddy boy. You just bought yourself a ticket to a low spot in hell."

"You killed them all, didn't you?"

Whooping and springing up into the air with a grimace on his face, he snapped off a kick at my testicles. A miss. I did a couple of basketball moves and eluded him. Then again. He began to wise up and alternate his blows, slashing with his hands, then kicking, then slashing, putting the combinations together the way his conscienceless master had taught him.

He riddled me with slaps and punches. He popped me in the thigh once and skirred a good one across my nose. Blood began dropping out of my nostrils and flowing across my lips. It tasted like a particularly dirty and bitter brand of sweat.

I threw a lamp at him, then a small chair, then a table, each movement electrifying my right shoulder in an excruciating series of prickling pains, as if I were tearing stitches out with my teeth. The tiny table swiped across his back and cartwheeled beyond him. He ducked, stumbled, held his back with one hand, swore, and came at me quicker and clumsier than ever, the nimbleness abandoning his limbs.

Scuttling over to a large conference table in a corner, I managed to get it between Sam and myself. I grabbed it with both hands and sledded the six-by-twelve table at Sam's legs. He wasn't expecting an attack, and it caught him by surprise, slamming into his thighs and almost knocking him down.

Before he could sidle around it, I went through a door that led into a copier room and then through that into the warehouse. The lights were all on. I scrambled through the stacks of cartons and past steel wire baskets of shiny unlabeled cans, passing various spots where I might have stopped and drygulched him.

I was scared. Sam was good.

The pop to my nose hurt as much as anything had in a long while. I would be one very lucky buckaroo if it wasn't broken.

A door banged behind me. The lights blinked off and then came back on. Sam was so panicky he didn't even know if he could see, had flipped the lights off by mistake. That was good. He was almost as jittery as I was.

I grabbed three cans out of a bin and lobbed them in Sam's general direction. I doubted if I would connect, but I might slow him down. I heard all three clip the concrete in a syncopated stutter. All misses.

Making my way to the other end of the warehouse, skipping across rows of stacked merchandise so he couldn't track me, I found the door where Hung Doan and his cronies had been waiting Sunday morning. I heaved it open and slogged into the dog food factory. The lights were on in there, too. I saw no trace of Emmett Anderson. I only hoped that when we barged in on him he would have a gun.

Then I saw the wooden stairway along the wall. I had never noticed it before. My guess was it led up into an old office complex, something that was probably vacant or reserved exclusively for storage now.

I scrambled up the steps, breathing hard, my throat aching. I mopped a gob of blood off on my sleeve, stunned at how badly I was bleeding. The reddish torrents were pattering down my shirt front and my pants as well. In fact, I was leaving a trail of dribbles like an errant painter with a hole in his paint can.

It was a dead end.

I was in a high, dusty, unused room overlooking the factory. It had been the boss's office once. Now it was stacked with cartons of files, thirty years of files. I had broken one of my own maxims and forged into the unknown at a time when I needed all the hole cards. It only showed how weary I was. A cartoon belonging to one of the former occupants hung on one wall. It read: "It's nice to be important, but it's more important to be nice."

Sam was at the top of the stairs behind me before I knew it. He had moved silently and efficiently, holding his breath on the climb. He was paying for it now, standing in the doorway in a half-squat, arms cocked for action, his lungs pumping overtime.

I moved toward him, feigned a left hook and kicked at him. He sidestepped, breathed harder, and kept his beady eyes on me.

He was good at not telegraphing what he was about to do. Very good.

He launched a kick at my face. I stepped back and felt the wind from his foot on the wetness on my face. When he landed he slipped. I laughed until I saw what he was slipping on. It was *my* blood. Good strategy. Bleed him to death. Another pint or two and he might fall down and kill himself.

Coming in fast, he struck at my face, missed, connected hard with my ribs and then did some sort of flying pirouette and knocked me down with his leg. My knee felt like a glass jar somebody had just shattered with a ball-peen hammer.

I rolled. It didn't take me far. Sam knew he had me now. He wasn't even concerned about getting it over with. It was all finished but the goodbyes.

He came close, bent over me, made a fist and held it up next to his grinning teeth. My south end began to pucker.

As he rammed his fist at my solar plexus with all the force he could muster, he heard the click—but he heard it too late. He completed the blow.

We stared at each other, our faces inches apart. He had dosed himself from a mouth spray before meeting Deanna. It was wearing off now. It took him a moment to figure out what had happened. I had flicked open the switchblade and he had crashed his fist straight into it.

He gaped in disbelief. He had punched straight down on

the pointed knife blade. It was buried to the hilt between the middle two knuckles of his right fist.

Hissing, he flew back, propping up his right arm at the elbow, gaping at the horror. After the blade had entered between his knuckles, it had kept right on going, had shimmed under the palm of his hand and continued into his wrist, piercing right up under the tendons. I could see the welt it made under his skin, as ugly a thing as I ever viewed.

"You have to be careful around knives, Sam."

Unbelieving, he sucked air through his teeth and carefully held the wicked apparition a foot in front of his eyes. He winced, whimpered, and finally wailed.

I crawled away, picked my broken body up and braced it in the doorway.

He knelt. I thought at first it was to pray, but he used his good hand to hoist up his jeans past one stitched white cowboy boot inlaid with designs in turquoise. Then he dug into the boot. I wasn't thinking. It felt like I hadn't been thinking for a year. Everything had gone wrong. And my mind was as dull and dumb as a medical resident after a 48-hour shift.

Laying a porcine look on me, he withdrew a small, lumpy, ugly revolver from his boot, reached across his pudgy body, pointed it at me and jerked the trigger. A splinter of wood exploded off the doorway and whirred past my face.

I dove for the stairs.

He squeezed off more rounds, but I didn't bother to keep track of how many. A crazy vertigo ripped my consciousness from its roots. I was falling. Tumbling. Twisting. Spinning down the stairs. Some giant brat had picked up the dog food factory and was rolling it down a hill and I was inside whirling like a pebble in a tire. Twirling and spinning until I was a broken mess. Until I was asleep, dreaming a fantasy about Deanna and her swimming pool and her luscious bare swimmer's shoulders. It seemed like we swam together almost forever.

Chapter Twenty-six

I REGAINED CONSCIOUSNESS the way a lazy bubble rises to the surface of an oil tank, with a slow, fluid and inexorably wavy motion.

An emergency paper blanket, its plastic wrapper crinkling, was propped under my head like a rolled cigar and an old scratchy wool army blanket was tucked tidily around my outstretched legs. My ribs sang at me when I inhaled and exhaled.

Listening to them was so much fun I kept right on inhaling and exhaling.

Half my face was swollen and tight. My right shoulder felt as if it had been torn out of its socket and hastily reinserted by a giant ghoul, but my mind was amazingly limpid.

Lying in what must have been the exact spot where I had crashed and burned, I looked across the aisleway at a long flat conveyor system lined with metal rollers. The thunderous machine that ran the conveyor was on, though the conveyor itself was motionless, thousands of gleaming tin cans queued up. Several other motors in the empty plant were humming, clanking or whinnying. The humid smells of cooked grain assailed my senses.

Exploring the back of my skull with my fingers, I discovered a lump just over and encroaching upon my left ear. It felt like a rotten pomegranate. It took a while before I recalled what had happened.

I had lunged for the stairs, lost my footing and knocked myself silly on the tumbling descent.

220

According to my watch, which had slid around the wrong way on my wrist, over three hours had passed. It was after midnight.

It wasn't until I shifted my weight that I realized how bruised and shattered I was. By rights, I should waste the rest of the night in a hospital bed. Maybe the rest of the week.

Moaning, I rolled onto my face and folded upward until I was on my hands and knees. Using my left arm, I gripped a piece of the apparatus above me and hoisted myself up. I stood alone in a factory full of buzzing machines, feeling the heat blasts from the large cylindrical baking ovens I knew were around the corner.

It took more than a minute before my blood pressure was constant enough so I could move without fear of listing and fainting.

Woozy and disoriented, I looked around for signs of Sam Wheeler. I tottered across the way to where one of the machines had what I would have sworn were bullet pocks stippling its green paint. On the glassy smooth concrete floor I spotted a drop or two of blackish blood and five empty .44 shell casings. Bending laboriously, I picked them up one by one and clicked them together in my fist. I sniffed them. Freshly fired. Sam had not shot at me with a .44. His gun had been a smaller caliber, possibly a .38. These shell casings were from another weapon, somebody else's.

"There you are," he shouted.

The old man strode toward me in his studied bowlegged gait, grim and somber, and more mellow than I had seen him in a while. He picked the brass casings out of my hands, bobbled them like popcorn seeds in a cooker and slid them into the pocket of his long white lab coat. They clinked like a handful of broken teeth. "Forgot about these."

"Where's Wheeler?"

Emmett Anderson didn't reply, only grasped me gently by the chin and the top of my head, tilting my skull and inspecting the damage. "You took a pasting, there. Big guy like you? Seems like you should have been able to take a little smartass fat boy.''

"I might have taken him, but I had a bum horoscope for today. Where is he?"

"Don't fret. Ain't no big boogyman gonna jump out and snatch you. You mosey back to the office with me, I'll get another chemical ice pack for that face. I had one on you, but it give out after a spell. Can you walk?"

Mildly insulted at the inquiry, I said, "I can walk. I can't jog, but I can walk.''

Tall, dignified, and a bit sad-looking tonight, Emmett Anderson strode in front of me, picked up the trappings with which he had been caring for me and led me to the glass-walled office in the center of the plant.

During the trek I noted that almost every machine used in the canning process was either turned on or looked as if it had been run recently. Behind the modern labeler sat an old-fashioned wooden-slatted hand truck. On it were four huge steel mesh crates of chrome cans waiting to be labeled. Probably three or four hundred pounds of cans.

In the glass-walled office Anderson cleaned me up with alcohol wipes, working to the brassy sound of a female country-western singer on the radio. Then he peeled my shirt away and swabbed out the knife wound on my shoulder. To keep from screaming, I clenched my teeth until old fillings squeaked and pinged in my mouth.

"How'd you get this?"

"Hung Doan and his friends. I went up to see them this afternoon. Seems like they were dealing drugs. Doan took a couple of pot shots at me. His colleague decided I was full of hot air.''

"So he stuck you?"

"Just a scratch.''

"Another quarter-inch and he would have pinned you to a wall. Your little tussle with Wheeler probably didn't help this incision any."

"Somebody made a big mistake and taught him how to fight.''

"I noticed that when I spoke to him. That's why I pulled out this." Anderson lifted the lab coat and, using two fingers, patted the ornate walnut handle of a Ruger .44 caliber pistol tucked into his belt. "Trouble was, the little shit had one of his own."

"He nick you?"

Anderson touched a finger to a dark lumpy spot on his scalp. It was already scabbing over pretty good. "It ain't nuthin'. What brought you down here?"

"I'd ask you the same thing, Andy."

"Me? I knew Mark didn't do himself in. And it hurt that he died up there in ICU. It hurt real bad. I spent most of last week up there in the hospital room waitin for him to wake up. That little fart Reverend came in and gave me a couple of lectures on the power of prayer. Even then I wanted to put a corkscrew in his eye. At one time Mark . . . he was like a son to me. We been bickering of late, but I was hoping we would be pals again, know what I mean?" He squinted his gray eyes at me.

"I think so."

"I thought on it and I thought on it, but it wasn't until you found that bugger in our freezer that it hit home. You know that box you found him in? That was a zany old ice-making contraption Sammy Wheeler used right back there in that same corner of the freezer years ago when he delivered ice blocks out to his folks' store. Hell, that box had been kickin' around here for ages and I don't think but three of us here knew what it was used for."

"And Sam was one of the three?"

"Yep. He used to throw a tarp over the box just the way it was done today. I drove out to his place this evening. Figured to do a little sleuthing myself. Followed him here to the plant. That really piqued my curiosity. Then I seen Deanna come in. Then you. I went around back and slipped in that way."

"So you were here all along? How much did you hear?"

"Not a damn thing. I was too far away. I figured you two

was in a ruckus, but I couldn't quite get a bead on it until he fired."

"So where is Sam?"

"I was like you. I thought I could beat him to death. Little fat boy. Surprised the hell out of me. I saw you boogy down the stairs. Then he tried to put one into your eyeball. Took aim and tried to slide one right into your occipital bone. I called out to him before he could fire. He saw me and the party commenced. Guess I took a stray across my scalp. After he emptied his pistol, I had the goods on him. I figured to punch out his lights. But he got close and jumped up in the air and did some sort of whirly thing. Almost took my head off with his boot. I think if he hadn't had them tight jeans and cowboy boots and a knife buried in his hand he would have decapitated me."

I was surprised he hadn't. A karate expert pitted against an old man. And the old man was standing here chatting; the karate expert was missing. Anderson obviously could take care of himself. Back in his prime, he would have been a man not to run up against.

"What happened to Wheeler?"

The old man didn't reply, merely went about his work— shutting the ovens down, turning off the machinery, flicking switches a machine at a time. I traipsed behind him, tagging along through the whole factory area. There was absolutely no sign of Sam Wheeler. Not a gun, not a cowboy boot, not a Bible in sight.

When everything was shut down and he had cut most of the lights, Anderson grabbed the wobbly handle of a dolly that was loaded with baskets of jumbled, unlabeled dog food cans. He towed it into the warehouse section.

"You been in here working, or what, old man?"

"Takes my mind off things. I come down here and do things once in a while."

He shut the main breaker off in the warehouse, led me through the office complex and outside to the parking lot. It was dark and Harbor Island was deserted. Three vehicles were in the lot. My truck. Anderson's Mercedes. And the

Chrysler that belonged to Sam Michael Wheeler. Until this moment I still cherished the notion that the old man had driven Sam Wheeler off, that he had left of his own volition, was scampering off to find a lawyer.

After the old man accompanied me to my truck, I said, "Where is he?"

He had been wheezing, so it took him a while to answer me. When he did it wasn't with words. He turned around and stared at the Trinity Building. I did the same.

"In the ice?" I asked.

The old man squinted in the darkness, an expression partially of satisfaction, partially of angst.

"You wouldn't do a thing like that?"

He grunted.

"What? Did you shoot him?"

Anderson wheezed as he spoke. "Didn't have any shells left. But he didn't know that. I made it as slow as a day in perdition. He knew it was coming and he whimpered like a puppy been boot-stomped. You would have enjoyed it."

"Don't count on that. Did he tell you anything?"

"Couldn't talk fast enough. Fact was, he didn't even get it all out in time. Didn't bother me none. I ain't writin' none of this in my diary. I save that for important things like when the milkman run over the cat."

"He told you he killed Mark?"

"Admitted he did that. Killed that detective and the girl up at the lake too. Admitted it all. No one else involved, just him. Started going into some hogwash about being an almost perfect double for Mark. Something about being mistaken for him a couple of times, especially when he was wearing clothes Mark gave him. I didn't catch it all. A false beard? You know anything about that? He wanted to stand in the bottom of that goddamned grinder and talk all night but I told him I had business to attend."

"The police are going to want to know where he is."

"Tell 'em to use this," said Anderson, handing me a small, chrome-plated implement. Breathing hard, he hobbled to his car, fired up the engine and drove out of the lot.

I watched the Mercedes sail down the midnight-dark street until it disappeared. The old man said Sam Wheeler had been standing in the bottom of the grinder. Not the enormous cast-iron meat grinder that chunked beef quarters into bite-size tidbits so the rest of the machinery could handle it and grind it into dog meal? Those steel mesh baskets had been stuffed full of freshly packed dog food cans. Cans that had been packed tonight. Fish flavor? Chicken flavor? Baptist flavor?

I looked down at the instrument in my hands. A can opener.

Good Lord.

Chapter Twenty-seven

Two WEEKS LATER my face had pretty much knitted up, and so had most of the other legion knots, bumps, and contusions that had been inflicted on me.

My only souvenirs of the case were a purplish, puckered indentation on my right shoulder and a tiny dark echo that kept ricocheting inside my head like the refrain to an exasperating song I couldn't rid myself of. The echo was a woman's laughter—nervous laughter, like water boiling over rocks.

I hadn't seen Deanna since the night at the plant, had been told she had left town to visit her mother.

It took a bit of convincing, but with Kathy's wooing thrown in, Ralph Crum finally came to believe that the Reverend Wheeler might have had something to do with both Beatrice Hindenburg and Kandy Darling. One of Darling's ex-roommates identified a photo of Wheeler as the man Kandy had been seeing for the past few months.

At the Galaxie Motor Court Inn both the proprietress and the two geeks next to Unit 12 identified a full-color picture of Wheeler as the man who had visited there several times with Beatrice Hindenburg.

Reluctantly, Crum had somebody dust the motel room and they found both Hindenburg's *and* Wheeler's fingerprints. They didn't find any of Daniels' prints. That was the point that began to sway Crum.

At the Daniels roost on Lost Lake they found Wheeler's

prints on the stereo and the toaster, as well as a track from his Chrysler in the muddy yard.

When Ralph Crum made an effort to interrogate Wheeler and found that he had vanished, the district attorney's office put out a warrant for his arrest. He was implicated in two separate murder cases and now he was missing. I never told anyone else what had happened to him—not Kathy, not the cops, not my telephone analyst. They found his car at the plant, but nobody knew what to make of it.

What was the point? The world didn't have to know how Wheeler had died. I got nauseated thinking about it myself. I went back to the plant a day later and searched it thoroughly. I found a pair of rings I recognized as Wheeler's, his wristwatch, the cowboy boots, his jeans and shirt. Anderson had stripped him down to his BVDs and made him stand in the grinder.

The machine was about the size of a double bed, tall, with a funnel-shaped apparatus on the top. Threatening Wheeler with an empty revolver, Anderson must have made him climb into the funnel and sweat. Sam had talked his head off, hoping it would save him. Anderson must have mercilessly switched on the machine and waited for the scrambling minister to get a piece of his anatomy caught in the whirring blades at the bottom. One piece would be all it would take. The blades would pull him in and do the rest.

Then the old man had processed the results the same way he would have processed a hunk of beef.

The suicide-murder ruling in the Daniels case was officially changed to murder-murder, though the case would never be officially cleared.

I squandered my time turning down a couple of teenage runaway cases where the parents swore their children were prostitutes. I also declined to make a secret tape recording of a man's wife making loud love to one of the neighbors in The Highlands so the disgruntled husband could play it over a loudspeaker at his wife's company picnic. I was glad I stayed out of it. A week later there was a shooting at a company picnic out at Lake Sammamish.

When Kathy Birchfield's workload finally slacked off at Leech, Bemis and Ott and she got some time to spend with her old friends, she and I made bleary-eyed appearances at the month-long Seattle Film Festival. She began attending almost nightly with me. Together we indiscriminately viewed everything that wasn't already sold out. The crowds were chatty, vibrant, cosmopolitan—dressing and speaking weirdly enough to hold our interest if the movies were duds. We heard directors and actors tout their latest extravaganzas.

One night after a subtitled horror flick from Bulgaria, Kathy met a gentleman she knew from her business dealings, and, as per our standing agreement, she went off with him to share a bottle of red wine and some inspiring whisperings. I skulked home alone.

The next night at a delightfully goofy French comedy about two best friends sharing the same woman, Kathy told me he had been no great shakes and in fact, she hadn't gone home with him, but had abandoned him at the bistro where they had sipped wine for an hour.

After the final credits rolled on the French comedy and we had dutifully clapped in appreciation and began filing out, I heard something strangely familiar. It was a bubbly, effervescent laughter coming from somewhere in the crush behind us.

The echo that had been zinging around inside me for weeks suddenly grew louder.

I whirled and spotted the top of her strawberry-blonde head bobbing in the crowd behind us. She was conversing animatedly with two other women.

Outside on the sidewalk, I pulled Kathy Birchfield to the edge of the building. She gave me a startled look.

"Last night was your turn," I said, scouring the crowd as it thinned out and straggled past. "Tonight is mine."

"You see a friend?" Kathy asked, as she caught a glimpse of Deanna Daniels strolling past, sandwiched between her two chums. "Oh, Thomas. Not this again. Not *her.*"

"I'm going to take her home. Maybe you could find your own way."

"Sure, you can try. But I hate to see you get dumped on when all these people are watching."

"Dumped on? I can feel the electricity from here. Dumped on?"

"You need help telling when somebody is giving off signals, Thomas. I'll help you all you need. But you can't tell by yourself. You see, when two people are giving off the right chemistry, it's obvious to almost everyone around. I myself would know if she liked you. You just have trouble reading the signals."

"Let's just go say hi."

Reluctantly, she followed my lead. We caught the trio of women as they were about to bend into a Volvo station wagon, doors winged open.

Softly, I said, "Hello, Deanna."

All three women turned around at once, but only Deanna reacted. She dropped both hands to her sides, sighed, and suddenly ceased smiling. Deanna glanced at Kathy, nodded timidly and then focused fully on my face. Under the streetlight she looked better than she ever had.

Kathy looked up at me to see how I was taking my rebuff.

Introductions were made, ponderously, politely, and we all smiled and finally Deanna stepped close, looked up at me and said, "I had to be away by myself for a while."

"Sure."

"I heard you were hurt."

"I'm okay." I winked. "You wanta see my scars?"

"Maybe we should *all* go have coffee somewhere," suggested one of Deanna's companions gaily.

Deanna Daniels slowly turned around and looked at her friends. "No, I don't think so. You'll have to excuse me, but I have some things to talk over with Thomas. I'll get home some other way. Thanks, girls."

"You sure, DeeDee?"

"I'll drive you home," I volunteered, sounding a bit too eager.

Kathy caught the zeal in my tones. She bobbled her eyebrows at me when she thought nobody else was looking and bestowed a slow, sinking, sideways look like a mother eye-scolding a toddler.

Deanna stepped over and grasped my arm possessively. I grinned. First, I grinned at Kathy and then I grinned at all concerned. "I'll call you tomorrow, Kathy. Good thing you brought your car, huh?"

"Yeah," she said, gaping in disbelief. "It sure was." Her little red two-seater was parked a block away. Deanna and I stood on the sidewalk amid the thinning movie theater crowd and watched her wheel away. She tooted at us and zipped past.

"She's pretty," said Deanna.

"Yeah, I know."

"You two must know each other very well."

"Real well."

"So," said Deanna, giving my arm a squeeze.

"So."

"I'm nervous."

"Me, too."

"I missed you. I didn't . . . Maybe I shouldn't have left, but I had to get things cleared up in my head. I needed a spacer."

"I understand. I was a little on the rotten side."

"No, you weren't. I believe I know exactly what you were thinking."

"Rotten."

"Okay, you were rotten. But you had a certain right to be."

We ended up in a late-night restaurant on Broadway, one of those atmospheric joints with blue and orange lighting, cigarette smoke piped in through the air-conditioning, where they put tiny chairs and tiny tables out on the side-walk when the weather permitted so the customers could suck exhaust fumes while they sucked Bloody Marys.

Deanna had a Scotch and water and I swigged my usual soft drink.

"Everything is so mixed up in my head," said Deanna Daniels, touching me across the table. I fingered the freckles on the backs of her hands. Wherever she had been during the past two weeks, she had been getting sun. "Sam ran away? Is what the papers were saying true?"

"I'll lay it all out for you, Deanna. Your husband wasn't exactly Mr. Faithful, but he was not cradle robbing. *Sam* was. With girls. Teenagers. But he was too cheap to get an apartment or go to a motel . . . at least not until it was absolutely necessary. At first he took these young girls out in his car. When that got old he used your place at Lost Lake. Then he began using Mark's office. He had keys to the building from years ago. One day he was up there and Mark walked in on him. He probably heard him coming, took Mark's gun and stood behind the door. When Mark walked in they had words. Mark threatened to expose him. So he shot Mark. Then he put the gun in Mark's hand and shot the girl, making it look as if Mark had fired both shots.

"No doubt he had some clever scheme hatched up to get rid of both bodies, but Emmett Anderson walked in about that time and Sam scampered out the back way. I was watching the plant too, but he must have had his car parked around the back by the railroad tracks. He could go out that way and nobody would see him from in front."

"You mean Mark was killed almost on a whim? Because he happened to show up at his own office at the wrong moment?"

"That's right. I'm not ruling out some ulterior motives either, like maybe the fact that if Mark was gone, Sam might have you all to himself. Surely, that crossed his mind.

"He'd been thinking a lot about Mark lately. He looked like Mark and he wore Mark's castoff clothing and I guess somebody mistook him for Mark a time or two, because he got himself a neat little theatrical beard and wore it when he checked into the motel. And he signed himself in as M. Daniels. I guess he figured it was safer than using a complete alias like Elmer Fudd or something. In fact, it saved him for a while. The detective who followed Beatrice Hindenburg for her father surely would have tried to blackmail him if he'd known he was the Reverend Samuel Wheeler.

"When I came to your house and got the keys that first morning, somebody called Hung Doan and told him his personal enemies had hired a torch to come in and burn down his livelihood. Only two people knew I was going to be there that morning—you and Sam.

"After I spoke with Kandy Darling she must have got to thinking. She must have known Sam and Beatrice were seeing each other from time to time. And surely Sam had taken her up to Mark's office, too. Maybe she didn't actually figure anything out. Maybe Sam just panicked. But he took her up to your place at the lake, beat her up and then killed her."

"God," said Deanna. "He must have just been a little bully at heart. But how could he preach one thing and live another? Does that make sense to you, Thomas?"

"Life is a bitch."

"What about this other person that got killed? The detective?"

"Teets had followed Beatrice Hindenburg. In fact, he had seen them together in Wheeler's car. But he mistook it for a Cadillac. After he saw me he must have run the plates and decided if the Reverend Wheeler was running around with sixteen-year-old girls like Beatrice, maybe he had a little spare cash. Sam met with him, probably at the closed-down Trinity Plant, and killed him. Later, when Kathy and I went to the plant, Sam locked us in the freezer by jamming the door with a forklift."

"This whole thing is the worst experience of my whole life," said Deanna.

"It wasn't one of my brighter episodes."

"One of my girlfriends told me I should find a cute little beach boy and take some of this insurance money and run off to the Bahamas for three months. You wouldn't want to be my little beach boy, would you?"

"Not my style." She laughed. It was high-pitched and agitated and several males at nearby tables looked over, wondering how I had captivated this entrancing woman. "I might go for a little midnight swim, though."

"A midnight swim? That might be just the ticket. But you're not . . ."

"Serious? Long-term? That sort of thing?"

"Yes."

"I don't know. You?"

"I don't know either."

On the drive to her place, she scooted across the seat and kissed my ear wetly. It resurrected hot memories.

"There's just one thing that bothers me. The police said all of Sam's assets are intact. His wife claims nothing is missing from the house. He's gone, but apparently he didn't take anything with him. Where is he?"

I shrugged. It was one of those suburban mysteries. The *Seattle Times* would run a feature article on it once every five years.

Of course they never would find him. The old man, Anderson, wasn't going to squeal on his own savage vengeance. And besides, his health was failing. I wasn't going to squeal on him. Before the courts could finish him, his own biology would do the job. What was the point in bothering everybody? The courts and police were already swamped. The newspapers already had enough grisly stories. He would be dead in another few months. I didn't have the heart or the righteous indignation to blab it to the authorities—not that they would have believed me, or been able to trace the corpse.

A task force of squeamish detectives wielding electric can openers and forks might get lucky and find part of some bridge work, or a scrap of bone, but I very much doubted it.

Wheeler was in cans, in packing boxes, on grocery shelves, in shopping carts, and in cupboards all up and down the coast. He was gone for good. Before the summer was over he would be spread across the lawns of five western states. I guess that's what they call the greening of America.

AN EXTRAORDINARY CREW REACHING FOR THE STARS . . .

FRANCIS R. SCOBEE, Commander: 46, aerospace engineer, Vietnam combat pilot. As a child, he drew pictures of airplanes. He flew more than 6,500 hours in 45 kinds of aircraft. "It's a real crime to be paid for a job that I have so much fun doing."

JUDITH A. RESNIK, Mission Specialist: 36, with a doctorate in electrical engineering, she was the second American woman in space. "I want to do everything there is to be done. . . . I'll never get old."

ELLISON S. ONIZUKA, Mission Specialist: 39, engineer, Air Force test pilot. He grew up in the coffee fields of Hawaii, dreaming of spaceflight. "I'll be looking at Halley's Comet . . . one of the best views around."

MICHAEL J. SMITH, Pilot: 40, a much-decorated Navy flier, he won his pilot's license before he knew how to drive a car. "I can never remember anything I wanted to do but fly."

GREGORY B. JARVIS, Payload Specialist: 41, engineer, satellite designer for Hughes Aircraft Company, he was bumped from two previous flights. Now his moment had finally come. "I feel very, very comfortable. I'm excited, but not nervous."

RONALD E. McNAIR, Mission Specialist: 35, MIT physicist, second black American in space, karate expert, musician. "True courage comes in . . . believing in oneself."

CHRISTA McAULIFFE, Teacher: 37, she won a nationwide campaign to select the first teacher in space, and captured the hearts and imaginations of all Americans. "I touch the future. I teach. . . . We're reaching for the stars."

By the staff of
The Washington Post

✦✦✦✦✦✦✦✦✦✦✦✦✦✦✦✦✦✦✦✦✦✦✦✦✦✦✦✦✦✦✦✦✦

CHALLENGERS:

THE INSPIRING
LIFE STORIES OF THE
SEVEN BRAVE
ASTRONAUTS OF
SHUTTLE MISSION 51-L

✦✦✦✦✦✦✦✦✦✦✦✦✦✦✦✦✦✦✦✦✦✦✦✦✦✦✦✦✦✦✦✦✦

PUBLISHED BY POCKET BOOKS NEW YORK

Another *Original* publication of POCKET BOOKS

POCKET BOOKS, a division of Simon & Schuster, Inc.
1230 Avenue of the Americas, New York, N.Y. 10020

ISBN: 0-671-62897-6

First Pocket Books printing March, 1986

10 9 8 7 6 5 4 3 2 1

Printed in the U.S.A.

Contents

Acknowledgments

Shortly after the space shuttle *Challenger* exploded on January 28, 1986, *The Washington Post* assembled a team of reporters and asked them to find out about the seven men and women who were killed on Flight 51-L. Soon after that, Pocket Books approached *The Post* with the idea for a book about the *Challenger* Seven, men and women whose dreams and motivations provided insights into the history of the U.S. manned space program and the history of American life over the past twenty-five years. Those details came out of hours of interviews with people who went out of their way to help, including family and friends of the seven astronauts who were still coping with the shock of the accident. Without them, there would be no book.

A dozen *Washington Post* reporters worked on the book, some of them visiting the small towns where the astronauts grew up and the large space complex in Houston where they worked. Researchers spent hours checking one fact after another and editors struggled under tight deadlines to make sure the book's chapters, each written by a different reporter, hung together.

Thomas O'Toole, who has covered the space program for *The Post* for a decade, wrote Chapter One, on the glory days of the program in the 1950s and 1960s. Kathy Sawyer, who covered the fatal launch and watched the *Challenger* explode above her, wrote Chapter Two, on the development of the shuttle program and the decision to recruit women and minorities for the astronaut corps.

The biographical chapters on the astronauts were grouped by their roles: pilots first, mission specialists next, payload specialists last. Lee Hockstader wrote Chapter Three, on Francis R. (Dick) Scobee, the commander. Anndee Hochman wrote Chapter Four,

7

on Michael J. Smith, the pilot. Chris Spolar wrote Chapter Five, on Judith A. Resnik, mission specialist. Saundra Saperstein wrote Chapter Six, on Ronald E. McNair, mission specialist. Stephanie Mansfield wrote Chapter Seven, on Ellison S. Onizuka, mission specialist. Carla Hall wrote Chapter Eight, on Gregory B. Jarvis, payload specialist. Laura A. Kiernan wrote Chapter Nine, on Sharon Christa McAuliffe, payload specialist. Alison Muscatine wrote Chapter Ten, on the astronauts as a crew and on the explosion.

The epilogue is different from the other chapters: it is an essay on space exploration, the challenges it poses and the risks that it requires. It was written by Richard Harwood, a deputy managing editor of *The Washington Post* who helped supervise the preparation of this book.

Several editors, both at *The Washington Post* and at Pocket Books, deserve recognition—Alison Howard and Bill Elsen of the newspaper's national staff, Larry Kramer, Rem Rieder and Bill Hamilton of its metropolitan staff, Jeff Frank and Bob Thompson of its Style section staff, who edited chapters of the book; Ben Bradlee, executive editor, and Leonard Downie, managing editor of *The Washington Post*, who encouraged the project from the beginning; Sydny Miner, of Pocket Books, who helped with editing and worked with Gina Centrello, William R. Grose and Irwyn Applebaum of Pocket Books to coordinate production of the book.

Post researchers Ferman Patterson and Barbara Feinman were invaluable and tireless in their efforts to chase down facts.

A book of this kind, written so quickly after a tragic incident, raises questions that should be answered directly. Half of *The Washington Post*'s fee from Pocket Books will be donated to one of the funds set up after the explosion in honor of the astronauts. The remainder will be divided among *The Post* staff members who produced the book.

Pocket Books will also make a separate donation to one or more of these funds.

Steven Luxenberg
The Washington Post
February 14, 1986

****
CHALLENGERS
****

Chapter 1

THE FIRST DECADE: SHOOTING THE MOON

It was as if a state of war had been declared. America's eyes strained toward the skies, its ears tuned to a relentless "beep-beep" beamed toward Earth. It was October 4, 1957, and the Soviet Union had just rocketed into orbit an 84.3-pound satellite called *Sputnik*, which did no more than circle Earth every ninety minutes and emit a steady beep that seemed meaningless. But the sound stunned the world and profoundly shocked the United States, much as if a great national catastrophe had occurred. On no other day was America's faith in its technological superiority so suddenly shaken until twenty-nine years later when seven American astronauts, including the first citizen passenger, died in the explosion of the space shuttle *Challenger*.

Sputnik provoked anguish and anxiety. Who were these Soviets who had managed such a feat? How could a nation perceived by many Americans as backward and brutal best the United States at anything other than weightlifting? What would America do to regain its preeminence? President Dwight D. Eisenhower sought to soothe a bewildered public by promising that the United States would better the Soviet feat during the following year. "After all," he said consolingly, "the Russians have only put one small ball in the air."

That was not what Americans wanted to hear. Senate Majority Leader Lyndon B. Johnson saw events so differently that he took the Senate floor to declare: "It is not reassuring to be told that next year we'll put an even better satellite in orbit, maybe with chrome trim and automatic windshield wipers. I guess for the first time I've started to realize that this country of mine might not be ahead in everything."

Sputnik had an even greater effect on some of the fledgling rocket scientists in America's space effort. When the news reached William H. Pickering, then director of the Jet Propulsion Laboratory, he took a sledgehammer and wrecked the new asphalt driveway he had built himself at his hilltop home outside Pasadena.

No single event of the century ravaged America's self-image as did *Sputnik*. So rudely did the little sphere undermine the idea that the United States was the world leader in military, economic, and technological prowess that *Sputnik* changed the way Americans did research, supported education and taught their children. One historian placed the U.S. response to *Sputnik* "in the same category" as decisions that preceded the Truman Doctrine, the North Atlantic Treaty, intervention in Korea, the eyeball-to-eyeball confrontation with the Soviets over missile sites in Cuba and greater involvement in Vietnam.

Sputnik launched America on a search for itself that did not end until July 20, 1969, during the *Apollo 11* flight when Neil Armstrong became the first man to set foot on the moon, just as President John F. Kennedy had promised eight years earlier. Between *Sputnik* and that historic moment, the United States went on a spending spree in education and technology, pouring as much as fifty billion dollars into schools and laboratories from Long Island to Los Angeles and producing a generation of scientists and engineers who changed American life and restored the nation's image of itself. The upheaval was not easily accomplished. The route to the moon was strewn with obstacles.

Immediately after *Sputnik,* as Americans anxiously awaited a reassertion of their nation's technical prowess, U.S. rocket ventures did little to polish that image. Only sixty-three days after *Sputnik*'s launch and thirty days after *Sputnik 2* reached orbit, the U.S. Navy attempted to launch a satellite aboard a Vanguard rocket from Cape Canaveral, Florida. Vanguard lifted off for one second before losing thrust, falling back on the launch pad and exploding. Its satellite rolled away, transmitter chirping and being registered clearly on nearby antennas.

A disturbing number of Air Force missiles disintegrated even before leaving the Florida coast. One called the Snark had an advertised range of 6,500 miles. "But I don't think the first twenty-seven had a range between them of twenty-seven miles," one Cape veteran noted, referring to the Snark's propensity to crash soon after lift-off. The missile's fizzle rate was so high that *Time* magazine called central Florida's coastal area the "Snark-infested waters of Cape Canaveral."

The Navy, Army and Air Force feuded openly over which would be first to orbit a satellite. After the Navy's abortive attempt, the Army was given four days in January, 1958 to launch one from the Cape's Eastern Test Range. The Air Force announced that, if the four days passed without a launch, it would undertake "urgent" missile tests at the range, which was Air Force property.

For two of the four days, the jet stream unexpectedly moved south, creating hazardous winds 40,000 feet above the Cape. On the third day, winds died, and the Army launched *Explorer 1* but not before battling with the Navy over how the satellite would be tracked. *Explorer* weighed 10.5 pounds but, because it entered orbit attached to the final stage of its launch vehicle, a thirty-one-pound object circled Earth. The Navy had given the Army permission to install tracking radios at a Navy installation on Antigua in the Leeward Islands but would not allow them to be checked before the flight. Salty Caribbean air corroded the radios so much that Army trackers at the Cape blockhouse never received the signal that *Explorer* was on its way to orbit.

Explorer Project Scientist Alfred Hibbs remembers Army General Bruce Medaris drumming his fingers on a blockhouse desk about the time no signal came from Antigua. "Hibbs, is it up?" Medaris asked. "There is a ninety percent probability that the perigee (low point in the orbit) is higher than 200 miles," Hibbs told him. "Hibbs, is it up or not?" Medaris asked. "Yes, sir, it's up," Hibbs responded, making a wild guess that proved correct later that day, "and it's going to stay up for ten years."

Meanwhile, the Soviets widened the gap. On *Sputnik 2,* they had orbited a dog named Laika, and later they orbited and recovered dogs, rats, mice, flies and seeds. In 1959, their *Luna 3* spacecraft flew around the moon and photographed its hidden side for the first time.

On April 12, 1961, the Soviet program took another stunning leap forward as Air Force fighter pilot Lieutenant Yuri A. Gagarin, twenty-seven, became the first man to orbit Earth. His Vostok spacecraft made one orbit and returned to Earth 108 minutes after launch. Less than four months later, Air Force Major Gherman S. Titov circled the globe 17½ times, a feat that kept him in space for two days in *Vostok 2*. According to a popular joke of the time, the Leningrad Symphony Orchestra was next in line for an orbital mission. The only American to attain orbit that year was a chimpanzee named Ham.

America was in a foul mood anyway that year. First Gagarin, then the abortive invasion of Cuba at the Bay of Pigs, then Titov. The new young president, Kennedy, pleaded for ideas on how to catch the Soviets, but many of his advisers told him not to become obsessed by a space race. After the Bay of Pigs disaster, April 17, some advisers, fearing further national embarrassment, urged Kennedy to cancel the planned suborbital flight May 5 of Navy Lieutenant Commander Alan B. Shepard. A year earlier, Eisenhower's advisers had told him to try orbiting fifty chimpanzees before risking a manned venture. One even recommended moving the entire Project Mercury manned-flight program to Africa because fifty trained chimps could not be found in America. Eisenhower's science adviser, George Kistiakowsky, summed up the White House mood, saying: "Manned spaceflight will be man's most expensive funeral."

On April 28, 1961, Kennedy called a secret White House meeting to discuss Shepard's flight. Science adviser Jerome Wiesner spoke against manned spaceflight, declaring: "We can't afford to have a man go up in flames on the launch pad." Kennedy looked questioningly at Edward Welsh, director of the National Space Council. "Mr. President," Welsh said softly, "why postpone a success?" Kennedy asked, "Do you have that much confidence in Mercury?" Welsh replied: "As much as I have flying from New York to Hawaii." Shepard's flight was "go."

As the Mercury debate continued, Lyndon B. Johnson, now vice-president, asked German rocket pioneer Wernher von Braun if the United States could win a space race with the Soviets. The visionary von Braun had begun building rockets in Germany before World War II and, with many of his co-workers, was being recruited by the United States as early as 1944. He headed the developmental operations division of the Army Ballistic Missile Agency and told Johnson that, while he favored a space race, he did not mean one that counted winners by numbers of launches or numbers in orbit. Von Braun said a space race would take both nations beyond Earth's orbit. "The goal should be the lunar landing," he told Johnson. "The Russians will be ahead every step

14

of the way, but we can beat them to the moon if we start now."

A successful suborbital flight by Shepard was crucial before Johnson could recommend to Kennedy that a moon landing should be the space program's focus. Launched in *Mercury 3*, Shepard spent fifteen minutes and twenty-two seconds in flight before landing safely in the Atlantic Ocean. Even before Shepard was debriefed, Johnson was on the phone to National Aeronautics and Space Administration Administrator James E. Webb and Defense Secretary Robert S. McNamara to ask that papers justifying a lunar-landing program be prepared for delivery to Kennedy in three days. They produced a thirty-page document that went to the president on time and remained classified for twelve years. "It is our belief that manned exploration to the surface of the moon represents a major area in which international competition in space will be conducted," their report said. "The orbiting of machines is not the same as orbiting or landing of man. It is man in space that captures the imagination of the world."

That was exactly what Kennedy wanted to hear and, on May 25, he stood before Congress and delivered a challenge. Previously, he had described space as "the new ocean" and said "this nation must sail upon it." This time, he detailed his determination to sail farther on the new ocean than anyone, saying: "While we cannot guarantee that we shall one day be first, we can guarantee that any failure to make this effort will make us last."

Then, he fired the shot heard round the world: "I believe that this nation should commit itself to achieving the goal, before the decade is out, of landing a man on the moon and returning him safely to the earth. No single space project in this period will be more impressive to mankind or more important for the long-range exploration of space, and none will be so difficult or expensive to accomplish." The Apollo program to land man on the moon was born.

Kennedy had not underestimated the degree of difficulty. Despite Shepard's successful flight and a duplicate one by Air Force Major Virgil I. (Gus) Grissom on July 21, 1961, little had been done to remedy rocket fizzles and delays that plagued those early days of manned spaceflight. The flight of Marine Lieutenant Colonel John Glenn, America's pioneer in orbit, was delayed at least nine times, slipping from December 1961 to February 20, 1962.

During one long wait for Glenn's mission, several missiles exploded with what seemed like a special fury in the bright Florida sun. The explosions had nothing to do with a man shooting his estranged wife one night in a crowded cocktail lounge but prompted a British journalist to cable his London newspaper: "The distressed husband of a Cape Canaveral waitress shot her in a bar just a few miles from the spaceport last night. It was the only successful shot here this week."

NASA's road to the moon was littered not only with technological obstacles but also hindered by the agency's longtime adversary, the Air Force. In late 1962, the two were battling about the Air Force role in the Apollo program. NASA fought to have Congress buy the land north of the Air Force's Eastern Test Range at the Cape and deed the land to NASA for a spaceport. The Air Force sought to force NASA to continue using the test range, figuring that the service could control what launches would be allowed and when.

Unknown to the Air Force, NASA had Representative Olin E. (Tiger) Teague (D-Texas) on its side. Teague, a member of Congress since 1946, was chairman of a key subcommittee dealing with NASA affairs and was deeply committed to what was then called the Manned Spacecraft Center in Houston. When he asked the Air Force how it would supply services such as machine-shop work to a demanding civilian tenant such as NASA, the Air Force said it had an excess of service facilities at Cape Canaveral. Someone at NASA suggested that Teague check for himself.

Teague flew unannounced to Cape Canaveral and appeared at 7 A.M. one morning at the Air Force machine shop. He located the shop foreman, identified himself and asked him how busy he was. "We can't handle another work order," the unwitting foreman said. "We're so busy now we're working around the clock."

Seeking more evidence about the Air Force a few weeks later, Teague joined NASA Launch Operations Director Rocco A. Petrone to watch the agency launch a Saturn rocket from an Air Force pad at the Cape. Petrone had decreed that no one be allowed on the pad after a launch until an inspection team checked for loose electrical cables or spilled rocket fuel. Nevertheless, an Air Force general and two of his aides walked from the blockhouse to

16

the pad before the inspectors. "See that?" Petrone told Teague. "That's a good example of Air Force cooperation."

Teague said nothing at the time but, a week later, wrote into the NASA funding authorization bill that "NASA will buy and retain" 80,000 acres of land on Merritt Island just north of the Eastern Test Range. His subcommittee's Senate counterpart did not have the words "buy and retain" in its version of the bill and, just before Teague met a few days later with Senate conference committee members about it, his secretary logged three phone calls. They were from Deputy Defense Secretary Roswell Gilpatric, Air Force Secretary Eugene Zuckert and Air Force General Bernard Shriever. Ignoring the call-back messages, Teague walked into the conference room and told the senators: "I'll change anything in this bill but three words: 'buy and retain.'" NASA had won its own spaceport and full independence.

Long before the Apollo success story was written, the NASA program looked as if gremlins had prepared it. In the late summer of 1963, a few months before President Kennedy was assassinated, Congress cut 400 million dollars from the Apollo program budget. Meanwhile, the Soviets widened their lead, highlighted by the launch June 14, 1963, of Lieutenant Colonel Valery F. Bykovsky who, as his craft passed above the Soviets' Baikonur launch site two days later, was joined in orbit by Junior Lieutenant Valentina V. Tereshkova, the first woman in space. Senators Barry Goldwater (R-Arizona) and Howard W. Cannon (D-Nevada) demanded that Apollo be turned over to the Air Force. In late September, U.N. Ambassador Adlai Stevenson wrote a speech that Kennedy delivered at the United Nations. In it, Kennedy suggested that the United States and Soviet Union join forces to fly to the moon.

Members of Congress who had backed Kennedy's original moon-landing plan raised a huge outcry, and proponents of the joint effort faded away quickly. Stevenson denied writing the speech, and presidential assistant Arthur Schlesinger denied writing the key sentence about going to the moon with the Soviets. NASA Deputy Administrator Robert C. Seamans stepped in and almost defused the dispute by leaking his ignorance of it to the press. "Well, frankly, I'm not smart enough to run a giant program with the Russians," he said. "I have a hard enough time getting American engineers to talk to one another."

On the day that he would be shot to death in Dallas, Kennedy told Teague and Representative Albert Thomas (D-Texas) that the U.N. speech was a mistake. "You know, the space program needs more identification," Kennedy told them. "I plan on going to Cape Canaveral again to give it some." Those were believed to be his last words about the space program.

Kennedy's successor, Johnson, proved to be more committed to the moon-landing goal. It helped that NASA's Manned Spacecraft Center was in Houston, but the native Texan's commitment went beyond that. He felt that the space program's effect on national morale was as important as the way it stretched the country's technological reach. Johnson was also a true believer in the "hero" system, and what better heroes could be found than the "Original Seven"? They comprised the first U.S. astronaut group, and each strove to prove that he was made of what novelist Tom Wolfe subsequently immortalized as *The Right Stuff*.

Under Johnson, the space program began to move forward, and he embraced its successes. Shepard and Grissom flew the one-man Mercury craft downrange. Then Glenn was followed into orbit in 1962 by Navy Commanders M. Scott Carpenter on May 24 and Walter M. Schirra on October 3. The Mercury program ended May 15, 1963, with the flight of Air Force Major L. Gordon Cooper. The only "original" who never flew a Mercury craft into orbit was Air Force Major Donald K. Slayton, whose turn in space would not come until 1975. None of the originals suffered serious ill effects from weightlessness, and the idea was dead forever that fifty chimpanzees should be orbited before the first human.

More than a year passed before another manned spaceflight, and the Soviets maintained their edge. On October 12, 1964, five months before the United States would begin its two-man Gemini launches, a new Soviet spacecraft named *Voskhod 1* lifted off carrying three cosmonauts. They included a medical doctor and a scientist and, to conserve room, none wore a bulky spacesuit, relying on the craft's pressurization. The Soviets shook the U.S. again on March 18, 1965, when two cosmonauts flew *Voskhod 2* into orbit and Lieutenant Colonel Alexei A. Leonov stepped outside through an airlock in a spacesuit, becoming the first man to walk in space.

Five days later, Grissom and Navy Lieutenant Commander John W. Young inaugurated the Gemini missions and became the first astronauts to change their craft's orbital flight path. American astronauts spent little time actually flying their spacecraft because increasingly sophisticated computers guided most flights. The Mercury Seven had expressed dismay about traveling as passengers rather than pilots and forced NASA planners to program missions that allowed a greater human touch at the controls.

With the flight of Grissom and Young in *Gemini 3,* nicknamed "The Unsinkable Molly Brown," the United States began closing the gap with the Soviets. The ten manned Gemini missions, numbered 3 through 12 and ending November 15, 1966, proved conclusively that manned spacecraft could rendezvous and dock without mishap, that spacewalks were feasible and that crews could live and work for at least two weeks in weightless conditions without endangering themselves.

The Apollo program, named for the Greek god of the sun, was about to begin. Its goal was a walk on the moon, and crew members chosen for the shakedown flight were Grissom, Navy Lieutenant Commander Roger B. Chaffee and Edward H. White. Grissom had flown in Mercury and Gemini craft and was as well known to Americans as most Hollywood stars. During the *Gemini 4* flight in June 1965, White had become the first American to walk in space. Chaffee, thirty-one, was a space rookie who had studied at the Air Force Institute of Technology and was described as the crew's engineer. He was the youngest American named to fly in space.

The Gemini program's spectacular success, and the dawn of Apollo, lulled NASA and many Americans into thinking that the Soviets had been overtaken. In a few, heart-stopping moments like those that would characterize America's response to the *Challenger* shuttle explosion nineteen years and one day later, the space program experienced its first major disaster.

It was 1 P.M. on January 27, 1967, when Grissom, White and Chaffee stepped into an Apollo spacecraft bearing production number "204" and perched atop its Saturn 1-B rocket on Launch Pad 34 at the spaceport, by then renamed Cape Kennedy. Wearing spacesuits, the three were to perform a dry run for what was projected as the first manned Apollo flight a few months later. At 6:31 P.M., the men neared the end of the rehearsal, and a voice cried from the cabin: "Fire in the spacecraft!" Similar shouts followed, and blockhouse sensors indicated movement in the cockpit for several seconds.

Within a minute, the astronauts were dead as fire in the

pressurized pure-oxygen atmosphere pushed the cabin temperature to 2,500 degrees Fahrenheit. Extreme heat and billowing smoke turned back rescue attempts. The astronauts could not complete their rehearsed emergency-escape technique before being overcome. Despite an exhaustive investigation, no explicit cause for the fire was found.

The cost of making sure that such a tragedy would never recur was about $110 million, and the incident set back the Apollo timetable by almost a year. "Six months to work the changes brought by the fire," Apollo Program Director Samuel C. Phillips, an Air Force Lieutenant General, said, "and six months to explain it all to Congress." Three months after the *Apollo 1* fire, the Soviet program suffered a setback when cosmonaut Colonel Vladimir M. Komarov died during reentry of the first manned Soyuz craft. He had begun reentry procedures after apparent trouble maneuvering the ship and was killed when the Soyuz recovery parachute deployed but snarled, slamming the craft to Earth at about 400 mph.

No one remembers the *Apollo 1* fire with the intensity of former Apollo Spacecraft Manager Joe Shea who, in the four months afterward, went from working alongside the astronauts to a NASA headquarters job in Washington, then to industry jobs with the Polaroid and Raytheon corporations, NASA contractors. More than ten years after the blaze, Shea told a reporter, "We'd been concerned about fire. The way you handle fire is to keep anything that might spark, because the only way you'd start a fire would be by an electrical short of some kind, keep it away from anything that might burn, so there wasn't any chance something might sputter. Anything that could cause a spark and ignite something else was a hazard."

On the day of the tragedy, spacecraft 204 was a fire hazard. On their own, the astronauts had installed extra Raschel netting to hold equipment in place, but Raschel netting was flammable. They had added 4,000 square inches of Velcro to fasten other tools, but Velcro was flammable. After all, it was a test run, not a launch. "I remember saying that same day, 'Hey, let's pull that stuff out of there because it's an O₂ [pure oxygen] test,'" Shea said. "We were literally talking about that kind of thing the morning of the accident."

One of Shea's deputies suffered a nervous breakdown. Shea

spent the night with him and persuaded him to enter a rest home. The family minister arrived and suggested the same thing. The next day, the man was taken to a sanitarium in a straitjacket. Shea seemed ready for one, too. He threw himself into his work, making a four-week study of where the Apollo program stood and driving himself eighteen hours a day, playing handball for two hours and sleeping for four hours with the help of medication. NASA Administrator Webb and Deputy Administrator Seamans told him to take an extended leave. A press release was prepared saying Shea was doing so, but Shea refused.

"I said I'll abide by the decision of any competent psychiatrist," Shea said years later. "And so we set it up at the Houston Medical Center with two doctors. This one guy said: 'You're stronger for what you've been through.' That was fed back [to Washington], and they dropped it." On Shea's living-room wall five years ago, there still hung a painting of Grissom, White and Chaffee praying before a model of spacecraft 204.

If Shea learned strength through adversity, so did the rest of the Apollo team. While NASA and Congress held hearings on the fire, time stood still for the moon-landing program. Not until three months after the fire did NASA officials tell North American Aviation, the spacecraft manufacturer, what it wanted done to prevent another fire, and another two months passed before the two agreed on the changes. The space agency ordered refitting and fireproofing of Apollo's two-foot-high frame. That was completed in fewer than eight months on the next Apollo craft off the production line.

The two agreed on 5,800 changes in the way the spacecraft was built. These ranged from adding ten-foot aluminum trays to cover exposed wire bundles in the floor to adding forty-six aluminum panels to hide equipment bays and create "fire breaks" in the interior. The 300 feet of aluminum plumbing was strengthened at the seams and, where necessary, replaced with stainless steel. Flammable urethane foam on the astronauts' seats and arm rests was replaced with a new material called beta cloth that was fire resistant to 5,000 degrees Fahrenheit.

The biggest change involved the escape hatch. A single, hinged door that could be opened outward within five seconds by an inside pump handle replaced the double-door hatch that required about ninety seconds to open.

To effect these changes, North American Aviation stripped half of the parts from seven Apollo spacecraft under production in Downey, California. It also designed engineering and test methods for new parts and reconfigured the assembly line to include those parts. This was accomplished in the summer of 1967, and company officials flew to Washington to suggest delivery of the first new Apollo craft on May 1, 1968. NASA insisted on delivery by February 15. After four days of round-the-clock sessions, the company replied that it could do so by March 15.

North American Aviation put together a new Apollo management team. Under pressure from NASA Administrator Webb, the company's Space Division President, Harrison A. Storms Jr., had been replaced with onetime Martin Company President William B. Bergen, and at least six other top management moves were made. Bergen decreed that Apollo would no longer have one production boss, responsible to him. Instead, he gave each spacecraft its own boss and each boss was granted czar-like powers.

"We changed the charter on this job," one company official said. "If a spacecraft manager wants something, he doesn't ask for it. He just gets it." The first new czar was a stoop-shouldered engineer named John Healey, forty-one, who had come to North American Aviation to solve problems with the second stage of the three-stage Saturn rocket that would boost Apollo toward the moon. To Healey went the first new Apollo craft, named 101, and with it the tough task of getting it to the Cape on time. He placed his workers on a virtual wartime production schedule.

By the end of October, Healey was fifteen days ahead of schedule and setting new work standards at the Downey plant. "We had to make it happen," he said at the time, and that meant changing work habits. "We personalized the work crews," he said. "If I thought they were doing a good job, we'd get their pictures in the company newspaper, take them into the executive dining room for lunch and make them feel as important as they really are." If any of the six workers inside spacecraft 101 needed a part or a tool, someone outside got it, even if the someone was a company vice-president.

Healey mastered details, such as initiating a third shift for engineers so that, when an engineering problem arose on that shift, it was solved then, not on the first shift the following day. He

22

moved the spare-parts bin closer to where the craft was being built. "It's psychological," he explained. "When the work crews can see the parts they still have to put in, they work twice as hard installing the parts they have in their hands."

One worker told Healey that at least twenty-four hours were required to finish a plumbing job. "Do it in two hours," Healey replied. The angry man did so. Bonding fifty-four brackets to the floor had taken pre-fire crews sixteen days. Now, workers told Healey that they could do it in eight days. Healey gave them five and a half; they finished in four.

Healey was just as hard on himself. He worked seven-day weeks, going to bed no earlier than 1 A.M. each day and arising six hours later. By 8 A.M., he might have been miles from Downey picking up a subcontractor's part for the day's work. One day, he needed a new bellows for a pump and was told that "lead time" for the bellows was three weeks. "I need it before Saturday," he told the manufacturer over the phone. "Make up your minds. Yes or no. All right, call me back tonight." Hanging up, Healey winked at a visitor and said: "I'll get it, I've got to get it."

The dedication paid off quickly. The first rebuilt Apollo was delivered to the Cape forty days ahead of schedule. The first Apollo flight into orbit—the one that would have been flown by Grissom, White and Chaffee—was called *Apollo 7* and left Earth October 11, 1968, 8½ months after the fire and three months ahead of NASA's new moon-landing timetable.

By the time *Apollo 7* splashed down October 22 after an almost flawless flight, the space agency faced a new crisis. The next scheduled flight was that of *Apollo 8*, which was to carry the lunar landing craft and practice maneuvers in Earth orbit but actually became the first mission to the moon. What ensued before launch was a series of moves that could only be described as Machiavellian. No mission caused more dissent within the program nor ensured that the lunar-landing goal would be met than did the Christmastime voyage of *Apollo 8* around the moon.

As early as August 7, Apollo Spacecraft Manager George Low, who had succeeded Joe Shea, had recognized that the landing craft would not be ready for the mission and suggested looking at the "feasibility of a lunar orbit mission" without the lander. That meant flying to the moon with only the main Apollo craft and circumnavigating the lunar surface for the first time. Enthusiasm for the mission was unrestrained at the Manned Spacecraft Center in Houston, but George Mueller, then Director of Manned Spaceflight at NASA headquarters in Washington, was adamantly opposed. "Too risky," he said.

Mueller wanted at least one more mission in Earth orbit before a moon flight. Shea backed Mueller and ridiculed the plan, writing top NASA officials: "The lunar module is necessary for redundance. Even more than that, there is little sense in going to the moon to go around it. When you go to the moon, you ought to be serious about landing there."

Two things affected the eventual decision: Flight directors in Houston said the trip would be invaluable as a pathfinding flight for subsequent lunar crews and, more important, the Soviets were hinting at a one-man flight around the moon, a possible suicide mission because they had never practiced it. In a short time, three unmanned Soviet Zond craft were flown behind the moon in a "free-fall" flight path back to Earth. The first crashed on returning, the second fell far short of its Indian Ocean target and the third splashed down off the coast of Madagascar, its destination.

The Central Intelligence Agency told NASA that the Soviets might be planning to strap a volunteer cosmonaut inside a fourth Zond aimed at the moon soon after New Year's Day 1969. Nevertheless, Mueller remained opposed to a U.S. mission in lunar orbit. So Manned Spacecraft Center Director Robert Gilruth, Deputy Christopher Kraft, Low and Chief Astronaut Slayton met secretly at the Cape with von Braun, Kennedy Space Center Director Kurt Debus and Apollo Program Director Phillips. The plan to fly *Apollo 8* around the moon was reviewed and approved. Mueller was not told of the meeting.

Four days later, on the day Mueller left for Europe with NASA Administrator Webb, the plan was hustled to Washington. Mueller heard about the meeting and telephoned his objections from Paris, telling Phillips that he would be away for eight days and ordering him not to make a decision on the flight until then. "We all agreed to keep going," Low recalled. "We could not wait for a decision."

Providing a mighty impetus was fear that the Soviets would fly around the moon before Apollo and that delaying *Apollo 8* would imperil the goal of a moon landing by 1970. Speaking for the astronauts, Slayton warned: "This is the only chance we have to do this before the end of the decade." Von Braun minimized the risk of flying men for the first time atop the powerful Saturn 5 rocket instead of the smaller Saturn 1-B that pushed *Apollo 7* into orbit. "Once you decide to man it," von Braun said, "it doesn't matter how far you go on it." Saturn 5 was a mighty, thundering beast whose sound volume was compared with the devastating explosive roar of the Krakatoa volcano in 1883. Instruments more than 1,000 miles away had detected its first-stage air-pressure wave during a test-firing in November 1967.

New NASA Deputy Administrator Thomas O. Paine agreed that Saturn and *Apollo 8* should be pronounced "go," and the plan was approved. But one hurdle remained. In September, just after the rocket and command craft were moved to the launch pad, a hurricane appeared off the Florida coast and moved toward the Cape. "You'd better get that bird off the pad," Launch Operations Director Petrone was told, whereupon Deputy Director Paul Donnelly said: "You take that bird off the pad, and you can kiss going to the moon this year goodbye." Petrone gambled that the weather would improve and did not order the "bird" moved to shelter. He won.

On November 10, Apollo contractors were polled, and only one voted against a lunar orbital mission. Walter Burke of McDonnell-Douglas Corp. said he favored a flight that would take *Apollo 8* once around the moon at a great distance rather than ten times at an altitude of sixty miles.

The only postflight dissent came from two of the three astronauts aboard. Slayton, the original Mercury astronaut still awaiting a spaceflight, smuggled three ponies of brandy aboard the craft for the crew to drink in lunar orbit on Christmas Eve. Air Force Colonel Frank Borman, the mission commander, vetoed the brandy. *Apollo 8* returned to Earth with Borman, Navy Captain James A. Lovell Jr. and Air Force Lieutenant Colonel William A. Anders and unbroken seals on the three pony bottles.

Where were the Soviets? "They abandoned their moon program," Kraft told a reporter not long ago. "*Apollo 8* took the wind right out of their sails." The flight caught most of the world off-guard. *New York Daily News* Executive Editor Floyd Barger asked *News* reporter Mark Bloom: "When they say, 'All systems are go,' . . . how many systems do they mean?" *New York*

Times Publisher Arthur Sulzberger asked reporter John Noble Wilford: "How will they see when they go behind the moon? Will they drop flares?"

Apollo 8 did more than put the Soviets out of the moon race. It proved on the first try that the Saturn 5 rocket would power Apollo to the moon, and it reduced the number of pathfinder missions needed before chancing the first lunar landing. "I had always figured," von Braun said before *Apollo 8*, "that we would have to make as many as six unmanned flights on the Saturn 5 before risking a man in it." Instead, two were made, and the third launch carried the *Apollo 8* crew.

Those in charge of Apollo were convinced that their success was the result of attention paid to detail. The day before *Apollo 8* left for the moon, someone expressed a sudden misgiving. What if the antenna on the rear of the spacecraft did not lock into place in flight? If it did not lock, what would happen when the onboard engine was fired behind the moon to bring the crew home? Would the sudden forward motion swing the antenna down against the bell-shaped engine nozzle? And, if so, would the antenna break or the bell shatter?

An immediate test was ordered, but no spare antenna or bell could be found. Twenty people at the Cape got on the phones and, in three hours, found an antenna at a contractor's plant in California and a bell at a contractor outside Salt Lake City. A flatbed truck began taking the bell from Utah to the California plant, where a test was planned. By nightfall, the truck was stranded by a snowstorm in the western Rockies. Apollo planners called the nearest Air Force base and, within an hour, a long-range helicopter was flying the bell to California. "The happiest sound in the whole world," recalled the engineer who supervised the test, "was hearing that antenna bang up against the bell time after time without a crack."

The program gained momentum. The flight of *Apollo 9* from March 3–13, 1969, tested the lunar landing craft in Earth orbit and, two months later, *Apollo 10* took it within ten miles of the lunar surface. Von Braun said he had never believed that the program would come so far so quickly. He said he had "hoped" that a moon landing could be made on the 10th manned flight, which would have been *Apollo 16*.

Instead, the historic moment came during the *Apollo 11*

mission. Its crew members were civilian Neil Armstrong, Air Force Colonel Edwin E. Aldrin and Air Force Lieutenant Colonel Michael Collins. The prime landing site was the Sea of Tranquillity in the east-central lunar lowlands. The time was five months before the deadline set by President Kennedy in 1961.

Millions of Americans were tuned to radio transmissions between Houston and *Apollo 11* or watching television simulations on July 20, 1969, when Collins piloted the command craft in lunar orbit while Armstrong and Aldrin descended to the surface in the landing module, dubbed *Eagle*. At 4:17:43 P.M. EDT, the module touched down, and Armstrong radioed, "Houston, Tranquillity Base here. The *Eagle* has landed." In response, Air Force Lieutenant Charles M. Duke said from Mission Control, "Thank heavens. You've got a bunch of guys about to turn blue."

Within hours, a fuzzy television picture was flashed live but upside down from the module. Houston technicians righted the image. Viewers saw Armstrong step slowly down the module ladder. He paused at its last rung, then hopped to the surface at 10:56:20 P.M. EDT, saying: "That's one small step for man, one giant leap for mankind." Later, the article "a" was inserted in the record, amending Armstrong's words to "one small step for a man."

Aldrin followed Armstrong to the surface. The two walked there, radioed what they saw and felt, bagged almost forty pounds of rocks, erected a stiff American flag on a wire frame because there was no breeze to help display it and saluted the flag. They talked by radio-telephone with President Richard M. Nixon in the White House, faced a nearby television camera they had propped on a tripod and saluted him. "For every American, this has to be the proudest day of our lives," Nixon said. "For one priceless moment in the whole history of man, all the people on this earth are truly one."

At 12:57 A.M. on July 21, Aldrin reluctantly returned to the landing module after being ordered to do so. Fourteen minutes later, the hatch door closed behind Armstrong, ending a two-hour, thirty-one-minute moon walk.

Five more Apollo crews landed on the moon in regions ranging from a valley surrounded by mountains to a volcanic area flooded with lava. Three and one-half years of lunar exploration ended December 19, 1972, when the crew of *Apollo 17* parachuted its spacecraft *America* into the Pacific Ocean. That crew included geologist Harrison H. Schmitt, the only professional scientist sent to the moon and, like Glenn, destined to become a member of the U.S. Senate.

Eight Apollo crews flew to the moon, two on pathfinder missions in lunar orbit for the six crews who actually landed there. The *Apollo 17* crew returned to Earth with 249 pounds of moon rocks, raising the total haul to almost 1,000 pounds. Schmitt and Navy Commander Eugene A. Cernan had spent twenty-two hours and five minutes roaming the surface.

"*Apollo 17* goes into the record books as the perfect mission, the most sophisticated mission we've ever had," Program Director Petrone said. It was America's last moon-landing mission. "We won't be returning to the moon without a very good reason for a long time to come," a space agency official said after *Apollo 17* came home. "I see no good reason for going for at least the next twenty-five years." And no one has.

The U.S. and Soviet space programs began to focus on establishing more permanent work stations in space and longer manned flights. Leftover Apollo command craft had been earmarked for the three missions in 1973 and 1974 that took U.S. astronauts to Skylab, the nation's first manned space station. Built from one stage of the Saturn 5 rocket, Skylab was approximately the size of a small two-bedroom house and was launched unmanned on May 14, 1973. Three-man crews rendezvoused with Skylab, and each spent a longer amount of time working there, culminating in an eighty-four-day mission. On July 11, 1979, Skylab completed its 34,981st orbit and was guided to a fiery reentry, largely into the Indian Ocean, although pieces of it were recovered in Australia.

The Soviets had a series of successes with Salyut space stations reached by cosmonauts flying Soyuz spacecraft. For the first time, cosmonauts from Soviet bloc nations flew into space. Disaster struck once. After successfully occupying *Salyut 1* during a flight that began on June 6, 1971, cosmonauts Georgi Dobrovolsky, Vladislav Volkov and Viktor Patsayev were found dead after reentry, victims of cabin depressurization after Salyut and Soyuz separated.

The Apollo-Soyuz era reached its zenith July 17, 1975, when three Americans, including Mercury "original" Slayton, met two

Soviets in space, their craft linked. U.S. space planners had hoped through such experiments and Skylab to establish research bases on the moon or perhaps send astronauts to Mars. But Americans' enthusiasm for space adventure began to wane after the drama generated by Apollo, and the Vietnam war was steadily claiming a larger share of federal spending. For at least ten years to come, money allotted by NASA for manned spaceflight was earmarked for the reusable space shuttle.

Apollo flights also ended because space agency officials were aware of the risk of catastrophe if astronauts continued going to the moon. The Apollo program's most impressive statistic was its virtually accident-free flight record. On its eleven flights, the worst injury a crew member suffered was a cut on the forehead of Navy Commander Alan L. Bean on *Apollo 12*. A sixteen-mm camera bracketed to the cabin wall fell loose at splashdown November 24, 1969, and struck Bean, who was given six stitches.

The Apollo program's worst accident occurred April 13, 1970, on *Apollo 13*'s way to the moon. The crew's oxygen tank exploded, leaving the command craft dark and cold, "like a tomb," astronaut Lovell, the mission commander, said later. The inside temperature kept falling because the crew had to use vacuum hoses to circulate air through the cabins of the command craft and lunar landing craft, which were joined. The water supply was threatened. Humidity increased because the one working spacecraft, the smaller lunar lander, could not deal with all of the moisture. Then, a water gun broke, leaking a quart of water into the weightless cabin. "It took six towels to sop it up and two days to get our feet dry," astronaut John W. Swigert said later. "Man, were my feet cold."

Lovell, Swigert and Fred W. Haise, Jr. flew around the moon and were able to return safely only because they used reserve oxygen in the lunar lander and fired its engine to accelerate their slingshot orbit of the moon and hasten their return.

Cold feet were a cheap price to pay for a program as perilous as Apollo. Long ago, astronauts had voiced acceptance of risk when they climbed into a craft riding above rocket engines holding millions of gallons of fuel and blasted toward space at speeds that reached 17,500 mph.

Collins, who guided the *Apollo 11* command craft around the moon while his crewmates strode the surface, spoke for many in reacting to the explosion that took the lives of the seven *Challenger* space shuttle astronauts.

"The test pilot in me was not surprised when *Challenger* blew up," he said. "I have been expecting something like this for more than twenty years. But knowing it's going to happen doesn't make the moment any less painful. On the contrary, I feel I am part of a family that has just lost seven children and will lose more."

Chapter 2

THE SECOND DECADE: CREATING THE FLYING BRICKYARD

On April 14, 1981, some 500,000 gawkers, scientists and soldiers invaded the barren landscape of the Mojave Desert to witness a drama that, to their eyes, would last only about five minutes.

The thunderous cracks of a double sonic boom and a short white chalkmark across the azure sky at 50,000 feet announced the approach of the spaceplane *Columbia*. It was the first time anyone had tried to pilot a craft from space to a controlled landing on earth.

The glide path brought the two astronauts, John Young and Robert Crippen, in over Big Sur and the coast range, and over ghost towns with names like Ragtown and played-out mines named Silver King and Waterloo. As they banked left toward the old borax mines of Ronald Reagan's "Death Valley Days" and, in their own state-of-the-art pioneer wagon, zeroed in on the powdery white surface of a dry lake named Rogers, few in their audience comprehended the forces in play, the scope, complexity and sheer audacity of the event.

When Young and Crippen crawled into the space shuttle *Columbia* that day, they faced longer odds than any U.S. astronauts before them. Unlike their predecessors, they were riding an untried launch vehicle powered by highly-experimental engines and a propellant new to manned flight. With four computers onboard (plus a fifth for backup), the *Columbia* was far more automated than any spacecraft or aircraft in history (except perhaps certain exotic military planes). It was bigger, heavier and faster than anything of its type had ever been.

And yet it was a model nobody had really wanted. More a duckbill platypus than the swan NASA had in mind, this "bird" was designed by a committee of competing bureaucracies and politicians and built out of compromises and shoestring. The astronauts were in a position similar to that of the first person who ever looked at a cow's undercarriage and said, "Whatever comes out of those, I'm going to drink it."

Previous space projects had had heavenly names—Mercury, Gemini, Apollo. The shuttle's uninspiring official name was Space Transportation System (STS). It was essentially a truck with wings. But those who worked on it had nicknamed it "the Flying Brickyard," a reference both to its looks and its powerless plunge to landing.

The *Columbia*'s lift-off two days earlier, which attracted a million spectators to State Road 3 and other byways and beaches around the space center at Cape Canaveral, Florida, was three years behind schedule. The thirty-third U.S. manned mission without a fatality, it happened to fall on the twentieth anniversary of the world's first manned spaceflight, by Soviet cosmonaut Yuri Gagarin.

Everyone knew that riding a rocket was dangerous, which of course was part of the spectacle's attraction. But the real potential for danger was beyond the awareness of most Americans.

At launch, Young and Crippen were riding a delicately-controlled bomb—a 184-foot tall external fuel tank filled with liquid hydrogen and oxygen resembling a giant artillery shell, with a Roman candle packed with solid fuel on either side (the two largest solid rocket motors ever built). The spaceplane itself, known as the orbiter, rode piggyback on the tanks, a configuration which has been compared to insects mating.

The whole assembly, weighing about 4.5 million pounds, blasted off with a total thrust of 6.9 million pounds. The two solid rocket boosters fell off (to parachute down and be retrieved) after two minutes, when the craft was twenty-eight miles high. Six minutes later, when the spaceplane's main engines had used up the liquid fuel in the big external tank, and it had burned up in the atmosphere (its debris aimed at the Indian Ocean), the craft was moving about 17,000 mph, close to the speed needed to go into orbit and about twenty-six times the speed of sound.

The worst case scenario, officials said, was an explosion on or just above the launch pad. For the first time in the U.S. manned flight program, the astronauts' lift-off escape system, which would have allowed them to cut loose from the fuel-bomb during the first 2½ minutes of flight, had been scrapped because it cost and weighed too much. There were several other so-called abort modes for later phases of the trip—such as the spaceplane without its tanks and rocket boosters coming back to land at the space center, or circling the earth in low orbit to land at one of the emergency sites around the world.

After the *Columbia* had completed thirty-six revolutions of the earth, it was up to the computers to fire thirty-eight thrusters, each pointing in a precise but slightly different direction, to take the craft out of orbit northwest of Hawaii. Even Young conceded that the complexity of it left the pilots totally beholden to technology. "The human being," he said, "could never remember how to point thirty-eight thrusters . . . couldn't do it."

As the two pilots reentered the earth's atmosphere at Mach 26, their craft metamorphosing gradually back from spacecraft to airplane, they faced possible incineration as the resistance of the planet's atmosphere turned their craft into a fireball.

During their 4,000-mile glide back to the lake bed at Edwards Air Force Base, they were flying a powerless craft with, as one NASA engineer phrased it, "the glide ratio of a pair of pliers." Coming in at 200 mph, on a glide path seven times as steep as that of a powered jet airliner, they had 7½ miles of runway and no one could be certain they wouldn't need that much and more.

In tests leading up to this launch, the program had encountered engine fires, cracked turbines, faulty welds, mechanical breakdowns and other engineering mishaps. And the *Columbia*'s crucial heat shield tiles, designed to keep the craft from being incinerated on its way back to earth, had turned into a costly, continuing circus of embarrassments.

But from the astronauts' point of view, it was all part of frontier living.

"It will be a sweaty palm launch," Noel Hinners, a former top NASA official, said at the time.

When the *Columbia* made a breath-takingly flawless touchdown on the dry lake bed, it ended not only the suspense but a period of six years during which no Americans had flown in space.

Since the summer of 1975, when three astronauts had linked up in space with two Soviet cosmonauts, forty-three Russians had flown on missions.

The flight came at a time when America's confidence in its technological prowess had been shaken by a string of setbacks: the fall of Skylab, the failed attempt to rescue Americans held hostage in Iran, the Three Mile Island nuclear accident and the eclipse of the American auto industry by Japanese competition. President Carter had declared the national mood to be one of "malaise."

The public had been slow to get caught up in the shuttle's troubled progress, in part, perhaps, as one commentator put it, "we'd forgotten how the rhythms of national exhilaration go." But it finally rallied for the spectacle of the *Columbia*'s first flight.

President Reagan, just elected, summed up the spirit of rising optimism when he declared, "Today both our friends and our adversaries are reminded that we are a free people capable of great deeds."

Once again, a spacecraft carried with it the nation's pride. "It's majestic," murmured John Chancellor of NBC News to his electronic audience as he watched the *Columbia* touch down. "It looks like Los Angeles Airport, and it's coming back from space!"

"This flight proves again that the U.S. is number one . . . number one," said NASA's acting chief Alan Lovelace after *Columbia* landed.

A working shuttle rendered all other spacecraft obsolete, put the U.S., some said, a decade ahead of the Russians and led to the redesign of a whole range of hardware, such as unmanned satellites, to fit its 60 × 15 foot cargo bay. It was to be the end of the throw-away spacecraft, and the beginning of economical, self-supporting space transportation.

And it was to open the way for a whole new generation of astronauts—scientists, junketeering politicians and "ordinary people."

Rookie Crippen, who had waited twelve years for a space mission, said, "It was worth it. . . . But I know I won't have to wait that long anymore. We're back in the space business."

Days later, Young, hardbitten veteran of four space flights, a man who had been to the moon, told a press conference back in Houston, "This flight gives us what we've been trying to do the last ten years . . . It gives us routine access to space for the next twenty years.''

Despite the momentary euphoria, the shuttle could not escape the legacy of its troubled beginnings.

Beset with riots in the streets, body counts in Vietnam, assassinations, a decaying civil rights movement and assorted other social upheaval, many Americans had already become restless with their space program by 1969, when Neil Armstrong planted that first dusty footprint on the lunar surface. With the same foot he was effectively stamping out whatever was left of the program's *raison d'etre:* America had beaten the Russians to the moon. Mission accomplished.

It was no longer the age of Apollo, but of Aquarius. Never mind that Americans would fly missions to the moon for two more years. The country's most visible youth no longer had stars in their eyes but anti-establishment menace. The space program had already become a whipping boy for the budget cutters on Capitol Hill and in the White House. From now on, Cold War competition would not be enough to justify the astronomical costs of space exploration. A growing chorus of voices made it clear that the space community must now compete for resources with programs to feed hungry school children and clean up poisoned rivers.

The scientific community, for its part, was unloading a host of pent-up resentments against the space effort for shortchanging research both on the ground and in space. Some leading scientists, claiming it had drained money from other, non-space-related areas of research for too long, demanded that the space program's rationale be completely re-examined. Others who had been involved in the Apollo program itself complained that they were routinely treated as second class citizens, even having to wait in line behind the press at Houston's Lunar Receiving Lab to see moon photos. The moon missions had favored pilot-astronauts at the expense of scientist-astronauts who could do research aloft, they noted. (As of 1969, none of the seventeen scientists trained as astronauts had been assigned a mission.)

Space agency officials were slow to realize that their romantic visions had been eclipsed. Thomas Paine, the new NASA administrator, was determined to use the momentum of the lunar landing to propel the program on to the next logical ''big project,'' a manned mission to Mars. Other officials favored a space station plus various hardware including a shuttle to ferry freight and people to and from it, and some fancied a base on the moon's surface. They still cherished an image of earth as an island in the ocean of space. Historically, they said, island peoples have prospered in proportion to how well they use the sea around them. Accordingly, Paine, backed by the dean of rocketmen, Wernher von Braun, wrote of a new breed of "buccaneers" who would "stake out and create powerful outposts of stability, sanity and real future value for mankind in the new uncharted seas of space and global technology."

But all this was so much pie-in-the-sky to political realists. President Nixon, a nominal supporter of the space program but also a pragmatist, and one who didn't want to appear to be copying President Kennedy, appointed a Space Task Group chaired by Vice-President Spiro T. Agnew to examine the options.

In a report issued on September 17, 1969, just before the *Apollo 11* astronauts and their wives embarked on a world tour to be welcomed as heroes in twenty-two national capitals, Agnew bought the whole NASA package: a manned Mars mission "before the end of this century," and to implement it a manned space station, a space shuttle "bus," a nuclear rocket engine for long life in space and an atomic-powered space "tugboat" to push the station around, either on Earth, moon or Martian orbit.

"Manned exploration of the solar system leading to a manned Mars landing is inevitable," said Agnew. He added that, among the scheduling options, he personally preferred a Mars landing in 1986.

Some supporters of manned exploration were disappointed that the task force was not recommending a bold crash program comparable to Apollo to accomplish all this. Their disappointments had just begun.

The administration was divided internally. Nixon pointedly refused to endorse Agnew's recommendations while other Administration officials sorted out a unified position on space. Nixon had paid lip service to the space program, said one NASA official, but in the end, when it came to money, "we got the fish eye."

Liberals on Capitol Hill pounced on the high costs. They charged that the moon missions had wasted the taxpayers' money. Senator Walter Mondale (D-Minnesota) and others said the country needed to spend more on education and health and less on astronaut "playthings" and "manned showbusiness." Senator

William Proxmire (D-Wisconsin) said, "When the smoke is cleared from all this pomp and circumstance, the harsh fact remains that American taxpayers have paid twenty-four billion dollars for the privilege of seeing two of their fellow citizens walk on the moon. Even by Broadway standards, this is a pretty stiff price for front row seats." And Representative Joseph Karth (D-Minnesota), chairman of the House Space Science and Applications Subcommittee, called for more resources for unmanned research flights and described the manned program as an overfed "hungry pig."

Forced by congressional budget limitations to choose among its many space projects, NASA had to choose the shuttle. There was no point in building a space station without a means of reaching it. There could be no Mars mission without a space station. The shuttle was the only item that could exist without the other elements, and indeed it was the keystone of everything NASA wanted to achieve in space for decades to come: get in and out of earth orbit routinely, carry up unmanned satellites, study the earth's lands and seas, assemble one or more large space stations in orbit, then supply them.

A period of infighting followed among Congress, the White House budget office, and NASA over what kind of shuttle to build. The Air Force joined in the fray; it wanted a shuttle for military uses but didn't want to foot the bill itself. Concerned about what the Russians were building for space use, the Air Force needed, as one officer put it, "to be able to take a look at and deal as necessary with space vehicles of another country."

So, in 1971, NASA went shopping for a shuttle design that would please everybody. A series of them were considered and rejected, with Congress and OMB (where George Shultz was director and his deputy Caspar Weinberger was honing his reputation as "Cap the Knife") pushing for dollar savings; the Air Force concerned about the design's ability to carry out certain operations necessary for national security, and NASA hoping for something that would advance its ambitious vision of humanity's future in space.

If the old anthem was "one giant step for mankind," the new one was the rather less-lyrical "find the lowest cost per pound of payload in orbit."

Could they design a vehicle which, as one NASA official suggested, could reduce that rate from $500 a pound using

37

throw-away rockets to something like $5.00 a pound? Should it be large or small, fully or only partly reusable? Should its wings be delta-shaped or straight?

NASA, of course, wanted the swan—a luxury model with a fully-reusable orbiter to be launched atop a first stage that could also be piloted back to earth for re-use. Their orbiter would have been able to land at commercial airports and would have had its own space "tug" to boost it into the high orbit where unmanned commercial satellites fly.

The Pentagon also wanted a pricey model, but not necessarily the one favored by NASA. It wanted something which could land from virtually any orbit and was big enough to carry military payloads which were getting so large and complex that they had outgrown the unmanned expendable rockets then carrying secret cargo into space.

The shuttle's fate was influenced, to a degree, by a near-disaster in April 1970, when U.S. astronauts had what would be their most dramatic accident in space until nearly sixteen years later. A main oxygen tank on the *Apollo 13* mission exploded fifty-five hours after launch, blew a thirteen-foot-square hole in the side of the craft's service module and almost cost the lives of the three crewmen. The astronauts, abandoning their lunar landing, detached their command craft from the shattered service module and, after nearly a week of gut-wrenching tension, landed safely. The experience shocked people into contemplating what a real catastrophe in space might mean.

In a report on the accident which sounds eerily like the speculation surrounding the fate of the *Challenger,* the agency investigators blamed "an unusual combination of mistakes" by men on the ground, including the installation of the wrong thermostats, rough handling of the oxygen tank by ground crews and improper monitoring of preflight tests.

If the oxygen tank had burst on the launchpad, a "major conflagration" might have destroyed the vehicle, the report said. It suggested that the agency and its contractors had not learned the lessons of the *Apollo 1* fire in 1967, which killed three astronauts on the launchpad.

"We haven't talked enough about the risks," acting NASA administrator George Low told a reporter at the time. "I felt very strongly that *Apollo 8* was worth the risk and therefore we should take it. *Apollo 11* (the first moon landing) was worth the risk. But the risk stays constant and the gains diminish. At what time do you say the risks are so high and the gains so thin that you can no longer fly the missions? . . . In my opinion we can no longer justify it on a risk-gain basis.''

Because of concerns over safety as well as tight money, *Apollo 18* and *19* were canceled, workers were laid off and scientists who had counted on the missions were infuriated. At the same time, however, the sacrifice of these Apollo flights bought time and money for the shuttle while the debate over its design raged on.

By mid–1971, the whole space industry was in grim health. Spending was half what it had been in the glory days five years earlier, and so was employment. For the first time since the program geared up, manned flight accounted for less than half the NASA payroll. Only twenty-one of the forty-nine pilot-astronauts at Houston had been assigned a spaceflight. Said chief astronaut Donald K. (Deke) Slayton, "The best I can say is, if anybody wants to quit, I'm not going to discourage him. The facts of life are we don't need pilots. We've got more than we need.''

As the grandiose visions were pared down, Mondale and other legislators who had recently grounded the country's supersonic transport plane (SST) tried to kill the shuttle too.

NASA, groping for a way to reconcile the craft's still ambitious mandate with its increasingly pinched budget, commissioned a study by Mathematica, Inc, a think tank. Using data from the contractors who would compete to build the craft, Mathematica concluded that the shuttle would pay for itself if it could maintain a launch rate of more than thirty flights a year.

In 1972, with the presidential election approaching and mindful of the aerospace industry's economic funk, Nixon and Congress agreed on a shuttle design. In a statement released at San Clemente, the president promised that the craft would "revolutionize transportation into near space by routinizing it'' and "take the astronomical cost out of astronautics.'' He went on to say the shuttle "will make the ride safer and less demanding for the passengers, so that men and women with work to do in space can 'commute' aloft.''

The result of the war of wills was "a shuttle that no one wanted, except perhaps the Air Force,'' said military historian Alex Roland of Duke University, in an article in the November 1985 issue of *Discover* magazine.

The winning shuttle design was not for the totally reusable

model that NASA had wanted. Its development budget was 5.5 billion dollars (later reduced further), about half what NASA had hoped for. Initial cost estimates assumed sixty missions a year by 1985, well over Mathematica's promised break-even point. But at the time the *Challenger* exploded, NASA had retreated to a schedule that would not even reach twenty flights a year by 1990.

In 1981, as the *Columbia* prepared for launch, former NASA official Hinners said, "To take on a technological challenge like the shuttle with penny pinching as its major goal was just plain stupid."

The U.S. commitment to the shuttle meant a return to the course the space program had been following before it was diverted by *Sputnik* in 1957. At that time, the military was working on a primitive spacecraft called *Dyna-Soar*, which would have been launched into orbit by rocket and returned as a glider. It in turn was a descendant of designs brought to America by German scientists. They had worked on the winged V-1 rocket bomb and later World War II designs which evolved into the X-1, the first American rocket plane, which was carried aloft by a B-29 and released. But the crash program to the moon forced NASA to temporarily abandon development of the reusable rocketplane and turn to throwaway ballistic rockets already developed for military uses.

In late 1972, the most coveted single space contract of the decade—the prime contract to build the new reusable spaceplane —was awarded to North American Rockwell Corporation.

The giant California firm, which had also been the prime contractor on the Apollo program, was the lowest bidder at 2.6 billion dollars. Rockwell's cost-conscious management approach and its recent intense experience with manned spaceflight were also factors, NASA official Richard McCurdy said at the time.

But there was another aspect to the award, which foreshadowed the influence of the social forces that would soon transform the astronaut corps itself: officials took into account the fact that Rockwell had more blacks, more Hispanics and more orientals than its three competitors. A few years earlier, after black workers at the company had confronted management and demanded better promotions and pay, the Labor Department's Office of Federal Contract Compliance moved in and forced the company to develop an "affirmative action plan" to improve its record in the area.

"We're not crusaders for civil rights," McCurdy said. "But the fact that (Rockwell) moved forward on this front tells us something about how the company is thinking ahead, about how it's going to get along in its labor relations . . . You know, the shuttle contract isn't anything like buying a smoked ham for next weekend. We're talking about something that's going to be the space agency's lifeblood for some time to come."

There were other signs of change in the space culture. In December 1972, when *Apollo 17* took off for the final moon landing, Harrison (Jack) Schmitt, went along to become the first U.S. scientist-astronaut in space. NASA officials bumped Joe Engle, a skilled test pilot of the old breed, to make room for Schmitt. Engle had waited eleven years for a mission and this was his last chance. He said getting bumped felt like a kick in the teeth. "It was hard to swallow. But it made sense." In late 1977, Engle would pilot a prototype spaceplane, named the *Enterprise* after the starship in the TV series "Star Trek®," in test flights leading up to the first shuttle launch. The *Enterprise* was carried repeatedly aloft atop a Boeing 747 and released from as high as 26,000 feet, to see if it could glide to a landing.

After watching the launch of that final Apollo craft, Julian Scheer, who had long served as a top public affairs official with NASA, was moved to write a bittersweet farewell to the glory days of space exploration, capturing the public ambivalence on the subject. "There was a mixed feeling of pride and guilt toward the space program . . . It moved forward on our television sets and in our subconscious, almost a solitary symbol of something that was working. But the question of its rightful place in the scheme of things always hung over it."

During the years that the shuttle moved from budget documents and blueprints to the factory floor, Americans satisfied their appetite for high-tech adventure at the movies while NASA wrestled with the nuts and bolts. The space age was supplanted by the age of *Star Wars*, reality by fantasy.

Reality was von Braun, father of the rocket and dean of the American manned space program, leaving NASA to join private industry because the sense of urgency and challenge was gone.

Reality was the dawning public awareness that the astronauts were, after all, human. It was revealed that three *Apollo 15* astronauts had been reprimanded for accepting money for carrying 100 autographed envelopes with them to the moon. Fifteen of the twenty-seven Apollo astronauts had been getting five dollars for each autograph they signed. The Justice Department was investigating the "commercialization of the manned flight program."

And before long, reality was a series of snafus connected with the shuttle's development. In contrast to the moon program, budget pressures prevented NASA from pursuing parallel development of alternative designs and technologies for the shuttle. Instead, engineers had to commit themselves to a "success oriented" strategy which, in plain language, meant that everything had to work right the first time if they were to avoid serious delays and cost overruns.

The two biggest headaches were with the main engines and the tiles.

The engines were built to burn liquid hydrogen, the first time any fuel outside of kerosene had been used to carry men into space, and they were at the cutting edge of technology. Their pumps were being built to turn at 36,000 revolutions per minute, a then-unheard-of rate in a high-pressure pump.

"These pumps we are talking about are roughly the size of a trash can, and the amount of energy being released during combustion is equivalent to five million horsepower," said a specialist who reviewed the shuttle's problems for Congress.

The engines repeatedly blew up on the test stands, pumps exploded and exhaust nozzles melted right through from temperatures approaching 3,000 degrees Fahrenheit.

The problem of the tiles seemed more appropriate to a Jules Verne fantasy than a late-twentieth century drafting board. NASA needed something light which could be molded to fit the shuttle's contours, something able to withstand the inferno of re-entry, when temperatures reach up to 2600 degrees, and something cheap.

It settled on a unique solution: it ordered 33,000 tiles made of river sand from Leseur, Minnesota, considered the purest in the U.S. They were fired into glass in Richmond, Indiana; fiberized and strengthened in Chamco, Kentucky; and machined and sawed into individually-cut blanks in Palo Alto, California.

The tiles were white or black, and were precision-cut in varying shapes and dimensions depending on where they were located and

42

what temperatures they would encounter. Attaching them to the shuttle was another matter. Both NASA and Rockwell grossly underestimated the task. The tiling schedule doubled, then tripled, then quadrupled.

The tiles were put on using a space-age glue on a nylon felt backing. The spaces between tiles could be no more than 17/1000s of an inch. Any gap at all, and the heat could burn through. Some of the most difficult tiles, around the curvier nose area, had to be sculpted using the sort of machine used to copy statuary.

When the *Columbia* was moved to the Kennedy Space Center for testing, in July 1979, it was still 10,000 tiles short. The tiling, begun two years earlier and plagued by delays, was proceeding in three shifts a day, six days a week, and had achieved the rate, one dispirited NASA technician said, of "1.3 tiles per man per week."

Fitting the more difficult tile patterns was incredibly time-consuming. Each time a worker installed a tile, he fit a dummy tile to the space next to it and then sent the dummy across the country to the shuttle factory at Palmdale, California, where a tracing machine milled out a real tile which was then shipped back to the Cape to be attached.

A call went out for more tile-hands. College students, out-of-work field hands, faded flower children and others showed up for the jobs. Ultimately, tiling the *Columbia* took roughly 335 man-years.

Some tiles had fallen off the *Columbia* during its relatively gentle flight across the country atop a jumbo jet. No one was sure they wouldn't start coming off during the shock of liftoff, triggering a "zipper effect" that might unravel whole sections. After the *Columbia*'s historic first landing, it was noted that astronaut Young bounded immediately down the stairs to the runway, heedless of protocol. He explained later that he was anxious to see if any tiles had fallen off.

The program was also affected by what critics charged were NASA's sloppy management practices, rapid turnover in top positions and chronic rivalry among its main space centers around the country (which more recent management had been trying to straighten out), all of this complicated increasingly by the military's concerns about secrecy.

In 1978, the shuttle's test problems, delays and cost overruns were such that some members of Congress tried to kill the shuttle.

It was saved mainly because the Carter administration needed it to carry up additional spy satellites for the Pentagon as the SALT II negotiations with the Soviets progressed.

Still, for some people, the magnetic pull of the space frontier managed to transcend all the difficulties—as it always had.

In January 1978, NASA admitted the largest single group of astronaut candidates to the citadel at Houston, the first new class in ten years and the eighth in the space program's history. The class shattered the mold of the old breed of astronaut, the white male brotherhood of *The Right Stuff*. It included one Asian-American, three blacks and six women. Its fifteen pilots were outnumbered by twenty others with new astronaut titles—"mission specialist" or "payload specialist."

Chosen from more than 8,000 applicants, the newcomers represented the shift in emphasis, fueled by the public demand for practical results from their space dollar, from the wonder of flight itself to "what the payloads do." It also reflected official efforts to build public support for the program by involving ever broader segments of the population.

The agency had first recruited scientists as astronauts in 1964. But some had flunked out or dropped out of the program, impatient or frustrated with their limited roles; one candidate even discovered he was afraid of flying. "This time, the agency wanted applicants who understood what would be expected of them and were willing to devote most of their careers to the program," said Carolyn Huntoon, Johnson Space Center's Deputy Chief for Personnel Development. The newcomers committed themselves to fly the shuttle for ten years, the intended operational lifetime for current design.

"They had to be very good in what they were doing. And yet they had to be willing to give it up to do more general things," Huntoon said. "They had to understand that they would be Indians when they got here. That's a little bit difficult to accept when people have excelled in their fields."

The civilians were to be paid, based on education and experience, between $21,800 and $33,800 a year. The military pilots would continue at their current pay levels.

Jeffrey Hoffman, a Harvard PhD among the thirty-five, said, "Most of my scientist friends think this is a frivolous thing I'm doing, but it's been my dream all my life, to go into space."

Rhea Seddon gave up a lucrative career as a surgeon for an astronaut job at starting pay of $24,700 a year. "Some of my doctor friends will never get over it," she said. "They think I'm crazy."

The new astronauts would earn their keep by handling and deploying satellites, repairing damaged ones in orbit, conducting a variety of onboard experiments for a variety of customers, operating telescopes and conducting photographic surveys of the earth's resources.

The new class also reflected the country's social revolution.

Said Huntoon, "I think because people were feeling a little bit bad about the way they had treated women . . . (the administration) said, 'It's a federal job and we're going to open it to all races, sexes, religious backgrounds and ages.'" Later NASA accepted several European applicants.

The selection of Sally Ride, a member of the class of 1978, to be the first American woman in space helped rekindle public interest in the program, as officials hoped it would. Ride had almost followed a career as a tennis pro, but as a graduate student in physics at Stanford, she found another calling: research into X-ray astronomy and free-electron lasers, one of a number of devices it turned out NASA was considering for transmitting energy from space stations to earth.

Early in 1977, she had spotted one of NASA's ads in a campus daily. NASA was looking for young scientists to become astronauts in the new category of "mission specialist." Until that moment, Ride had never thought about such a career path. It hadn't existed. "It never occurred to me," she said. "I thought I was going to get a job . . . doing research in free-electron laser physics and then work at a university, doing research and teaching. That's what physicists do." She knew nothing of the requirements to be an astronaut. "I didn't know whether they were going to throw us into a centrifuge or hang us from the ceiling by our toes."

In fact, much of the program's mystique seemed to be crumbling as it opened to a wider range of people. The physical standards had been considerably loosened compared with the old days. Glasses were okay if they corrected vision to 20/20. A history of significant illnesses such as epilepsy, diabetes or heart disease was grounds for elimination, but there was no limit on the age at which an astronaut, once selected, could fly. In fact, men in their late fifties would soon be flying on the shuttle. One astronaut, a former Navy test pilot and nuclear engineer who had been rejected by the program in 1964, was accepted in 1978, at age forty-two.

The shuttle's cockpit chairs moved up and down to give smaller astronauts better access to all switches. The cargo bay doors were made easy to open, in case a woman with poor upper-body strength had to do it. And a suction toilet was designed to accommodate both sexes.

The chosen ones no longer went through survival training in which they were left marooned on islands and had to survive by snaring and eating wild lizards. (All the shuttle's landing strips, it was noted, were near civilization.) Since the shuttle pulls only three times the force of gravity at lift-off, the whirling of astronauts in a face-flattening centrifuge was dropped. Tight money limited an astronaut's flying time to fifteen hours a week.

Some passengers would not even have their own space-suits. In case of an emergency requiring a transit through the void of space, they would roll themselves up inside tiny airtight spheres and their suited crewmates would float them across like beachballs.

As early as March, 1970, NASA officials had talked publicly about taking people who were neither scientists nor pilots, people with no special training at all, on a space ride. A person who was "simply in good health" would be able to go, administrator Paine said at a news conference. "We will even be able to take healthy newsmen if we can find any," he quipped. And by 1979, scores of print and television reporters had applied. Even some astronauts were heard to make remarks like, "My ninety-two-year-old aunt could do this." But it would be some time later before a NASA administrator would manage to push the idea all the way to the White House and presidential approval. That feat was accomplished by James M. Beggs, who took over the space agency in 1981 and nurtured the idea of citizen participation.

On August 27, 1984, in a speech to a group of educators, President Reagan endorsed a NASA advisory council recommendation, announcing, "It's long been a goal of our space shuttle, the program, to some day carry citizen passengers into space. Until now, we hadn't decided who the first citizen passenger would be. But today, I'm directing NASA to begin a search in all of our elementary and secondary schools and to choose as the first citizen passenger in the history of our space program one of

America's finest—a teacher. . . . When that shuttle lifts off, all of America will be reminded of the crucial role that teachers and education play in the life of our nation. I can't think of a better lesson for our children and our country.''

The announcement provoked charges that it was a politically motivated public relations stunt.

In 1985, two members of congress who hold some of the space program purse strings and a Saudi prince would ride into orbit as the first non-scientist, non-pilot space passengers, beating the officially designated ''astro-teacher.''

But the notion that astronauting had become a pursuit for just anybody was as false as ever. Most of the veteran astronauts had long expected a fatal accident in space and some had argued against giving valuable seat space to the untrained.

In some ways, the standards for spaceflight were actually rising. The new-generation astronauts were better educated and more at home with computers than their predecessors. The test pilots among them had flown faster high performance aircraft than the old breed. Nineteen of the newcomers were veterans of Vietnam, racking up a combined total of more than 2,900 combat missions. ''Almost every one of these new guys has shown before they even got here that they could perform under stress,'' said Young, the astronaut boss. ''They've got a depth of experience that wasn't even available to us fifteen years ago.''

They needed it. The shuttle was ''an order of magnitude'' more complex and tricky to fly than the Apollo craft he had taken to the moon in 1972, he said. And the NASA selection panel still looked for a special brand of self-assurance, poise and grace under pressure in its astronaut candidates.

The newcomers were treated to an initial whirlwind of photo sessions and training rides in T-38 jets, and weightlessness training in the KC-135 ''vomit comet.'' But the training soon settled down to classroom lectures on engineering and computer science, charts and manuals and diagrams about every inch of the shuttle, and instruction in a variety of sciences important in space such as geology and biochemistry.

After the first year of classroom training came a period of apprenticeship to veteran astronauts, when the fledglings learned the engineering tasks that would become their special responsibility on shuttle flights—tasks that took them far from their own original scientific interests.

Later, when one-by-one they were assigned to specific shuttle missions, their schedules became for months a blur of fifteen-hour days, of grueling, round-the-clock sessions in the shuttle simulators, visits to contractors' factories to see equipment, technical briefings and studying stacks of manuals outlining every minute of the flight.

Almost all of them would have flown on at least one mission by 1986. The shuttle fleet had grown to four orbiters, with the addition of *Discovery*, *Atlantis* and *Challenger*.

In the old days, Donald K. (Deke) Slayton, one of the first seven astronauts, had served as superboss, deciding which of the others got to fly on the rare missions. The atmosphere was compared to that of a harem, with each one finagling for a night with the king. And, said Slayton, himself then grounded with a heart condition, "The flight is the king."

After the first shuttle successes, as the pace of flights picked up, some of that competitiveness that had characterized the old astronaut corps disappeared and allowed the newcomers to become a more tightly-knit group.

Still, the standing mandate of the old brotherhood of *The Right Stuff* was too entrenched not to weigh on the new generation: keep cool and don't screw up.

The workaholic grind (stripped of the glamor of the Apollo days) later began to take a toll that stunned the corps. For twenty years, one resignation a year had been the average. But within a sixteen month period in 1984 and 1985, at least eight astronauts quit their jobs, often citing the pressure on their family life. "There's a payoff to astronauts working sixteen-hour days, six or seven days a week, and that is they get to fly in space," said John M. Fabian, who resigned two months after he won his third shuttle assignment. "Their families don't get that payoff. All they see are the missed dinners and the trips out of town to Cape Canaveral or some contractor's factory in California."

NASA officials argued that a brisk training pace, keeping the astronauts physically and mentally honed, was one reason the U.S. had never had a fatal accident in space. In any case, the lure of space travel has never failed to attract long lines of ardent volunteers ready to ante up anything that's required for a ticket to ride, knowing they ride as trusting dependents of millions of machine parts and thousands of human minds and hands.

Four of them formed close friendships as members of the

iconoclastic class of '78: Francis R. (Dick) Scobee, Judith A. (J.R.) Resnik, Ellison S. Onizuka and Ronald E. McNair. Three more—Michael J. Smith, Gregory B. Jarvis and Sharon Christa Corrigan McAuliffe—came later, to seek and win the remaining seats on Flight 51-L, to pay the price that so many willing others had escaped by who knows how much.

What fueled their passion for this curious and risky world, their January rush to meet the future with such headlong eagerness?

Chapter 3

FRANCIS R. (DICK) SCOBEE

On an October day in 1966, a squadron of excited young pilots sat in a classroom at Moody Air Force Base in Georgia, staring at a blackboard in the front of the room. It was the last day of a year-long pilot training course, and the room was abuzz with nervous chatter. The blackboard listed the assignments available to them, and their choices would determine what paths their careers would take for years, perhaps decades.

It was a time-honored Air Force ritual, and the pilots knew the routine. Invariably, the top of the class, given first crack, chose fighter planes, the supersonic hot rods of the sky. The rest, disappointed, were left with "the heavies"—Air Force lingo for multi-engined heavy aircraft—and packed their bags for remote air bases where they would learn to fly huge planes with names such as the Caribou (C-7 cargo propeller plane) or the BUF—the Big Ugly Fella, as the B-52 bombers were known. The pilots marked their forms and submitted them, hoping for the best.

Dick Scobee, who was graduating second in his class, had his pick of assignments. He was a natural choice for fighter jets—who would pass them up? But Scobee jotted down: "C-141," a heavy.

When the assignments came through a week later, Scobee's classmates were dumbfounded at his choice. Almost all of them wanted to be fighter jocks, heirs to the great tradition of aviation's barnstorming days and the aces of the two world wars. How could anyone pass up the chance to fly the world's fastest jets in stupendous displays of aerobatics? What's more, fighter pilots dominated the ranks of NASA astronauts, the most elite group in the history of aviation, as if it was their birthright.

Heavy pilots were another breed. Dubbed "trash haulers" by the fighters, heavy pilots lumbered about in their huge planes, hauling men, cargo, trucks and ordnance. Many pilots, including heavies themselves, insist it's easy to tell the two breeds apart. Fighters wear their emotions like flak jackets, chase women and bust up bars. Heavies are more even-keeled, more methodical: their job is to deliver passengers and cargo safely. The best heavy pilots achieve the maximum finesse from the minimum effort in the cockpit, notice problems quickly and correct them unflinchingly. They are smooth as glass in the air and set their crafts down as if their cargo was a crate of eggs.

It was an unglamorous and, for the most part, unloved job, but somebody had to do it. Besides, given the accident rates of fighter pilots, there was a better chance of surviving the experience. There was something to be said for remaining alive, the heavies would console each other. They formed their own informal fraternity—the bus drivers of the skies!

Scobee fit the image of a heavy to a tee: He was competent and sober, determined but not overly ambitious. He was six-foot-one and sturdily built, handsome in a wholesome, you-can-rely-on-me way, with a Cary Grant jaw, even features and a sincere smile that began as a hint at the corners of his mouth and then spread broadly across his face. He was deeply self-confident but without being cocky; his self-assurance emerged gradually through a veil of soft words and modesty. For all his ease in the cockpit and with other pilots, he seemed to go out of his way to divert attention from himself.

And no wonder. Scobee was unaccustomed to the limelight. When he received his wings in 1966, he was twenty-seven years old, several years older than most brand-new Air Force pilots, many of whom get their training immediately after graduating from college. He had signed up as an enlisted man in the Air Force shortly after graduating from high school, and spent six years working as a mechanic on propeller planes at a base in Texas. "The only reason I tolerate you," an enlisted friend told Scobee years later, after his career had blossomed, "is because you were brought up right."

In Air Force parlance, Scobee was a "mustang," an enlisted man who had managed to break from the ranks to become an officer and a pilot. That was commendable, all right, but it still left the odds stacked high against him. Every time he'd come up for promotion, he'd be in the upper reaches of the age bracket; men the same age would always be a rank or two more senior. It was unusual, even for enlisted men who became officers, to become pilots. And if they became pilots, it was almost unheard of that they'd reach the lofty confines of test pilot school at Edwards Air Force Base, cradle of the fabled *The Right Stuff*. As for the chance of such an upstart someday joining the elite family of NASA astronauts, well, the odds were better that a squadron of fighter pilots would stay sober for a year.

In the 1940s, the little town of Auburn, Washington, twenty-five miles south of Seattle in the shadow of Mount Rainier, was a community of just over 4,200 people. Surrounded by farms, it was supported by the Northern Pacific Railway, whose yards at the town's edge were an important source of jobs. Francis R. Scobee, a strapping railroad engineer, and his wife, Eddie, moved there from the Cascade Mountain town of Cle Elum, Washington, soon after their oldest son, Dick, was born on May 19, 1939. The Scobees lived near the center of town, in a small, two-story, dark-brown clapboard house on Fourth Street, just a block from Auburn's only high school. The house was modest and homey—there was a pool table downstairs—but it was a step up from the sprawling rows of shanties across from the busy rail yards that were homes for hundreds of railroad workers and their families.

Auburn was changing, however, shedding one generation's technology for the next. In Seattle and other Green River Valley towns north of Auburn, the fastest-growing employer was the Boeing Company whose factories had turned out thousands of military planes for the armed forces during the war. In the mid-1950s, the company began to manufacture the 707, America's first commercial jet. As Boeing supplanted Northern Pacific as the region's principal employer, Auburn was swept up in the change. The area's high school graduates entering the work force were eschewing the rail yards in favor of the hangars and tarmacs. Jobs in the growing airplane industry were plentiful, and if a family didn't have a relative who worked for Boeing, it certainly had a friend who did. For boys growing up in the valley in those days, weaned on newsreel footage of the heroism of America's

World War II aces, dreams of flying a jet airplane were not so far-fetched.

Dick Scobee got the bug for airplanes and flying as a toddler. At the age of two or three, his parents gave him a toy car, the kind of wheel-about vehicle that parents hope will burn off kids' energy. Scobee's was a hybrid: it had a pair of wings. The winged car sparked his imagination. In class, when he'd finish his lessons, Scobee would take out a thick black pencil and sketch airplanes. As he got older, the sketches became increasingly sophisticated, the Spitfires and P-38s replaced by fantastic, futuristic contraptions. After school, Scobee spent his afternoons building wooden models of airplanes. By the time he was in high school, so many of the models hung by string from his bedroom ceiling that a visitor had to bob and weave his way through the room, taking care not to dislodge a propeller or collide with a heavy bomber.

A well-groomed, well-mannered boy with shining blue eyes, thick dark hair and a shy smile that accentuated his apple cheeks, Dick Scobee was well-liked in high school. Schoolwork was difficult for him, but he made up for it by working hard; his grades, while never straight-A's, were above average. He was a lineman on the football team but didn't start, was a shotputter but quit the track team his senior year. He was rarely sick; in three consecutive school years, he didn't miss a day. In school, Scobee kept a low profile and liked it that way; he didn't like people making a fuss over him, and he wasn't out to impress anyone. His was a quiet 1950s boyhood in a quiet town: swimming and inner-tube rides in the Green River, hiking in the Cascades, hay-stacking in the summers, a job as a box boy at a local Safeway, bowling, double-dating and hanging out at the Rainbow Cafe on Auburn's Main Street. He spent hours overhauling and polishing his car, a mid-1940s Ford sedan, and fished with his father and friends in Puget Sound for steelheads, a type of trout.

When Scobee was a senior at Auburn High in 1957, he approached his guidance counselor: how could he win a scholarship to the Air Force Academy in Colorado Springs? The counselor told him he had to know a U.S. Senator personally—which was untrue. Scobee gave up on the idea. When he posed for his graduation photo at the end of that year, he wore a bow tie and dark jacket. Underneath the photograph is the italicized caption: "Serious and dependable."

A few of Scobee's classmates went to college, but not many needed a bachelor's degree to work on the farm or for the railroad or Boeing. Lacking the money for college, Scobee went to work for Boeing immediately after graduation, filing blueprints in the company's Seattle plant. The job lasted about three months.

In October 1957, he and a close school friend, Larry Brooks, signed up to enter the Air Force as enlisted men under the "buddy system." They were sent to Kelly Air Force base in San Antonio for training as mechanics. It was not exactly a well-trodden route to fame and fortune—nor was it intended to be. Both men planned to stay four years, learn what the Air Force had to teach them, then return to Auburn, where Scobee had a girl friend and expectations of landing a permanent job with Boeing. A few months later, Brooks remembers, a "Dear John" letter from the girl friend back in Auburn that changed all that. There was no longer any reason for Scobee to return home. He was eighteen.

One autumn Saturday in 1958, about a year after Scobee arrived in San Antonio, he went to a hayride at the Mayfield Park Baptist Church, not too far from the base. It was an old-fashioned hayride, with bales arranged on the back of a flatbed truck. He found himself sitting next to a curly-haired girl, who introduced herself as June Kent. She was a little taller than five feet, and just sixteen years old, but mature for her age. As the afternoon faded to dusk, the truck arrived at a garden, where there was a picnic under flickering lanterns. June and Dick wandered away from the crowd into a remote spot of the garden. There was a creek nearby, the evening was balmy, and the two talked about how beautiful the natural scenery was. He asked if he could call on her at home the next day, Sunday—she lived in a community just south of the base—and she agreed. Soon he was picking her up regularly from her high school, taking her to hamburger drive-ins, chatting over shakes.

They shared a fascination with airplanes. "I remember we talked about the camber of a plane's wing," said June. "He had always had a fascination with airplanes, and they seemed to be like a miracle to me. I was curious about what made them work, and he could explain it to me."

June Kent was a serious-minded young woman, the daughter of a construction worker who lived where he could find work in the South and Southwest. She had shared responsibility for raising her younger brothers. In Scobee she met a young man every bit as earnest and reflective as herself. They talked about things she had never discussed with anyone: life and death, airplanes and flying, friendship and the future. They talked about their goals. Both wanted a college education. For the time being, Airman First Class Scobee wanted to be the best mechanic he could. He had a quiet determination to do well—always looking pragmatically at how to improve a situation—that never seemed quite to spill over into overt ambition. She trusted him instinctively. He was not concerned about the appearances of what he did, or about impressing others; rather, he wanted to live up to his own standards and that seemed a far more exacting standard. It was an attractive quality.

On a spring day in 1959, as they ate burgers at a drive-in restaurant, Dick presented June with a ring and proposed marriage. She said yes, but not right away—she wanted to wait a few years. Soon afterwards, though, they decided there was no sense waiting, and two months later they were married at the Mayfield Park Baptist Church, site of the fateful hayride. He paid for the ring and the wedding from his small savings, and they had a small ceremony attended by her friends and family and a few of his friends from the base. The couple honeymooned in Auburn, where June met Dick's family. She was sixteen, he was twenty.

They returned to their San Antonio garage apartment, and Dick resumed his job as a mechanic on the C-124 Globemaster cargo propeller plane. It was a time for sorting out options. One of the top priorities, they agreed, was for them both to begin work toward a college degree. "I decided if I were to get anywhere in life, I probably ought to start going to school," Scobee said in a 1984 interview. He and his wife started attending night school at San Antonio College, but June soon quit after their first child, Kathie, was born in January 1961. Going to school at night demanded a fair bit of overtime and schedule-juggling, trading off with mechanics who would handle his evening work shifts if he would take their weekend assignments. At school, he took a smattering of basic college courses—English, algebra, social sciences—before deciding to concentrate on engineering.

The Scobees' lifestyle was simple. The family's monthly budget included forty dollars for housing, a forty-five dollar car payment and twenty dollars for groceries. Planning for a new pair of shoes was a major endeavor. Some of their friends were occasionally disappointed when they found June and Dick reluctant to splurge for a movie.

By 1963, Dick Scobee had two years of college credit from his studies at night school, and had set his sights on one day getting his bachelor's degree and perhaps becoming an officer when he found out about the Airman's Education and Commissioning Program, aimed at producing officers from the enlisted ranks. He applied and was accepted within weeks: the Air Force sent him to the University of Arizona. He spent two years there, studied hard, sometimes falling asleep on the living room couch with the alarm set so he could arise and study before class in the morning. It was a time of building confidence. In 1964 his son Richard was born. The following year he graduated from Arizona with a degree in aerospace engineering.

The Air Force's idea was that since Scobee had come from a maintenance slot as an enlisted man, he would be returned to maintenance as a supervising officer. Scobee, eyeing the unfolding war in Southeast Asia and sensing a chance to capitalize on his longstanding dream to become a pilot, had other ideas. "[The war in] Vietnam was ginning up pretty good and they needed pilots," he said in an interview nearly twenty years later. "I asked if there were any chance of going to pilot training and they said yes."

It was a turning point in Scobee's career, and the manner in which it came about was typical of Scobee's advancement: there was never any grand design, never a preordained game plan. His focus was on the immediate and on the potential next step. Failing that, he had a fall-back plan—in this case, to become a maintenance officer. But there was never much thought of some resounding ultimate success; Scobee was too practical for that.

Scobee was commissioned as a lieutenant in September 1965, and went directly to an eleven-month pilot training program at Moody Air Force Base in Valdosta, Georgia. Almost immediately, he loved to fly planes as much as he had loved watching and sketching them; his classmates said he had "good hands." For a young man who had always found school work painful, it was a surprise to find flight training, which entails intensive academics, to be enjoyable and to come naturally. "I remember he would say it was nice to be doing something that you're good at," said June. "He'd say that he and the airplane could feel as one, a part of each other. He'd say he felt fortunate to be able to make his avocation his vocation."

Scobee's decision to fly heavy planes was in character. "His focus was always on the job that needed to be done," said June. "He didn't care about what plane it was. He enjoyed them all, every plane he's ever flown. The focus was on the job rather than the image."

Scobee trained briefly in Oklahoma, then at Charleston Air Force where he learned to fly the C-141 StarLifter, a large jet cargo transport plane. In November 1967, he was sent to Vietnam. His experiences in the year he spent flying there, in the 535th Tactical Airlift Squadron, were never a prominent conversation topic for Scobee, even with his wife. But the decorations he received—the Distinguished Flying Cross and the Air Medal among them—spoke loudly enough of Scobee's bravery in flying C-7 Caribou twin-engine cargo plane through enemy fire and awful weather. A week after *Challenger* exploded, June received a letter from an Air Force captain in New Hampshire who had served with Scobee in Vietnam. "I remember Dick from my Vietnam experiences," the letter said. "He saved my life when he kept the enemy at bay while I belly-landed my fighter. He was a brave and strong man." June never heard her husband mention the captain or recount the incident.

When Scobee returned from Vietnam, he spent more than two years in Charleston, flying C-141s and other large transport aircraft, frequently on overseas supply missions, while June took classes at Baptist College at Charleston. In 1971, he received a form letter informing him that he was eligible for Air Force Aerospace Research Pilot School at Edwards Air Force Base in California. The school held out no promises of acceptance, but said it was looking for a broader field of applicants within the Air Force. Scobee spent several months talking about the opportunity with his wife, but June Scobee was concerned; test piloting was dangerous business.

"Don't test pilots someday become astronauts?" asked June. But Scobee reassured her: no, he said, he could never be an astronaut because of his height. Astronauts had to be five feet ten inches tall or less to fit into the space capsules, and at six feet one, he was just too tall. It was an indication of how little Scobee knew about the astronaut program; the original five-foot-ten height limit for astronauts in the *Mercury* and *Gemini* programs had been lifted six years earlier.

In any event, Scobee had little reason to expect an easy entree to

CHALLENGERS

test pilot school. For one thing, he was a "slick-wing"—in the military lingo, a pilot who lacked the seven years' pilot experience that brought a star to be clipped to the uniform above the Air Force's silver-plated wings. For another, at thirty-two, he was on the verge of being too old for the program. The test pilot school is among the most elite programs in the military. Hundreds of pilots apply; fewer than twenty-five a year are accepted, and most are twenty-eight or twenty-nine. For applicants older than that, the Air Force, which spends hundreds of thousands of dollars on each pilot in the course of the eleven-month program, was forced to ask tough cost-benefit questions: Will the Air Force get its money's worth? Will the pilot stay in the military for long, or resign and earn an additional $10,000 or $15,000 a year doing the same job as a test pilot for Lockheed or Northrop or Boeing? The older the applicant, the harder those questions became. Moreover, the Air Force Academy graduates always seemed to have an edge. They had a knack for rising to the top, for filling the most prestigious Air Force jobs at the Pentagon and the plum test pilot jobs at Edwards.

Balanced against the doubts that Scobee's application must have raised was the fact that he was a superb pilot—a heavy, yes, but a superb pilot all the same. That was the principle criterion for admission to the school, which prided itself on taking the cream of the Air Force's aviator crop. In July 1971, Captain Scobee entered the test pilot school at Edwards. He'd been an officer for less than six years, and a pilot for less than five. He entered Class 72-B as one of the oldest—and one of the junior-ranking—students in the class. It wasn't long before his classmates affectionately dubbed him "the old man."

The decision to apply and to go to test pilot school was a major turning point in the Scobees' lives. For the first time, Scobee would be applying for a job—without any obligation to do so—that entailed substantial implicit danger. Test pilots sometimes die, and in the closely knit community of test pilots at Edwards, where most of the Air Force's aircraft testing is done, many families have come to expect to lose an average of one friend every year.

Test pilots and their wives deal with the risk of death in different ways. Some pretend it isn't there. For many, the exhaustive training, simulator time and technological expertise lent an aura of caution to the job, or at least a conviction that the risks have been

58

pared down to manageable dimensions. Some may even imagine that they are invulnerable. Of course, there are no guarantees for test pilots, even for the best ones. But then, as test pilots invariably contend, there are no guarantees for pedestrians, or commercial airplane passengers, or motorists on the highway.

The Scobees confronted the risks head-on, talked about them, made their peace and moved on. "We really wrestled with life and death," said June. "We were very close, it was a wonderful marriage, each other's best friend. But after we wrestled with it, each day after that seemed to be a special gift to us. Each day was an extra day. And we both realized that not to do something that you enjoy could be a life and death situation . . . You resolve that we will all die sometime. And Dick had said that the years that we had been married were the best years a man could ever have—what more could a man ask for? Once you've wrestled with death and got that out of your system, you really become able to face life and enjoy life more."

Dick Scobee himself was matter-of-fact about the dangers he faced. "You have to risk something to gain something," he said. "When you find something you really like to do and you're willing to risk the consequences of that, you really probably ought to go do it." It was a functional creed, or at least a mainstay of psychological survival for the work Scobee would soon undertake.

A number of flukes of geography and tradition conspire to make Edwards test pilot heaven. For starters, there's the Mojave Desert climate: more than 300 sunny days a year. The air is dry, clear and generally still in the morning. Pilots at the base are generally airborne at the first light. They can glimpse the Pacific coast to the west, San Diego in the south and all the way to Nevada in the east. Bounded to the south and west by the San Gabriel mountains and the southernmost range of the Sierra Nevadas, which converge in a V just north of Los Angeles, the desert sprawls northeast to Death Valley and into Nevada. In the midst of the desert floor is the forty-four-square-mile Rogers Dry Lake, a playa scrubbed smooth and hard by the wind and ideal for emergency landings.

As every young pilot knows, Edwards barren and desolate though it is, is steeped in aviation history. Known as Muroc Army Air Field until 1950, it was the test site of the nation's first jet, the Bell XP-59A, in 1942. In 1947, then-Captain Charles E. (Chuck) Yeager, flying a Bell XS-1 rocket aircraft there, became the first man to break the sound barrier. Edwards was thereafter enshrined as the proving ground of *The Right Stuff*, the cradle of derring-do.

On top of all that, every aircraft in the Air Force inventory is tested at Edwards. Pilots there determine and test the dimensions of what pilots like to call the plane's "envelope"—its limits: How fast must it go to become airborne? How much runway does it need to land? How tight can it turn? What makes the engines flame out? What makes them stall? It's exacting, precise work, and the pilots who have mastered it comprise a special brotherhood and share a camaraderie rooted in refined skills, technological prowess, and a shared understanding of risk, on one level or another.

In 1971, when Scobee entered the school at Edwards, the daredevil days of the 1950s and 1960s when the Air Force winked at pilots playing roulette with their lives—not to mention the multi-million-dollar transonic machines they were flying—were over. Things were tighter, more controlled; there had been a professionalization of the test pilot corps. A new premium had been placed on precision, on discipline in the air, on mastering the new and fast-changing technology. "It's not like the white scarf old days when you jumped in an airplane and go with it," Scobee said in a 1984 interview with United Press International. "It's very analytical." The new breed of test pilots looked back on *The Right Stuff* days mostly with awe, but also with a little condescension. There seemed to be a New Stuff, and Dick Scobee was its perfect embodiment.

Scobee emerged as one of the best in his section of twelve pilots. Without doubt, he was the pick of the eight heavy pilots in the group and he had no trouble flying the souped-up fighter planes. He flew the heavy planes as they were meant to be flown; he was confident and capable, always meticulously prepared and seemed to be able to handle any job. "Dick wasn't a real hell-raiser like a lot of us," said David L. Ferguson, a fighter pilot who was his classmate and friend. "But anything he did he just did an exceptional job."

Scobee had gained confidence since his high school days, but hadn't really changed very much. There was still the shy smile, the businesslike and amiable manner, the easy laugh—all made him supremely well-liked. He didn't drink much, but didn't judge his friends who did. "He was so straight, it made an Irishman sick," said Mike McMorrow, an enlisted flight engineer of Irish descent who said his feelings about Scobee after working closely with him for three years following pilot school amounted to "sly hero worship."

After more than 700 hours in class and 150 hours in the air, Scobee graduated from test pilot school in June 1972. He did not win the prize awarded to the class' outstanding member, nor was he one of the "distinguished graduates" singled out by the school for special recognition. But it didn't matter; the best jobs for test pilots were at Edwards, and Scobee landed one. Despite the eight years of enlisted service, "the old man" had wound up right where he wanted to be: testing planes at the focal point for aviation achievement.

Although more than half the nation's astronauts were graduates of the test pilot school at Edwards, the members of Scobee's class saw NASA as a distant prospect at best. Not that they all weren't dying to be astronauts. *Apollo 11* had landed on the moon just three years earlier, and the space program was near the height of its considerable prestige. But the space agency had selected its last regular group of nineteen pilots for the astronaut program in 1966. Eleven scientists had been chosen the following year, and seven more pilots were picked in 1969 from a special program canceled by the Air Force. NASA had plenty of astronauts, more than enough to man (and they were all men) the scheduled Apollo missions.

After graduating from test pilot school, Scobee flew C-5's, testing the largest airplane in the country. He was then assigned to test the E-4, a converted Boeing 747 designed to serve as the airborne command center for the president of the United States in case of nuclear attack. Scobee and his flight engineer, McMorrow, were in charge of marrying the more familiar technology of the cockpit to the rebuilt, redesigned remainder of the plane.

Some of the testing Scobee carried out on the E-4 was extraordinarily difficult. He had to fly the plane perilously close to a leading fuel plane, which would extend a boom back toward a nozzle under the 747's nose. The procedure was extremely hazardous under the best conditions—and test pilots are not particularly interested in examining the best conditions. Rather, the idea is to take the plane to its limits, to find the point at which systems don't work, to push at the tolerances—or in Air Force lingo, to poke at the edges of the "envelope." On paper, test pilots know the procedure works. But what happens if, in midair refueling, one of the aircraft is off by five degrees in space? What if it's off by ten degrees? What if there is a tolerance of only a foot or two in space? The mental stress of the job is tremendous; there are good pilots who cannot do it day after day. Test pilots are typically given a "card" that outlines the precise steps they are to trace in a given flight, so that the plane locks onto a certain profile. Scobee could fly the cards in his sleep.

In 1975, Scobee was selected as a test pilot to fly the experimental X-24B, one of a line of "lifting bodies"—wingless aircraft with rounded contours whose fuselages would generate enough lift for gliding flights. Lifting bodies, the forerunners of the space shuttle, were designed to reenter the earth's atmosphere intact, minimizing the heat generated by foregoing large wings and other "sharp" angles, and land on the earth as any other glider might. His task was to pilot it on a glide flight, and make a safe landing in the desert. In two such flights, Scobee flew the plane flawlessly, landing smoothly at Edwards.

Air Force officials knew the handful of pilots selected to test the lifting bodies would have a leg up when NASA got around to choosing its next batch of astronauts. And when the call went out in 1977 that the space agency was looking for a new crop of astronauts, Scobee applied. He told people his application was just a lark, but friends knew he was excited about the chance to fly the shuttle. In January 1978 he was selected.

"There wasn't a conscious decision," he told a television interviewer in 1983. "When I was a test pilot at Edwards it was kind of a logical progression in my career and it was one of those things that happened at the right place, at the right time . . . I'm convinced that you have a lot of gates in your life, a lot of directions you can take. And they're influenced by yourself and by other people and you just end up at a place and a time. And any other place and time, I wouldn't have gotten into the program."

Scobee moved his family to Houston, retired as a major after twenty-two years in the Air Force and bought a home in Clear Lake City, a residential neighborhood adjacent to the Johnson Space Center. Wary of the driving habits of Houstonians, he sold a motorcycle that he had enjoyed riding around the flat desert roads at Edwards, and settled into a quiet lifestyle as part of the NASA family. He was content in his personal life, and he delighted in the achievements of his wife, who had taken a doctorate in education from Texas A&M University and was a visiting assistant professor of education at the University of Houston. His daughter Kathie, meanwhile, was married and had her first child in 1985, making Scobee a grandfather. His son Richard chose the path his father had been unable to follow and entered the Air Force Academy in 1982.

Scobee's first mission, as second in command of the *Challenger*'s Flight 41-C, came in 1984. Ironically for Scobee, who sidestepped publicity whenever possible, the flight was one of the space shuttle program's most celebrated successes: retrieving and repairing the Solar Maximum Mission satellite—the so-called Solar Max. The weeklong mission, beginning April 6, 1984, went off approximately as planned—until the landing site was changed because of bad weather in Florida from Cape Canaveral to Edwards. Alerted just hours before the *Challenger* was to land, Betty J. Callister, an old friend of Scobee's who was a secretary with NASA at Edwards, draped a large banner from a building in plain site of the deplaning area. "Dick," it declared, reviving a longstanding office joke, "if we knew you were coming we would have baked a cake." Alighting from the *Challenger*, Scobee saw the banner, smiled and waved. Then he stood aside, leaving the limelight to his crewmates. In the familiar photograph after the flight, Scobee and the crew appear in T-shirts announcing themselves as the "Ace Satellite Repair Co."

The flight thrilled Scobee, and he couldn't wait to go again. "We're all doing handstands, yelling, 'Take me! take me!'" he told an audience on a speaking tour after the 1984 flight. A classmate from his pilot training class in Georgia—a fellow heavy pilot named Craig Morrison—called to offer congratulations, and Scobee was typically modest.

"Once a 'trash hauler,' always a 'trash hauler,'" he said.

"Yeah, but you're doing it 180 miles up in the sky," said Morrison.

"Well," said Scobee with a chuckle, "there are a few perks in it."

While he was familiar enough with the complex technology of the space shuttle to understand its inherent dangers, his more immediate concern was to avoid any mistakes at the controls of the giant craft. Scobee had logged 6,500 hours of flying in forty-five types of aircraft, but no previous flight had been as thrilling as the mission to space. In an interview conducted by his wife appearing in the March 1986 issue of *Science and Children*, a magazine of the National Science Teachers Association, he said sleeping in space was like dozing on the world's greatest water bed; the shuttle's lift-off was like riding a runaway railroad train. He dreamed of the United States colonizing the moon, of everyday space travel, of humans living in space. Without space exploration, he said, man would go the way of the dinosaur, his resources depleted and his natural curiosity stifled.

Scobee looked fine on TV. The screen captured his obvious honesty and sincerity; it was hard not to like the man. But with television and print reporters alike, he wasn't interested in wedging himself into the hero's mold the media had cast for him. Scobee wanted to be respected for his technical expertise, but he would gladly have skipped the interviews and color commentary. Publicity, he said, is like a pre-flight physical: you can come out behind or even, but you can't come out ahead.

He was uncomfortable hearing himself praised as a national hero. As he was always quick to say, he was just doing a job. "It's an enjoyable profession," he told an interviewer in 1983. "But some people would like it and some wouldn't. It's like any other occupation. . . ."

Chapter 4

MICHAEL J. SMITH

It was October 1959, a brisk Thursday afternoon, and the Beaufort High School Seadogs were playing the Havelock High School Rams. Coach Tom Hewitt groused on the sidelines, watching his junior varsity team as it struggled to avoid its first loss of the season.

The Seadogs, their white pants grass-stained nearly the color of their kelly-green jerseys, had the ball on Havelock's forty-yard line. They were behind, 7-0. Hewitt was keeping a particular eye on his freshman quarterback, Michael J. Smith. Long summers in the Little League infield had trained Smith to throw in a strong arc, and during early practices he had tossed the football as if he were sending it to second base. Hewitt had spent hours teaching Smith to crook his right arm tight and throw from the ear.

As Hewitt watched, Smith's concentration seemed to break, and his gaze drifted from the forty-yard line to a spot beyond the field, the spot where a Marine Corps jet began its slow, growling ascent from a runway at the Cherry Point air station. The plane lifted over the trees, slicing the sky with a bone-shuddering roar and trailing a plume of dark smoke.

Transfixed, Smith called a time-out.

Hewitt's own concentration snapped, and so did his temper. "If you want to play football, play football!" he yelled from the sidelines. "And if you want to watch planes, you come over and get on the bench with me and you'll have all afternoon to look at them!"

Smith stayed on the field. Several plays later, Beaufort scored a touchdown, went for a two-point conversion and beat the Rams, 8-7.

The junior varsity Seadogs had only one defeat that season, and few remember their record. Smith's fascination with airplanes became a local legend. In Beaufort, a fishing village of 4,500 in the middle of North Carolina's coastline, a good story traveled fast and got told often. On the Seadogs' home field, a mile from Beaufort-Morehead City Airport and twenty miles from the Cherry Point base, airplane interruptions became part of the rhythm of practice. When single-engine Pipers or military jets churned up from the runways, Smith often stopped running wind-sprints or practicing hand-offs and watched the planes until they disappeared above the pines.

Twenty-seven years later, after Smith was killed in the explosion of the space shuttle *Challenger*, former coaches and family and friends came back to Beaufort to mourn, and they exchanged the airplane stories again.

They reminded each other of how Mike Smith had pursued his dream of flying, moving methodically through the Naval Academy, a fast-paced graduate program, flight training, test-pilot school, ending up at NASA, always succeeding, always stretching for the next step. They told each other, repeatedly and emphatically, that Smith had died in the joyous exercise of the only kind of work he'd ever wanted.

At a memorial service, they recalled his words to an interviewer just months before his death: "Whenever I was conscious of what I wanted to do, I wanted to fly. I can never remember anything else I wanted to do but flying. To tell you the truth, it's been wonderful. I could not ask to have a better career than I've had. Flying's been fun."

A fierce sense of purpose carried Smith from his parents' poultry farm to NASA, a drive as precocious as his love for planes. Smith discussed his dreams with only a handful of close friends and relatives; others knew only that he loved to fly and that his path beat a straight line toward that goal. When each accomplishment came, and it always did, there wasn't much to say but, well, of course.

If self-discipline can be absorbed, Smith could have gulped it from the air of Beaufort, where the fishermen's lives were locked to the movements of the sea and the farmers' lives to the rhythms of the weather. His parents, Robert and Lucile Smith, had a small poultry-and-produce farm, 13½ acres of chickens and cabbage on the edge of town. Hard work, and the right circumstances, yielded tangible rewards. In 1953, a good cabbage crop bought the family a television set; seven years later, another bumper crop bought a black Chevrolet.

Robert Smith was not a speech-maker, but he counseled his children—Mike, the oldest, Patrick, Tony and Ellen—to be honest and to work wholeheartedly. As a freshman football player, Mike was not the most gifted athlete to cross the Beaufort field, but he practiced fiercely; in his spare time, he ran, lifted weights and jumped rope to build his strength. He hung a tire from one of the hen houses in the Smiths' yard and practiced passing, tossing the football through it again and again.

In the 1963 Beaufort High School yearbook, *The Mainsail*, Smith's list of achievements was among the longest in the class of sixty students: junior varsity football his freshman year and varsity the next three, football co-captain his senior year, baseball, science club, sophomore class president, student council president as a senior, hall patrol, banquet waiter. He was pictured on other pages, too, tall, grinning and slightly awkward-looking in the tie and jacket, voted by his classmates as the "most outstanding," the "best all-around," and possessor of the best physique. Beneath his snapshot, a fair-skinned, angular face under crew-cut dark hair, the book read: " 'Tis not in mortals to command success; but he'll do more, he will deserve it."

Smith did do more; he landed a coveted appointment to the U.S. Naval Academy in Annapolis. In Beaufort, they were pleased with the news of his achievement, but they weren't much surprised. They would have been surprised if Robert and Lucile Smith had raised a lazy son. Lucile's family, the Safrits, had come to Beaufort in the 1930s to start a sawmill and were known around town as unassuming, hard-working people. The Smiths, originally from nearby Bachelor, were story-tellers and dry wits, plain folk who cherished their families.

Lucile handled the business end of the egg-and-produce operation—the sorting and weighing and bookkeeping. Her quiet manner hid ingenuity; when their brick house was enlarged in 1955 so all the children could have their own rooms, she drew the plans, designing rooms with built-in closets and drawers. Robert Smith worked the farm and reserved every Thursday morning in the summertime for a fishing trip at the Neuse River. Only a crisis could take him away from home, even briefly; when Mike, in a bout of frustration and homesickness early in his freshman year, called home and threatened to quit the Naval Academy, his father drove the black Chevrolet 600 miles to Annapolis, talked his son into staying in school, and drove back again that night.

In the Smith household, there were chores in the morning—the chickens' 6:30 A.M. feeding, gathering the eggs—and after school as well. Sunday services and Sunday school and the Methodist Youth Fellowship were mandatory. Often, between the youth meetings and the evening service, Smith followed the Reverend John M. Cline to his study and sat for ten or fifteen minutes, asking questions, talking about his day. One Sunday, Mike greeted Reverend Cline with a wide grin and the news that he'd flown his first solo flight. It was his sixteenth birthday.

Smith's fascination with planes couldn't be sated by gazing at them from a football field. He wanted to sit in them, feel the throttle and the rudder pedals, take them into the air. Each year, Mike and his brothers went with their father to the Armed Forces Day air show at Cherry Point. There, parked on the tarmac, wings glinting in the sun, were the newest and sharpest of the nation's air fleet, planes with cryptic numbers—FJ-4B, A-4, F-8, F-9F—and wild, fierce names—Fury, Skyhawk, Crusader, Cougar. The pilots stood snappy in uniform, answering questions and letting the boys clamber into the jets, dangling their legs toward the rudder pedals and craning to see over the controls.

The air show's crowning moment was a Blue Angels performance. For forty-five minutes six bright blue F-11 Tigers looped and rolled over, flew upside down, arranged themselves in a precise "V," cut the sky with their quick lines. It was meant to dazzle, and it did.

At home, in the side yard, Smith tried some of the fancy maneuvers with gasoline-powered models he bought at the E.J.W. Bicycle and Sports Shop and built himself. These planes, made of balsa wood and cloth, were bigger and more intricate than plastic models; they had three-foot wingspans and names like *Blue Flight Streak* and were meant to fly in simple circles, anchored by a wire. Smith soon got bored, and tried to make the models loop and dive. Plane after plane faltered and crash-landed on the grass.

By the time Smith was a high school junior, Alan Shepard had become the first American to enter space on the back of a Redstone rocket. But for the moment, Smith was more interested in the planes at nearby Beaufort-Morehead City Airport. As soon as he was old enough for seven-dollar-an-hour lessons and a job to finance them, Smith reported to George Huntley's building supply store on Saturday mornings; when work was over, he headed to the airport.

Each Saturday for six months he flew for an hour in a single-engine Aeronca Champion, sitting in the front seat of the dual-control plane with Bob Burrows coaching gently from the rear. The first time out, they sat on the runway for thirty minutes and Burrows just talked about the instruments: this is the altimeter, showing how high we are in twenty-foot increments; this is the throttle to adjust the engine; this is the tachometer, counting the engine's revolutions per minute; this is the oil-pressure indicator, the fuel gauge, the compass.

On the ground, the Aeronca looked like a gray-and-maroon insect with a thirty-five-foot wingspan. As Smith tried his first takeoffs, Burrows gave quiet guidance: "You've got the wing down too far; you're giving it too much rudder . . . okay, easy now." The control wheel jumped under a heavy hand; it took the lightest touch, fingertips, really, to guide the nose up, climbing to 400 feet, then 700, leveling out at about 1000, heading north with the Newport River on the left and the North River to the right. A chaotic landscape melted into neat blocks—the green was farmland and the blue was water and the white was the steeples of town.

They practiced turns and climbs, glides and stomach-jolting stalls, takeoffs and landings and more takeoffs. They flew low enough to see the latticed porches of summer houses on Atlantic Beach, high enough that Cape Lookout resembled an elegantly curved finger dipping into the ocean.

The morning of April 30, 1961, Burrows stayed on the ground. He told Mike to take off and fly in a circle, touch the runway twice more as if to land, then make a final landing. "If I don't stop you, then come back for me," he said. Burrows had called Robert and Lucile the night before, and they watched, hidden at the end of the airport so Mike wouldn't be nervous. If *they* were nervous, they didn't say so.

The solo took twenty minutes, and Mike came off the airstrip grinning. He got his student license validated that day. After that, his friend Jeffrey Salter, who worked at Huntley's and longed to be a Secret Service agent, sometimes chipped in half the rental fee and went up with him, looking down at the fishing boats, listening to Mike explain how the Aeronca worked. Later, in basic flight training for the Navy, Smith's head start helped; many of his classmates knew planes on paper but fumbled on the runways, while he seemed a natural at the controls.

At home, Smith always seemed to have a project going. Once he used an erector set motor to mechanize his room. He could open and close the door, turn the lights on and off, raise the shade, all while sitting in bed. He was a perfectionist even when the results would not necessarily be noticed. One morning at Huntley's, he and Salter unloaded gallon cans of paint, twenty or thirty cases of them, and Mike insisted on shelving them with their labels facing out, all the handles the same way. Jeffrey's cans were a hodge-podge, and Mike made him rearrange them.

Everyone at Huntley's carried hinged rulers in their back pockets, and the boys made it a game to "draw" them like pistols, seeing who could extend his ruler to its full length first. One day Smith took a stiff, brand-new one home at night and worked the hinges until he could unfold it in seconds from his pocket, its sections clicking open like a string of dominoes. Salter tried to cheat, greasing the joints of his ruler with graphite, but Smith won the next day's draw anyway.

On the job and the playing field, Smith held himself to rigid standards, but he knew how to pull a practical joke. On slow summer afternoons when the boys were young, they busied themselves with what George Huntley's wife called "prankin'," telephoning someone they knew, muffling their voices and announcing that five pounds of shad would be delivered on the lawn by six o'clock. Smith once dragged a reluctant Salter with him to Greenville for a blind date, touting the girl's charms throughout the ninety-mile drive, then announcing just outside the city limits that her friends called her "motormouth."

In the twelve-grade school, a group of boys—Mike and Pat, Jeffrey and Daniel Nelson and a few others—formed a knot in first grade and stayed friends. They were the "drugstore cowboys," hanging out at Guthrie-Jones' for grilled cheese and vanilla Cokes. They were the ushers at Ann Street United Methodist Church, occasionally slipping out after the service started, zooming to the dance halls at Atlantic Beach to see who was there, and dashing back to the pews in time for the last "Amen."

Most of their close friends were Beaufort boys and girls, but summertime at the beach brought new faces, girls from upstate visiting their aunts' summer houses. On one trip to the beach, during football camp his sophomore year in high school, Smith met Jane Ann Jarrell, on vacation from her Charlotte home. They made a striking pair. She was petite, with pale blond hair, and he was tall, dark and blue-eyed. They saw each other two or three times and exchanged addresses when the summer ended. She went home to Charlotte, Mike returned to Beaufort and the routines of classes and football; as the year wore on, he lost touch with Jane.

Smith's high school accomplishments, a grade-point average that ranked him third in the class, and a recommendation from U.S. Representative David N. Henderson, who knew a family friend, won him a spot at the Academy. In Beaufort in 1963, appointment to a military academy said all the right things about a boy: that he was bright and tenacious and had good connections. When Smith set his sights on Annapolis, his friends and brothers urged him on, making sure he didn't drive too fast or after a few beers; they wanted his record to remain spotless.

Compared with life in Beaufort, where Mike was independent and usually disciplined himself, the Academy regimen was a bit of a cold surprise. The rules were clear and no-nonsense: no dates the first year, no riding in cars, everyone up and to meals and to bed at the same time. The Academy became another test, and Smith strived to ace it. He graduated 108th of 893 students in 1967.

The *Lucky Bag*, the Academy's yearbook, echoed his high school accolades: "A hard worker and a gifted student, Mike has excelled whether it be in the classroom or on the athletic field. . . . Mike's friendly smile and good-natured personality have aided him in developing many close friendships . . . with these attributes, Mike is certain to be a success in any field, be it in or out of the Navy."

Smith was a sharp student, but not a grind, with a quick, fundamental grasp of engineering and aerodynamics. Some friends, like Hugh Wolcott, always seemed to leave their studying to the last minute; the night before a final, Wolcott sometimes showed up in desperation for a cram session with Mike, who explained the equations and made them sound easy.

Smith's energy level became well known among classmates and colleagues. Seven years after the Academy, when both he and Wolcott sweated over control panels and magnetic tapes of data at the Naval Air Test Center, Wolcott would drag himself home exhausted, wanting only to pop open a beer and collapse on the couch. Mike would stride brightly into the house, pick up his woodworking tools and get to work on a table or a picture frame.

His junior year at the Academy, Mike received a postcard with a picture of an Eastern Airlines "Whisper Jet" from Jane Jarrell, the girl he'd met at the beach in high school. She was then an Eastern stewardess, living near Washington, D.C., and they began to date. On June 17, 1967, ten days after Mike graduated from the Academy, they were married in Calvary United Methodist Church in Charlotte.

Smith didn't announce his plans to Academy friends, or to his family, but no one had doubts about the brightness of his future. Right after the wedding, he headed to Monterey, California, farther from home than he'd ever been, one of twelve Academy students studying aeronautical engineering in a brand-new accelerated program at the U.S. Naval Postgraduate School. The California air was balmy, good for playing tennis or biking all year round, if you had time, and the campus was stunning, Spanish-style buildings with tiled roofs and a lake with swans and peacocks, if you had a minute to look at them. Most of the 1400 students had come to the postgraduate school after flight training and a combat tour; their curriculum included some refresher courses and stretched over two years. Smith and his classmates did it in a breathless nine months and remembered it as a flurry of activity: "Hello welcome to the U.S. Naval Postgraduate School what would you like to write your thesis on?"

Smith and the others in the accelerated program, ensigns of twenty-two or twenty-three, were the "kids" of the graduate school, six or seven years younger than some of their classmates. To them, the lieutenants and their wives seemed distant, separated by a gulf of age and sophistication. One of Smith's classmates from the Academy, Garth VanSickle, was in the same advanced program, and his wife marveled with Jane at the older women, who occasionally went out at night, leaving their husbands at home, and drank wine—imagine!—at the Wives' Club meetings.

The young couples stuck together for whatever social life the men could squeeze in between morning classes, afternoon labs and long hours at the library or computer center at night. Jackie VanSickle learned how to punch computer cards, so she could at least seize a few hours of conversation with Garth under the computer center's fluorescent lights. The curriculum was rigorous, but compared to the ordered two-step of the Academy, life was relaxed. No uniforms here, or anyone checking the sparkle of your shoes, just mandatory coats and ties for the students and instructors, a sort of Ivy League style and university atmosphere.

While Smith was there, a young instructor named Dave Wooten challenged his thinking in the classroom and won his friendship outside it. Smith asked Wooten to be his thesis adviser, and Wooten grew to respect the young ensign as one of his best students: methodical, bright, but not flashy about his intellect. He liked Smith personally, too, respected his values. Other guys at the school, working like hell and cramped in tiny Monterey apartments, talked of the days when they could afford Corvettes; Smith once called Wooten and chattered gleefully for 15 minutes about his new power saw, as excited as if he'd won a lottery.

By this time, in 1968, earth and lunar orbits were frequent and Wooten's lessons in aerodynamics took on the air of a current event. He taught his students how basic formulas could be pressed to far-reaching applications: the same equations of mass and gravity and centrifugal force that explained how a single-engine Aeronca got off the runway in Beaufort and arced over Cape Lookout could be manipulated to tell you how fast a satellite was traveling, and why it stayed up. Smith's work was good, his writing lucid, and he could see the usefulness of the complicated formulas. On paper, it was tedious work, but the delicate data of flight would take on life-or-death magnitude later, flying an attack mission over North Vietnam or landing on a carrier in a dark ocean.

In the meantime, Smith couldn't stay out of the air. He joined a local flying club in Monterey, rented a Cessna 150 and took VanSickle up for his first ride in a light airplane. For some, the delight and mystery of flying might have vanished over time, sapped by the study of vectors and acceleration. For Smith, it was always a thrill: the spread of the ground beneath, the shudder of the plane under his hands, the heady instant, hovering on the edge of an aircraft's capability. Test pilots called it "pushing the outside of the envelope." Smith had been doing it all his life.

Between Smith and the space program lay a dozen years of work. First there was graduate school, ending in March 1968, then a hectic six years of basic and advanced flight training, a stint as an advanced jet training instructor and a Vietnam tour on the carrier USS *Kitty Hawk*. He and Jane moved frequently—from Monterey to Pensacola, Florida; Meridian, Mississippi; back to Pensacola, then to Kingsville, Texas, and Whidbey Island, Washington. Garth VanSickle's moves mirrored Smith's, and Jackie commiserated with Jane over the purchases put off, the cartons that never seemed to get unpacked. Mike was on his way to Kingsville when Jane gave birth to their first child, Scott, on January 12, 1969, in Charlotte. Five months later, Smith received his aviator wings and began a stint as instructor in the advanced jet training command.

After the thick pines and marshes of Beaufort and the lush weather of Monterey, Kingsville felt like a desert—dry and windy, flat land and no trees. But Mike and Jane soon had company; his brother Pat, now a Navy pilot himself, and his wife, Gay, moved in just a few blocks away. Nearly every night, the four ate dinner together at one house or the other.

As instructor, Smith became known for his high standards, boundless energy and compassion. He taught students the vagaries of the TA-4 Skyhawk as relentlessly as Coach Hewitt had taught blocking and as gently as Bob Burrows had taught flying. His skill as a teacher later impressed Senator Jake Garn, a veteran Navy pilot, as he trained for an April 1985 shuttle launch. The day Garn was assigned to his crew, NASA officials introduced him to Smith, saying, "Senator, this is your mother hen." Smith lived up to his introduction, giving Garn his home phone number and encouraging him to call if he had questions, walking him through the maze of buildings at Johnson Space Center and tutoring him in the unfamiliar phrases—main engine cut-off, T-minus-three, go with throttle up. Smith chatted easily about NASA, about the shuttle, but it took prodding to make him talk about himself.

After teaching in Kingsville, the next three years tested Smith's forbearance with some of the most difficult tasks of aviation and the stress of an overseas tour on the carrier USS *Kitty Hawk*. In the spring of 1971, he was at the RAG, the Replacement Air Group, where newly qualified pilots trained in the aircraft they would fly during combat. The idea of the training squadron was to learn the A-6 Intruder from the inside out. Smith often stayed up past midnight, poring over textbooks about the landing length of the A-6 from different altitudes.

Training for the squadron was more than a matter of textbook perfectionism; the practice had urgent application, even before the test of flying in combat. It was in the training squadron that pilots made their first night carrier landings. If landing on a carrier in the daytime was like lighting on a tabletop in a lake, night landings were like executing the same thing in a bottle of black ink. On paper, a night carrier landing meant "reduced visual cues." In the air, it meant the horizon line melted, the sky and sea merged into an identical bluish-black.

The ship was the main source of light on the sea, a deceiving, dancing dot that muddled your sense of distance, so a smart pilot averted his eyes until he was three-quarters of a mile from deck, reading the gauges and listening to words of guidance crackle over the radio. "You're three-quarters of a mile, call the ball," the voice would say, and only then could you safely lift your eyes from the quivering needles, heading, throat clenched, for the safe, well-lighted place of the carrier deck.

A night carrier landing took all the concentration you could muster; it was perhaps the only time in your life when a daydream could not creep between your thoughts. You were single-minded, like a machine. When the engine had growled to a stop, the wings folded, the aircraft parked neatly on the deck, you turned again into a human being, quivering, thankful, drained.

At the RAG, Smith met Bill Newton, who was training as a bombardier-navigator. Garth VanSickle was there, too, and the three lived within blocks of each other. They flew from the carrier in ink-darkness and daylight, practicing for the war their wives watched each night on the evening news. If the wives feared anything—the familiar name ringing horribly from a list of casualties, or the uniformed stranger at the door to say, "I'm sorry, ma'am, but . . ."—they did not say so, not to each other, not to their husbands. Risk, and the thrill that came with it, was one reason for choosing the work; Smith told an interviewer two months before the *Challenger* flight that he'd selected the Navy over the Air Force because "I thought I might like to fly off aircraft carriers rather than off runways."

But the men had no death wish. What they had was the fierce faith of competence. There is a saying in the Navy: "There are old pilots and there are bold pilots, but there are no old, bold pilots." In a job that seemed, to outsiders, the height of recklessness, the men wielded their skill like a shield; it was what they relied on to ward off death. Fatal risk became a matter not of chance, or bad luck, but a variable to be metered and mastered. When an accident did happen, they talked of the "cause factors," how to prevent the next one. That presumed the "next one" could be prevented, and that it wouldn't be their plane. Once, when Smith and Bill Newton were on the accident investigation board after their Vietnam tour, a pilot who'd made it through combat unscratched was killed during a practice bombing run. The wing of his A-6 fell off 16,000 feet over the bombing range, sending the aircraft into a rapid spin. Both the pilot and the bombardier-navigator died in the fiery crash when it hit the ground.

There were ways of coping with the danger, and one was to joke about it. When Daniel Nelson, Smith's childhood friend, was in the Navy, some of his buddies used to say each time their planes touched ground, "Well, we've cheated death again in an aircraft built by the lowest bidder."

Still, a Navy pilot had to be realistic, especially if he had a family. Before Smith left for his Vietnam tour in 1972, he sent his brother Pat a list of things to do in case "something"—the vague word for the unspeakable—happened. There were insurance documents and phone numbers in the package, a list of who Mike wanted to be pallbearers . . . in case. He left for an eleven-month tour on the USS *Kitty Hawk*, flying combat missions over North Vietnam. His friend Bill Newton went, too, and their friendship strengthened in the cockpit of an A-6, Smith piloting in the left-hand seat and Newton the bombardier-navigator on the right.

Sometime in 1973, Smith applied to, and was accepted at, the U.S. Naval Test Pilot School at Patuxent River, Maryland. When the news reached Garth VanSickle, on cruise near Japan, it did not surprise him. Test pilot school was the next logical step for Smith.

The rigors of Test Pilot School didn't drain Smith's energy, or his sense of fun. One day, he piloted an F-4 Phantom with Hugh Wolcott, an old friend from the Naval Academy, in the backseat. He was testing the plane to see how it handled a stall in midair, drawing back on the stick until the nose stuck up and the plane hung like a hummingbird, shuddering, then pushing the stick forward to lower the nose, picking up speed and gentling it back to level flight. Wolcott got bored with the lazy maneuvers and said, "Come on, Mike, pull on it," and Mike did, hard, so that the nose somersaulted up and over and Wolcott found himself doing a headstand over Maryland's Eastern Shore. Smith righted the plane again: "You mean like that?" he asked, smooth as pie.

All his life Smith had aimed for the achievement that lay just out of reach, and grasped it, and plugged on inexorably for the next. By the time he was accepted at NASA, his future pointed in two equally bright directions. Based at the Naval Air Station in Oceana, Virginia, his family—now including Alison, born in 1971, and Erin, born in 1977—in a two-story Colonial near the water, Smith had advanced to maintenance officer, then operations officer, of Attack Squadron 75. He didn't announce that he was readying for application to NASA, but he didn't have to, at least not to anyone who saw him running relentlessly on the flight deck of the USS *Saratoga*. He applied for the 1978 astronaut class, and didn't make it. When the next call came from Houston, in May of 1980, Smith was in line for command of the attack squadron—a major career step for a Navy aviator and the first notch on the path to admiral. Smith pondered the choice the way he always handled things—methodically. He sat on Bill Newton's back patio in Emporia, Virginia, talking through the pros and cons, the ifs and buts.

In its infancy, the space program hadn't created much stir in Beaufort, where, for most, the frontier extended only as far as the fishing boats strayed from shore or the occasional exotic destination of a ship that docked in the harbor on its way to somewhere else. Pat was eleven and Mike was twelve when Lucile Smith called out the back door one October afternoon in 1957, telling her sons that the Russians had just sent a satellite into the heavens. By Smith's senior year in high school, John Glenn had orbited the earth, but talk of space remained somewhat remote. The notion of becoming an astronaut was discussed not unlike the prospect of becoming president of the United States—enthralling, but not quite realistic.

Smith's love of flying sometimes prompted jokes about space travel from others, including his bubbly young English teacher, Jackie Waters. "There may have been times," she would say, "when you wanted to send me to the moon because of all I required of you." Smith would grin, standing in her classroom, one hand shoved in the pocket of his blue jeans. "When you get on the moon, I want you to remember, you owe it all to me," she teased.

If Smith set his aim on the moon, or beyond, he didn't say so. His career progressed quietly in the proven path of the first astronauts—basic flight training, combat flying, test-pilot school

—as surely as if he had read their résumés and set out to match their credentials. After the historic "one small step for man" in 1969, Smith saved ecstatic front-page headlines like "MAN STEPS ON MOON!" and framed them.

To those who knew him well, Smith's intent to join NASA was clear, if unspoken; as the astronaut corps became the plausible zenith of an aviation career, it only made sense that Smith would strive for it. No one doubted his discipline, and few envied his accomplishments. He never told his family about the decorations he received on his return from Vietnam—the Navy Distinguished Flying Cross, the Vietnamese Cross of Gallantry with Silver Star, thirteen Strike Flight Air Medals and others. They did not learn of the medals until Smith spoke in 1980 at the dedication of the North Carolina School of Science and Mathematics in Durham, and someone read his Navy biography as introduction. If they admired Smith for having the "right stuff" to be an astronaut, they loved him for also having the "nice stuff"—a private manner, gentle humor, simplicity of purpose.

Now, as Smith faced the choice, NASA exerted a pull as strong as gravity. But the road toward admiral was a fierce lure, too. As the barbecue smoked in Newton's yard and the spring day turned into dusk, they wrestled with the decision aloud, weighing the effect of each choice on Jane and the children, on the time Mike would have at home, on the opportunities it would open afterward. "Gosh, Mike, you don't have any bad choices," Newton told him.

When the acceptance call from NASA finally came, surprising no one, Smith startled some at the space agency by asking for a moment to think it over. Then he called Jane. Then Jane called Jackie VanSickle. Mike had the operator break into their conversation to announce his decision: they were going to Houston.

Later, some friends would say the choice was never in doubt, that Smith's destiny was wired to the astronaut corps from the time he flew his first solo over the Beaufort airfield. NASA was the highest challenge an aviator could reach, and Smith had worked for it: How could he turn it down? But there were other considerations. For Smith, who had lived in the same house for the first eighteen years of his life and then never stayed in one place more than four years, who had moved eight times since he married, NASA also meant a return to stability. Squadron command would have meant more deployments, more long stretches away from

Jane and the children. In Houston, they could count on at least five years in one place, stable schooling for the kids, a house they wouldn't feel bad about fixing up.

He delivered his decision with characteristic Smith understatement. Phoning his brother Tony's home in Beaufort, he reached Kerry, his sister-in-law.

"Guess what. We're going to Houston," he said.

"Aw, no, you're not," she answered.

"Oh, yes, we are. I made it."

Shortly after that, he talked to his childhood friend Jeffrey Salter, who had followed his dream to the Secret Service. "You'll do a little flyin' on the way there, a little on the way back, but you won't be flyin' that thing," Salter teased. "You've got to be crazy, going up there with a Roman candle strapped to your butt."

"Well, jumping in front of someone to take a bullet isn't the smartest thing I've ever heard of, either," Smith said. From the inside, neither job felt particularly brave. Salter got up in the morning, put on an earphone and kept an eye on the president. Smith flew planes. The work was what you did; if you were lucky, and persistent, it was also what you loved.

Even as the family settled in Houston, Smith's mind kept moving, his eye toward what would come next. He told Pat he was looking forward most to his second launch, scheduled for September, when he would be mission commander and could pay more attention, free from the giddy novelty of the first trip. In an interview with a reporter from Beaufort's local paper, the *Carteret County News-Times*, Smith said, "I hope, after this trip, I will fly [in space] again in six months to a year. I want to fly two or three more times, if they will let me." He had talked to an old friend, now with the Naval Space Command in Dahlgren, Virginia, about working in that office once he'd left NASA. He had talked with Newton, who left the Navy in 1975, and tossed around the idea of buying a financial services company and going into business together.

Six months before his first flight, scheduled for January 1986, was set to launch, Smith brought his entire family back home for the first time since they'd moved to Houston. Much had changed: both Robert and Lucile had died, the farm had gone, and his brother Pat had left the Navy and now flew as a spotter for a commercial fishing operation. Pat lived with his wife and two children in the old house. Jeffrey Salter's mother approached Mike at a party during his visit. "Mike, you've lost your mind, going up in that thing," she said.

"Don't worry," he told her. "It's just as safe as getting in any other airplane and flying."

Mike told them about the less serious side of NASA training, particularly how it felt to be weightless. He and Jane talked about life in Houston, about the boat house Scott and Mike had built behind their home, about the yard-maintenance business Scott and Alison had started. They talked about plans for a giant reunion of family and friends at Cape Canaveral in January, before flight 51-L lifted off.

Later, the whole family piled into a rented Continental and cruised down Front Street, the radio blaring "City of New Orleans," one of Mike's favorite songs. "I'll be gone five hun-der-ed miles when the da-ay is done," Arlo Guthrie sang. Then they headed back to Houston, with a promise from Pat to mail a replica of the Beaufort flag and a pledge from Mike to take it into space, have all seven *Challenger* astronauts sign it, and bring it home again.

Chapter 5

JUDITH A. RESNIK

In April 1981, four years after NASA began seeking astronauts who didn't look like John Glenn or fly planes like Chuck Yeager, a petite woman dressed in pink sat in front of a television camera. Judith Resnik, a new breed of astronaut, was in a makeshift NBC studio at Kennedy Space Center in Florida to talk about the first-ever launch of the nation's space shuttle. Resnik, a spectator for this momentous flight, took her cue from morning anchor Tom Brokaw.

In a firm, clear voice, she told millions how engines and rockets would lift and thrust the shuttle *Columbia* into the Florida skies. Astronauts, trained like herself, had studied for months to prepare for this ambitious roll in the atmosphere. They had trained in airplanes, buckled themselves into tethers and swung through the air. For hours, they practiced in spaceflight simulators and, through the days, studied the science they hoped to advance in space.

Columbia's crew was ready for whatever would arise during this mission, Resnik told Brokaw. He smiled and asked a question he hoped would lighten the serious talk.

"But what do you say when you meet a guy and he says, 'You're too cute to be an astronaut?'"

Resnik, thirty-two years old, recipient of a doctorate in electrical engineering and a fellow in biomedical research, one of six women chosen out of thousands of people who applied to the space program in its days of expansion in the late 1970s, responded quietly. "I just tell them I'm an engineer."

More silly fluff followed, breathless chatter that Resnik contained with efficient, one-line responses and confided later she disliked. Would there be romance in space? What would NASA do if romance occurred? Was she a tomboy growing up? Would she *really* not tell someone in first meeting that she was an astronaut?

Resnik, who later became friends with Brokaw, politely threw out a verbal shrug.

"Not unless he asks."

Judith Arlene Resnik would travel into space three years later, in a journey described by friends as the pinnacle of a lifetime fascination with science. For her, the voyage was but another progression. Blessed with a logical mind that achieved perfect college board scores, Resnik always worked hard to achieve. She was methodical, thorough. Whether it was the performance of a Chopin prelude as a child or the maneuvering of a space shuttle's mechanical arm as an adult, Resnik's execution was the result of hours of practice.

Born on April 5, 1949, in Akron, Ohio, she was the only daughter of a father who delighted in her confidences and a mother who demanded a regimen of weekly cooking lessons, daily piano sessions and pixie haircuts. When her family crumbled in a painful divorce while she was in high school, Resnik took small steps toward independence. She sneaked out on dates. She grew her hair long enough to reach the bottom of her spine. She applied to a technical college, which few women attended, to study science—which even fewer women tried.

Years later, following a decade of change in which she married, and then divorced while studying at one of the nation's top research institutions, she seemed to realize how the discipline of her childhood helped her evolve into a scientist sure of her talents and herself.

She recognized that she was able to become an astronaut only after the women's movement nudged NASA into expansion; conscious of her own efforts, however, Resnik later came to credit nothing and no one but herself in getting the job. She was proud of her accomplishments. That pride clearly was tempered with an awareness that she was but one part of a team, whose players were always determined by NASA. Work was exhilarating and, to her delight, so were her fellow space pioneers. They challenged her, made her laugh, led her to define and defend her own sense of science and then, always without rancor or regret, to accept the NASA way.

Resnik, an intensely private person, maintained a serious,

no-nonsense face during interviews and public appearances in which she represented the space program. With people she trusted—and NASA was one entity she trusted entirely—Resnik showed humor, chuckled over double entendres, and even gushed about her favorite TV star, Tom Selleck. Resnik told nearly every close relative and friend in the last few years that she would stay in Houston "as long as they will have me." At age thirty-six, she had an active social life that included dates with pilots and then a steady relationship with Frank Culbertson, Jr., a pilot-turned-astronaut. She made friends with the wives of several astronauts. On holidays, she was invited to their homes.

"Any place that Judy had been before, she was always so much brighter than anyone else, in high school, in college," her stepmother Betty Resnik said. "Until she got to NASA, people were always looking up to her. When she got there, though, there were all these intelligent people with the same interests . . . she had found what she called 'her family.' They worked hard but they played hard. I think those had to be the happiest days of her life."

Work—the act of producing something of worth—always seemed to hold a certain allure for Resnik. When asked long ago to write a poem for her Hebrew class, she penned a singular message of faith:

"Blessed is the match that is consumed in kindling a flame. Blessed is the flame that burns the secret fastness of the heart."

It was an afternoon in 1963 and Judy Resnik was ready for her weekly cooking lesson. One time, she had learned how to slice radishes so they looked like roses. This day, she would learn how to bake chocolate chip cookies. Barbara Cheek, a twelve-year-old neighbor, stopped by just before the mixing began. There was a bowl of sugar, a bowl of chips, a bowl of flour, two eggs, a stick of butter and extra bowls for mixing set out on the kitchen table. Cheek saw that, under the instructions of Judy's mother, Sarah, even Nestle Tollhouse cookies had become a science. "There were all these little bowls everywhere. . . . It was so highly organized. I thought it was fascinating," Barbara Cheek Roduner recalled.

For Judy Resnik, every day was organized in the white wood and brick raised-ranch-style home, set on a corner lot, in an affluent suburban section of Akron. She had a schedule: a time to study, a time to play piano, a time to go to Hebrew school at the Beth El Congregation. Sarah, a homemaker, pushed Judy to memorize the alphabet before she went into kindergarten. Little Judy, as her father, Marvin, called her, could read at a third-grade level by the time she got to first grade. In the middle of that school year, she was promoted to second grade.

Friends remember Resnik during her years at Fairlawn Elementary School and Simon Perkins Junior High as someone who worked to please three masters—her mother, her father and herself. She methodically fulfilled her mother's commands but turned to her father to teach her how to find pleasure in her work. Sarah taught her how to make a bed and wield a hot iron across cotton shirts. Marvin approached the girl with a different message, one that was an appealing blend of humor and insight—with gestures as simple as creating a nickname that lasted a lifetime or as grand as buying a complete set of Nancy Drew books when Judy let it be known she enjoyed the adventures.

"We were close," said Marvin, an optometrist who later decorated his office with pictures of a NASA-suited Judy in space and holding a sign that says "Hi, Dad." "As close as we could be with her reticence."

Sarah Resnik wanted the best for her children, Judy and her younger brother Charles, and thought it could be achieved by teaching them discipline and organization. But she also recognized when the children needed compassion. One day the family dog, Pansy, was struck by a car and died. Judy, then in junior high, was inconsolable. Sarah telephoned two neighbor girls and asked them to spend the evening with her daughter. Those two, years later, still carry the memory of a solemn Sarah and a tearful Judy who met them at the door. Judy led the girls to a corner of the family living room and chanted the Kaddish, the traditional prayer of mourning in the Jewish religion.

Such moments of closeness later seemed to elude mother and daughter. After her parents' marriage began to disintegrate in 1965, Judy found herself at odds with her mother, who was given custody of the two children. Judy went to court so she could live with her father. It was a breakup that took two years to resolve and left a cleft between the two women, both strong-willed and determined.

As Judy coped with the pressures at home, she found relief in the world of figures and formulas. The study of math and science were gaining importance in a nation obsessed with a space race in the 1960s. Friends and family do not remember Resnik showing any special interest in space shots that were televised on black-and-white screens then. Few girls her age did. But Resnik took advantage of the expanded science curriculum that her high school had as an answer to an America in search of new technology.

Harvey S. Firestone High, a wide-halled, rambling brown building meant to accommodate the baby boom in Akron, was a public school that opened in 1962 with extras supplied by the Firestone family. In one wing was a swimming pool; in another, a planetarium. Such luxuries sparked a reputation among other city schools that Firestone was the place for "The Cake-eaters," the students who had money and whose parents could afford to send them to Stanford, Harvard and the Massachusetts Institute of Technology.

Judy Resnik was one of those kids, an "A" student who wore white blouses and plaid skirts, and smoothed her dark wavy hair into a pageboy that she set on empty orange juice cans like so many girls did then.

But in most ways, she stood apart from the crowd. She made the National Honor Society, had a perfect grade-point average and was a member of the French Club, the Math Club and the Chemistry Club, organizations that the popular girls avoided. Years later, after she had been selected as an astronaut and returned for her twelve-year reunion, Resnik remarked to a friend that a former cheerleader had asked her for an autograph. Judy was smiling and clearly pleased.

Other students accepted and respected her studiousness, often asking her for help. Resnik responded with a low-key ease that her teachers found gracious in one so young. Some, like Donald Nutter, who taught Judy trigonometry, solid geometry and advanced-placement calculus during her junior and senior years, took secret advantage of Resnik's gifts. He graded students' exams by checking his key to Resnik's paper. If she had an answer wrong, he checked his own calculations to see if he, the teacher, erred. Six times in two years, he found he was wrong. "We had a lot of girls who took upper-level science," Nutter said. "But many girls never had a good image of themselves in those fields. That young lady did."

Resnik's talents went beyond academics. She took a typing class and, perhaps because of her piano playing, perhaps because she had double-jointed fingers, Judy was soon typing ninety words a minute, with no mistakes. She took other business courses, and by the time she was done, her speed of 125 words a minute had won her an award. Her typing teacher was amazed.

In the middle of her junior year, Judy's parents filed for divorce and her father moved out. Judy buried herself in work. Teachers who taught her could not recall that she ever talked about changes in her life. But the hurt inside Resnik was keen. A handful of friends knew there were tears and angry words at home. As the breakup progressed, Sarah Resnik became more demanding and restrictive, quizzing both children about how they spent time away from home.

Judy began to quietly rebel. Occasionally, she sneaked to a movie with a boy she had met from nearby Copley High. On some weekend nights, she and her girlfriends cruised the Skyway Drive-In Restaurant looking for boys. She continued to see her father by visiting his apartment during her school lunch break, holding onto their relationship. They bantered about the fortunes of the Cleveland Indians, mimicked his receptionist's high-pitched German accent or made arrangements for Sunday morning bowling matches.

Resnik also made decisions in those tumultuous ten months that would forever affect her life. A talented musician, she opted not to pursue piano as a major. She instead turned to the steady logic of math after consulting with her father, who agreed she had an aptitude to master it. With the recommendations of her teachers and her own high marks of excellence in hand, she applied to the Carnegie Institute of Technology in Pittsburgh, since renamed Carnegie-Mellon University.

Carnegie has always attracted top science students from across the United States. In 1966, that meant young men. But Judy Resnik was undeterred. She joined them, would come to best most of them and love one of them.

There is an image of Judy Resnik that Angel Jordan, once chairman of the engineering department at Carnegie-Mellon and now provost, remembers with a chuckle whenever he passes through the white-domed entranceway of Hamerschlag Hall. He sees a young woman, five-foot-four, long hair flowing, pulling a dog on a leash across the tiles of a first-floor office. She greets the secretaries, lets the dog dart under a conference table and walks into his office. "Angel, I am here," she would say in a lilting voice. "Do you have a moment?"

"Of course," he said. And the moment always spun into a half hour of conversation, laughter and ideas.

"If I was busy when she walked in, she would talk to the secretaries. As she talked, she'd pull out some experiment she was working on and lay out the dishes on the table right here," he said, pointing to a busy intersection in the center of three rooms. "Sometimes she would talk for too long. . . . She felt she was welcome here always."

Resnik blossomed at Carnegie Tech. Beginning as a math major, she switched to the more practical study of electrical engineering before her first year ended. She pledged a sorority, Alpha Epsilon Phi, and later led her sisters in song during meetings held in the lone women's campus dorm, Morewood Gardens. She belonged to student committees and once was runner-up to the homecoming queen. Photographs of Resnik from that time show a young woman, wrapped in a fake fur coat, looking mischievously into the camera. Even through the hues of a faded photo, she sparkles.

Weeks after arriving on campus, she was asked out by a young man who shared a room with a fellow from Philadelphia. But she found the roommate, Michael Oldak, far more attractive. Oldak, a blond-haired sophomore studying electrical engineering, had an engaging personality, a consuming interest in sports cars and a shaggy-haired dog named Elissa that followed him across campus. Before Christmas break, Oldak and Resnik were dating. By the end of the year, the dog was following both of them to classes and Judy had learned to tinker with car engines. Friends said they seemed headed for marriage.

Resnik, who had never had a serious boyfriend before, pursued the relationship with Oldak with a fervor none of her hometown friends had ever seen. Nearly two decades later, they called it comparable to the effort she made in gaining acceptance to NASA. She studied with him, joined clubs with him, even navigated for him when he drove his TR-6 in sports car rallies. Michael brought out laughter in Judy, who now came home wearing jeans with a touch of fringe. She also was quite taken with the warm family life he had, friends remember. "She took her studies very seriously but was devoted to Michael. . . . Michael was her extravagance during those years," said Emily Cutler Vos, who shared a room with Resnik during their sophomore year.

In Judy, Oldak saw a girl with "a calm determination" and a

strong sense of privacy. "She was not a workaholic but a person who would decide that she wanted something and go after it. . . . When she decided to apply to NASA (years after her undergraduate study), she found out who was the head of the Air and Space Museum in Washington and got an interview with him. She learned everything she could about whatever it was she wanted," he said.

Judy concentrated on her studies and avoided activities that might thwart them. Carnegie Tech was then strike central for western Pennsylvania colleges caught up in the nation's turmoil over Vietnam. Though Resnik watched some of her friends gather for protests on the "cut," a lawn that stretches through the middle of the urban campus, she did not hold up any protest banners herself.

Women's rights, too, were beginning to seep into the consciousness of America. Resnik, taught as a young child that only the best was acceptable, did not believe she needed a movement to gain respect for her efforts. She was already at Carnegie Tech, where women attempting to excel in the sciences were awarded special attention. Resnik, perhaps because of the closeness she enjoyed with her father, prospered in classes dominated by men. She was able to develop a smooth sense of professionalism with them that could be used two ways: as a conduit to quickly convey a sense of competence and as a shield to deflect questions about her personal life.

The young woman still held a strong belief in her religion during her college years. She observed Jewish holidays by not attending class, unless a test was scheduled, and only "then with some guilt," remembered Vos, her college roommate. As she grew older, she no longer practiced the religion, but she never stopped being Jewish. She simply refused, throughout her life, to allow people to categorize her. After she became an astronaut, Jewish publications appealed for interviews. Resnik declined most. "I am an astronaut. Not a woman astronaut. Not a Jewish astronaut. An astronaut," Resnik said in her later years.

Resnik's private nature meant her friends knew only bits and parts of her personality. All mentioned her closeness with her father and her estrangement from her mother. Some described her as only quiet. Others admired her for entering a profession dominated by men. Her friends remember her vibrancy, but professors recall Resnik did not greet people with a smile when she saw them in those years at Carnegie. The smile would come, slowly, with conversation.

Resnik did not seem, at first glance, to be the kind of girl who wanted adventure. She had to be persuaded by Oldak to ride the thunderous roller coaster at Kennywood, an amusement park in nearby Duquesne that teemed with high school students on class trips or celebrators roasting lamb on grills set up for made-up holidays like Croatian Day. They returned to the park another time, though, and Resnik, grinning, said she wanted to ride the train first.

"To a great extent, Judy was just like everyone else," Oldak said. "She was not a superperson. She was a person with super talents. She grew up with a father who liked to joke and a brother she felt very close to. . . . When she became an astronaut, she didn't want to be pigeonholed as anything close to greatness. 'I am who I am,' was her attitude. 'I'm doing the job I want to do. But I'm like everyone else.'"

Something that always gave Resnik pleasure, during her college years and while at NASA, was her piano. After a day of studying, she would grab a stack of sheet music, some Bach, some Chopin, and descend on the grand piano in the red-carpeted lounge of Morewood Gardens, playing movingly for two or three hours at a time. Later the first piece of furniture she and Oldak bought after their wedding was an upright Steinway.

As Resnik advanced in college, she also climbed in class standing. She graduated in the top of her class and as a member of every honor society, the same year that Oldak, who had stayed on an extra year to complete a double degree, received his diploma in electrical engineering and business administration.

A month after graduation, Oldak and Resnik married in an orthodox Jewish ceremony held July 14, 1970, the only day her synagogue in Akron had available. Resnik wore white lace and Oldak stood tall in a black tuxedo. Friends left the happy, formal affair murmuring how deeply Judy loved Michael.

In a few years, however, the young woman would need other challenges.

Just outside the nation's capital in a cluster of red-brick and granite buildings, men and women explore some of science's most intriguing questions. In the halls of these laboratories, known as the National Institutes of Health, scientists from around the world mull over mutants, string together theories and harness computers to record endless data. One day in 1974, Judy Resnik Oldak arrived to help search for the answers.

She came, primarily, because she wanted a doctorate and NIH had offered her a fellowship in biomedical engineering that would lead to a Ph.D. from the University of Maryland. She decided to focus on something her father, the optometrist, could appreciate: the retina.

Every weekday, in a narrow office on the fifth floor of Building 36, Resnik followed a meticulous routine. She'd kill a frog, extract an eye and uncover the retina, the part of the eye sensitive to light. Then she shone a light across it, bleached part of it and analyzed it to see how the light had affected it. She had to run the tests, which were slow and tedious, again and again to produce a consistent finding on which she could base her doctoral thesis. In 1977, her work and writings were accepted.

Resnik later came to regard those three years, aimless in a way and at times frustrating, as a passage of life in which she searched for more than a diploma. She struggled between old dreams and new realities. Personally and professionally, she began changing directions.

After her graduation in 1970, she and her husband had followed similar career paths that, at first, allowed her to grow. Both worked for RCA Corporation in Moorestown, New Jersey, and took night courses in electrical engineering at the University of Pennsylvania. But that changed the next year when Oldak was accepted into Georgetown University Law School in Washington.

Resnik transferred to an RCA office in nearby Virginia and went to night school. Oldak went to law school full-time and had a part-time job. Many who knew Resnik believe she immersed herself in her career to avoid motherhood. She and Oldak seemed to be going in different directions; it took a toll on their marriage. In 1975, they separated.

"She felt she didn't have the freedom as a woman that she really wanted. She felt constrained by other commitments in her life," said Professor Robert Newcomb, who recruited Resnik to the electrical engineering program at the University of Maryland in 1974 and was a member of the committee of professors who judged her doctoral work in 1977. "She said she was going through a lot of turmoil over what to do. . . . There was a big change in her once she was divorced. There was a happiness . . . I think that was the key to getting into the [space] program. Had she been married, I don't think she would have done it."

After the separation, Resnik moved to an apartment in the Maryland suburbs of Washington and lived there through the divorce in December 1976. The couple still talked on the telephone every few months, a pattern that continued over the years. When Judy applied to be an astronaut, Michael—who as a youngster had dreamed of being an astronaut—was enthusiastic and encouraged her. Judy asked him to be a reference for her application and he eagerly agreed. Judy later invited him to her first launch in 1984. When Michael asked her to take into space the tags of the dog that followed them around the campus of Carnegie, she agreed.

It was a painful divorce for both of them, her friends said. As she had done before in times of stress, Resnik threw herself into work.

At NIH, her colleagues regarded her as an outstanding researcher. They remember her arriving early, about 7 A.M., wearing a blue or white sweatsuit and immediately getting started. Her hair piled on top of her head, she would spend hours over her microscope. Dr. Jeffery Barker, now chief of the lab, worked alongside her. At times, she turned to him for help in interpreting data. Resnik never told him what she planned to do after her research was done. There was one conversation, however, that led Barker to believe that she questioned whether she was in the right field.

"Once she pulled me aside and said, 'Where do you get your ideas [for research] from?'" Barker said. "I told her that if she had to think about where ideas come from, she ought not to go into that kind of science. . . . It's the kind of question somebody who is very adept at carrying out someone else's ideas asks. And she was extremely talented at carrying out complex tasks."

She also began to realize she had no real life outside the laboratory. When she was married, many of her friends were people she had met as Oldak's wife. On her own now, she needed to learn over again how to make friends. She reached out to people who could understand her new lifestyle.

Connie Knapp, whose husband, Jeff, graduated law school with Oldak, invited Judy to join them and other friends for beachhouse weekends in Bethany Beach, Delaware. The two women became close friends. They spent their days in the sun and their nights eating steamed crabs, playing Monopoly, reading and talking in the dark of the screened-in porch. "She loved to eat. She loved to eat a lot," Knapp said, laughing. "I would eat three crabs. Everybody else would eat six. Judy and Jeff would just keep eating. She loved crabs."

She also loved the sun. Before the others were awake, Resnik ate breakfast, packed away some fruit and a Coke, grabbed a beach chair and ran to the sand. She was short on cash, living on a college stipend, so she bought drugstore hand lotion rather than suntan lotion; for entertainment, she read books and walked to the ice cream store.

Resnik easily caught the attention of men who roamed the beach. They would try to strike up conversations which she attempted to ignore. Her friends watched with amusement as Resnik developed a defense. She learned to zing the obnoxious. "I never saw her get angry. Impatient, yes . . . she'd definitely rise to the occasion and show off her smarts if she needed to," Jeff Knapp said.

One day in the summer of 1977, Connie Knapp saw Judy, lying flat on her stomach in the sand, writing on a piece of paper. "What are you doing?" Knapp said. "Applying to be an astronaut," Resnik replied. "I looked at her and said: 'You're doing what?'"

Her work at NIH wasn't fulfilling. She had come to miss the task-oriented sciences she tackled at RCA, where she designed radar control and small rocketry circuits. When NASA decided to expand its astronaut ranks in 1977, searching for more scientists and for women and minorities, Resnik mailed her application and called her father and step-mother.

"Daddy, I'm going to try to be an astronaut," Resnik said.

"Good," he said. "Because you're going to get it."

Although Resnik applied for other jobs, she devised a thorough, methodical plan to beat out the thousands of competitors for a NASA berth. She interviewed former astronaut and fellow Ohioan John Glenn, wandered through the halls of the newly opened National Air and Space Museum, read every piece of information about the program she could find and mapped out a regimen of diet and exercise. She cut her hair to look more professional. She went into the early interviews believing she had little chance, but soon learned she was in the top 200 of the more than 1,000 women who applied. She began studying for a pilot's license.

In the months leading to the final selection, still unsure of her future, she earned her doctorate and left academia for a job with Xerox Corporation in California. She waited for word from NASA. She underwent a physical that, she told friends, revealed a thyroid problem. Wasting little time, Resnik sought out a medical expert, who examined her and wrote NASA that the problem was minor.

Resnik's friends and family still remember the sound of their phones ringing impatiently one January morning in 1978.

It was Judy. "I did it."

Six astronauts are lying on their backs, waiting for the first launch of the space shuttle *Discovery*. It is June 26, 1984, at Kennedy Space Center's Pad 39-A, and the launch had already been delayed once. Five of the crew members—pilot Michael Coats, mission specialists Resnik, Steven Hawley and Richard Mullane and the first commercial crew member Charles Walker—had never been in space before and were anxious to go. Commander Henry Hartsfield had been on one earlier shuttle, but he felt special about this trip with its high-spirited crew.

The team had become known as the Zoo Crew during its training for the 2.5-million-mile, 150-million-dollar trip. They got along well, played with double entendres, teased between assignments and even planned a few surprises to liven this adventure.

Two were in store for Resnik and one was already hidden in the lining of the ship's bathroom curtain. It was a poster of Tom Selleck, pinned so that Resnik would see it when she had to use the bathroom. The crew members figured it would be a good match to the coffee cup she had. "Excuse No. 1," were the words written across the cup, "I'm Saving Myself for Tom Selleck." The other was something that mission control had planned: on a wakeup call one morning, the University of Maryland Victory Song would be piped into the orbiter.

Resnik, who had joined the space program in 1978, would be the second woman in space, following the journey of Sally Ride on the *Challenger* in June 1983. Resnik showed no disappointment about NASA's decision to make her number two. She simply told friends that she was glad not to face the public relations hoopla that Ride endured. She had enough of the stuff she hated—the speeches, the interviews, the parties—without being the first anything. "I am just pleased to have a flight assignment," Resnik said in an interview. "I feel that I am very fortunate to be any woman in space, any person in space."

For her own flight, Resnik was unrelenting in her drive to excel. She practically lived in the Johnson Space Center simulator during the last months. She developed a deft touch with the remote manipulator system, a derrick-like arm that she would use to lift a solar panel into space. Conscious of the need for stamina, she ran and lifted weights.

In the months before flight, she even agreed to an interview with her hometown paper, the *Akron Beacon Journal,* to comply with a NASA public relations request. She disliked television interviews because she could not control what would happen next. In newspaper interviews, she was impatient because, inevitably, the questions turned personal. None of the reporters she had met ever had enough questions about the technical nature of the mission.

"Did anyone influence you or do you feel that you are where you are today because you are self-motivated?" the interviewer asked her.

"I am where I am today because I just happened to make the right decision at the times when the decisions were presented to me," she said.

"Do you credit the women's movement at all?"

"No, I don't credit anyone."

In her eight years at NASA, Resnik had created a life that revolved around work and a social life with other astronauts, pilots and secretaries at the space center. She prepared gourmet dinners with a food processor that her friends kidded she wore out, spent evenings at Frenchy's, the Italian restaurant near the space center that hung astronauts' photos on the wall, and hitched rides on a T-38 training jet from Houston to Washington and back again in a day to log training hours.

Those quick trips had a zany quality to them. Resnik, in her NASA jumpsuit, would take a cab from Andrews Air Force Base to NASA headquarters in Washington. At lunchtime, she would rip off the NASA tag, held on by Velcro, and meet her friends at a casual restaurant. Other diners thought she was a mechanic.

Resnik changed during those years, in temperament and looks. Her attempt to set her hair in a shorter, smooth coiffure failed in the Houston humidity. She let her hair curl naturally, giving her a less formal and more fashionable look. People who knew her before she entered the program were struck at how quickly she tied her future to NASA. Two months after she was accepted into the program, Resnik spoke about the qualities that made a good astronaut in a statement that might have been written by a public relations firm. "The important thing is to be dedicated enough," she said in a Xerox company newsletter. "I believe I'm both dedicated enough and qualified enough to do whatever NASA calls on me to do."

Later, though, Resnik confided to a few that she was wary of opening the shuttle to nonscientists; time in orbit was too precious to waste. Congressmen would just be "invading their space," Resnik told her friend Connie Knapp during a visit in 1984. "What are we going to do with these people?"

In public, Resnik spoke out only positively about the new effort by NASA. What NASA wanted, Resnik supported. What NASA asked, she did. Resnik trusted NASA to protect and support her.

On the day of her first flight, that trust was tested. Strapped on their backs, at 8:43 A.M., the Zoo Crew listened as the countdown rolled to T-minus-thirty-one seconds.

"Hang, on, gang, here we go," Hartsfield said.

T-minus-6.6 seconds and *Discovery*'s three main engines began groaning to life. T-minus-4 seconds and a loud bang was heard.

Suddenly, fire flashed out of the back of *Discovery*. An alarm went off. There was smoke. Then silence. Giant water hoses began spraying thousands of gallons of water into *Discovery*'s engine nozzles. The whine of the engines changed pitch abruptly, sounding like a beast in pain. It was a launch abort, the first in shuttle history and the second ever in American manned space-flight.

When it was safe, about forty minutes later, the astronauts emerged from the shuttle. They all gathered, grinned and shook hands with the launch crews. No one was hurt.

Later, it was found that a fuel valve had malfunctioned. The NASA system of computers and detectors had "safed" it and aborted the launch, NASA spokesmen said. The astronauts went on leave for two days. All returned to say they were unafraid.

"I was disappointed," Resnik told an interviewer later. "But I was relieved that the safety systems do work. It was unfortunate that we had to check them out. But it built a confidence in the whole system."

CHALLENGERS

This is the official emblem for the Space Shuttle
mission 51-L. (NASA)

The Space Shuttle *Challenger* lifts off from Pad 39-B at the Kennedy Space Center in Florida. Moments later the craft exploded, killing the crew of seven. (AP/Wide World)

SPACE CREW—Here is the seven-person crew of the Space Shuttle *Challenger*. From left, front are: astronauts Michael J. Smith, Francis R. (Dick) Scobee, and Ronald E. McNair; and from left, rear: Ellison S. Onizuka, Sharon Christa McAuliffe, Gregory Jarvis, and Judith A. Resnik. (AP/Wide World)

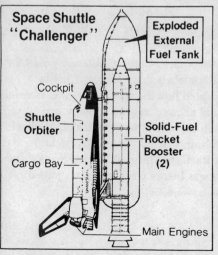

Space Shuttle *Challenger* exploded shortly after liftoff from Kennedy Space Center, January 28, 1986. Graphic locates the external fuel tank which exploded. (AP/Wide World)

Crewmembers of the Space Shuttle *Challenger* posed for this gag photo last fall when space teacher Christa McAuliffe was accepted into the space program. Wearing graduation caps and dressed as grad students are (clockwise from bottom left): Ellison Onizuka, Michael Smith, Ronald McNair, Christa McAuliffe, backup teacher-astronaut Barbara Morgan, Francis Scobee and Judy Resnik. This was before Gregory Jarvis joined the crew. (UPI/Bettmann Newsphotos)

Challenger commander Francis R. Scobee in the jet trainer. (NASA)

Scobee displays a New Hampshire tee shirt after arriving at the Kennedy Space Center.

(AP/Wide World)

Challenger pilot
Mike Smith.

(AP/Wide World)

McNair, Scobee and Judy Resnik arrived at the Kennedy Space Center for a dress rehearsal of their countdown.

(UPI/Bettmann Newsphotos)

Mike Smith
with family in
Houston, Texas.
From left: wife
Jane; daughter
Erin, 8; daughter
Alison, 14;
Smith; and son
Scott, 16.

(AP/Wide World)

Judith Resnik.

(NASA)

Judith Resnik, left, and Christa McAuliffe.
(AP/Wide World)

Astronaut Ronald McNair.
(NASA)

Ronald McNair holds his son, Reggie, in this photo taken
February 11, 1984 just after McNair had returned from a
Space Shuttle mission aboard *Challenger.* (AP/Wide World)

Ellison S. Onizuka on the day of the tragedy.

(Photo by Paul Larkin)

Astronaut Gregory Jarvis. (NASA)

Jarvis making a public appearance on behalf of NASA.
(NASA)

Christa McAuliffe floats aboard NASA's KC-135 "zero gravity" aircraft. (NASA)

Teacher-astronaut Christa McAuliffe. (NASA)

Christa McAuliffe takes a breather following a busy day's training. (NASA)

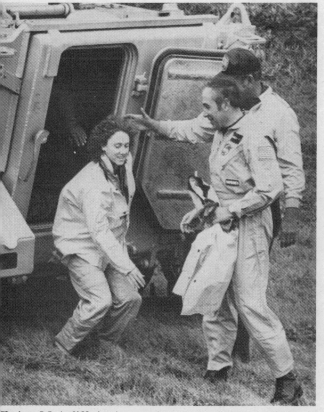

Christa McAuliffe is given assistance by Gregory Jarvis,
who became her friend during the training, as she jumps
from a launch-pad evacuation vehicle.
(AFP; Photo by Jonathon Utz)

President Ronald Reagan ordered flags at half-staff for a week in the aftermath of the Space Shuttle *Challenger* accident. (AP/Wide World)

Chapter 6

RONALD E. McNAIR

It wasn't much of a swimming hole, just a deep, round cavity dug in the center of a large cow pasture on the edge of Lake City, South Carolina, behind the Pine Bay Dairy. Really an irrigation pond, it had been scooped out of the earth by a bulldozer to help keep the parched farmland moist in the tiny tobacco town. The cool waters seemed inviting when the temperatures topped 100 degrees as they often did in the muggy South Carolina summers. And there was no pool in town for the Negroes, as blacks were called in the early 1960s.

Too bad the pond at the cow pasture was taboo. According to local folklore, a man was drowned, dragged under by a whirlpool, sucked down and down. "No one was going to swim at the cow pasture, no way," Harry Wright remembers of those days when he and his friend Ronald McNair were eleven or twelve years old. "You'd get a beating if you did."

One day around sunset, when Wright and some friends were out in the cow pasture stalking redbirds and sparrows and crows and squirrels with their BB guns, they looked over and saw Ronald McNair jumping off the dirt embankment, paddling away as if this were any old swimming hole and not the dreaded place where a man had drowned.

Wright wasn't really all that surprised. It was just the kind of thing Ronald would do all by himself, never telling anyone about it. Maybe that's why Wright wasn't shocked when nearly twenty years later his friend McNair told him that he was going to fly off in a giant glider sitting atop what McNair liked to call "six million pounds of fire and thunder." After all, hadn't Ronald McNair—he'd never been Ron to his friends and family growing up—always

97

been the smartest kid in Lake City? Hadn't he been the captain of the football team, the president of the senior class, the best saxophone player in the Carver High band? Didn't he talk about thermodynamics and read books on calculus when the other kids didn't know what those words even meant? Wasn't he a black-belt in karate who could break five cinder blocks with his forehead?

"Don't ever tell Ronald he can't do something," McNair's father Carl liked to say. "I've tried it, and I always came out on the short end."

The emergence of the talented, determined McNair as a space explorer was easy to understand in 1986. But in 1950s South Carolina, the very idea that Ronald E. McNair, a black man, could become an astronaut was as amazing as a man soaring 170 miles above the earth and whirling around the planet at nearly 300-miles-a-minute.

As in many rural towns in the South, integration came slowly and somewhat quietly to Lake City, a town of about 5,100 people when McNair was born there on October 21, 1950. The town, set in some of the South's richest tobacco country, did not elect its first black councilman until 1969. The high school was fully integrated in 1970, three years after McNair had graduated.

Segregation was taken for granted; it was a system in which everyone knew his place. When McNair and his friends went to the old Propst's Theater to see movies on Saturday afternoons, they sat in the segregated balcony. When they wanted candy or popcorn, they could not go to the concession stand. They had to take their money to the lady at the ticket booth, and she got them what they wanted. Later, when they walked up Main Street, past the railroad tracks, to buy comics and ice cream at M&D Drugs, they knew just what to do there, too.

"We used to have to stop right here," McNair's classmate, Dozier Montgomery, said as he retraced their steps, stopping near a small freezer at the front of the store. "You were black and you could get your ice cream from here. But they had stools there. . . . The white kids could sit at the counter and get their ice cream there. You'd go home and say, 'Mama, why I have to stand there and I couldn't sit down?' And many times Mama said, 'Well, that's just how things are right now, but they're working on it, you know. Be patient.'"

Sometimes, the atmosphere grew ugly. When McNair was about four years old, the home of Walter Scott, the president of the local NAACP, was shot up one night and big crosses were painted on the gas station where he worked. There had been a Ku Klux Klan rally that night, said Scott, and later when the shooting started he and his family had lain on the floor of their home, as bullets came through the picture window in the living room. It was not the kind of thing a child in the neighborhood forgot.

McNair never forgot those days—not after he left Lake City; not after he earned a Ph.D. from the Massachusetts Institute of Technology, one of the few blacks in the large student body; not after he had seen raw racism in Boston; not after he was picked as one of the country's first black astronauts in 1978.

After his selection, McNair climbed into the pulpit at Trinity Baptist Church in Los Angeles, where he worshipped, and told his audience about growing up in "one of those places where the railroad track right through the middle of town drew a color line," where "there wasn't very much for black kids to do during the summer vacations . . . except go to the field." He told of picking beans and cucumbers, tobacco and cotton in the sweltering summers. He told of working as a delivery boy and being warned he could not read his school books on breaks, even if he sat in the trash boxes behind the store. He told of a public library that wasn't really public.

"Somehow it seems these situations never end," he told the congregation. "It's always somebody trying to get in the way. Always somebody trying to limit us." But the rest of his message was upbeat. Many people, he reminded his listeners, including their parents and his parents, had made sacrifices to open new opportunities; it was up to the young to grasp them. "We need to get away from some of this stereotype mentality that we carry. . . . This is the modern age, and we just can't do the same old regular things we used to do or think that way."

McNair was a symbol of that modern age, of NASA's decision to discard the image of its astronaut corps as a white, male brotherhood of flyers. He was one of three blacks and six women picked as part of a new class of thirty-five astronauts in 1978. Black magazines such as *Ebony* and *Black Enterprise* wrote articles about McNair and his two black colleagues. McNair's hometown held Ron McNair Day. His alma mater, a black university in North Carolina, honored him, too. There were invitations to speak at MIT and before lawmakers in South Carolina and Massachusetts.

In one way, at least, McNair warmed to his new role. It was a way to reach young people. The freshly-minted astronaut, with his quiet air, ready smile and walk that conveyed a sense of urgency and confidence, traveled to speak in grammar schools like Brooklyn's P.S. 5 in the inner-city Bedford-Stuyvesant section. He recruited black students for graduate science programs, traveling to Washington, D.C., and southern California. He was always ready to jump on a plane, always willing to add one more stop to his schedule. It was as if he had cracked the code, and he wanted others to be able to do it, too.

When Dozier Montgomery's fifth-grade class wrote McNair a letter shortly before he took off on his first shuttle mission in 1984, he sent a three-page handwritten reply, carefully including each child's first name.

"Yes, I did go to the very school you are now attending—from second through fifth grades. Yes, it is true, astronauts are usually from New York, Los Angeles, Philadelphia and Boston. But let the fact that there is one from LAKE CITY, S.C., serve as a lesson to you that it doesn't matter where you come from, who your relatives are, how much money you have, or who you are; whether or not you reach your goals in life depends entirely on how well you prepare for them and how badly you want them. . . ."

It was signed, "Your friend, Ronald E. McNair NASA Astronaut 'Homeboy'."

On the football field behind Carver High in 1965, Coach Jack T. Williams sized up the new recruits. One of them was about five-foot-eight, 145 pounds, with glasses and what Williams called the "look of a Phi Beta Kappa candidate.

"This guy's not gonna pan out," Williams remembers thinking. And then he put him through some hitting drills. "He was vicious," Williams recalls. "Total football player."

McNair became a starter, number 21, playing linebacker for the Carver Lions that year, his junior year in high school. Williams always had trouble telling McNair apart from his older brother, Carl, who also came out for the team that year. So he took to calling them the Gizmo brothers, Big Gizmo and Little Gizmo.

But in most circumstances, there was something that seemed to set Ronald apart from the others, and all the teachers noticed it.

"Determination. Anything Ronald set out to do, he did," said Williams. "He didn't lay back and wish."

Like Judy Resnik, he took advantage of NASA's decision to open the space program to women and minorities, and like her, he was an accomplished scientist and a talented musician. But if Resnik was a woman who had found herself by getting into the space program, McNair was a man who always knew who he was and exactly where he was going. McNair's father likes to say he "was born that way." But, of course, it wasn't that simple.

Ronald's mother, Pearl, was a grammar school teacher who went back to college for her master's degree when Ronald was about ten years old. She instilled in him the love of books, the reverence for learning. His father, Carl, was an auto repairman. "You wreck 'em, I repair 'em," was his blunt way of describing his job. There was a gentle dignity about him, and an eloquence that belied his ninth-grade education. McNair, after he became an astronaut, would say diplomatically that both parents had motivated him equally, but his boyhood friend Harry Wright believed that Ronald's father had given Ronald an essential tool—what Wright called "mother wit," the sort of street wisdom that has nothing to do with book learning.

Ronald's father, for instance, got someone with a typewriter to change the date on Ronald's birth certificate, so that Ronald could start first grade at the age of four, the same year as his brother who was ten months older. Ronald's mother, a teacher, wanted nothing to do with the caper. But, his father recalled, "He was more than ready, and I didn't see any sense in keeping him home."

His father tried to keep track of his three sons, even dropping by their school on occasion. His visits exasperated Ronald's seventh-grade science teacher, Rosa N. Conner. He would stick his head inside the classroom and say, "I'm just checking on my boys." He held regular homework sessions with the boys, which, years later, Ronald described as "a big comedy hour." He said he once believed his father "was the world's greatest expert in grammar" but later changed his mind. "I don't really think he knew the stuff, but he was so clever that he made me think he knew it," Ronald said.

In the late '50s, Carl McNair began going to New York City for lengthy periods because there was not enough work for a black auto repairman in Lake City. Carl McNair said he returned for holidays and important occasions in his sons' lives. He said he and his wife "had the kids in common. It was good for the family." During the summer Ronald often spent time with him in New York, there were "periodic father-son talks" with all three boys, and always Carl McNair tried to tell his sons about "my past experiences, [about] being uneducated, how much I missed out on."

Ronald often asked his father to send him books about calculus or other subjects that weren't available at home. In school, he already was finding the assignments too easy and asking the teachers for more advanced work. "He worked the devil out of me to keep feeding him," said Elouise Cooper, McNair's seventh-grade English teacher. "We didn't have gifted and talented programs then. Everyone was all piled together, all fifty kids, maybe more in one class." But Cooper found works to stimulate Ronald's searching mind. While his classmates were reading less challenging fare, she gave him *Beowulf*, an 8th century epic poem in Olde English usually read by college students.

Grade-conscious and serious, McNair already was a perfectionist. "When he passed up a paper, and got less than 100, he wanted to know why, what was wrong with it, if it were something he didn't understand," Cooper remembered. Somehow, he escaped being the class grind. Maybe it was his speed in track or his ability on the football field. Maybe it was playing in the Carver High band. McNair had a girlfriend and a sweater with the big Carver "C" on it, Dozier Montgomery recalled. "He was all right."

He was also a participant—sometimes the instigator—in high school pranks. Archie Alford Jr., another high school friend, recalled the time the two took as much sodium as they could find in the chemistry lab, filled a sink with water and threw it in. "It started fizzling, and it blew up in a big black cloud, . . . and we were scared we'd get caught," Alford said. "McNair cut crazy just like the rest of us. If you saw five of us walking down the street together, you wouldn't know he was the brain."

McNair was hungrier for knowledge than the rest, and the teachers did their best to feed him. Carver High, a rambling one-story brick building a few blocks from the McNairs' Moore Street home, was a place where teachers and students improvised. Ragged books were passed down from the white schools. When the students wanted to start a track team, Coach Williams recalled, they scraped and leveled a track around the football field themselves. In science class, when there was no hydrochloric acid for their experiments, the students brought vinegar from home as a substitute.

In school, the youngsters were taught to revere education, and the teachers had the tools to make the lesson stick. "I paddled when I had to," said P.C. Lemmon, the former principal of Carver High. "And I didn't have to worry about parents beating my behind because I beat their kids' behinds." Dozier Montgomery remembers something else about Lemmon. "He always told us, 'Never say, That'll do. If you can do that, you can do better.' It must have stuck with Ronald."

Black students were taught they had to be twice as good to make it. They learned that college was the "only channel, the only way out," said McNair's friend Harry Wright. Perhaps a third of McNair's 1967 graduating class of about 150 went off to college. As was the tradition in the region, their ministers helped them get into black colleges affiliated with their churches. According to Wright, the Baptists went to Morris College, the Methodists to Claflin and the African Methodist Episcopalians to Allen University. All three schools were in South Carolina.

"But Ron and I knew if you went to school here, you'd fall in the same syndrome . . . end up coming back here a teacher," said Wright, who went off to Virginia Union in Richmond and came home to become a juvenile probation counselor. Both McNair and his brother Carl chose North Carolina Agricultural & Technical State University, a black school known for its engineering and science programs in Greensboro, about 170 miles from home.

McNair always had liked math and science. But, he once told his college adviser and physics professor Tom Sandin, that wasn't the only reason he chose his major. McNair recalled asking his high school teachers what the most difficult college major would be. When they said physics, that's what he picked.

He also picked karate as an extracurricular activity. He started in a class of about 200. At the end of the first semester, there were five left, McNair once said in an interview. At the end of the second year there was one. It was the start of a lifetime pursuit for McNair, as he worked his way up to the highest level, black-belt, and then through its successive categories of skill.

It was not so much a means of self-defense as another challenge, another way to hone his sense of discipline and grace under pressure. Bob Maloney, who met McNair at MIT and took a karate class from him, said McNair reminded him of a Samurai warrior when he fought in tournaments. "There was none of this Muhammad Ali circling," said Maloney. "He fought people who outweighed him by forty or fifty pounds and his style did not change. . . . When he fought he went straight ahead."

That style would serve him well in the space program and in the years at graduate school.

As he neared his senior year and decided to apply to MIT, Sandin recommended him for a Ford Foundation Fellowship that would pay his way to the more sophisticated world of Boston. The Ford Foundation "was looking for blacks who had not only intellectual abilities, but leadership abilities," Sandin recalled. He remembered one phrase he had written in the recommendation: "If you can't give this to Ron McNair, you can't give it to anyone.' "

Columns. Ten of them looming tall and majestic under the words "Massachusetts Institute of Technology." Engraved on the limestone wings of the huge classical edifices, the names of the greatest scientists of past generations—Darwin, Newton, Pasteur, Lavoisier, Faraday, Archimedes and on and on. The buildings themselves, built around a graceful courtyard on the banks of the Charles River in Cambridge, were enough to put anyone in awe.

As if that weren't enough, there was the academic reputation. Getting an education at MIT is like taking a drink of water from a firehose, or so the saying goes. Ronald McNair later joked that when he arrived at the university, he'd heard "even the janitors had master's degrees."

He came there first as a junior, fresh from North Carolina A & T as part of an exchange program in which MIT sent professors to black Southern colleges, and the colleges sent their most promising students north. Later, after getting his bachelor's degree in physics and graduating *magna cum laude* from A & T, he returned to pursue a doctorate in physics. "It was his entrance into the white world," said Harry Fleming, his high school economics teacher. And what an entrance it was. For McNair and other blacks, Cambridge and nearby Boston was not the gracious center of liberalism and culture that many whites found when they came.

In 1971, there were only about 200 black students among MIT's enrollment of 7,700. Many of the blacks, one of them recalled, arrived thinking of the Boston Symphony and Harvard Yard.

Instead they heard the sound of racial taunts and discovered white working class enclaves like South Boston and Dorchester where they dared not walk.

It was a time of deep passions stirred by a fight over integrating the public schools. All about the city, there was an acrid air of racial tension. No matter where McNair went, it seemed like he could not escape the issue of race.

He grew up as the fledgling civil rights movement took root in the South. In 1962, just before McNair turned twelve, James Meredith, armed with a court order and protected by U.S. marshals, entered the University of Mississippi—the first black ever to do so. When McNair was fourteen, Martin Luther King Jr. and a small group of blacks tried to register at the Hotel Albert in Selma, Alabama, setting off a violent attack in which King was punched and kicked. But, in a sense, McNair had been insulated from racial strife by parents who did not talk much about segregation or racism, by a town that was not quite part of it all.

The bloody riots that Meredith's registration set off and the attack on King somehow seemed far away from Lake City. "This was a little town where they would still get together when some big issue was on television . . . about blacks and whites. The blacks and whites would stand there and talk about it. 'Did you see that on TV last night? Did you see what they did?'" said McNair's friend Dozier Montgomery, mimicking the whispers he'd heard as a youth. "They didn't even realize what was really going on was *you.*"

In McNair's own home, the teachings were the same. "We didn't think segregation," his father recalled. "They were raised to think a person is a person. We never made a distinction."

But in Boston, the racism was raw. "The first time I was ever called a nigger to my face was in the Boston Common," said Bill Quivers, who like McNair was an MIT grad student in the 1970s. He got to know McNair well in the karate class McNair taught at the St. Paul A.M.E. Church, off Massachusetts Avenue a few blocks from the campus.

McNair had his run-ins too, two of them in Harvard Square, the congested, noisy jumble of streets and shops right next to the entrance to Harvard College—"One of those more enlightened areas of town," Quivers said with a wry smile. One time at a bus stop, "some guy kept messing with him, calling him all kinds of names. . . . He was just waiting for the bus." Another time,

Quivers and a group from the karate class were coming out of the Wursthaus, a popular Harvard Square hangout, when a group of whites started taunting them.

The whites had been drinking. One of them jumped McNair, who turned on him and wrestled him to the pavement. That seemed to end the fight, Quivers said. The men went off, but one returned moments later on a motorcycle. "It started up again. Ron had the guy on the hood of a car. It was pretty funny. Ron did throw a punch, and his glasses got messed up. And this time it did end," Quivers said.

The incident that shook McNair the most, according to Quivers, occurred when Ronald was caring for a friend's apartment in a white Boston neighborhood. McNair was going to the house when someone sicked a dog on him. He managed to outrun the dog and get inside, uninjured.

" 'Why me? I wasn't doing anything, minding my own business, and this guy sicks a dog on me,' " McNair told his friend. Quivers shared McNair's disbelief. "Sure, we'd get these racial incidents," Quivers said, "but there was something about a dog being set on you; it bothered him a lot for a while."

Although it was a volatile time in Cambridge, a time marked by protests over civil rights issues and the Vietnam War, MIT was not a center of student demonstrations. McNair did not join protests over civil rights or the Vietnam War in his college days as far as anyone can remember. He had other things on his mind. Five years earlier, when his high school chemistry teacher asked the students to write an essay about what they'd be doing in a decade, McNair, in his typically confident way, wrote that he would have a Ph.D. in physics. The decade was half over. There was a deadline to meet.

MIT was a high-pressure, demanding new world. The valedictorian from Carver High wasn't as prepared as the students from Harvard and Stanford and Cal Tech. Said Michael Feld, McNair's MIT physics professor and Ph.D. adviser, "It was predictable that he'd have a tough time. Given his fairly inadequate background, it took tremendous determination to bring himself up to speed, but he was able to muster that kind of resolve."

There were gaps to fill, even undergraduate courses to take, and there was a sense of isolation. Said Quivers, "The secret of getting through this place is study groups. You study together . . . and being the only black in a couple of hundred students in a class, it's just hard to fit into a group." There was also the self-generated pressure, particularly for a perfectionist like McNair, accustomed to being the class star. He took his undergrad courses in advanced physics and electrical engineering, and spent endless hours doing laser research for his thesis in the lab in the battleship gray basement at MIT.

Just as McNair had avoided being a grind in high school, in grad school he never became a "tool," the MIT term for students who did nothing but study, "you know, like an old, worn-out, used-up tool," said Quivers. McNair had his saxophone and taught a karate class at St. Paul, a comforting green clapboard building near MIT. The class became a sort of extended family for McNair and the others who were so far from home. At a St. Paul pot-luck dinner, McNair met Cheryl Moore, a pretty teacher with a shy manner from Jamaica, New York. They were married at the church on June 27, 1976.

Despite his steady progress at MIT, there were setbacks along the way. When it came time for his physics qualifying exam—the five-hour monster that everyone must pass for a doctorate—McNair flunked and had to take the test again. That was a minor problem, compared to what was in store. One night on his way out with Cheryl, he set his karate bag on the car. It contained the notebook that had every scrap of data he had collected for his doctoral thesis during more than a year of experiments.

"He had put it down and went around the side of the car," Cheryl recalled. "I don't remember how it happened, but he came back and it wasn't there. It was just a split second. It was not that he cried, or beat on the car. He just kind of got very quiet. Ron generally thinks a lot . . . thinks first and reacts later. He thought and said, 'That was my whole paper, but we'll see.' That was really it. By the time we reached our destination, he'd figured out how he'd replace it."

Michael Feld, Ronald's adviser, said other students might have decided to remain an extra year in school to replace the lost data, but not McNair. He just did the experiments again, faster, "in three or four months not even batting an eyelash." He completed his doctorate on schedule, and went on to California to continue the work he loved.

Physics, he later told an interviewer, "is something very different from the world I grew up in; it is a nice playground where I can go and play. We are all trying to unravel mysteries about our universe. It's a totally different world. Once you have grasped a concept, it gives you a very euphoric feeling."

The time was October 1957. Ronald McNair, just about to turn seven, rushed out of his ramshackle house on Moore Street to gaze in amazement at the sky, trying to see *Sputnik,* the Soviet satellite that made history by going into orbit around the earth. He was worried the mysterious contraption might fall, and he watched from the yard so he could get out of its way. How, he wondered, could something so big stay in the heavens?

It was not the first time—and certainly not the last—that McNair looked at the unknown and wanted to understand.

Riding down the highways and country roads with his father when he was only three, he studied the letters on the signs—his grandmother had already taught him the alphabet—and wanted to know what they meant. Later, there was what his younger brother Eric called the "family physician" phase when Ronald practiced on his siblings, but not with any toy stethoscope from a doctor's kit. Ronald had big, thick medical books. "If something was wrong with Carl or me," Eric McNair recalled, "we'd go to him and say, 'I got this pain,' and he'd look in his book and give us his professional diagnosis."

There was also the time when the three brothers, who'd always been very close, went hunting with their BB guns. "We shot a bird . . . and Ron and Carl performed an operation on the bird. They opened him up, took the BB out, sewed him up and nursed him back to health," said Eric, about four years younger than Ronald. But it was no humanitarian gesture, he added with a mischievous grin. "No, it was more for the science of it," just wanting to know how it all worked.

No one seems to be able to pinpoint precisely when McNair's questing mind turned to the wonders of physics, but that science seemed to be the perfect match for his skills and personality. It combined the logic he so loved in mathematics and the formidable challenge of a discipline whose mission was nothing less than to explain how the universe works.

"The mother science," McNair's MIT colleague Quivers, also a physicist, called it. "Chemistry, biology, they all have their roots in physics. Everything else is just sort of physics in different disguises."

McNair once told an interviewer that "the most satisfying thing about physics itself is the feeling of having understood and unlocked something heretofore unknown. You have worked on a problem, and now you have found a solution. . . . [It] is a good feeling like no other. It goes so far as to negate all of the hard times and frustrations that you have encountered in trying to find the solution.''

When McNair, at twenty-six, earned his doctorate, with a thesis on laser physics, he also picked off one of the plums of his field and joined Hughes Research Laboratories in California. There he was able to do advanced laser research at one of the world's foremost centers for such work. And the Malibu setting could not have been better: a white stucco building, nestled in the green hills above the Pacific. It was so picturesque that it was in demand by film producers who wanted to use it as the set when a scene called for a futuristic research facility.

He'd been there only a short while when a brochure came in the office mail, inviting scientists to apply as mission specialists in the space program. McNair wasn't even sure why he had gotten the brochure, his wife, Cheryl, recalled. "He brought it home and said, 'What do you think about it?' I told him, 'Well you have the credentials. You're qualified, so try it.'"

When brother Carl first heard about Ronald's plans he was struck by the enormity of Ronald's aspiration, particularly given their background. When Ronald told him, "I'm going to be an astronaut," Carl remembered replying, "Sure, and I'm going to be the Pope." Carl, now a data processing consultant in Atlanta, said he thought back to their days growing up in Lake City. "There were no Mercedes, no Jaguars. There's now one black doctor. I don't know of any black attorneys. . . . You didn't have any of the old-time role models."

McNair went about the application process in his usual methodical, meticulous manner. When Carl asked why he thought he would be chosen from among the 8,000 aspirants, McNair answered, "Because I applied." It was not a cocky answer, but a confident one based on the knowledge that he had left nothing to chance.

Midway through the application process, when things were looking good, he called Bob Maloney, his friend from grad school days in Cambridge who was on the staff of the House Appropriations Committee. He said, "Bob, I have the academics, the physical part, but do you think politics would play a role?"

Neither one was sure if it would, but Maloney agreed to help him get recommendations from U.S. Senator Edward W. Brooke, a Massachusetts Republican, and several Representatives. "It just made Ron feel he had touched every base. It was consistent with his personality."

Looking back now, a few high school and college chums recall McNair talking about wanting to be part of space exploration. But those closest to him don't remember space travel being his burning desire. Eric said he and his brother watched the space shots, and with Ronald "it was an edge-of-the-seat type thing. . . . He would be really into it." But at that age—Ronald was eleven years old when John Glenn became the first American to orbit the earth—all the kids marveled at the gleaming rockets and the astronauts that hurtled into the sky.

In January, 1978, McNair got the call from Houston. Cheryl was standing next to him in their Marina Del Rey apartment. "When the phone rang and he signaled me that it was NASA, we both sat there," she recalled. "I could hear the conversation and I knew." In the summer he joined Resnik, Onizuka, Scobee and the rest of the class for training.

Eric believes that for his brother, flying into space was an extension of his first love. "It was science. It was another wonder," said Eric. "His fascination was not with space, but a fascination in finding out why things happen as they do."

Back in Lake City, the house on Moore Street where he had grown up wasn't even there anymore. The weather-beaten home, whose roof had always leaked when he was a kid, had fallen apart after the family moved to a new place across town.

In Houston, the house McNair bought for his family in 1984 was made to last. Red brick trimmed in rich brown wood, located in an affluent suburb, it had a price tag of 145,000 dollars and all the nice things that went with that—a family room with huge windows that caught the glint of the afternoon sun, a grassy yard, protected by a vanilla-colored fence, where Reginald, then two, and Joy, who was on the way, could play as they grew up. Edward H. White Elementary School, named after one of the astronauts killed in the *Apollo 1* fire in 1967, was close to the McNairs' subdivision, and there were tennis courts and a park with swings and jungle gyms within easy reach.

Early each morning, McNair drove the family car out curving

Lake Shore Drive, past Taylor Lake, then on to NASA Road 1, which offered a straight shot to the Johnson Space Center, only five miles away. By then, in the summer of 1984, he had been with the space program for six years.

Like everything that had come before in his life, the program had its own set of challenges and McNair met them in his usual way. NASA had a military style, and MIT and the Hughes physics lab weren't the best places for basic training. McNair needed to learn not only how to work through channels but where the channels were, and "how far you can push [for something] and still keep everyone happy," said Alan Bean, who was the chief of the astronaut office when McNair arrived in 1978 with Judy Resnik and the others. Some caught on faster, said Bean. Some of McNair's classmates—Sally Ride, later America's first woman in space, and Resnik—were quick studies at the new game.

"Some people never get the hang of it, but he did," said Bean. "He'd watch and recognize why things worked, [things] that hadn't worked back at school." Bean remembered McNair as the "most quiet person" in the class. While others tried to make their presence known, tossing out opinions, polishing their images, McNair held back, taking it all in. Said Bean: "He was learning things his own way. I liked it."

If it was difficult being among the nation's first three black astronauts, McNair didn't talk about it with his colleagues, even with his friend Charles F. Bolden Jr., who became the fourth black astronaut in 1980. Lieutenant Colonel Bolden, a graduate of the Naval Academy and a flyer, said that by the time people like himself and McNair get to the space center, being in a white environment "is old hat. . . . You don't see that you're one around so many or four around so many. I don't think Ron ever thought about it."

McNair was assigned to his first mission in 1983 and when the shuttle *Challenger* lifted off into the Florida skies on February 3, 1984, McNair became the second black astronaut to hurtle into space. The mission was the first in which men flew freely in space—with no lifeline to attach them to their mother-ship. Two of McNair's fellow astronauts, Robert Stewart and Bruce McCandless, donned jet-powered backpacks over their spacesuits and left the craft. McNair joked, "You guys look like two of the Three Stooges" as Stewart tried to fix a tiny camera on McCandless' helmet by hitting him in the head with a hammer.

McNair, working as part of the team from inside the shuttle, helped pave the way for future astronauts to fly untethered in space so they could retrieve and repair damaged satellites. As part of his duties, McNair, sometimes sporting a jaunty beret, filmed scenes for a movie to be shown in planetariums. When President Reagan called to talk to the astronauts and the questions turned to science, it was McNair who gave the answers.

The mission also was plagued by problems. Two communications satellites deployed by the crew were later lost in space. And there was a personal disappointment for McNair, who had cajoled the NASA establishment into letting him take a tiny soprano saxophone aboard. He wanted to send a message back to earth by playing "What the World Needs Now is Love." He recorded it, but the tape was accidentally erased.

McNair returned to a celebration in Lake City, where the main highway was renamed Ron McNair Boulevard. He was given the keys to the city in Greensboro, North Carolina, and his native South Carolina awarded him the Order of the Palmetto, the state's highest honor. In a speech to the South Carolina legislature that day, he talked of going to the launch pad before sunrise and "seeing this gentle beast majestically peering toward the sky," then lying strapped in before the countdown, and "for the life of me I could not make myself believe that this thing was real." It looked and felt, he said, like the replica of the space shuttle where astronauts train.

"The countdown continued—three, two, one—at T-minus-zero I got a boot like I've never felt and the vibrations simply shook every nut and bolt in the whole place, and that . . . vehicle literally lurched, leaped off the launch pad and we were on our way. It was a great ride. . . . I can do that all day, every day, for a month," he said.

That was the public Ronald McNair. The private Ronald McNair at home in Lake City didn't talk much about his experiences. After the big celebration, as he settled in for a game of pinochle with his old buddies from Carver High, they asked him about the view from space. McNair thought back to the days when they were young and fantasized about such things. Then, he said simply: "It looks like the way we used to talk about it. Now deal the cards."

At another time, allowing a rare glimpse at his innermost

feelings, he said something that Howard Friedrich, a friend from Hughes Laboratories, will never forget: "You know, Howard, I was just born to be up there." Friedrich recalled, "He couldn't wait to get back."

On the ground both before and after the flight, McNair kept up the breakneck pace learned at Carver High. He taught free karate classes at an inner-city church. His son Reggie was a student, and often he'd take Joy along, stopping to change her diapers during breaks.

He still played the saxophone, for a time in the Contraband Swing Band, a group formed by NASA employees, and sometimes on Sundays he jammed in nightclubs open to polished amateurs. At times, he took Cheryl and Charlie Bolden and his wife along to Cody's or Rockefeller's in downtown Houston, rooms filled with people and smoke and the sound of Kirk Whalum, his favorite saxophonist.

He attended Bible study classes at Antioch Missionary Baptist Church, where he was a deacon, a member of the church's governing board. And sometimes Bolden teased him about sounding like a Baptist preacher, because of his rich, booming voice and eloquent style.

Though many friends described McNair as fearless, Bolden believed that McNair, not unlike Bolden himself, had private, almost indefinable fears of hurtling into the skies. Bolden said it was nothing like a young child's fear of the dark or the fear that someone is going to hurt you. It is a "fear of dealing with the unknown." As for his friend, he said, "I know he feared God . . . but he understood. He put fear in the proper perspective."

Indeed, in a speech in 1984 at the Los Angeles church where he once worshipped, McNair told the congregation that he "would not climb up on top of that big piece of smokin' hardware, strap myself down in that seat, sit down and wait for the count to zero, . . . and sail out of this world unless I knew that Jesus got in first."

In November, 1985, mere months before the *Challenger* exploded, Ken Barnett, a friend from California, visited Houston. McNair took him into one of the shuttle replicas, housed in a hangar at the space center. Barnett, a pilot, sat in the cockpit. McNair's son Reggie got to play co-pilot. "I actually asked him,

'What happens if something goes wrong?' " Barnett recalled. "He said, 'You ride it out, or go down with the ship.' "

McNair was just a little boy when the civil rights movement began opening doors for his people, and when it nudged open the gates at NASA, McNair was ready with the skills and credentials to walk inside. He had never been what Bill Quivers, his friend from MIT, called a "hellraiser" on civil rights issues, but when he finally made it he didn't forget how far he'd come.

There are more than 30,000 physicists with doctorates in the nation, and McNair was one of perhaps 135 who are black. With that accomplishment, he already was an example for young blacks, but few would have clamored for words of wisdom from a bookish black scientist. No, the title astronaut before his name suddenly gave him a way to make them listen.

So he was always quick to jump on a plane and fly to San Francisco or New York City or Fayetteville, North Carolina, to talk to a group of scientists or students. Whenever he went to colleges, he'd try to set up a side trip to a grammar school or ask that some youngsters be bused in for his talk.

That's what he did in Cambridge for a speech at MIT in 1984.

In Kresge Auditorium, he told the students about turning down the chance to come to MIT in an exchange program in 1969 because he feared the competition and was content at his North Carolina school. A little while later, he said, he changed his mind.

"It is at that moment I became a winner. Not because I went to MIT. Many people go to MIT who are not winners. Not because I finished MIT. Many people finish MIT who are not winners. But I became a winner because I was willing to hang it over the edge. The unknown was mysterious. The unknown is frightening," said the man who once jumped into the pond at the cow pasture where no one else would venture. "You can only become a winner if you are willing to walk over to the edge and just dangle it, just a little bit. That's why I say to you students . . . be a winner. Hang it over the edge."

Chapter 7

ELLISON S. ONIZUKA

It was 1:30 in the morning by the time Ellison Onizuka finally made it home.

He had been late from work before, but this was different. It was the first time he had seen his family since returning from the *Discovery* shuttle mission in January, 1985. The phrase "back to earth" had a new meaning for the thirty-eight-year-old Air Force colonel and aeronautical engineer, as he sat in his Houston living room after his first space flight. On the couch next to him were his two pretty teenage daughters. Across from him was his wife, Lorna.

No one said a word.

"It was so quiet. We just sat," Lorna Onizuka recalls. "I told him I understood. I respected the fact that it was something he could only share with himself. What he felt was greater than anything he could say."

For Ellison Onizuka, this eloquent silence represented the end of an ecstatic journey to the unknown, the culmination of what Lorna calls a lifelong "quiet grooming." Was it so many years ago that he had lain on his back in a lush Hawaiian coffee field, looking up at the stars? Or heard the other boys laugh when he had told them, "I will fly in space someday"? If the gods do indeed punish us by answering our prayers, Onizuka accepted it as part of the bargain.

"What are your goals now?" Lorna asked softly.

"I haven't really thought about it," he sighed. "I'm just grateful for what I have."

By dawn, his daughters had fallen asleep in his arms. Ellison was still awake, wired by the memory of what he had just witnessed: the vast, empty miracle of the universe.

115

Lorna no longer feared for him. They had faced the demons together. "I don't know how or when it stopped," she says, "but he was not afraid."

The longing that had fueled their lives for a decade was spent. Lorna switched off the lights. Ellison had finally dropped off to sleep.

"There was no more need for being anxious. He had reached what he wanted to be."

He was born Ellison Shoji Onizuka on June 24, 1946, in Kealakekua, Hawaii, and was raised in the town of Keopu, a small farming community dotted with coffee plants and macadamia-nut trees. It is part of the lush paradise known as the Kona Coast, not far from the world's most active volcano, Kilauea Iki. Within a half mile stretch, there are five houses and two country stores. One of them is The Onizuka Store, located on a narrow winding road on the slopes of Mount Hualalai.

Ellison's grandparents emigrated from Japan in the late 1800s, from Fukuoka Prefecture on the island of Kyushu. They labored on the sugar plantations, eventually settling along the Kona Coast. Their son Masamitsu—Ellison's father—married a Japanese woman, Mitsue, and in 1933 they built the small store in Keopu, with three bedrooms in the rear.

The sign above the tiny store advertises "general merchandise." It is mostly a grocery store, but tourists can find aloha shirts, pants, slippers and other household items there. "Whatever you wanted or needed, they had at the store," says Ray Takeguchi, Onizuka's second cousin and boyhood friend.

Ellison was the third of four children. He had two older sisters, Shirley and Norma, and a younger brother Claude. The family would have been considered poor by any standard, Takeguchi says, but "they were the wealthiest people anyone could ever hope to have, in American values and achievement."

The elder Onizukas were firm believers in the work ethic. "They told us if we wanted to get ahead, we had to work for it," says Ellison's older sister, Shirley. Besides helping out at the store, the children were put to work on their grandfather's coffee farm, and later on the family's eight-acre parcel of land. "It was a good, country-style upbringing," according to Claude.

As a toddler, young "Ellie" liked to cut out paper planes from old catalogues and boasted to his grandmother, "When I grow up,

I will drive an airplane." The Saturday morning television space shows, so popular around this time, were tailor-made for boys like him. There was "Tom Corbett, Space Cadet" and his rocket ship, the Polaris; "Space Patrol," with Commander Buzz Corey; and of course "Flash Gordon."

Ellison attended the eighty-student Honokohau Elementary School. His principal remembers him as a quick learner "who always dotted his I's and crossed his T's." Vacations, from August to November, were spent harvesting the coffee. Often, the boys took breaks and went swimming or body surfing, or maybe exploring in a few nearby caves.

In 1959, at the age of thirteen, Ellison took a field trip with several classmates to watch the eruption of Kilauea Iki. As the red-hot lava shot 1,900 feet in the air, wrote Dale Van Atta in a 1984 story for the Japanese edition of *Reader's Digest,* he "was preoccupied, not with the beauty and wonder of the eruption, but with how to control all that energy. He was looking at it the way an engineer might."

By 1962, when Wally Schirra splashed down near Hawaii after a six-orbit flight, young Ellison was hooked on the Mercury space program. He told his grandfather he wanted to become an astronaut. His grandfather laughed at him. So did his scout leader, Norman Sakata. "He wasn't the Buck Rogers type," Sakata says.

But he definitely was the Boy Scout type.

"He was cautious. He never made mistakes, this boy," Sakata recalls. Normally, it takes six years to make Eagle Scout; Ellison made it in four, receiving his badge as a member of Explorer Post 26, in Holualoa. "He was the kind of person who wouldn't accept second best."

As chairman of the post's constitution committee, it was Ellison's job to write the bylaws. Under "objectives," he came up with the following: "To encourage better citizenship; to promote student leadership; to develop social and moral character; to curb delinquency; to serve the community, state and nation; to stimulate independency to alleviate the burden of parents." The last objective, hand-written at the bottom of the typed list, was "To encourage physical fitness."

He played in the outfield on a Little League baseball team. Later, he became interested in the 4-H program, and eventually, as a high-school senior, was elected president of the Hawaii 4-H Club Federation.

Whatever he undertook, he was always prepared. "If he had an assignment to do, it would be well planned. Methodical. Whatever the assignment, everything was well thought out," says Sakata. "He was efficient. A very detailed person. When you asked him a question, before he'd say anything, he'd stop and think."

While he took pride in his cultural background—serving, for example, as president of the Junior Young Buddhist Association—he did not think of himself as primarily Japanese or Hawaiian. Ellison, says his cousin Ray, was simply "the all-American boy."

At Konawaena High School, he made the basketball and baseball teams, and what he lacked in natural ability he made up for in perseverance. "He wasn't a star," says Sakata of Ellison's varsity baseball career, "but he loved the sport." A friend called him the spark behind a fifteen-game winning streak that brought Konawaena High a division championship. "He was not the type of leader to tell people what to do," Ray Takeguchi says. "He led by example."

Another boyhood friend, Walter Harada, remembers that many of the boys didn't know exactly what they wanted to do when they grew up. Besides, the Kona Coast was a seductive paradise. "I warn you," wrote visiting novelist Jack London, "if you have some spot dear to you on Earth, not to linger here too long, else you will find this dearer."

But Ellison knew he could not linger.

"Most of us were trying to decide what we wanted to do in college," Harada says. "Ellison had his mind set pretty early. He was going to be an aerospace engineer. He couldn't think of doing anything else. He knew where he was going to school and what he was going to do. The rest of us were groping."

Still, he never mentioned his dream of becoming an astronaut to his friends.

"I don't think he told many people. Maybe he felt we'd think he was crazy." Besides, Harada explains, "it wasn't fashionable at the time. Not many people were thinking about it."

"It was like somebody from here saying they wanted to be a major league baseball player," says high school classmate Gary Oura. "The highest you get up in the air here is commuting on an airplane to the next island."

"I don't think he was a dreamer," says another classmate, Stanley Oker. "He did things with foresight. He planned."

118

In fact, Onizuka was a dreamer *and* a pragmatist—not the type to leave his future to fate. The "quiet grooming" had already begun. When he left Hawaii, he promised to return one day. But there was something he had to do first.

Under his picture in the senior yearbook, his classmates wrote: "Wind enkindles the great."

Since no university in Hawaii offered a program in aerospace engineering, Ellison Onizuka enrolled at the University of Colorado at Boulder—a thousand miles from home—where he was awarded a two-year ROTC scholarship. On September 25, 1964, soon after he arrived, he took time to write to Norman Sakata.

"I hope this letter greets you and your family in the best of everything. How is the Explorer Post functioning? I'd like to thank you for the fine send off you gave me and also for the fine guidance you gave me during my four years with you. Now that I am all alone by myself, I find that everything is strange in adult life. I am alone to make all of my own decisions and carry on my expectations. But all of those experiences and words of encouragement that you gave me right along have given me the confidence to do whatever has to be done. . . . ''

On the same day he wrote a separate letter to the Explorers themselves.

"I would like to take this opportunity to convey my sincere and heartfelt thanks to all of you for the fine farewell banquet you dedicated to the departing seniors of 1964. All the discipline and guidance that were acquired on my journey to the castle of the Eagles are a major part of my priceless treasure chest, today. As a member of the Air Force ROTC, I find that all the training that I got as a scout in marching, discipline, care of a uniform, *esprit de corps,* and initiative imbued confidence and the drive to be a top notch officer in the 155th cadet corps into me. . . . Congratulations on your successful sponsorship of your recent 'pot luck' dinner and the tremendously successful Fishing Derby. I received a clipping of the Derby and good news of your dinner from my brother and parents. My Dad is proud to be your committeeman and he was awfully pleased with the dinner that you carried out. . . .

"My heart shall be with you always, for as the saying goes, 'Once an Eagle, always an Eagle.'"

Later that first year, Onizuka learned that his father had died of a heart attack. Grieving, he returned home for the funeral.

Back on campus, he found himself—as he had been in high school—both popular and respected. "He was one of the most personable people you've ever met," said Robert Culp, one of his University of Colorado professors. "He was always this cheerful happy face that everybody liked. When he smiled, it was kind of a shy smile. He was not a slap-on-the-back type guy. He was always so positive, so enthusiastic. He didn't grouch about anything."

He was a member of the engineering club and the student government, and was named a "campus pace-setter." He was listed in *Who's Who in American Universities and Colleges*.

If Onizuka had any obvious fault, it was perhaps that he was too trusting. When a friend asked to borrow a term paper to study from, Ellison gladly gave it to him. Only later did he learn that the friend had copied the paper verbatim.

He let it pass, even though he knew he had been taken advantage of. He told a friend, "People will come to their own time, a time when they will have to face the consequences of their acts."

Later in the school year he wrote to Mr. Sakata and the Explorers again.

"Now that a new year has come, I surmise you are in the midst of planning a very challenging program for 1965. . . . Don't forget the top notch scouting spirit which places all of you and Post 26 in the ranks of the elite. . . . The prestige of Post 26 is the envy of many people, so I hope you'll continue to keep faith in scouting and serve Kona in 1965. In whatever you do, remember to 'stand tall, walk tall, and most of all think tall.'"

* * *

By his junior year, mutual friends had introduced Onizuka to a pretty young Hawaiian woman, Lorna Leiko Yoshida, who was studying at the University of Northern Colorado Teachers College in Greeley, Colorado.

Lorna had already heard of Ellison Onizuka. She had been involved in the 4-H program back home, but the two had never met.

"I guess I was comfortable with him from the very beginning," she says. She was attracted by his sense of humor, his mischievous nature. "I saw him as kind of klutzy." But above all, she remembers, she was drawn to him because of "his old cultural sense of honor. A great deal of pride, and above all, humility."

He was also ambitious. As Lorna put it, "He was always running, never walking."

He earned his bachelor's degree in June, 1969. He and Lorna were married in Denver on June 7, and Lorna left school without getting her degree. Several months later, Ellison earned his master's degree, and soon their first child, Janelle, was born.

Ellison was a proud father and a competent one, remembers Lorna. The baby was so tiny that Lorna was afraid of her, and Ellison got up in the middle of the night for the feedings. He also bought dozens of nipples and boiled them in a saucepan on the stove, because that's what he had seen in the movies. One night, the tired couple left the pan on the burner and went to sleep. In the middle of the night, they both woke up to the smell of burning rubber. Running to the kitchen, they discovered that the nipples had all melted into each other.

They scooped the burnt mass from the pot and kept it on the counter for years, a souvenir of early parenthood.

In 1970, Onizuka was commissioned as an Air Force second lieutenant and assigned to McClellan Air Force Base in Sacramento, California, where he developed a new helicopter lift technique for retrieving downed aircraft. Almost immediately, he applied to the Air Force Test Pilot School at Edwards Air Force Base, California. There wasn't a program for engineers, but he thought training at Edwards would be his best chance to get into the space program.

Finally, in 1974, he was accepted. He worked as a flight test engineer in forty-three different types of planes, logging more than 1,600 hours of flight time. On March 11, 1975, the Onizukas' second daughter, Darien, was born.

It was a hard life for the young couple. While Lorna was bogged down in motherhood, Ellison's day began at dawn, when he would climb out of bed, gulp a cup of coffee and head for the classroom for a flight briefing. He would be in the air until noon, stop for a quick lunch, then attend classes from 1 to 4 P.M. He would dash home for dinner, then go back to the school for an analysis of the day's flight. By 10 P.M., he would stumble home.

"I think we lived kind of a blah life," Lorna recalls.

As a flight test engineer, Onizuka didn't actually fly the planes; he was usually in test pilot Roy Martin's second seat, taking flight data. "He was very easy to fly with," Martin says. "He was well organized, and he was never afraid. He had faith in the pilots, that we knew what we were doing. He had a lot of confidence in us."

The school at Edwards is highly competitive. Tempers flare and egos clash as trainees cram at least two years of work into one. Onizuka thrived in the intense atmosphere. His classmates awarded him the Propwash Award, generally given to the one student who inspires and motivates the others—in other words, the most eager beaver. But the year took its toll on his personal life. Families at Edwards, as Roy Martin says, "kind of have to take care of themselves."

"I'm not a martyr," Lorna says. "We had our spats."

For the next three years, Onizuka stayed on at the school as an instructor. The family lived in a comfortable, one-story stucco house on base and socialized with the other military wives and children. There was a Happy Hour every Friday afternoon, parties on Saturday nights.

Every year, Onizuka put on a real Hawaiian luau—complete with a roasted pig—out in back of the officers' club. The broad-chested and heavily muscled engineer ("I built them up working in the cane fields," he'd say) would dig a pit and place the pig in the dirt. Then he'd cajole engineer Rick Olafson or another friend into coming with him to a swamp outside the base, to chop some leaves for the barbecue pit. "If we're gonna do it, we might as well do it right," he'd insist, handing Olafson the machete and wading in. The two would be waist deep into the water before Onizuka was satisfied.

"These will do," he'd say.

He kept up his interest in baseball, and coached the Little League team on the base. Once, when one of the boys—a southpaw—was sent onto the field with a right-handed glove, Onizuka gently chastised the boy's mother, then went home for his own glove and gave it to the boy.

Most of the men at the school were Vietnam veterans. And all had the same dream: space. "We were all exposed to the glamour of the space program at a very impressionable age," explains Martin. "It had a very large impact on all of us. Space was the last frontier. We all wanted to be a part of that."

When the space program began taking applications in 1977, nearly everyone in the school applied. "It was a very keyed-up time for all of us," Martin remembers.

Ellison didn't tell Lorna he was applying. In fact, he did it at the last minute, and the next day sent his secretary a dozen roses for getting his application in on time. Now an Air Force major, he was one of 8,079 military and civilian experts vying for thirty-five slots in the program. By the late '70s, however, NASA was eager for minority astronauts, and Onizuka was in the right place at the right time. He knew that being of Asian descent might help him get into the program.

"It didn't hurt him any," said Joe Guthrie, former commandant of the test pilot school. "It helped him. He used to always say if he didn't have slanty eyes, they never would have picked him."

By October, he was chosen as a finalist and underwent a battery of interviews and physical examinations at NASA's Johnson Space Center in Houston. Amid all the hoopla, he was typically reticent. "He really didn't talk about it," his wife recalls.

Rick Olafson also applied for the program, and went down to Houston at the same time Onizuka did. "He was in the best physical shape he had ever been in," Olafson says. "He had really worked hard, running, getting his weight down. He worked hard, he said, to be as prepared as he could be."

When he returned home, Lorna asked him how it had gone. "There are so many qualified people," he told her wearily. "Whether they choose me or not, I'd be happy just meeting them."

On the morning of January 16, 1978, Onizuka's car wouldn't start, so he took the bus to work. After he left, Lorna looked out the window to see a strange car in the driveway. The men in it were looking for her husband. They tried to follow the bus, but lost it. By the time Onizuka walked into his office, a group of friends had assembled in the doorway: the word had already gone out that the astronauts were being notified one by one. And the phone was ringing.

He picked it up. "Congratulations," said NASA director of flight operations George Abbey. "You've been selected." Onizuka looked up and flashed a thumbs-up sign.

His friends cheered.

Later that day, he sought out Roy Martin. Onizuka knew that Martin was bitterly disappointed. The two friends shook hands. "I'm sorry," Onizuka said, choking back tears.

Lorna, meanwhile, was having her wisdom teeth taken out. That morning, she had been frightened about the surgery. Her husband had teased her mercilessly, telling her how painful it would be. In the afternoon, she heard the news. That night, several friends stopped by with champagne. But "It wasn't a whoop-de-doop," Lorna says. Ellison "was not jumping up and down or anything. He felt bad for the people who weren't chosen, who he felt were qualified who didn't make it."

"So many people are not going with us," he said.

Lorna was worried about the dangers. Being a test flight engineer at Edwards was one thing, but this was different. She had lived with fear before; this was more like stark terror. Ellison took her aside. "Everything's a risk," he said softly.

Back in Hawaii, Claude Onizuka was driving to work when he heard on the radio that his brother had just been chosen as the first Hawaiian for the space program. "It never dawned on me that he would become an astronaut," he says. When he got to work, he called his mother. The line was busy. Then he tried his sister Shirley. The line was busy. "We were all trying to get through to each other," he laughs.

Family, friends and relatives all had trouble picturing their shy, gentle "Ellie" orbiting the earth. Says his cousin Arnold Onizuka: "He didn't fit the mold."

The next week, Ellison and Lorna drove to Houston to look for housing. Lorna was upset. It was the first time she had left the children. When she cried, Ellison, in mock anger, threatened to leave her by the side of the road.

"I'm going to make you walk home."

Once they got to Houston, she says, "we discovered how really poor we were." They found a small, brown brick tract house on Shadwell Drive and put a deposit down. It was the first house they ever owned. The city was nice, Lorna thought, but not as friendly as the base had been. It was a large environment and civilian life was a shock. Instead of the commissary, she shopped at the Piggly Wiggly. They decorated the house and added a garden out back.

Ellison taught his children how to plant vegetables with the same Boy Scout zeal that had driven him to seek perfection all his life. The familiar refrain, "If you can't do it well, don't do it at all," was often heard around the house. His bond with his daughters was strong. "They attached themselves to him the way I had," Lorna says. Ellison was the leader. Every Saturday, he and Janelle went to feed the ducks. Perhaps because he was absent so much, the days at home were precious.

"He tried hard to make time for us," Lorna says.

Onizuka dove into the training regimen, sometimes working 70 hours a week. In 1979, he was certified for a shuttle ride. As the flight's trouble shooter, he was expected to handle a wide range of duties, from keeping the power systems operating to fixing the toilet. And he had to be ready for any space walks that might be needed to do repairs.

Through it all, he kept a sense of humor. "It's hard not to laugh," he said, "when you're standing on the ceiling."

His fellow crewmen called him "El," and joked with him about being the first Japanese-American astronaut. He said he would be the first man to eat sushi—his favorite food—in space.

Once he was assigned to a shuttle crew he received a letter from Mr. Sakata and sent back this reply, dated November 22,1982.

"Thank you for your very thoughtful letter regarding my recent assignment to the STS-10 crew. I am very pleased with my selection and most honored to be able to serve on our nation's first Department of Defense mission. Getting to this point in my career was an effort on the part of many people who have had an influence in my life. . . . It is only because of people like those at the banquet that others like me can grow up in the coffee fields of Kona and fly on the Space Shuttle. As Alan Shepard once said, 'It's so easy to reach out and touch the moon if you're standing on the shoulders of giants'—you are all 'giants.' Thank you for helping me to 'Be Prepared.' ''

Norman Sakata says he knew his pupil would go far some day. But he never dreamed he would leave the earth.

Onizuka was scheduled to be aboard the shuttle *Discovery* on a mission beginning December 6, 1984. As a mission specialist, he would track instruments during launch and re-entry, monitor scientific experiments and deploy a satellite using the shuttle's fifty-foot remote arm.

The launch was delayed until January, 1985.

"He's looking forward to the mission. He's ready," Onizuka's mother told reporters at the time. "I'm happy for him because it's what he wants to do and what he's been working for. I'm not really nervous," she added. "I pray that it will be a safe and successful mission." His mother, brother and sisters came from Hawaii for the launch. The Onizuka Store was closed down for ten days, the longest shutdown period in its fifty-two-year history.

On the flight, Onizuka took along a Buddhist medallion—"It was something he felt secure with," says Lorna—and pilot wings belonging to his friend and former instructor, Colonel Ray Jones. His first shuttle mission was also NASA's first fully-classified manned space flight—the so-called black-out flight. While in space, he helped release a 300-million-dollar spy satellite for the Pentagon. The mission ended January 27, one day early, because of predicted bad weather at the Kennedy Space Center.

The outpouring of sentiment for Ellison Onizuka was overwhelming. He was toasted and cheered and paraded. He served as grand marshal of Nisei Week festivities in Los Angeles, the oldest Japanese-American cultural event in the country. On his uniform were the various medals he had won. During the parade he stopped often to shake hands. And on various trips to schools, he had to be dragged from the classrooms because he was so intent on telling the children to get ahead. Keep working, he'd say. If he could make it, so could they.

At the University of Colorado, he spoke to a group of students. "I have to pinch myself to see if this is real," he said. "This is something I've always wanted to do. Everything I've done has been deliberately to apply to become an astronaut." Calling the shuttle trip "the ride of a lifetime," he said, "There are no surprises—but the intensity is higher."

At a March testimonial dinner in Hawaii, attended by more than 1,000 friends and family members, Onizuka told the crowd: "Being an astronaut is a great experience. I owe it all to you all who have helped me along the way. Your love, support and aloha spirit have made it all possible. Thank you for being there when I needed you most."

He was proud of the space program, saying it made America "second to none." It wouldn't stop here, he added, "because there is still a long way to go."

If he had been afraid, he hadn't let anyone know. The only thing he complained of was the noise the shuttle made on lift-off—and the tremendous amount of vibration. "He still remembered that noise," says Albert Ikeda, his old teacher. "It was loud and so forceful going up. The loudness and the pressure, pushed against the seat. He said he looked out of the aircraft and saw Kona and realized how beautiful it was. He had some very good memories."

"I still have to pinch myself to convince myself that the dream came true," Onizuka remarked.

"He loved space," says one old friend. "He said he didn't want to come down."

He was dubbed "The Lindbergh of the Big Island." People asked for his autograph, treated him as a celebrity. He was revered by school children and considered a hero in Japan. Still, he was the kind of man who kept his trophies in a box in the attic, and crossed his shoes to hide the holes in his soles.

"I'm not a hero," he told Lorna. "I'm just a man."

"After the first shuttle mission, he was just Ellison," his brother Claude says.

Says Lorna: "I don't think he really changed."

He went back to Kona as often as he could. On one trip, he built a wooden frame to hold mailboxes by the side of the road across from The Onizuka Store. "I laugh when I think about when he built it," his mother says. "His daughter, who was then about six years old, was afraid her father would be hit by a passing car, so they made a sign that said, 'Danger, Man At Work.' She stood out there holding the sign, and I chuckle every time I think about it."

The work, as always, was first rate. "He did a good job," his mother says, "it's going to last a long time."

A month before the scheduled lift-off of *Challenger* he wrote again to Mr. Sakata.

"Thank you for your interest and continued support of my participation in the Space program. We are looking forward to having all of you at the Kennedy Space Center for STS 51-L. Our training is continuing at the usual hectic pace that occurs in the final thirty days of preparation.

"With the launch coming up in about twenty-eight days and the crew going into quarantine on January 16th, the schedulers and trainers are busy trying to get everything done. We are all anxiously anticipating the tenth flight of *Challenger* which will accomplish a week of orbital activities.

"Your schedule must be just as hectic with the Annual Boy Scout Recognition and Installation Banquet approaching on January 8th. I have enclosed a message which I'd like you to read at the banquet. . . ."

Onizuka was excited about his second shuttle trip. But the night before he was to leave Houston for Cape Canaveral, his daughter Janelle had a soccer game in Dallas that he didn't want to miss. He got home at 9 P.M., changed and drove to Dallas with Lorna. They caught the tail end of the tournament and instead of driving right back, decided to follow the school bus carrying the team because Ellison was afraid the driver would get lost. He was right. They all got lost and didn't get home until three in the morning. He slept for forty-five minutes, then got up for his last trip to the space center.

Lorna knew that her husband was torn between his family and his career. "I felt so guilty because I used to nag him all the time," she says. The prospect of another shuttle trip frightened her. "I used to get anxious and excited. That's why he never talked about it."

Several days after he left for Florida, Onizuka called his wife. He had forgotten to bring his University of Colorado class ring. It was his good luck charm for the shuttle ride. He asked Lorna to bring it to Cape Canaveral.

Once at the Cape, the astronauts were officially in isolation. They were ordered to keep fifty feet from their children. The wives were an exception, and Onizuka made a habit of sneaking out to see Lorna. "He'd tell them he was going to run home and get some clothes," she laughs. "He'd stay for a few hours, then sneak back."

Onizuka called his brother two days before the launch. "Everything was going smoothly," Claude remembers being told. "They were ready to go."

The astronaut always called home before he left the pad. This time was no different. A godawful hour, Lorna complained. He talked with the girls. They were laughing and crying at the same time. He spoke softly to Lorna. They talked about all the mistakes they had made with each other. He was gone so much of the time, and she had nagged him.

Before his first shuttle launch, Onizuka had put together a book for Lorna, in case anything happened. Included in the material were insurance papers and letters to the two children. There were instructions to Lorna on how to handle family business. During that launch, the book was kept in a safe in the crew quarters. Onizuka asked his wife several times if she had remembered where it was. "I was very uncomfortable with that and he knew it," she says.

This time, he didn't mention the book. But he did something that Lorna now thinks is strange. He told his daughters what he had written to them in the letters. Later, she found the book. He had taken it from the safe and brought it home. As always, he had been prepared.

Chapter 8

GREGORY B. JARVIS

In a black leather-bound yearbook of a small high school in upstate New York is a picture of a teenage boy in a football jersey with a buzz cut and a giddy grin. Across the country is another picture of the same man, taken more than twenty years later, showing him clad in a NASA flight suit in a KC-135 weightlessness training plane, legs spread-eagle, the soles of his feet to the camera, a styrofoam cup of water in his hand with water globules stuck on the ceiling.

On his face is the same giddy ear-to-ear grin accompanied by bright eyes and an openness that made his expression electric.

Gregory B. Jarvis was never dashingly handsome. As a teenager, he was all angles and nose and ears; in high school, girls thought he was cute. Adulthood softened the angles and grayed his temples. It also pulled back his hairline—which he would note when it would get him a laugh. "You look at an astronaut," he said after he was selected, "who is just about a perfect human being, and here you are, your hair falling out, and they call you."

Shortly after he was selected as one of two engineers from Hughes Aircraft Company to ride the space shuttle, a Hughes manager threw an office surprise party. Stephen Cunningham, one of the two alternates for the shuttle, remembers that the manager "said he was pleased that we had been selected, but his opinion of astronauts had gone way down."

The room broke into laughter. "But it did reflect a lot of people's opinions," Cunningham mused. "Astronauts are not real people."

Nobody knew he didn't fit the prevailing image of the astronaut better than Jarvis. Not that Jarvis cared. This was a chance to glimpse a world for which he'd spent years designing satellites. He never envisioned going, but he and his colleagues watched with awe and perhaps a tinge of envy as the space couriers carried the engineers' products into orbit.

If he ever yearned to be part of the daredevil astronaut fraternity, he never told anyone. It's unlikely he ever agonized over an unpursued career; in the eyes of his friends and family, he appeared to be that rare soul—a man of few regrets.

"He had a real zeal for life. He lived every minute like it was his last," said his younger brother, Steven Jarvis. "He always seemed to be having such a good time. I guess I was always jealous of that."

The fraternity to which Jarvis belonged was the group of engineers that built the enormously expensive and complicated satellites put into geosynchronous orbit 22,300 miles above the earth.

He was also a competitive, intense man who hated to lose. He had a voracious appetite for doing everything—he cycled, played squash, cross-country skied, and compulsively signed up for local college courses in whatever subject caught his fancy. He was undaunted even when he failed. He plugged away at classical guitar lessons and played terribly.

He was bright and where he wasn't facile, he made up for it by being determined. Years later, after he had been selected for the shuttle, he came back to speak at a commencement at his *alma mater* in Buffalo and said, "All of you recall the student with whom you had classes who worked a little harder to achieve perhaps the same grades some of you got with minimal effort. In business, industry, or the academic settings where you will embark upon your careers, you will find this same student—working harder, willing to take on the extra and perhaps dull or unpleasant tasks."

Those people, Jarvis told the new graduates, are the ones who "reach for the stars."

With him almost always was his wife and college sweetheart, Marcia—his partner in the adventures of his life. "I married my best friend," he said. The couple was devoted to each other, and, apart from a puppy who won Jarvis' heart and a place in his house, they were their own family, free to travel the world or walk the nearby beach, free to challenge trails whenever they pleased.

But there just weren't enough days and weeks. Greg gave up

bicycle racing because he didn't have time to train. He started one night course three times before finishing. He simply wanted to do everything, and when there suddenly appeared a chance to go into space, his response was in character: go for it.

Greg Jarvis was born in Detroit on August 24, 1944. Two years later, the family moved to Mohawk, New York, a lulling story-book of a town with modest clapboard houses and hills rising in the distance. In the winter, there are mounds of snow piled to the sides of the road, and carrot-sized icicles drip from porches.

With a population just under 3,000, Mohawk has a commercial center about one block long, dominated by a gas station and convenience store on one side and a clump of storefronts on the other. Mohawk was the hometown of A. Bruce Jarvis, Greg's father, and the elder Jarvis had returned with his young son and wife, Lucille, known to everyone as Tele, to run the pharmacy and, further down the road, a restaurant.

Mohawk is Republican territory, between Syracuse and Albany, a mix of blue collar and professional where people find employment at the Duofold underwear manufacturing plant down a side road off the main street or at the large Remington Arms plant in the adjacent town of Ilion (where Greg Jarvis' mother and stepfather now live). There's also Mohawk Data Sciences, Herkimer County Community College in Herkimer, on the other side of Mohawk, and the school and offices.

Some people stay: one of Greg's former high school girlfriends, Lyn Drury, is a Republican Committeewoman and a supervisor of the Motor Vehicles Department of Herkimer County. Rosemary Conigliaro, who taught Jarvis, has been at Mohawk Central for thirty-eight years. "I wasn't born here and I wouldn't leave," she said of the town she has come to love.

Greg grew up in a modest white- and green-trimmed house on a corner across the street from the school grounds. In the basement, his father had set up on plywood tables an elaborate train set complete with switches and bridges and mountains.

While Greg immersed himself in school and the activities there, his father worked long hours at the pharmacy.

There was a built-in distance between Greg and his two siblings. Steven is five years younger; Alan is seven years younger. Alan, who lives in Springfield, Massachusetts and works at the nearby

Old Colony Envelope Factory, has the fuzzier memories of Greg, the brother who played his saxophone in his bedroom.

Steven and Greg were never close, but Steven was drawn to Greg in a symbiosis of admiration and competition. "We were always kind of competitive all throughout life—we were so similar."

Among Steven's remembrances of Greg, one stands out vividly. It was during his older brother's football practice—Greg was blocking, another teammate got in the way of his block and the player ended up with a broken leg.

"He's the only guy I know who broke the leg of one of his teammates at football practice," said Steven years later with amazement. "Not on purpose. That's just how intensely he played."

Eventually, Steven would attend the same college as Greg, major in the same field—electrical engineering—and move to southern California to work for a rival aerospace firm. Instead of enhancing a lifelong friendship between them, it fostered a lifelong competition.

Mohawk Central School—which in the aftermath of the *Challenger* explosion will be renamed in honor of Gregory Jarvis— seems tucked into a pocket of the town. There, in a class of eighty-nine, Greg played football and baseball, managed the basketball team, worked as newspaper publicity manager, played saxophone in the band, and was a member of the Math Club and National Honor Society. He even managed to be in the senior play.

"That was the nice thing about it," said Charles Baron, the former team quarterback. "You could be involved in everything."

Jarvis is remembered as the guy in the back of the class, with the clever one-liner, never a troublemaker but something of a well-meaning prankster. When the National Honor Society was assembled for a yearbook picture, Jarvis, standing in the back line of the group, pinched a friend and told him to "pass the pinch" along. Eventually, the whole group was giggling and grinning and the yearbook photographer complimented them on their perkiness in posing.

There were record hops on Saturday nights during football season and a date was walking a girl home from the basketball game on Friday. In his freshman year, Greg used to walk Lyn

Drury—then Lyn Burgess—home from basketball games. Though he gave her a necklace for Christmas, their wisp of a relationship was over as nebulously and gently as it started.

"My mother remembered him as polite and very quiet. She said she didn't know how we got along." Drury said with a laugh. "I was not quiet."

Greg Jarvis was remembered for stuffing all his math assignment papers into the pages of his math book until it was wadded full.

"Full of fun . . . mischievous . . . serious when it comes to math . . ." the text under his senior yearbook picture read. "I can never remember Greg depressed," said Paul Richie, a high school and college friend who is now a social worker in Buffalo.

This was the era of the Mercury astronauts—John Glenn, JFK and tickertape parades—but the space program hadn't touched the reality of their lives. "Space," said Lyn Drury, pondering all the notions the word conjures up. "It wasn't anything that any of us thought we could do."

Greg's chemistry and physics teacher, Harold Whitebread, doesn't remember Greg ever talking about space. He was still teaching at the high school in the winter of 1986 and had a student who was determined to be an astronaut. Whitebread had been invited by Greg to watch the launch but declined because of school commitments.

"Was he a super brain?" mused Whitebread. "Did he study all the time? No. He was smart. I think it came pretty naturally to him."

The most vivid memories of Greg's high school classmates were of football glories, for Mohawk was a small, scrappy team, driven by a demanding coach. They were especially driven in the 1961 season for a game against rival Oneonta that Mohawk won, 13-0—a great victory.

When a story in a newspaper, accompanied by a current photograph of Jarvis, announced that he had been selected to fly on the space shuttle, former teammate Paul Richie wrote him a letter: "Congratulations. Hope your space shuttle flight is as thrilling as that day we beat Oneonta. Where's your hair?"

Marcia Jarboe, a sophomore at U.B., the State University of New York at Buffalo, was helping her freshman brother, Bill, move into his dormitory room one fall day in 1965, when her brother's resident advisor, a junior named Greg Jarvis, caught her eye. Greg was one year older than Marcia.

"He was so cute," Marcia said. "He kept hopping up and down the stairs, seeing how everyone was doing."

In the living room of the house they shared in Hermosa Beach, California, pictures of Greg kayaking stood on the mantle; others were secured in a thick album. She took out a photograph and smiled at the face. "You see that grin on his face in all the pictures now," she said, "like it was plastered there from the time he was a kid and he grew into it."

Jarvis had been at U.B. for two years. He had survived the transition from a small high school to a huge state university—wrestling with his course work in engineering, and working his way through college. He was a member of ROTC for four of the five years he stayed in the engineering program. ROTC paid some of his expenses in exchange for military service after graduation.

Greg was on a busy, erratic schedule, sometimes studying from 2 to 5 A.M. He was determined to pay his own way through college. It was not a matter of money, but of independence.

"He worked in every library in school," said Marcia. "He worked in the physics library, the engineering library." He worked at the entrance desk in dormitories—those being the days when students signed in and out and phones rang on a central switchboard—and he worked the weekend hours that no one else wanted.

There had been a flirtation with teaching history, but by college he was in engineering for the long haul and it was not easy going. He had to repeat some courses. "He was not a Dean's List student," recalled Marcia. "He had to work hard to get grades. He was very intense about his work."

But there was still the high school cut-up in the college student. "He also screwed around a lot," Marcia said ruefully. There were hockey games on the long hallway of his dorm with stale bagels serving as pucks. "That's what I liked about him. He never grew up. He could live to be 100, and he'd never grow up. Life was never dull."

When they had time together, they'd play gin rummy. Marcia was terrible at it, and the loser—who was always Marcia—took the winner—who was always Greg—out for the banana splits that

135

he loved. "Finally I said to him," says Marcia, " 'If we're going to keep doing this, and I'm going to keep losing, let's go out for a pitcher of beer where everyone else goes.' "

By the time he graduated, they had discussed marriage but Marcia had another year of school. Greg was headed to Boston, to Northeastern University, for graduate work and spent the summer in Mohawk. One night, while talking wistfully of Marcia with his family, someone suggested he consider marrying her. So he got up from the dinner table at the restaurant and called her on the spot to propose.

They were married the following June, in 1968, after Marcia's college graduation. They drove in Greg's pink Rambler with red-and-white bucket seats for a brief honeymoon in Tarrytown, New York.

While Greg was doing master's work at Northeastern and working at Raytheon, the couple lived in a basement apartment on Beacon Street. "One weekend, we didn't have any money," Marcia remembered. "We shook out the piggy bank and we had fifteen cents. So we split an ice cream cone." They amused themselves by walking along the Charles River or going to outdoor concerts, toting along a blanket to spread on the grass.

After getting his master's in 1969, he owed the Air Force four years of service. Vietnam was not in his future; because of his engineering training, he was assigned to the Air Force's Space Division in El Segundo, California, just south of Los Angeles. As his mother (by now divorced from his father) waved the couple off to California, Greg reassured her, "We'll be back." "No, you won't," his mother said. She turned out to be right. They found an apartment in nearby Hawthorne and Greg began military service.

He complained about the slow, bureaucratic pace and he chafed at some of the rules. Once admonished for not shining his shoes, he said, "You want performance or you want style? You don't get both."

"He wasn't meant to stay in the Air Force," Marcia said. But he did like his work, especially with satellites. His brother Steven remembers coming out to visit Greg while he was still in the Air Force. "It was the first time I realized that space was his life," said Steven Jarvis.

Jarvis was involved in the evaluation of proposals that aerospace companies submitted to the Air Force for satellite communications projects. Ironically, Jarvis came to the attention of Hughes Aircraft Company in the process of Hughes losing a proposal to build a satellite communications system for the Air Force. But Hughes and Jarvis were impressed with each other. When he left the Air Force with the rank of captain, he had interviews with several aerospace companies. He fretted to Marcia that maybe he wasn't good enough, but job offers were plentiful, and he started work with Hughes in the spring of 1973.

Meanwhile, Greg and Marcia had settled into Hermosa Beach, in a mustard-colored stucco house on a gentle sloping street where poinsettias grow in front yard gardens and the ocean is six blocks away. They bought it for one reason—the open beamed wood ceiling that gives the living room a cozy warmth.

"I never did anything athletic until we moved out here," said Marcia, a handsome, tanned woman with short dark hair streaked with gray. "Greg said 'Give everything a try and if you don't like it, fine.' And we kept up just about everything we started."

Marcia found a job as a dental assistant—the same job she held in early 1986—and the couple thrived. They took up hiking, skiing, sailing and snorkling. They once took an early morning hot air balloon ride across the desert, and, upon landing, toasted their excursion with champagne. They entered 10K races and went to all the cycling events of the 1984 summer Olympics in Los Angeles.

It was bicycling for which they reserved most of their spare hours and energy. In the garage behind their house, you could see the bikes: a Masi racing bike and a red tandem bike propped against one wall, and a Raleigh, the "work bike" that Greg rode the five miles north to work. The Raleigh stood next to a rowing machine, both of which blocked the way to the clothes dryer. Suspended above all this was Greg's "junk bike", a rusty, paint-chipped relic. Their car, a gaudy, turquoise '68 Dodge Dart, sat in the side driveway.

They belonged to a bicycle club, the Los Angeles Wheelmen. In October, they would make an overnight trip that began with a ninety-mile ride from Malibu northeast, past pumpkin fields and walnut trees, to Ojai. They soaked up the land and atmosphere. "If you cycle through the orange groves, you can smell the oranges," says Marcia. "You can see things close up that you can't see in a car." In 1980 they joined friends for a vacation and cycled 1,000 miles across Canada on a tandem bike, from

Kamloops as far east as Calgary and down as far as Rebelstoke. They did 100 miles a day, met friends over dinner to trade notes and spent nights in lodges near mountains or icefields.

At work, colleagues complained about the smell of the sweaty bike clothes he hung in his office on hot summer days—and he thought nothing of hanging upside down in his gravity boots on a runner's course at the corner of two residential streets. He was not neat. The arrival of Greg home from work meant a trail of shoes, backpack, and jacket across the house. "You could have the house clean and he'd come in and five minutes later, the house would look like you hadn't done anything," said Marcia.

Every year, the Jarvises bicycled to the staging area of the Rose Bowl parade in Pasadena. And when they arrived, Greg insisted they find the Clydesdale horses. "Greg used to say if he were ever reincarnated, he'd like to come back as a Clydesdale," Marcia laughs. "They were so pampered and so taken care of."

He played sports fiercely. During squash games, Marcia said, "When he didn't get the ball, he'd yell at himself—but they all did that." He often played with his brother, Steve: "I kicked his ass all over the place," said Steve. "He couldn't stand it. I was just a weekend player. He couldn't play at all. But he tried to do everything to perfection, and it got to the point where I couldn't give him a game."

The Jarvises also spent evenings at home, comfortable on the sofa, Greg's head in Marcia's lap, watching television. They decided against having children. "We liked to pick up and go when we wanted to go," said Marcia.

On the day before New Year's in 1973, bicycling along the beach, they saw a man with a box of five puppies. A little black one on top caught Greg's eye, they stopped to look and Greg said he wanted it. They named the black fluffy mutt—its owners had sworn she was a Labrador Retriever—Sirah, after the wine. They'd been winetasting recently.

The Jarvises filled their house with keepsakes. On the wall across from the brick fireplace hung large framed photographs they'd taken of the places they had explored together: Black Sands beach in Hawaii, underwater vistas in Cancun. And on one wall in the small dining room, alone, were three framed photographs of Yosemite, the place that Greg loved winter or summer. Yosemite was their refuge. "It was the one place we could go and unwind and forget everything else," said Marcia. "You're not that important when you look at the mountains and the waterfalls and the trees.''

Their favorite time of year at Yosemite was winter. They would follow cross-country trails deep into the woods. ''It was just yourself and the sound of your skis,'' Marcia said.

Greg dreamed of retiring early—at about fifty-five—and living there. He had taken an accounting course at the local junior college and ''thought it would be neat if he could be an accountant and live all the time at Yosemite.''

He always told his wife that he wasn't going to stay an engineer forever. ''But I had my doubts,'' she said. ''He just loved what he did so much.''

Greg Jarvis' first project at Hughes was the Marisat program, a satellite communications system that Comsat had hired Hughes to build on a rush basis. Comsat wanted to lease service to the Navy and commercial shipping firms.

Jarvis joined the five-person systems engineering team working on those parts of the satellite specifically involved in communications. The group was expected to design and test the components —a long process in which the satellite is subjected to every condition it might encounter in space. Testing can take from four months to a year, and it's in this stage that you find the problems you didn't foresee. In chambers large enough to accommodate satellites, engineers simulate conditions of launch and orbit.

Jerry Dutcher, a Hughes engineer, worked with Greg and was technically his supervisor on the Marisat project, though Dutcher is amused by the idea of anyone supervising Greg: ''He was a very independent, competent guy.''

Jarvis got good reviews from Dutcher, who found him smart and hardworking, a self-starter with good technical skills. He was easy to get to know and disarming when he set out to make friends, but he wasn't always easy to work for. ''He was a driver,'' said Dutcher. ''He drove himself and others.''

When Marisat was done, Jarvis worked on classified military projects for several years—''defense satellites.'' But it was the Leasat (short for leased satellite) program to which Jarvis devoted five years. Leasat was a communications satellite that would be built by Hughes Aircraft and owned by Hughes Communications Incorporated, a subsidiary of the company. The satellite, intended for military use, would be leased mostly by the Navy. What made

Leasat different was that it was designed to be launched into orbit only by the space shuttle.

Jarvis worked on Leasat in various capacities from 1978 to 1983. In 1982 he became assistant spacecraft manager for Leasat, responsible for daily decisions regarding the design, construction and testing. "You're the guy living with the satellite on a day by day basis," said Dutcher. By 1983, he was managing the testing of three Leasats.

Because the satellite was being tested around the clock, it was not unusual for Jarvis to get a 2 A.M. call from technicians, reporting some problem. Once he was called at 1:30 A.M., went to work, returned home at 3, got another call an hour or so later, returned to Hughes and came home at 6 A.M. His wife didn't even realize he'd been gone twice.

He ploughed good relationships with people. He treated the secretaries well, respected the technicians, and got a lot out of his colleagues. They called him the "Silent Tornado." But he had definite ideas about how he wanted things done and locked horns at least once with a superior, though he had a way to deal with that. "Greg would stick around until after the supervisor went home and do it the way he wanted it done," said Dutcher. "You come in the next morning and the job was done. What could you do?"

The satellites were his babies. He would give Marcia lovingly guided tours. "You'd look at all these pieces," Marcia said. "He knew what each part that he worked on did. And maybe there was an antenna he'd worked on really hard that he'd point out."

Satellites even led to an instance of rare sibling sharing between Greg and Steve Jarvis, the two competitive brothers. Steve had become an engineer with TRW, one of the aerospace firms competing with Hughes for government contracts. "When we got together, we'd sit around and just look at each other," said Steve. "I don't know if he ever knew how much I respected and admired him." But once, when Hughes needed to test Leasat at a TRW facility, Greg called Steve and asked him to come down and take a look.

"It was the first time he'd taken time to talk about his work with me," Steve said. "He was beaming. It was a strange moment."

The shuttle itself fascinated Greg Jarvis. He and Marcia would rise at 4 A.M. to watch televised lift-offs. "They were beautiful, they were graceful," said Marcia, whose vision of space is vivid and poetic.

Jarvis was no avid skywatcher, but he took an astronomy course at a nearby junior college at the beginning of the decade, and bought a chart of the skies. Once, Greg and Marcia went up to Yosemite and, standing in a snow-covered meadow, flashlight in hand, Greg Jarvis pored over the chart and scrutinized the sky.

At Hughes, engineers watched with more than detached interest as shuttle missions took off. Since the program started in 1981, the spaceplanes have carried nineteen Hughes-built satellites.

"I don't think it really entered his mind at the time that anyone besides an astronaut would go," Marcia Jarvis mused. "And then it was mostly military people—flyers and commanders. You had to be a pilot."

Years after the dawn of the American manned space program, Greg Jarvis would tell his wife that space had always intrigued him. "I never really said anything about it, but I was really interested when things first started," he told her. "I thought it was really exciting." He never dwelled on it, but if he had any regrets, it was that he'd missed a chance to learn how to fly.

When he was growing up, his father, in partnership with a couple of others, owned a Piper Cub and a Cessna 172, flying the small planes out of an airstrip south of Mohawk. Jarvis knew he would never have been a professional pilot—he was color blind—but he certainly could have flown his father's plane. "He told me once that he could kick himself a thousand times over for not having learned to fly," Marcia Jarvis said. "He said, 'I should have given it a shot.'" In recent years, he suggested to Marcia that they try hang gliding, but they never did.

"For people who've grown up in the last twenty to thirty years, you start out with space travel being a fantasy—'Buck Rogers,'" said Jerry Dutcher. "And in our lifetime, we've seen it turn into something that's real. Though most of us realize we won't go out there, working in our field is the next best thing to being there. . . . It's a way to spend your life on the periphery of the space program."

These guys at Hughes were not flyboys, and they knew it. They were systems engineers. They loved their association with the space program and reveled in the success of the technology. But their career choices had been made, and being an astronaut was a fantasy to be entertained watching the stars in the California sky.

But then NASA announced a new policy to customers who were paying millions of dollars to ship up their satellites via the shuttle—it would allow a payload specialist from the company to go along with the product, and Hughes (which pays NASA about 30 million dollars to launch each Leasat) was offered two slots. In April of 1984, Hughes posted notices that engineers could apply to accompany the Leasat.

"Typical Hughes," said engineer Bill Butterworth, Jarvis' alternate. "Very low key announcement: 'By the way we're going to fly two people into space. If you're interested, fill in the adjoining coupon.'"

No matter how casual it sounded, 600 Hughes engineers grabbed at it. "I called it the most coveted prize in recent history," said Butterworth. Alternate Stephen Cunningham heard about it in his vanpool. Engineer John Konrad, a confirmed "spacehead" who grew up on "Star Trek," read about it just days before the deadline for applications. Konrad—chosen, like Jarvis, for a future mission—had dreamed of being an astronaut before giving it up to get an advanced engineering degree from Caltech.

When Jarvis found out about the competition, he was nonchalant.

"Are you going to apply?" Marcia asked him.

"I'm thinking about it," Greg said.

A couple of weeks later, Marcia inquired again: "Did you pick up that application?"

"I keep meaning to pick one up," Greg said, brushing it aside, "and I forget."

A week or so passed, and Marcia asked again. "Yeah, I filled it out," Greg said. He turned it in the day of the deadline.

"I think both of us were a little reluctant to apply," said Konrad. "Think of the total disappointment if you don't get it."

It was a one-page application that asked only for basic job information. There were no essays in which to wax eloquent about man in space, and Hughes already had some ideas about who they wanted: someone with five years experience in the industry, someone who had worked in various aspects of the satellite program—someone like Greg Jarvis. Jerry Dutcher called him the "sentimental favorite." And he knew people thought he was a "shoo-in." "I think in his heart, he wanted to believe it, but he couldn't let himself," said Marcia.

One early June day in 1984, Marcia Jarvis had a "dumb"

feeling that Greg was going to find something out. Later that day, at her dental office, she got a phone call from Greg: he'd gotten it, he told her calmly. She shrieked in her office. She went outside into the alley and let out a less constrained whoop of joy. "I really wanted to go too," Marcia said. " 'Stow me away in a locker,' " she told Greg.

When Greg came home, he told Marcia not to tell anyone for a month. Hughes hadn't officially announced it yet and NASA would have to do physicals on the people Hughes had selected. But by that time, Marcia had already called all their friends and told all the neighbors. It took a while for Greg to realize how his life had been changed. "He was so cool and calm for the first couple of days," Marcia said. "And then one night we were lying in bed and he couldn't go to sleep at all. I said, 'What's the matter.' He said, 'I just realized. I'm really going to go up on the shuttle! No kidding! I can't believe it!' "

And from that point, Jarvis reveled in it. So did John Konrad and their two alternates—Bill Butterworth, Jarvis' alternate and Stephen Cunningham, Konrad's alternate.

Jarvis was 5'9", balding, and despite his athletic endeavors fighting extra pounds. Konrad, then thirty-four, was nearsighted and, at 6'5", too tall to stand up in the spacecraft. They were besides themselves at being picked, and delighted in their non-astro-jock status. They had no intentions of molding themselves into anything else.

A reporter who covers NASA interviewed Jarvis and Konrad and remembered thinking, "You think of astronauts as cool. These guys were not cool. They were so excited."

Hughes tried to give them lessons on interview etiquette: don't touch yourself, don't put your hands in your pockets, stand a certain way. "They gave up on us pretty quickly," said Konrad. "We were a couple of engineers. Public relations wanted us to present ourselves as best as possible. But we were going to be ourselves."

In September 1984, the two chosen Hughes engineers and their alternates traveled to Kennedy Space Center for a safety walkdown—a vertical tour of the shuttle and its safety features. It started with an elevator ride to the top of the gantry and continued with stops at various levels along the length of the spacecraft. Nothing quite prepared them for the spectacle of the *Challenger* ship up close. The four were engulfed in emotion. Jarvis took a look at the ship and proclaimed, "The only thing small is us." Later, they talked for the first and last time as a group about the risks.

"We all recognized that if something went wrong with the shuttle, we couldn't pull it over to the side of the road," said Konrad. "That was the night we recognized the risk, dealt with it, and filed it away. The mission still justified the risk."

There was no question they were in, no question they wanted to do it.

"It was exciting and big and, yeah, we could die," said Cunningham who kept a journal of his experience. "We didn't consider it riskier than flying in an airplane. Greg specifically shared that he wasn't particularly concerned with what happened to him. He was concerned about what would happen to Marcia."

None of the four knew each other very well, but Cunningham and Butterworth, as the alternates, said they would help people left behind. "We talked about taking care of people—it was all direct and sort of impersonal," said Butterworth. "Business-like."

In November 1984, Hughes Aircraft invited various officials and observers to watch NASA launch a Hughes satellite at Cape Canaveral. At the cocktail party the night before, Jarvis spoke, nervously but openly. As he talked about what an honor it was to be chosen, he momentarily choked up, overwhelmed by the realization of what he was about to do. He paused, collected himself and continued his speech.

In January 1985, Jarvis and Butterworth moved to Houston to begin training for Mission 51-D. Butterworth and his wife, Jenny, moved into an apartment near Greg and Marcia's.

It became quickly apparent that there would be little for Jarvis to do with his satellite. He may have helped design and test it, but he was to have no part in deploying it. That made sense—Hughes knew the satellite, but NASA knew the shuttle.

But Dan Brandenstein, originally the commander of the mission, scheduled for late March 1985, made both Jarvis and Butterworth feel part of the crew. The Hughes engineers were included on a social level, too; in January, they were invited to a Superbowl party with the crew.

They went through all the standard practice maneuvers—weightlessness training, exiting the shuttle, preparing food.

"Jenny and I were out walking the dogs," said Marcia, "and we saw this black plume of smoke. We thought, 'Gee, they said they were going to practice firefighting but . . .'" An hour later, Butterworth and Jarvis returned to their apartments, drenched. They had been learning how to handle fire hoses as a crew, so NASA provided gasoline fires on which to practice.

Several weeks before the scheduled March launching date, Mission 51-D was postponed until April, prompting a complex reshuffle of crew and payloads. 51-D got a new commander, pilot, and mission specialists but there was still room for two payload specialists. One would be McDonnell Douglas engineer Charles Walker—from the original crew of 51-D. The other might have been Jarvis, but Senator Jake Garn (R-Utah), a member of the appropriations subcommittee that handles NASA, trained with the new crew of 51-D and took Jarvis' place.

"It was one of the few times I've ever seen him disappointed about anything," Marcia said. Without a mission, Jarvis returned to Hughes and his work. In the summer of 1985, Jarvis sometimes would pass Konrad in the hall. "Have you heard anything?" Konrad would ask.

He was told he might be able to go on the August shuttle mission—but then he found out there wasn't enough room for any payload specialists. In September, he was told he would fly in December. Jarvis returned to Houston for the crew picture and by the time he got there, he was told he'd been bumped by another politician—Representative Bill Nelson (D-Florida), chairman of the House subcommittee on space science and applications. But this time, he found out that he would be assigned to the January flight of the *Challenger*—Mission 51-L.

It took a while for it to sink in. After a half year of disappointment, he would have to gear up again. Because he had already trained with one crew and had work to do at Hughes, he commuted between Houston and Los Angeles, splitting the week between the two cities. It wasn't until New Year's Day, 1986, that Marcia and Greg flew to Houston to begin preparations in earnest.

Assembled at an airstrip at the Johnson Space Center for a press conference, each flight-suited crew member spoke briefly. When it was Jarvis' turn, he walked up to the microphone and said, "I am so happy to be here."

In the few weeks before launch, Jarvis worked on setting up the experiment he would take into space. He would investigate the

145

reactions of fluids to various shuttle maneuvers and simulated spacecraft movements.

The motion of liquid fuel tanks in orbited satellites can have a destabilizing effect on the satellites. Hughes designed their satellites to compensate for that, but Jarvis' experiments would help them to manufacture more efficient and cost effective satellites. It wasn't crucial research, but for Hughes the trip was a combination of public relations and unprecedented first-hand observations of the shuttle in action.

Pre-launch time was also spent getting to know the crew. Jarvis was perhaps closest to Christa McAuliffe, and he and Marcia became good friends with McAuliffe's alternate, Barbara Morgan and her husband, Clay, a smoke jumper and fiction writer.

Bill Butterworth couldn't train with this crew, so Jarvis went out of his way to include Butterworth when the alternate came to Florida to see Jarvis.

Once the crew was at Cape Canaveral, they tried to amuse themselves through the numerous launch delays. Jarvis started writing the long-delayed master's thesis for the business management degree he'd been working on. On Sunday, January 26, the launch having been postponed another day, Jarvis put the time to good use.

Spouses were allowed to have dinner with the crew, and when Marcia walked in, Greg handed her a large envelope.

"You're going to be so proud of me!" he told her.

"Why, what did you do?" she asked.

"I finished my paper!"

The day before, Saturday, there had been a lunch gathering of crew and invited friends at a beach house. It was a relaxed time. Jarvis had invited the Butterworths and Jenny arrived early. She and Greg went for a walk on the beach, and later, when Bill Butterworth and Marcia showed up, Greg found a quiet corner of the house where he and Bill settled down to discuss the experiments that he would be carrying out.

Business concluded, Greg and Bill reminisced about the whole experience and Greg talked about how lucky they were to be chosen and how he could hardly believe it was finally, really going to happen.

Then Greg paused for a long time, as if he were thinking about something.

"Don't worry," Butterworth said. "I'll take care of Marcia for you."

Greg smiled. "I know you will," Jarvis said. "I know she's in good hands."

"To say there's a chance that he could have been on the shuttle in April or in December—we're both sort of fatalists," said Marcia Jarvis in her living room, where a picture of her husband in flight suit was on a nearby bookshelf.

"When your time comes, it comes, and if you're doing something that you really like and your time comes that's a better way to go than being sick in bed. We never had any fear with this program. It never crossed our minds.

"Do it again? Yeah, we would. We wouldn't have changed it. I hope they continue the program. They have to. It's a good program."

And Marcia, in the winter of 1986, wondered about the Rose Bowl parade. "Who knows?" she asked with a playful smile. "Maybe next year I'll go up there and see a big horse with a grin on its face."

Chapter 9

SHARON CHRISTA McAULIFFE

There she was in the Roosevelt Room at the White House, gulping back tears as she clutched a small statue of a student and teacher gazing at the stars. There she was in Houston, strapped into the cockpit of a NASA T-38 supersonic jet, a black mask pulled up to the bridge of her nose, a white crash helmet pulled down to her eyebrows, her smiling eyes saying she loved the idea of all those G-forces coming at her. There she was at home in Concord, New Hampshire, her arms around her blond daughter while her son looked on. And on a cold morning at the Kennedy Space Center, there she was, smiling delightedly as she accepted a shiny red apple from a NASA technician before she climbed into the *Challenger*.

Sharon Christa McAuliffe, the Teacher in Space, was a public relations dream not only for NASA, but for educators, mothers, wives, Sunday school teachers and the Girl Scouts. She radiated enthusiasm and equanimity from that moment at the White House in July 1985 when the nation learned that McAuliffe had won a ride on the shuttle.

"It's not often that a teacher is at a loss for words, I know my students wouldn't think so. I've made nine wonderful friends over the last two weeks," she said of the other finalists who stood behind her. "When that shuttle goes, there might be one body"— she paused to press a finger to her mouth as she fought the tears—"but there's going to be ten souls I'm taking with me."

With those words, McAuliffe, a high-school social studies teacher, became part of the public domain and the flight's trademark, dogged en route to the history books by reporters and photographers, autograph seekers, star-struck school children and just plain admirers. It was the end of the era of "the right stuff," author Tom Wolfe said, and the beginning of the age of Everyman in space.

McAuliffe's competitors had included a pilot, a mountain climber, a Peace Corps volunteer and a former pro-football player. But McAuliffe was the girl next door who married the boy she met at fifteen and built her life around the daily routines of wife, mother and teacher. She was an ordinary person with a chance to do an extraordinary thing.

"I would like to humanize the Space Age by giving a perspective from a non-astronaut, because I think the students will look at that and say, 'This is an ordinary person,'" she told a reporter shortly after her selection. "This ordinary person is contributing to history, and if they can make that connection then they're going to get excited about history, then they're going to get excited about the future. They're going to get excited about space."

As she worked her way toward the countdown, she learned about the rigors of spaceflight and celebrity; she also learned what it meant to be tired and lonely despite the attention. None of it changed her. She was the same Christa Corrigan who had bounded into a classroom at Marian High School in Framingham, Massachusetts, more than twenty years ago, a little late, a little flustered, captivating classmate Steven McAuliffe. She was the same free-spirited Christa McAuliffe whom colleagues at Concord High had seen hopping a ride on a friend's motorcycle, hair flying from underneath her helmet. She was the same Mrs. McAuliffe whose students would show up at her home late at night with leftover pizza and a need to talk. She was the same confident wife and mother who liked to sit by the pool at the Concord Country Club, eating a sandwich, drinking a beer, surrounded by family and friends.

"I have a pretty realistic view of who I am and what my limitations are and what my goals and values are in life," she said at one of several crew news conferences. McAuliffe's friends only laughed when FBI agents showed up at their doors to conduct a routine security check for NASA: she had taken no wrong turns.

Christa was born to Ed and Grace Corrigan on September 2, 1948, in Boston, the day before Ed was to start his sophomore year at Boston College. The family lived in a small apartment near Fenway Park, where the Red Sox still play baseball, and the story goes that Grace Corrigan washed her baby's diapers by hand and ironed them dry to recycle her small supply. The baby, known at first as Sheri Christa, suffered from asthmatic bronchitis and was hospitalized at six months for chronic intestinal problems. Medical bills forced Grace and the baby to live with her mother in Waterbury, Connecticut, while Ed stayed in school. Later, the family was reunited in a small apartment in a public housing project in Boston where they remained until Ed earned his degree in industrial management.

There were four more children—Christopher, Steven, Lisa and Betsy—after Christa, and the Corrigans eventually settled in Framingham, a middle-class suburb west of Boston. Ed Corrigan became an assistant comptroller for Jordan Marsh, a department store chain. Grace Corrigan, a lean, handsome woman who had been a fashion model, immersed herself in community and church activities, and family friends say Christa's vivacious personality was a gift from her mother. Christa would say later that her mother was the greatest influence in her life.

Childhood portraits show a fresh-faced, wide-eyed little girl in a party dress, with ribbons in her hair. Christa attended modeling school for a short time, appeared on a television fashion show and was crowned queen of Framingham's Saxonville Playground. A childhood acquaintance, Robert Beck, remembered that the boys in the schoolyard used to call Christa Corrigan "chipmunk" because her cheeks puffed up when she smiled, framing her prominent two front teeth. She remembered being prone to motion-sickness—and never outgrew it. ("I still get sick when I look at any ride that goes around and around," she would confess after her selection by NASA). It was the feeling that comes at the top of the roller coaster, the feeling that bothers astronauts at zero gravity.

As the oldest of five children, Christa helped raise her brothers and sisters: babysitting, listening to them, advising them, bringing home treats to put under their pillows. "She never made us feel like we were tagging along," Lisa Corrigan Bristol told a Concord reporter. Christa took dance and piano lessons and attended Christian doctrine classes for Roman Catholics. In the seventh grade, she watched on a black-and-white television as Alan Shepard became the first American in space, crammed inside a tiny Mercury capsule for a fifteen-minute–twenty-two-second suborbital ride into history. When she sent her application to NASA twenty-four years later, she recalled her introduction to the space program:

"I remember the excitement in my home when the first satellites were launched. My parents were amazed, and I was caught up in their wonder. In school, my classes would gather around the TV and try to follow the rocket as it seemed to jump all over the screen. I remember when Alan Shepard made his historic flight— not even an orbit—and I was thrilled."

In 1962, Christa Corrigan entered Marian High, a co-educational Catholic school run by the Archdiocese of Boston. The girls wore the traditional plaid skirts and gray blazers, the boys wore jackets and ties, and the nuns wore long black habits with starched white bibs and heavy rosary beads dangling from their waists. A stone statue of the Virgin Mary stands on the school lawn, and crucifixes hang in the classrooms, where self-discipline was as much a part of the curriculum as religion, Latin, English and history. Sister Mary Denisita, an elderly nun, remembers Christa as buoyant and eager, devout but not "a goodie goodie," an average student who worked hard. Those who knew her said her accomplishments were the product of determination more than sheer brainpower. She entered wholeheartedly into the life around her, and the list of activities after her name in her senior-class yearbook is one of the longest: glee club, student council, orchestra, girls' basketball, ceramics, German club, the senior play.

Steven McAuliffe first saw Christa Corrigan in homeroom during their sophomore year at Marian, and a friend introduced them a month later in a downtown drugstore. When they were sixteen, friends say Christa told Steve that if he asked her to marry him, she would say yes. He did, and she did, but they agreed that the wedding could wait until they had finished college. Steve's yearbook picture shows a handsome, clean-cut teenager, staring firmly into the camera. In her picture, Christa Corrigan is wearing a white blouse with an open collar, and her hair sweeps gently over her forehead into a flip, the popular style of the day. She wears a demure, school-girl smile, not the beaming, toothy grin that the nation would come to know.

Steve enrolled at Virginia Military Institute. Christa had decided to teach and enrolled in the class of 1970 at Framingham State College so she could live at home and save her parents the cost of room and board.

"When I was in junior high," she told the Manchester (New Hampshire) Union Leader a month after her selection, "I remember somebody sitting down and talking about career choices and saying I could be a nurse, a secretary, a teacher or an airline stewardess, nothing else."

Framingham State is a small, liberal arts college on a hill overlooking Route 9. The parking lots are always full. Christa was a day hop, a commuter in a Volkswagon bug dividing her time among home, school, a part-time job as a trucking-company clerk, babysitting and visits to Virginia Military Institute to see Steve. But, unlike many other commuters, she made time to participate in campus life: she joined the debate club and the glee club, had a part in the musical "The Pirates of Penzance" and helped organize Framingham's first outdoor rock concert.

In the late '60s and early '70s, college life lost its innocence to the Vietnam War, the invasion of Cambodia, the killing of four students at Kent State University, and the assassination of Martin Luther King, Jr. and Robert F. Kennedy. Christa was not a flag-burner or a speechmaker or a protest organizer, but she demonstrated against the war and, like many other students, wore a black arm band to her graduation ceremonies.

"I became aware of an awful lot in those years," she told an interviewer much later. "I developed a healthy distrust for authority. I guess I was hoping to change the world." She was fifteen when one of her first heroes, John F. Kennedy, was assassinated in Dallas. "My generation was all caught up in that Kennedy charisma," she said once. "He was always telling young people how important it was to do something for your country and how you can make a difference. . . ." Later, she would add other heroes to her list, people such as Britain's Prime Minister Margaret Thatcher or the slain Indian Prime Minister Indira Gandhi who she felt had somehow broken the mold. But her real inspiration seemed to come from the journals and diaries kept by the families—particularly the women—who lumbered west in wagon trains across the great valleys and plains of the American Frontier.

The pioneer diaries, which she read as part of a Framingham course on the American frontier, are vivid stories of hardship and death, testimony to the extraordinary strength of spirit and commitment required of the frontier men and women. She saw these tales as the common man's version of history, simple and poignant. The women's stories about their overland journeys seemed to be especially painful chronicles of their cross-country burdens. Years later, in a course she taught at Concord High on the history of American women, her students read from a collection called "Women's Diaries of the Westward Journey":

"Cold; breaking fast the first thing; very disagreeable weather; wind east cold and rainy, no fire. We are on a very large prairie, no timber to be seen as far as the eye can reach," wrote one woman, pregnant with her eighth child and on her way to Oregon in 1853. Her child was born along the roadside. "Evening—have crossed several bad streams today and more than once have been stuck in the mud. . . . Came twenty-two miles today. My head aches, but the fire is kindled, and I must make some tea, that will help it if not cure it. . . ."

The graves of other mothers and children marked the frontier trail. "In the afternoon we passed a lonely nameless grave on the prairie. It had a headboard," another woman wrote as she traveled with her family from Iowa to California. "It called up a sad train of thoughts, to my mind, it seems so sad to think of being buried and left alone in so wild a country with no one to plant a flower or shed a tear o'er one's grave. . . ."

In her application to NASA, she observed that much of American social history is preserved in the moving prose of pioneer journals and diaries.

"This social history of the common people, joined with our military, political and economic history, gives my students an awareness of what the whole society was doing at a particular time in history," she wrote. "They get the complete story. Just as the pioneer travelers of the Conestoga wagon days kept personal journals, I, as a pioneer space traveler, would do the same." Later, she told an interviewer, "Those diaries and journals are the richest part of the history of our westward expansion—without them, it would just be how many Indians were killed and the number of settlements started."

Christa graduated from Framingham State in the spring of 1970 with a degree in history, and in August, she and Steve were married. In their wedding portrait Steve McAuliffe wears a white, double-breasted dinner jacket with dark trim. His hair is short, and he wears glasses. Christa, standing beside him, wears a long-sleeved, lacy white wedding gown. Her hair is smoothed back, and her face is framed by a headband of daisies. It is a very traditional portrait in a very turbulent time.

With 500 dollars, the McAuliffes set out for Washington, D.C., where Steve began classes at Georgetown University Law Center. Christa taught American history, English and civics at junior high schools in suburban Maryland and worked for a time as a waitress at a Howard Johnson's restaurant to help pay the bills. Their first child, Scott, was born in September 1976 when Christa McAuliffe was twenty-eight. Two years later, she earned a master's degree in education administration from Bowie State College, writing her thesis on the acceptance of handicapped children in the traditional classroom environment. During those early years in Maryland schools, she developed the teaching technique that would become her trademark: the field trip. She believed that the best way for her students to learn was to see.

After law school, Steve spent four years in the Judge Advocate General's Corps—the Army's law firm. In 1977, his military service concluded, he was offered a job in the U.S. Justice Department in Washington, but Christa insisted that they raise Scott in a less power-packed environment. Steve later told *The Boston Globe* that Christa had said, "You can live where you want, but the child and I will live in New Hampshire."

As a youngster, Christa had camped with the Girl Scouts in rural New Hampshire, and she had skied at New Hampshire resorts a short drive from the Corrigan home in Framingham. She remembered the serenity and self-confidence that lingers with visitors to northern New England, far from the crowds and hectic pace of metropolitan Washington.

Those memories were rekindled at Christmas time in 1977 when the McAuliffes went to the rural community of Bow, New Hampshire, on the Merrimack River to visit good friends who had moved there from the Washington area. Steve said later that his wife fell in love with the state again, and they agreed to give up their big-city life. He took a job with the New Hampshire attorney general's office, and the family moved to Concord, the capital city of 32,000 residents that Christa McAuliffe once called a "Norman Rockwell kind of place."

Concord sits in the Merrimack Valley in south central New Hampshire, seventy miles northwest of Boston. Downtown, beneath the capitol's gold dome, a statue of Daniel Webster stands on the statehouse plaza on Main Street. Weekday traffic is steady, and drivers stop politely to let pedestrians cross between shops and banks and offices. Not long after the McAuliffes arrived in 1978, Concord embarked on a cosmopolitan facelift, renovating old buildings or erecting new ones for clothing boutiques and restaurants for a young, professional clientele. Not all of the ventures succeeded, and there was grumbling that Concord was losing its small-town identity without settling on a new one.

A trailer park sits along the main highway into town, which leads to old frame houses in the center city where the streets have names like Harvard, Princeton and Yale and many of the larger homes downtown have been carved into apartments. In the middle of town is a popular YMCA where devoted followers show up for a grueling, lunchtime aerobics class taught by an ex-Marine. The state hospital for the mentally ill is on Pleasant Street as it heads out of town, and farther up the road is the huge, wooded campus of St. Paul's School, an elite prep school.

The McAuliffes moved into a three-story Victorian home in an area known as The Hill, an enclave of large, stately old homes a short drive from downtown. Their house on Park Ridge is tall and narrow with a small yard, less grand than some of its neighbors. A wall in the second-floor hallway is a gallery for several generations of family photographs, and paintings by Grace Corrigan, who earned an art degree at Framingham State years after Christa graduated, hang in the McAuliffes' house.

Family life is the backbone of the community. Many parents spend their weekends with the children's baseball, soccer or ice hockey leagues, and city officials take pride in the public schools, which are among the best in the state. Concord is the kind of place where family obligations come before professional ones, where working parents came home for lunch, where the clerk at the newstand knows customers by name.

In September 1978, Christa McAuliffe began work as an English and American history teacher in a Concord junior high school but was laid off in June, a casualty of local budget cuts. Her second child, Caroline, was born in August 1979, and McAuliffe was back in the classroom by October, substituting at Bow Memorial School for Carol Mulligan, a middle-school teacher recuperating from a kidney transplant. Mulligan said McAuliffe told her then that she had thought she would be content to stay home with her children but soon discovered that it did not satisfy what Mulligan described as her "incredible energy."

McAuliffe tutored four students in Concord the following semester and in September 1980 began teaching again in Bow, where she joined the Bow Education Association, a union representing about fifty teachers. First as a member of a contract negotiating team and later as the association's president, she led the union through a round of salary negotiations.

In the fall of 1982, McAuliffe left the Bow school system to teach social studies at Concord High School, two blocks from home. That year, Steve McAuliffe joined the prominent Concord law firm of Gallagher, Callahan and Gartrell, and the McAuliffes settled into the busy life of a professional couple with small children. Steve, who relished his work as a trial lawyer, spent long hours at the office. Christa, who quickly established herself at school, was often seen going back and forth, with Scott and Caroline in tow.

As her mother had done in Framingham, Christa immersed herself in community activities, joining the Junior Service League of Concord and raising money for Concord Hospital and the YMCA. She had starred as Granny Greenthumb in a community play, and she and Steve were members of the Court Jesters, a local volleyball league. Sometimes she jogged at dawn or played doubles at the tennis club. Her interest in the church was revived when Scott grew curious about religion, and she began teaching Christian doctrine classes at her parish church, St. Peter's.

McAuliffe was always scurrying around, always a few minutes late for a meeting, never idle, always busy. She seemed to rest only in the summer, by the pool at the country club with her children, reclaiming family time lost during the school year. And every summer since 1979, she had spent a weekend at New Hampshire's Camp Wabasso with friends from her childhood Brownie troop in Framingham.

Each year, an underprivileged child stayed at the McAuliffe home as part of a program called "A Better Chance." When Steve, a self-described cynic, warned Christa about the potential legal liabilities of such visits, Christa would toss her head back and laugh. "Sue me," she would say. She believed that some children needed help and that she was there to help them. One night, a girl called to say she'd been thinking of suicide. Christa told her to come over and watched all night as the girl slept in the bunk bed below Scott's.

Concord High is a large brick building whose main entrance is framed by stone pillars. The social-studies teachers began their day at small desks in a large, brightly lit corner office on the second floor where pictures of Christopher Columbus, Albert Einstein and President Reagan hang on the walls. There is a globe, a book of maps, a stack of newspapers, an assortment of textbooks on desks and floor. The teachers check in at 7:30 A.M. and hurriedly organize their papers and lessons, until the 7:55 A.M. bell signals the start of the first class.

Down the carpeted hall, past long rows of beige lockers, is Room 305 where Christa McAuliffe taught most of her classes. There are tables instead of desks, and above the blackboard is McAuliffe's standard classroom decoration—covers from *Time* magazine. Her standard teaching tool remained the field trip. McAuliffe took her students on so many field trips—to the police station, the courts, the prisons—that other faculty members complained that her students were missing too many other classes.

She brought in speakers—members of congress, lawyers, judges, and suggested setting up an independent study program at the local court. She assigned students to watch the stock market or dress up in period costumes or keep journals like historians. School Principal Charles Foley considered McAuliffe one of the best teachers at Concord High School, and so did her peers. After observing one of McAuliffe's classes, Foley had no recommendations, no criticisms to offer: "It's reassuring for me as principal to watch a first-class teacher at work," he wrote in his evaluation.

For a teacher who liked to learn by doing and taught the same way, NASA's teacher-in-space program was an irresistible adventure. "In her mind, there was no way that she could let that go by," said Eileen O'Hara, her friend and colleague who taught for McAuliffe while she trained for the shuttle flight. As was her style, McAuliffe waited until the last minute to complete the eleven-page application.

More than 11,000 teachers applied, seventy-nine of them from New Hampshire. In April 1985, McAuliffe and Robert Veilleux, an astronomy and biology teacher from Manchester, were selected as the state's two finalists. "I'm not naive enough to think that I am the best in my profession," she told a reporter later. "I happen to be from a small state that didn't have as many applicants as California, for example. There is a lot of luck in being at the right place at the right time," she said. She told Eileen O'Hara that her goal was just to make it to Houston, as a finalist.

In essay questions on the application, McAuliffe plainly described why she wanted to be "the first U.S. private citizen in space."

"As a woman, I have been envious of those men who could participate in the space program and who were encouraged to excel in areas of math and science," she wrote. "I felt that women had indeed been left outside of one of the most exciting careers available. When Sally Ride and other women began to train as astronauts, I could look among my students and see ahead of them an ever-increasing list of opportunities.

"I cannot join the space program and restart my life as an astronaut, but this opportunity to connect my abilities as an educator with my interests in history and space is a unique opportunity to fulfill my early fantasies. I watched the Space Age being born, and I would like to participate," she said.

McAuliffe's proposal for a special space shuttle project had an appealing simplicity: a space journal, an ordinary person's chronicle of a new frontier like the diaries kept by America's earlier pioneers. "My journal would be a trilogy," she wrote. "I would like to begin it at the point of selection through the training for the program. The second part would cover the actual flight. Part three would cover my thoughts and reactions after my return.

"My perceptions as a non-astronaut would help complete and humanize the technology of the Space Age. Future historians would use my eyewitness accounts to help their studies of the impact of the Space Age on the general population."

McAuliffe—who was about to become the subject of an extraordinary number of photographs and film clips—proposed to NASA that she record her daily activity aboard the orbiter on videotape and slides. She knew that her students were always hungry to *see*. "A visual message would have a greater impact on an American public than just the written word," she wrote.

By late June 1985, McAuliffe and 112 other teachers were in Washington for interviews. Besides four former astronauts, the judges included actress Pam Dawber who had appeared in "Mork and Mindy," a television show about a man from outer space; former pro basketball player Wes Unseld; Robert Jarvik, the inventor of an artificial heart, and the presidents of three major universities.

On the teachers' first day in Washington, there was a discussion of the risks involved in a shuttle mission. Alan Ladwig, manager of NASA's spaceflight participant program, described the six million pounds of thrust needed to lift *Challenger* off the launch pad and the highly volatile chemicals used to produce that thrust. David R. Zahren, a Maryland teacher, recalled that it was like reading the warning label on a bottle of oven-cleaner: You read the warning and used it anyway, believing that nothing would happen.

By July 1, McAuliffe and nine other finalists were on their way to Houston. At the Johnson Space Center there, they were given medical and psychological tests and had a brief taste of weightlessness aboard a NASA KC135, known as "the vomit comet." On July 12, McAuliffe and the other finalists watched in an observation room behind Mission Control when a *Challenger* flight was aborted by a valve failure three seconds before blastoff. Ladwig turned to the teachers and reminded them of the risks. He asked if anyone wanted to withdraw from the competition, and they all said no. Ladwig said Scobee also met with the ten finalists and talked at length about the dangers involved. "He didn't want to give anybody the illusion that they were on any kind of joyride," Ladwig said.

When Vice-President George Bush announced a week later in Washington that Christa McAuliffe was NASA's unanimous choice to be the first teacher in space, her competitors were not surprised. McAuliffe was personable and spunky and enthusiastic. She handled the press with unstudied aplomb. Americans would be able to see themselves in her and like what they saw.

The media blitz was under way, and McAuliffe accepted it as part of the deal. McAuliffe was whisked around the city in taxicabs from one television interview to another, from "ABC World News Tonight" to the "MacNeil/Lehrer NewsHour." During an interview with "Cable News Network," she told a reporter that she was not afraid. "I really see the shuttle as a safe program," she said.

Back home in Concord, McAuliffe's friends and neighbors were overjoyed. Her selection came during "Old-Fashioned Bargain Days"—three days when Main Street is closed to traffic and shopkeepers sell their goods on the sidewalks—and the announcement fueled an already festive atmosphere. A local disc jockey, already broadcasting live from a stage on Main Street, interviewed shoppers for their reaction to the news that one of Concord's own would make history.

The next day, there was McAuliffe, riding in the Lions Club Soccer Parade, sitting up on the back of a convertible with Caroline and Scott on either side of her. She wore NASA's cobalt-blue jumpsuit and a red, white and blue cap with a picture of the space shuttle on it. She was smiling from ear to ear and flashing the thumbs-up sign.

"Atta girl, Christa!" her new fans shouted from the parade route. "Go for it!"

Steve McAuliffe bought a video camera and began amassing a library of tape, even photographing the press photographing her. Christa went to Los Angeles and appeared on the "Tonight Show" with Johnny Carson, where the band played the Air Force anthem: *"Off we go into the wild blue yonder . . ."* In August, at a band concert on the statehouse plaza in Concord, the mayor declared Christa McAuliffe Day and gave her a tiny Concord flag—the city has no key—and a pewter plate from the governor. She conducted the band in "Stars and Stripes Forever," as the crowd clapped along.

Christa traveled to Washington later that month to begin preparation of the two "live lessons" she would teach from the shuttle. The Public Broadcasting Service would carry the lessons by satellite, and schools with satellite dishes could arrange through NASA and a project called "Classroom Earth" to receive daily transmissions from *Challenger*. During the first lesson, which she called "The Ultimate Field Trip," McAuliffe planned to conduct a tour of the flight deck, the shuttle controls, computers and the payload bay area. On the middeck, where McAuliffe would sit with Onizuka and Jarvis during blastoff, she planned to show her students what NASA literature called "the kinds of equipment and processes which help human beings live comfortably and safely in the microgravity environment of the shuttle." In other words, McAuliffe planned to explain how astronauts sleep, eat, dress, brush their teeth—even how the toilets work.

In the second lesson, called "Where We've Been, Where We're Going and Why" McAuliffe planned to use models of the Wright Brothers plane and a space station to discuss why the United States is exploring space.

McAuliffe also planned to conduct several experiments while she was on the shuttle including growing beansprouts and dropping Alka Seltzer in water to watch the effects of weightlessness on effervescence. She also planned to take along a screwdriver, a toy car and a billiard ball for other experiments that would be filmed in the flight, narrated by McAuliffe on her return and distributed as educational films.

In September, McAuliffe left Concord to begin training with the shuttle crew at the Johnson Space Center. She worried that the "regular" astronauts would think she was thumbing a ride, that they would resent her. She wanted to be accepted and set out to do that in one important way: she would not pretend to be an astronaut. She wanted no special treatment. She would learn to take care of herself. She knew how to measure up. She also knew that she was not burdened with the professional pressures faced by the other six crew members, whose lives and careers were in space. When this adventure was done, McAuliffe intended to go home to Concord and teach.

Houston was hot and humid when McAuliffe moved into a furnished one-bedroom apartment off NASA Road 1 in an adult community called Peachtree Lane where NASA had previously rented apartments for private contractors in the space program. Peachtree Lane became home for eighteen weeks for McAuliffe and her understudy, Barbara Morgan, a second-grade teacher from McCall, Idaho. The two women were next-door neighbors on the second floor. Morgan's husband, Clay, a writer, was there for much of the training period, and Greg Jarvis lived in the same complex.

There could be no comparison between the rich New Hampshire countryside in autumn and the dull, flat land of Houston in any season. McAuliffe's apartment—a bedroom, a living room, a galley kitchen and a dining room that she converted to a study—overlooked a small grassy area with a grill, a picnic table, a pool and a jacuzzi. The heat and dampness made her so homesick that by November she had taken to setting the air conditioner in her apartment low enough so she could wear a sweater and jeans.

But the toughest adjustment was the separation from her family. She had brought some momentoes from home, including family pictures. Steve often sent samples of the childrens' school work, which hung on the walls. "While Christa Trains, Steve Plays 'Mr.

Mom' " one New Hampshire headline said. The article described
how Steve, accustomed to long hours in his law office, had
mastered the rudiments of microwave cooking. Christa called
home almost every night. She missed the parental ritual of tucking
the children into their beds. She worried about finding time to hem
the curtains she had sewn for the family's new playroom. But the
couple felt the separation was worth it.

"You know, you're talking about a human being free of the
bounds of gravity orbiting the earth," Steve told a reporter.
"There aren't very many human beings that have done that. So I
think most of us feel that whatever the price in terms of
readjustments, of my taking on things that I probably should have
been doing before and hadn't done, whatever those prices are they
certainly pale in comparison to the opportunity."

"It's hard being away from home," Christa wrote to a former
teacher in October, "but we realized it was a tradeoff for a chance
in a lifetime."

In training, McAuliffe never lost that gee-whiz attitude, saying
over and over that she couldn't believe NASA was going to let her
go up in the space shuttle. But there she was, leaving the crew
quarters one day, striding behind Ellison Onizuka, arms swinging
as she flashed a gaping, excited smile. "It's just such an exciting experience," she said once. "I still can't believe I'm really
here."

McAuliffe was a different breed from the other women—driven,
professional scientists, who had made space their life's work. She
remained mindful that she was not an astronaut but a "flight
participant," not a technician but a teacher, a communicator. She
chose her words carefully and enunciated each one precisely, at a
fast clip and sometimes with a teacher's sing song. She spoke in
crisp, complete sentences.

"Good morning, this is Christa McAuliffe, live from the
Challenger and I'm going to be taking you on a field trip," she
recited during a rehearsal for her televised lessons. "I'm going to
start out introducing you to two very important members of the
crew. The first one is Commander Scobee, who is sitting to my
left, and the second one is Michael Smith . . ."

The publicity abated while McAuliffe trained, a reprieve she
must have welcomed. NASA limited interviews to two hours or
less a week. McAuliffe's apartment was always off limits, as were
telephone calls after hours. Along with her shuttle skills, she

quickly learned some of the lessons of celebrity. She learned that she did not have to rush to every interview, because without her there was no interview, that not every autograph seeker planned to hang her portrait above the mantlepiece—some autographs were being sold instead. Critics of the Teacher in Space program said that McAuliffe was a public relations pawn, that she was being used by the Reagan administration to gain favor with teachers and by NASA to gain favor for the space program. McAuliffe believed she was improving the public's perception of teachers and enhancing the public's interest—especially children's interest—in the space program.

As the novelty of her selection wore off and her training wore on, the media's interest in McAuliffe dimmed—except at *The Concord Monitor*.

The Monitor has a small staff, thirteen reporters and a handful of editors, and a small circulation, about 21,000 readers. Publisher George Wilson is a tall, aristocratic-looking man who has lived in Concord with his family for twenty-four years. Editor Mike Pride had just returned to the *Monitor* from a Neiman journalism fellowship at Harvard University when NASA picked McAuliffe, and he and Wilson knew that this would be a very big story for a small town.

They assigned Bob Hohler, a sports writer who had recently joined the news staff, to cover McAuliffe full time, and they decided to publish two special supplements. One, "Christa's Challenge," was written for junior high school students. The other had two sections, "A Teacher in Training" and "The *Challenger*'s Countdown." In the end, the newspaper's work provided a painfully detailed account of an extraordinary period of space history.

"Christa's Challenge" produced a wealth of facts about spaceflight, from rescue procedures (the astronauts would be transferred from a disabled shuttle in space to another vehicle in a thirty-four-inch-wide cloth ball with its own air supply) to cuisine (astronauts pick their menu after sampling a hundred foods, forty-five drinks and condiments before the flight). There was also a feature called "Kids Ask Christa":

Q: What do you like least about your training?

A: There's nothing that I don't like. Everything is new and fun, and remember that I'm getting ready for the ride of a lifetime!"

She would tell her own students that she was reaching for the stars—and so should they.

From Houston, Hohler wrote extensively about her training, much of it focusing on what to do in an emergency. After her selection, McAuliffe's life-insurance premium rose so dramatically that she canceled the policy. Later, she accepted a gift of one million dollars in coverage from a Washington, D.C.-based company.

Much of McAuliffe's training involved studying workbooks on such things as how to get in and out of the shuttle, how to cook, how to use the bathroom, how to operate cameras. The books also showed her which of the shuttle's 1,300 switches to avoid.

"Frankly, we want to teach her how to stay out of the way," NASA's flight training director Frank Hughes told Hohler. When McAuliffe passed a test after each workbook, she was rewarded with a flight in a T-38 supersonic jet or a session in the huge shuttle simulator or another session of weightlessness. It was the T-38 that gave McAuliffe her greatest thrill. In a gleeful telephone conversation with her friend Eileen O'Hara, McAuliffe described how Scobee had once let her take control of the machine for some dives and rolls. O'Hara said Scobee was the only crew member McAuliffe mentioned to her. He and his wife June, a teacher, had adopted her, McAuliffe said, and tried to make her feel at home.

McAuliffe made notes for her "pre-mission" journal which were scattered around her apartment or dictated into a tape recorder. "I've got notes spread all over the place," she told friends. During the flight, she planned to record her observations on a dictation machine small enough to fit in the palm of her hand, a technique used by astronauts on previous shuttle missions.

During breaks from training and homework, McAuliffe would page through *Good Housekeeping* magazine or work on her needlepoint. She liked to browse through a greeting card store near her apartment in Houston. Once she baked pies for the shuttle crew with fresh MacIntosh apples that she and her children had picked in a New Hampshire orchard. When they had the time, McAuliffe and Morgan went to the movies or roamed through the Armand Bayou, a nature preserve near the space center. McAuliffe played volleyball in a space center league.

Life at Peachtree Lane sometimes had the makeshift qualities of a college dormitory. When McAuliffe, Morgan and their public relations manager, Linda Long, were preparing dinner for a *New York Times* reporter and photographer, they had to hunt around for the right baking pan for shrimp and a bowl for the Caesar salad. McAuliffe and Morgan bought an ironing board that they shared with Long, who let them use the washer and dryer in her apartment. Jarvis occasionally visited for a glass of wine and talk about family and friends.

In November, Steve and the children visited (Caroline said the most exciting part of the trip for her was eating tuna fish in the NASA cafeteria). McAuliffe missed them and was sometimes weary, but she saw her odyssey in the space program as a single year of her family's life. She made clear that when her post-flight commitments to NASA were completed, she intended to return to Concord and her classroom. Meanwhile, plans for her homecoming there had gone somewhat awry.

The trouble began in December when *The Monitor* reported in a front page story that the city government had set aside $26,700 to plan an "Olympic size" celebration for McAuliffe in early March and later criticized the plans in an editorial headlined "Hype-hype-hooray." McAuliffe made clear through intermediaries that she did not want money, especially taxpayers' money, spent on a homecoming. Embarrassed officials of the Christa McAuliffe Homecoming Committee withdrew their request for the money and scaled back the plans to a small parade, a speech to the legislature and maybe a service-club luncheon.

Meanwhile, a network of neighbors continued to help Steve McAuliffe care for his children while Christa was in Houston, occasionally bringing them meals or even taking Caroline out to buy a needed pair of shoes. He joked that he knew how Prince Phillip felt, playing second fiddle to the queen, and that he had reinvented the Snickers candy bars as a breakfast food. But he knew the real value of his time alone with his children.

"I was one of those fathers who always came home after the kids were in bed," he told *The Monitor*. "I've really been surprised at how I have gotten to know them in a different way. . . .

"This is tough, really hard," he said. "I was really frantic for the first few months, but now I'm starting to get pretty comfortable. When it comes down to it, it's good to know you can make it on your own if you have to."

In a letter to Sister Mary Denisita, Christa wrote that Steve was doing "a super job" taking care of Scott and Caroline.

"He's getting to know his children better," she said, "and they are delighted to have Daddy's attention. It's going to be a wonderful year for all of us."

Chapter 10

THE CHALLENGER SEVEN

The land that stretches for fifty miles south of Houston to the Gulf of Mexico is brown and drab and flat. Man-made embellishments —water towers, shopping centers, gas stations, hot tub stores, utility poles—have sprung up haphazardly, a sign of the area's fast and unplanned growth. These are the outskirts of Houston, Texas, one of America's new frontier cities. It is a boom area, built on oil money and the success of a new genre of entrepreneurs who have made and lost and remade fortunes by gambling on high-stakes business ventures.

It is the hub of the new Southwest, a symbol of America pushing forward, of the American ideal of taking risks to achieve a dream. Once dominated by the frontier spirit of old Western cowboys, Houston has come to embody a new pioneer spirit of hi-tech, futuristic corporate cowboys. For the past twenty-five years, the sprawling city has embraced and promoted a pioneering American enterprise: the space program, personified by an elite corps of men and women whose dreams are to push technology to its limits and to explore the dangerous frontiers of space.

Houston has not been able to resist molding itself around the symbols of the space age. The city's baseball stadium, one of its spiritual emblems, is called the Astrodome; it opened in 1965, four years after Houston was designated the headquarters for America's blossoming space program. Even the name of the team was changed to match the city's new identity: The Houston Colt 45s became the Houston Astros.

In this setting, Astronaut Group 8 came to train for the space shuttle in the sweltering humidity of July 1978. Thirty-five men and women who hailed from towns in New England and California and Hawaii—towns with their own special histories and vivid sceneries—settled in the steamy outskirts of Houston, in communities twenty-years-old or less. Subdivisions with names such as Clear Lake and El Lago sprouted up on what was largely pastureland until 1963, when the Manned Spacecraft Center opened. By the time the new astronauts arrived, hastily constructed condominium developments and fast food outlets lined four-lane NASA Road 1, the main link to Interstate 45 and a 25-mile drive to downtown Houston.

The trainees in Group 8 found their real homes at the center itself, a 100-building complex with 10,000 employees, set apart in appearance and in spirit, an oasis in the midst of the hodge-podge of NASA Road 1. Its neat green lawns sparkled against the dull Texas landscape. There was an order and simplicity to the place. Streets were named Avenue A, Avenue B, Avenue C. Buildings were modern cement-and-glass structures identified by numbers, rather than names. Man-made ponds and trees and walkways fit symmetrically into landscaped quadrangles. In all, the space center had a feeling of uniformity and coherence. It was a comfortable setting for pilots and scientists who wanted to master the precise and technical intricacies of space travel. In the solar system of communities revolving around Houston, the space center was a planet unto itself.

Two worlds, one public and one private, coexist at the complex, now called the Johnson Space Center. Tourists—nearly 1.5 million each year—are an integral part of NASA's efforts to build its public image. They visit Mission Control in Building 4, the nerve center for all manned flights; they walk up to the enormous Apollo Saturn rocket in Rocket Park; they inspect a scaled-down replica of an Apollo spacecraft and a full-size lunar module, as well as view moon rocks, photos from space, and films about space missions; they see the simulators used to train crews for the shuttle. They can eat in a cafeteria with NASA workers, including astronauts in training, using meal trays emblazoned with the NASA logo. At the gift shop they buy every imaginable souvenir, including chartreuse punk sunglasses with NASA printed on them.

The fantasy of space adventure holds a special allure for children, who crowd into exhibit halls and stare at facsimiles of spaceships. In the visitor's center, one wall is reserved for paintings, poems and stories about space submitted by children from around the world. "Dear Space Commander," begins a letter from seven-year-old Matthew Thomas Schottnick of Bloomington, Illinois. "I would like to go to the moon. Can I please make a reservation?" Since the space center opened, thousands of children have signed up to be members of the Young Astronaut Program. Christa McAuliffe's nine-year-old son, Scott, is one of them; his local chapter traveled to Kennedy Space Center in Florida to watch her fateful lift-off.

The other world at the space center, not on public display, is the training program that dominated the experiences of the thirty-five members of Group 8, selected from among 8,079 applicants who responded to the space agency's announcement in June 1977 that it was looking for men and women of different races to diversify its astronaut corps. Before the announcement—ever since Alan Shepard's first flight in 1961—NASA's astronaut corps had consisted only of white men, most of them military pilots. Now, the new NASA welcomed, as mission specialists, Judith A. Resnik, an engineer at the Xerox Corporation; Ronald E. McNair, a black physicist from South Carolina on the staff of the Hughes Research Laboratories in California; and Ellison S. Onizuka, an Asian-American engineer in the Air Force. At the same time, NASA did not turn its back on the military—it chose twenty-one pilots, including Dick Scobee, for Group 8, and more in 1980, including Michael J. Smith.

NASA had good reasons to select the five astronauts who later became part of the crew on shuttle flight 51-L. Scobee was closest to the archetypal space pilot, but even he was different from the fighter jocks who manned the first American spaceships. He was a methodical and humble man, whose finesse in handling large, heavy planes made him an attractive candidate when NASA was looking for shuttle pilots. Onizuka, a lieutenant colonel with a background in aeronautical engineering, had a jovial personality that made him one of the best-liked members of the astronauts corps. Smith was a test pilot who had advanced quickly in the Navy and was close to being promoted to commanding officer of an attack squadron when he applied to the space program. Faced with two possible career paths, he chose NASA in hopes of bringing more stability to his family while continuing to pursue his only real dream: to fly.

Resnik and McNair, too, were ideal candidates. They met the qualifications sought by NASA, which included a bachelor's degree in science, three years of professional experience or a graduate degree, height between five feet and six feet four inches, and vision no worse than 20/100, correctable to 20/20. Beyond that, they were uncommonly smart, highly professional and fiercely motivated.

Both had another quality that NASA valued in astronauts who had to work in the stress of the space program. Resnik and McNair were conservative in temperament and style, team players unlikely to undermine or bring embarrassment to the agency. Hardly publicity seekers, they seemed content to set their own goals and meet them through hard work. Both shunned labels that were frequently foisted on them. McNair used his own experiences as a model for children, particularly black children, but he always considered himself a professional above all else. Resnik once told an interviewer: "Firsts are only the means to the end of full equality, not the end itself."

NASA selected the crew for shuttle 51-L in two stages. In early 1985, five astronauts in the permanent corps who were up for rotation were assigned to the flight. Four of them—McNair, Scobee, Resnik, Onizuka—had been to space once before, on successive shuttles beginning in mid-1984. Each also had a specific skill that matched the activities planned for the 51-L mission. Scobee had already piloted one flight and NASA wanted him to take the role of commander. McNair's background in physics was crucial for observations of Halley's Comet. Onizuka was going to help deploy a large communications satellite that would be carried in the orbiter's payload cargo area. Resnik had helped develop and was deft at operating the shuttle's moveable arm, a pole-like machine that would be used to release the mission's payload, a $100 million NASA communications satellite, into orbit.

Smith was excited about going up for his first trip, but was already looking ahead to his second flight, scheduled for the fall of 1986, when he would be the commander. "He figured the first time he would be so excited he would miss alot of things," said his younger brother, Patrick. "He was really looking forward more to the second time."

The other two members of the crew had not been picked yet, but the five professional astronauts knew they would be a teacher and an industry engineer—the result of NASA's new policy allowing civilians on shuttle flights. Some of the astronauts were quietly disturbed that NASA had decided to let civilians with no experience share something they had competed for and worked toward for years. Already NASA's promotion of civilian space travel had eroded some of the mystique of the astronaut corps. "If you're alive and breathing," veteran astronaut John Young had said, "you can fly [on] the shuttle."

Apart from highly orchestrated training schedules designed to ensure that crew members rehearsed tasks for their mission, and regular check-ups in the six weeks before a lift-off, there were no prescriptions for exercise or lifestyle. There was hardly a reason to impose more discipline on the crew of 51-L; most were conscientious to a fault in learning the technical aspects of their flights and in staying in good shape. Scobee was an avid cyclist. Resnik had taken up racquetball and weight-lifting. Only Onizuka, who enjoyed beer and macadamia nuts, had a physique that might have benefited from a more rigorous diet. But he, too, jogged miles every day to stay in shape.

Given the changing image of the astronaut corps, the entrance of an ordinary person into their ranks was, on one level, difficult. The engineer from private industry was one thing—Gregory Jarvis, at least, was trained in aerospace engineering and had worked on the Leasat satellite project for Hughes Aircraft. But Christa McAuliffe, the teacher, while likeable, gung-ho and as committed to the mission as the other members of 51-L, was far from the prototypical NASA astronaut. She was more emotional, high-spirited, and outgoing than the rest, and slightly disorganized. In a group of pragmatists, she was something of an idealist. While Scobee and Smith flew combat missions in Vietnam, and Resnik and McNair were not active politically during the turmoil surrounding the Vietnam War in the late 1960s, Christa McAuliffe demonstrated against the war. The others seemed to regard politics as a distraction from more serious professional pursuits. McAuliffe didn't. She was sympathetic to the underprivileged and to women's issues; as president of the teacher's union in New Hampshire she campaigned for higher teacher salaries. Somehow, she would have to fit into this group of deadly serious, highly focused astronauts.

McAuliffe's task was particularly difficult because she had to bear the burden of the publicity that surrounded her mission. She was picked because she seemed to embody the public's image of the model teacher. Among the ten teacher finalists evaluated by the agency were several pilots. But NASA wasn't looking for a teacher-pilot. It was looking for a teacher-ordinary person. In a public relations sense, the agency could not have made a better choice than Christa McAuliffe.

By necessity, the other crew members had to go along with more than their accustomed share of public appearances and news conferences. While this was no imposition for most of them—after all, when they joined NASA they knew they had to play the role of goodwill ambassador for the space program—one crew member chafed at the idea of being a celebrity.

Judy Resnik hated publicity and had shunned it throughout her life. It was one of the reasons that she had not been selected as the first woman to fly in space. That honor fell to Sally K. Ride, another member of Group 8. Ride and Resnik were equally motivated, disciplined and hard-working. But Ride could tolerate publicity, and made the public believe she enjoyed her role. Resnik disdained it. With other astronauts and scientists, Resnik cracked jokes and laughed when they called her "J.R." or "Roseanne Roseannadanna," but in public she resisted showing her personal side. When an interviewer asked a personal question, particularly one that seemed frivolous, her irritation showed. After her 1984 flight, when she was filmed in shorts and a T-shirt, her wavy brown hair floating in the weightless atmosphere, an interviewer asked how she could keep her hair coiffed in space. "No comment," she said.

The following year, she was asked about the publicity generated by the teacher mission. "I feel like a potted plant," she said.

During the three months before the shuttle *Challenger*'s scheduled January 1986 launch, the crew members designated for flight 51-L spent most of their time training separately, not as a crew. They came to know each other professionally and occasionally ate dinner together or went on a picnic, but they did not form close relationships with each other. Scobee, Smith, McNair and Onizuka had families in the nearby communities. As the pace of the training increased, time with their wives and children became more precious. Resnik was dating another astronaut and, while well-liked, she was private and independent by nature. It was different for McAuliffe and Jarvis. The space center was not home to them and they left behind families when they came to Houston to start their training for flight 51-L.

When Jarvis and McAuliffe arrived, in early September 1985, they received cobalt blue flight suits and had their pictures taken with the rest of the crew. Jarvis had been through training twice before since his selection in 1984—he was bumped off two flights to make room first for Utah Senator Jake Garn and then for Florida Congressman Bill Nelson—and this time he only spent a few days each week in Houston. McAuliffe settled into the nearby Peachtree Lane Apartments, across from a Putt-Putt miniature golf course and a Burger King. The modern garden apartments were secured by a gate that could only be penetrated with a plastic identification card, a prime consideration for a woman coping with the demands of the news media. Barbara Morgan, a teacher selected as McAuliffe's backup, rented the apartment next door. During the following months the two of them, sometimes joined by Jarvis, shopped together at the Kroger, drank margaritas at Rick's Turtle Club, and tried to lead lives as normal as possible.

McAuliffe was particularly conscious of trying to keep in contact with her children and Steve, who visited her once during the training period at the space center. Her five-year-old daughter, Caroline, had never quite grasped what her mother was doing. Shortly after McAuliffe's selection, a television reporter asked Caroline if she was glad her mother was going to space. "I want mommy to stay at home," Caroline replied. During the autumn months, when the family, except for Christa, was in New England watching the foliage reach its peak of color, Caroline asked her mother on the telephone: "Mommy, are you in space yet?"

While the professional astronauts prepared for more complex activities in space, McAuliffe underwent training designed specially for her. Ten teacher finalists who convened over the summer had drawn up ideas for eight elementary experiments. Using their proposals, NASA's Bob Mayfield met regularly with McAuliffe and designed a series of simple scientific experiments for McAuliffe to conduct on live-television from space. Mayfield had hoped McAuliffe would take a leading role in designing the equipment for them, but she was so busy with her other training and with a relentless publicity schedule that she was only able to meet with him for a few hours a week. Early on, Mayfield became worried that she wasn't learning the experiments. He could tell she was tired, and he began to wonder whether NASA's grand public relations scheme was headed for failure. To his surprise, McAuliffe managed to juggle her responsibilities and to learn the experiments flawlessly. He realized that she was able to concentrate on a number of things at once and still absorb what he had been saying to her in their lessons. "My feelings turned from resentment to total admiration," Mayfield said. "She turned out to be an A+ student."

The crew members typically began working at 8 A.M. and were scheduled for various training activities throughout the day, except for a break at lunch. At night, most of them would study at home. For McAuliffe and Jarvis the most critical task was adapting to the near zero-gravity of space. Once weightless, failure to perform activities that were second nature on earth could be comical, but also disruptive to a more experienced crew whose responsibilities on board required concentration and precision. A piece of bread allowed to crumble would become a spray of crumbs floating aimlessly around the cabin that could jam Dick Scobee's instrument panel in the upper deck. A pen placed on a surface of the cabin or a stray fork left on a meal tray would rise into the air, potentially distracting Judy Resnik as she performed delicate maneuvers with the shuttle's moveable arm. Juice allowed to drift from a container would turn into a ball that would float until it hit a wall and divided into two spheres, leaving a sticky mess that the crew would have to clean up.

To avoid such disruptions, NASA trained McAuliffe and Jarvis in a KC-135 training jet nicknamed "the vomit comet." The jet accelerated to high speeds and then dipped sharply before pulling up quickly, giving the "vomit comet's" passengers the feeling of weightlessness for as much as thirty seconds. First-time space travelers often suffered from "space adaptation syndrome," a lethargy sometimes accompanied by vomiting (but not nausea) that can last for a few days until the astronaut adjusts. In rehearsal after rehearsal, McAuliffe and Jarvis learned simple exercises such as drinking and eating—putting Taco sauce on beef steak and spreading peanut butter on seedless rye bread.

The Johnson Space Center had a range of training facilities and simulators that bore eerily close approximations of what astronauts experience 200 nautical miles from earth. Training became more intense during the final forty-five days before launch, when the crew went through repeated simulations and familiarizations or, in NASA parlance, "sims" and "fams." Scobee and Smith, the commander and pilot, flew in a T-38 jet to practice radical maneuvers at high speeds. Onizuka and McNair, the only crew members who might have to walk in space, spent hours in the "Wet F"—the weightless environment training facility—where they were dropped into a twenty-five-foot deep swimming pool in full space gear. Moving about under water was the closest thing on earth to moving in the near zero-gravity of space.

The crew began to train as a unit in December. McAuliffe and Jarvis, who had offices in a building apart from the rest of the crew, joined the five others in one big office in the Astronauts building. Jarvis began spending the entire week in Houston to prepare for his role on the mission, which was to examine the properties of fluids in space. He and McAuliffe spent more time together and became good friends. Jarvis was like an older brother, kidding her to relieve the tension of training and spending evenings with her in games of Trivial Pursuit. By then, McAuliffe proved that she had adjusted to the pace of NASA life. She showed nearly infinite patience with her public relations responsibilities, which NASA halted for the final sixty days of training. She also managed to maintain a semblance of family life, going home at Thanksgiving and Christmas for holiday reunions with Scott and Caroline and Steve in Concord.

McAuliffe also made great strides in winning acceptance from the crew. Ultimately, she managed to become one of them without losing her own personality, baking apple pies for the crew. The strongest indication of her acceptance in the group came when the crew assembled for an official NASA photograph. They greeted McAuliffe wearing mortar boards with tassels and carrying Cabbage Patch school lunch pails and red apples.

By the final weeks, subtle personality differences had begun to emerge. Scobee, the commander, was the most serious, setting the tone for the rest of the crew. McNair and Onizuka relished their moments of fun. In 1984, before his first flight, McNair showed up for a photo session wearing a black beret and sunglasses, carrying a movie clapboard with bold letters: Cecil B. McNair. Onizuka, a loyal alumnus of the University of Colorado, gave Mission Control specialists kona coffee and macadamia nuts from Hawaii before his flights (he also took coffee and nuts on board, along with his class ring). In return, Mission Control agreed before 51-L to let him put a University of Colorado emblem on the satellite that was going to track Halley's Comet. Onizuka won over the quieter Smith, and the two became good friends during preparation for the mission. Smith respected Onizuka because he "kept the right perspective," one of Smith's friends said.

The astronauts who knew Resnik managed to get past her tough exterior. "She had a great sense of humor," said Michael Coats, a member of her first crew. "We used to joke around and Judy was right in the middle of it." But sometimes Resnik could be stubborn. If she disagreed with someone she said so. "She always got her two bits in, but when she was done arguing, she would smile and that would be it," said Coats. He thought she was a special person.

Twenty-four times before flight 51-L, NASA had sent shuttle missions into space with no loss of life. The agency's safety record was so good that the public hardly gave a second thought when McAuliffe was chosen for a shuttle mission. Americans seemed to regard space travel as no more dangerous than flying or driving, activities whose safety also depended on sound machinery and responsible, well-trained human beings. Many Americans knew victims of car wrecks. Fewer knew people killed in airplane crashes. Virtually no one knew someone who died in a space accident. There had been only seven space-related deaths in the nation's history, and only three happened in a spacecraft.

"I feel, probably, safer doing something like that than driving around New York streets," McAuliffe said before the flight. When a friend of Mike Smith's told him six months before the launch, "Mike, you've lost your mind." Smith disagreed. "Don't worry," he told the friend. "It's just as safe as getting in any other airplane and flying."

But the danger of space travel was real to NASA, and the agency took enormous precautions before allowing shuttles to launch. The shuttle's computer system, with 2,000 sensors and data points, was so sensitive that it had delayed flights because of minor technical problems that probably posed no danger in space. The shuttle itself—the orbiter, the external fuel tank, and the solid rocket boosters—was constructed with enough back-up equipment that most mechanical or technical failures could be tolerated in flight. By the time a shuttle blasted off a launching pad, its crew and the experts in Mission Control had rehearsed every maneuver, every minute of the mission, over and over again. All of this was reassuring to the public, including Steve McAuliffe. When flight

51-L was delayed several times because of bad weather, he told one interviewer: "I have found [the delays] very comforting. It seems to me that it demonstrates beyond anyone's normal patience that they are not sending them up unless everything is perfect."

While laymen were comforted by NASA's precautions, the astronauts knew there were certain risks that no backup system could overcome. "You're really aware that you're on top of a monster, you're totally at the mercy of the vehicle," Onizuka told a friend from Edwards Air Force Base. The test pilots, like Scobee and Smith, were well acquainted with the danger of flying sophisticated aircraft at high speeds. Flirting with death was part of the test pilot ethos, part of their lore. "Progress is marked by great smoking holes in the ground," astronaut Chuck Yeager, the first test pilot to break the sound barrier, once said. These pilots saw themselves as crusaders for civilization, people willing to perform new tricks with technology so that mankind could march forward. Danger was a given in their line of work; they didn't dwell on it.

Each astronaut seemed to cope with the possibility of death in his or her own way. On one level, Mike Smith felt that his skill as a pilot was the key to averting disaster. Still, when he joined NASA he reminded relatives that flying in space was a risky business. To Judy Resnik, something was "only dangerous if you aren't prepared for it or if you don't have control over it or if you can't think through how to get yourself out of a problem." Supremely confident of her own abilities, she didn't consider her job unusually dangerous. "I'm a big girl," she told an interviewer. "It's just as well that we don't discuss it."

"You resolve that we will all die sometime," explained Scobee's wife, June, summing up the astronauts' psyche. "Once you have wrestled with death and got that out of your system, you really become able to face life and enjoy life more."

Despite the shuttle's safety record, there had been potentially fatal mishaps on several flights whose crews included some of the astronauts assigned to 51-L. On Scobee's first mission as the *Challenger*'s pilot in 1984, bad weather forced the orbiter to divert to a back-up landing site in California a few minutes before it was scheduled to touch down at Kennedy Space Center. On a flight of the shuttle *Discovery* several months later, Mission Control aborted the lift-off with four seconds to go because lethal liquid hydrogen had burst into flames on the craft. The shuttle was flooded with thousands of gallons of water to douse the flames. Forty minutes later the crew, including Resnik, emerged, their space suits sopping wet.

By Christmas 1985, final preparations were underway for flight 51-L. The crew's mood was upbeat. Shuttle astronauts relished the chance to go in space. It happened only a few times during their careers, and each trip lasted only a few days. "The flight is what we are here for," L.J. Lawrence, a NASA official, said. "All the crap in between is a pain in the neck."

Thirty days before take-off—known as T-minus-30 at NASA—the crew members appeared for the last time at a joint news conference at the space center. "I'll be looking at Halley's Comet," Onizuka responded when asked what he would be doing on the mission. "They tell me I'll have one of the best views around."

They also began to make arrangements for their families and friends to watch the launch. Smith sent out a computer-generated letter with suggestions of restaurants and hotels in the Cape Canaveral area. "Dear Folks," the letter began. "If you really want to see the launch, plan to be prepared to spend up to two extra days in case of bad weather or shuttle problems (I'm betting we launch on time)." Smith warned friends that he would be quarantined for the last week of training. Only intimate friends and spouses were given "personal contact badges" that allowed them to visit the crew. "I know that's good news for the ninety-five percent of you who are coming to see Jane," Smith joked at the end of the letter.

Judy Resnik's brother, and his family, planned to come with her father and stepmother. She had agreed to take her nephew's signet ring and her niece's heart-shaped locket on the mission.

Resnik had invited one special guest, actor Tom Selleck. She had never met him but sent him a letter asking him to come to Florida for the launch. Resnik's crush on Selleck was widely known, and at a crew dinner in Houston a week before the launch, someone asked if the actor had responded. Resnik confessed that his staff had called to say he probably wouldn't make it. Then, flanked by her boyfriend, astronaut Frank Culbertson, she began a monologue about Selleck's good looks. "Tom Selleck is so cute, and he has such a great body," she gushed. Culbertson pretended to look hurt. He flexed his biceps and looked at Resnik. "I may have to work on my body," he told her, "but there is no way Tom Selleck is getting a personal contact badge."

As 1986 began, NASA looked forward to its most ambitious year yet for the space shuttle program. The agency had fifteen missions scheduled at Kennedy Space Center and at a new west coast spaceport at Vandenberg Air Force Base. But a few days into the New Year, the first shuttle mission—a *Columbia* flight—was delayed a record seven times and then cut short by a day because of technical problems. These delays forced NASA to move the *Challenger*'s launch date back two days, from Wednesday, January 22 to Friday, January 24.

The *Challenger,* one of four squat-looking, 122-foot orbiters used by NASA in the shuttle program, was the workhorse of the group. It had flown nine of the twenty-four shuttle missions, and had survived its share of mishaps. Its maiden voyage in 1983 had to be delayed two months because technicians discovered highly flammable liquid hydrogen leaking from a faulty fuel line. Then it came within minutes of potential disaster on Scobee's mission in April 1984, when the landing site was switched abruptly on its descent to earth. On its subsequent mission in July, the countdown was stopped at T-minus-3 seconds when a heat sensor mistakenly signaled that one of the *Challenger*'s three main engines was overheating. In November 1984, the orbiter damaged its landing gear and one booster rocket when it returned from a mission and landed on the dry rock bed at Edwards Air Force Base. Then, during a retooling session at Kennedy Space Center in preparation for 51-L, workers lifted one of the orbiter's solid rocket boosters and heard a sharp crack. They discovered a broken pin on the handling ring.

Repairs made, the *Challenger* was pronounced fit a few days before Christmas and mounted to a 154-foot rust-colored external fuel tank and to two 149-foot white-colored solid rocket boosters. Assembled, it was placed on launch pad 39-B. For thirty-eight days, in colder than usual temperatures, the *Challenger* sat on the pad with its nose facing the sky, waiting to begin its tenth journey to space. "It is beautiful," Marcia Jarvis thought when, twelve hours before lift-off, the crew and their spouses were taken to a special viewing spot for a close-up look at the shuttle. "It looks like it was just painted white. It's like a Christmas tree. It's awesome."

The astronauts, in T-38 jets, and McAuliffe and Jarvis in a NASA jet, flew from Houston to Kennedy Space Center on Thursday, January 23, arriving in the late afternoon. By then relatives and friends had gathered at hotels in the area. McAuliffe's parents and children and eighteen students from Scott's third-grade class were there. On his backpack, Scott had written: "Christa's kid." United Air Lines had flown in 100 teacher-in-space semi-finalists—two from each state—to watch the countdown of the teacher mission. Smith's friends, responding to his letter, had come too, from North Carolina, Florida, Maryland, Virginia and Houston.

The Friday afternoon lift-off was already in doubt because of a sand storm at the emergency landing site in Dakar, Senegal, and ultimately NASA postponed the launch until Sunday morning.

It was a ritual at NASA that the spouses of the crew members hosted, at their own expense, some kind of pre-launch celebration —a brunch, a cocktail party or a reception for the crew. Steve McAuliffe, Marcia Jarvis, and June Scobee had a reception with light hors d'oeuvres at the Holiday Inn in Orlando. The crew also was feted at Patrick Air Force Base and again at a beachfront house on Cape Canaveral, where they ate barbecue and potato salad and drank Cokes and beer. Everybody was happy, despite the delays. "It was time to go fly and everybody was ready to do it," said Bill Butterworth, Jarvis' backup from Hughes.

At 11 A.M. on Saturday, January 25, senior NASA officials at the Kennedy Space Center in Florida met for the "L minus 1-day review." The meeting centered on the weather. The cold temperatures had continued, and rain was threatening the Sunday launch. A lift-off in rain was prohibited because rain drops could create dangerous pockmarks in the heat resistant tiles on the base of the orbiter that protect the shuttle from high temperatures during reentry. They called another meeting for 9:30 that evening, when updated weather forecasts would be available.

The evening review was equally pessimistic. Rain showers were expected into Sunday, so the launch would have to be delayed another twenty-four hours. After the meeting, Jesse W. Moore, associate administrator of NASA, told reporters: "We're not going to launch this thing and take any kind of risk because we have that schedule pressure. We'll sit on the ground until we all believe it's safe to launch."

The delays were frustrating and McAuliffe's mother, Grace Corrigan, told friends over the weekend that she had a case of bad nerves. "I'm getting a little more apprehensive as it gets nearer," she said.

On Sunday, Scobee and Smith took up a T-38 jet to rehearse landings on the shuttle runway and to practice high-speed maneuvers. That night the crew and their spouses had dinner together in a quarantined dining facility. As the meal came to an end, Ron McNair pulled out a large shopping bag. Inside was a magnum of champagne with a design of the shuttle etched onto it. McNair passed the bottle around with an etching pen, and each crew member signed his or her name on the bottle.

Later that night, McAuliffe had trouble sleeping. She called her friend Greg Jarvis. They left the crew quarters and found two bicycles with lights. In the dark, they rode around the complex, an activity not even contemplated under NASA training rules.

Monday morning, the rain had stopped. It was about forty degrees, but the sky was clear. Dressed in their space suits, the crew members made the six-mile trip from the crew quarters to the launch pad. The countdown was on schedule. For the first time, they crawled into the *Challenger*'s circular hatch at mid-deck. McAuliffe, Jarvis and Onizuka strapped into their seats, their feet pointing toward the sky and their backs parallel to the ground. Scobee, Smith, Resnik and McNair climbed a ladder to the upper deck, a cock-pit like cabin filled with control panels. Through the front windows they could see the cloudless blue sky. Apart from Scobee and Smith, who ran through a series of computer and mechanical checks at the controls, the others had little to do until they were in orbit.

With nine minutes remaining before lift-off the countdown suddenly stopped. A bolt on the handle of an external hatch was stuck. NASA technicians tried to remove the bolt, but couldn't. A battery-powered drill was sent to the launch pad. The bit was too small, and the batteries were dead. Four hours passed, and the crew sat uncomfortably in the flight decks. Jarvis grumbled that his leg was falling asleep and McAuliffe began to doze off. A hacksaw was found, and NASA technicians finally removed the bolt. But the weather had turned windy, with gusts too strong to ensure a safe lift-off. NASA postponed the launch until Tuesday morning at 9:38.

The new delay discouraged some of the 1,000 well-wishers who

181

had gathered to watch the countdown Monday morning. Some of Smith's friends and his brother, Pat, had to go back to their jobs. Jarvis' mother, Tele Ladd, returned home to New York.

The next morning the winds had died down. The crew woke up at 6:18 A.M. and a half-hour later ate a light breakfast in the crew dining area. NASA provided a pre-launch dessert: a cake decorated with the *Challenger* emblem and a design of the orbiter, along with each astronaut's name, in white icing. After a ten-minute briefing, the crew left for the launch pad in a NASA van. It was almost 8 A.M.

"My kind of day," said the commander, Scobee, when he saw the launch pad crew. "What a great day for flying." McAuliffe added: "We are going to go today, aren't we?"

At 8:23 A.M., after the launch pad crew helped them put on their vests and helmets and cleaned off their shoes, the 51-L crew members entered the orbiter once again. A launch pad technician handed McAuliffe a red apple. "Save it for me and I'll eat it when I get back," she said, thanking him.

The cold weather concerned NASA officials. The average temperature for shuttle launches was seventy-three degrees, and the coldest temperature ever had been fifty-one degrees. Earlier that morning, the temperature had dropped to twenty-seven degrees. Icicles had collected on the launch pad. By mid-morning the mercury had climbed only a few degrees above freezing.

The weather could affect rubber rings in the rocket boosters, which were needed to keep seals tight and prevent leaks of burning solid fuel. In 1982, NASA officials had exchanged internal memos warning that faulty seals during lift-off could be fatal to a shuttle and its crew. As a precaution for flight 51-L, Mission Control on Monday had consulted with the booster manufacturer, Morton Thiokol, about the effects of cold temperatures on the seals. The experts agreed the launch was safe, but lift-off was moved up two hours, to 11:38 A.M., to give the launch-pad crew time to repair a broken water pipe on the pad and to double check for icicles.

Inside the shuttle, Scobee and Smith sat at the control panels running through last-minute instrument checks. Only during the first two minutes and eight seconds of a flight—a fraction of the six-day, thirty-four-minute mission—was the crew completely at the mercy of technology. Lift-off was the trickiest time to control a failure in the system. The shuttle would be catapulted into the atmosphere on 2.9 million pounds of thrust. Its solid rocket boosters were filled with 1.1 billion pounds of solid fuel. The external fuel tank contained 529,000 gallons of liquid oxygen and liquid hydrogen. Six seconds before lift-off these highly explosive fuels would flow through seventeen-inch aluminum fuel lines into the shuttle's main tank. Once ignited, the fuel burned until it was used up.

With four minutes left on the countdown and the temperature now at thirty-eight degrees, Mission Control gave the crew a final reminder to close the airtight visors on their helmets. Thirty seconds later the shuttle began operating entirely on its own electrical power. "Ninety seconds and counting. The 51-L mission ready to go," said Hugh Harris, a NASA commentator whose voice came over the loudspeakers in the viewing stands four miles from the launch. Families and friends lined the viewing stand, their eyes fixed on pad 39-B.

"T-minus 10, 9, 8, 7, 6, we have main engine start," the NASA announcer said.

The *Challenger* pushed off the launch pad and cleared the tower. In its trail was a magnificent 700-foot column of white smoke. Cheers went up in the VIP stands. Sixty seconds later, shuttle flight 51-L was eight miles up and traveling just under 2,000 miles an hour.

Mission Control: *"Challenger,* go with throttle up."

Smith replied: "Roger, Go with throttle up."

Then there was a long pause. The spectators were confused. They saw a mushroom cloud of smoke nine miles above Earth, and a solid rocket booster cartwheeling off into the ocean. Inside Mission Control, computer screens became dotted with "s", signifying only static from the shuttle.

For forty interminable seconds, the NASA announcer was silent.

Then, "Flight controllers here looking very carefully at the situation. Obviously we have a major malfunction. We have no downlink.

"We have a report from the flight dynamics officer that the vehicle has exploded."

In the VIP viewing stand, children began to scream. Christa McAuliffe's sister shrieked and clutched her chest. "Daddy!"

cried one of Michael Smith's children. "I want you, Daddy. You always promised nothing would happen."

Hundreds of miles away in North Carolina, Smith's brother, Pat, was driving home from the Cape, fiddling with the radio dial to get a station that carried news of the lift-off. In New York, Jarvis' mother sat by herself in front of the television set. Further north, at McAuliffe's high school in New Hampshire, dazed students hung their heads in disbelief. Across the country, a public that had become inured to the danger of space travel watched as the seventy-four-second flight of 51-L was replayed and replayed and replayed on television screens, a minute of history now frozen in time.

In Washington, Vice-President George Bush and Communications Director Patrick Buchanan hurried into the Oval Office where President Reagan was working on his State of the Union address. "There has been a serious incident with the shuttle," Bush said. Buchanan was more direct: "Sir," he said, "the shuttle has exploded." Startled, the president got up from his desk.

"Is that the one the teacher was on?" Reagan asked.

A few minutes after the explosion, NASA officials ordered the families and relatives in the VIP viewing area down from the roof. They were taken to crew quarters, where they were left to themselves to wait for further information. Grace Corrigan kept repeating over and over: "The craft has exploded." Across the room, Ellison Onizuka's wife fainted. Her body, collapsing, brushed a light switch on the wall. The room turned dark.

Fifteen minutes later, NASA officials asked a representative from each family to gather in a conference room. "We don't know all the details," said NASA official George W.F. Abbey. "But it looks like there has been an explosion. I don't believe there is any hope for the crew."

It was the official confirmation.

They already knew.

Epilogue

THE CHALLENGES
UNDIMINISHED

When Neil Armstrong set foot on the moon seventeen years ago he described the voyage from Earth as a "small step for man." That profound truth was lost in the wonder and excitement of an historic and heroic moment. Many of us, unschooled in astrophysics, assumed that the stars would be next, that the path to the heavens now lay before us, awaiting only the pioneers. It was a romantic notion that has not been realized and will not be in the lives of Earth's present generations.

We have become more aware in the years since the moon landings of the vastness of space and of how puny our conquests have been. The journey to the moon covered less than 250,000 miles. The nearest star to our sun, Alpha Centauri, is twenty-five trillion miles away. At a speed of 25,000 miles per hour it could be reached in about 115,000 years. There are 100 billion to 200 billion of these stars in our galaxy and billions upon billions of galaxies in a universe of such immensity that its boundaries, if they exist, are presently beyond our ability to define them.

"We have inaugurated an age of discovery," historian Bruce Mazlish has written, "but it is not *The* Age of Discovery, and it lacks the props and resonance we were conditioned to expect. The major difference . . . is that in space there are no flora or fauna. There are no people on the moon to be conquered or converted. There are no new animals to grace the parks of a Spanish king, no exotic plants to nurture in the Royal Gardens at Kew. Columbus returned with naked savages. Lewis and Clark identified twenty-four Indian tribes, 178 plants, and 122 animals, all of them

185

previously unknown. . . . Space, in comparison, is 'empty,' and our chief harvest thus far has been in the form of rocks.''

The technology employed in the "small step" into the sky is impressive. But, as the *Challenger* tragedy reminds us, it has not immunized man from the perils of even timid exploration. Since *Sputnik*, the casualty rate among American astronauts approaches ten per cent, although none has perished in space. Virgil Grissom, Edward White and Roger Chaffee were incinerated in 1967 in an Apollo spacecraft fire. Ted Freeman, Charles Bassett, Elliott See and C. C. Williams were killed in airplane crashes during required training flights for NASA. Ed Givens was killed in an automobile accident. And now the *Challenger* Seven, blown-up in sight of their launching ground on a flight that would have taken them a mere 177 miles into space.

But for chance or luck, the toll over the years might have been far higher. During the *Gemini* flight of Dave Scott and Neil Armstrong in 1966, the space vehicle went out of control and for ten minutes "spun like a top" before it was stabilized through desperate and unrehearsed measures. A similar problem arose because of human error—a switch left in the wrong position— during the *Apollo 12* flight of Thomas Stafford, Eugene Cernan and John Young in 1969. That same year the *Apollo 12* spacecraft was launched during a thunderstorm and was struck twice by lightning, temporarily knocking out its computer and power systems. On the *Apollo 13* flight in 1970, an oxygen tank exploded; the crew survived only because of what was called a "technical miracle." Following the joint American-Soviet Union space mission in 1973, the American spacecraft developed serious problems during its return to earth. The cockpit filled with toxic gases choking and gagging the crew for more than five minutes as they struggled to find oxygen masks; one crew member was rendered unconscious.

Michael Collins, a member of the crew that made the first moon landing, has written of other perils in his memoir, *Carrying the Fire:* "Inside the cockpit, I get my first manifestation of weightlessness: tiny bits of debris, washers, screws, pieces of potting compound, dirt particles . . . are floating aimlessly about. In an hour or so they will be gone, sucked into the inlet screen of the ventilation system, but for the time being they are an amusing oddity as well as a sober reminder that this machine has been assembled by fallible hands which drop things which find their way into inaccessible and possibly dangerous crevices. . . . My own feelings were . . . in keeping with those expressed in a speech by Jerry Lederer, NASA's Safety Chief, three days before the flight. While the flight posed fewer unknowns than had Columbus's voyage, Jerry said, the mission would 'involve great risks that have not been foreseen. *Apollo 8* has 5,600,000 parts and one and one half million systems, subsystems and assemblies. Even if all functioned with 99.9 per cent reliability, we could expect 5,600 defects.''

The record of the American space effort reinforces the point. Between 1957 and 1984, there were 152 unsuccessful manned and unmanned space flights, a failure rate of nearly fifteen percent.

Then there are the human fragilities that Collins has described—the nausea brought on by motion sickness, for example. Frank Borman became one of its victims, afflicted by vomiting and diarrhea: "If a . . . space walker had ever thrown up while outside, it would probably have meant a messy death, as he would be blinded by the vomit trapped inside his helmet, and possibly asphyxiated by its clogging his oxygen supply circuit. The same, of course, would apply to moon walkers. . . .''

Other physical and psychological difficulties, arising out of long confinement in cramped spacecraft, have been encountered in recent years. Crew members have suffered bone damage as a serious side effect of weightlessness and the lack of proper exercise. The psychological pressures have been described by Soviet cosmonaut, Valery Ryumin, who participated in two six-month flights aboard the *Salyut* spacecraft. He quoted the American writer, O. Henry: "All one needs to effect a murder is lock two men into a cabin, eighteen by twenty feet, and keep them there for two months.'' Ryumin wrote in his diary: "Our problem is deeply human. We must now adjust to living together, away from the rest of the world. Robinson Crusoe, after finding himself alone on an uninhabited island, solved problems by himself accounting to himself. We have to solve ours together, taking into account the feelings of the other. Here we are totally alone. Each uttered word assumes added importance. One must bear in mind—constantly—the other's good and bad sides, anticipate his thinking, the ramifications of a wrong utterance blown out of proportion.'' It is reported that on one of his extended flights, Ryumin begged to be returned to earth after two months. Another cosmonaut concluded that "it is impossible to ensure psychological compatibility on a long flight."

Human and mechanical problems are not the only factors that have limited man's reach for the heavens. The spectacular success of the moon landings—the "heroic era" of spaceflight—has been described by John Noble Wilford of *The New York Times* as "a triumph that failed, not because the achievement was anything short of magnificent but because of misdirected expectations and a general misperception of its real meaning. The public was encouraged to view it only as the grand climax of the space program, a geopolitical horse race [between the United States and the Soviet Union] and extraterrestial entertainment—not as a dramatic means to the greater end of developing a far-ranging spacefaring capability. This led to the space-program's post-Apollo slump."

At its peak in 1966, NASA commanded a scientific and industrial work force of 420,000 people and a budget of more than five billion dollars a year—pre-inflation dollars. By the early 1970s NASA's work force had shrunk to 160,000 and its budget had been cut in half. In comparable dollars, its budget twenty years ago was almost three times greater than today.

This is a result of many influences, scientific, political and cultural. We are frequently a fickle people with short attention spans, seeing the world as a nightly newsreel, skipping from event to event, remembering little. We are also, in the nature of democracies, quarrelsome and given to factionalism. Even before the moon landing series had been completed cynics were sneering. A 1972 column by Nicholas Von Hoffman in *The Washington Post* was headlined: Two Klutzes on the Moon. "What is this one," he wrote, "*Apollo 16* or *26?* No one cares. No one watches but the necrophiles who go to car races in hopes of seeing the drivers kill themselves. The only story left to be wrung out of this moon business is death. Those two klutzes up there on the moon breaking their equipment, bumping into each other, unable to repair what their clumsiness has damaged didn't look like scientists or lab technicians even. They looked like what they were, a couple of miscast yahoo military officers." Scientific factions appeared, expressing more elegant but similar views of men in space. As Dr. Thomas Gold, Cornell physicist, put it, "All experiments and observations can be done equally well or better by instruments rather than by men. For observations, the presence of a man is a disaster. He can't keep still enough."

A *New Republic* magazine article in 1984 argued the same theology: "Space travel has never quite lived up to its billing as a technological bonanza. The science and engineering feats it encourages have only limited use here on Earth. Trickle-down technology is not an efficient way to regain our competitive economic edge. And the spin-offs of space has given us such things as hand-held calculators, digital watches, phone calls via satellite, improved computers—just about everything except Tang —have come from programs that have one thing in common: they were unmanned . . . Building new ways to carry men into space offers little of value to earthlings."

When NASA proposed in the 1970s a manned mission to Mars there was little political support for the project and the government settled, instead, on the development of the shuttle, an unglamorous transport vehicle (the size of a DC-9) to haul cargoes into space. It might not send man's spirit soaring but, it was argued, it might pay for itself as an orbiting truck line.

The climate of doubt about NASA's purposes in the 1980s and beyond and about the future of space exploration is exacerbated by politics of the age. In the 1960s the government was able to sustain simultaneously a war in Southeast Asia, a war on poverty at home and a race for the moon. Today the political obsessions are with balanced budgets, fiscal restraint and American competitiveness in an international economy. Exhortations to "reach for the stars" are sublimated to cost-benefit analyses and to other claims on the nation's scientific and financial resources. The Apollo program attracted the "best and the brightest" engineers, scientists and test pilots. The Jet Propulsion Laboratory in California, the space center in Houston, the launch site at The Kennedy Space Center and the great aerospace factories were Meccas for creativity and adventure. Presidents and congressmen were singleminded in their support. But today there are other priorities and other frontiers. The great scientific and engineering issue is not whether men will land on Mars but whether, at an untold cost, a "strategic defense" system can be developed to protect the nation against intercontinental ballistic missiles. Military claims on the public treasury for space programs have risen astronomically. In 1982, appropriations to the Pentagon for projects in space surpassed for the first time those appropriated to NASA. Last year the Pentagon's space allocation was nearly double that of NASA—12.9 billion dollars versus 6.8 billion. Independent military "space commands" have been created to manage diverse and costly research programs, to launch and operate a growing array of reconnaisance, communications and navigational satellites and to develop an anti-satellite weapon which, in itself, poses formidable scientific problems. These programs are driven, in large measure, by military competition with the Soviet Union, the sort of competition for "prestige" and technological advantage that inspired the race for the moon more than two decades ago.

No comparable competitive engine drives the civilian space program in the 1980s. The superiority of American technology, exemplified by the shuttle, has become a truism; the drive to "beat the Russians" has lost all urgency. This is reflected in the fact that the powerful congressional space committees that nurtured NASA in its early years have since been downgraded to subcommittees. NASA's political support in the industrial community has been somewhat diluted as the great aerospace companies diversify and acquire new clients, notably the Pentagon. At the end of 1984, the aerospace industry had an orders backlog of 133.5 billion dollars; space vehicle systems accounted for less than 5 billion dollars of the total.

Irrespective of these developments, the prospect for bold, manned ventures into space in this decade might still be doubtful. It is a serious question whether the country's technological and scientific base is sufficient to support simultaneously a "Star Wars" program, an enormously expanded Pentagon space program, Stealth bomber and ASAT developments, a technological "overhaul" of America's industrial base to meet international competition and, at the same time, embark on a manned mission to some distant planet. The aerospace industry alone already employs nearly twenty per cent of all the scientists and engineers in the United States.

The matter of priorities thus arises from every side. The Federal government is mired in debt, searching desperately for budget-cutting and budget-balancing formulae, while diverse factions clamor for greater shares of the public treasure. In this political bazaar, the claims of space explorers have lessened resonance.

"What is left?" the historian, Mazlich asks. "The 'high' has been taken out of the adventure—a humanless space and a heroless program have seen to that. There are no heathen to missionize, nor little further military and national prestige to be gained immediately, and either paltry or very long-range economic gains to be reaped. . . . The forces justifying space exploration, therefore, have become discretionary. As a discretionary matter, and not a matter of unquestioned national purpose, the space program is now weighed against other discretionary expenditures—cancer research, urban renewal—and is often found wanting and wasteful by comparison. Until space colonization or stepped-up military conflict in space come along to rekindle public interest, the space program's chief ally seems to be leftover momentum: the fact that certain programs, planned long ago, happen to be under way.''

No matter; the passion for exploration, the mystique of space, the emotional pull of the stars and planets are powerful forces in the human spirit and psyche. The first flight of the shuttle, that clumsy and unglamorous cargo ship, drew a million people to the takeoff at Cape Canaveral in 1981; another half-million waited anxiously for its subsequent landing on the salt flats of Edwards Air Force Base; tens of millions watched through the medium of television. The *Challenger* disaster itself was a profoundly moving event throughout the world, evoking a kind of primordial grief and admiration for strangers who had dared to win—or lose—an unearthly prize. The subsequent reaction was further proof that the mystique of exploration is in the human bloodstream as the 20th Century nears its end. Public opinion polls revealed that two-thirds of the Americans were unshaken in their support for space programs, including, specifically, more shuttle flights. The families of the dead crew of *Challenger* Seven were among that majority.

Even now scientists, poets, politicians and eager pioneers are rallying for new adventure into the heavens, the long dreamed of manned mission to Mars. Let it be, Carl Sagan and others insist, a joint American-Soviet undertaking to discover not only the secrets of that planet but the secrets of friendship and brotherhood it might reveal: ''In the long run, the binding up of the wounds on Earth and the exploration of Mars might go hand in hand.''

The transcendent element in man's reach for the stars, however, is not the logic or rationality of it. It is something more elemental, an indefinable instinct encapsulated in the simple motto of the test pilots at Edwards—*''Ad Inexplorata''*. Toward the unknown.